RETURN TO SANCTUARY CITY

SCREENPLAY

By

Paul D. Escudero

This publication contains the opinions and ideas of its author. It is intended to provide helpful and informative material on the subjects addressed in the publication. The author and publisher specifically disclaim all responsibility for any liability, loss or risk, personal or otherwise, which is incurred as a consequence, directly or indirectly, of the use and application of any of the contents of this book.

WORKBOOK PRESS LLC
187 E Warm Springs Rd,
Suite B285 Las Vegas NV 89119 USA
Website: https://workbookpress.com/
Hotline: 1-888-818-4856
Email: admin@workbookpress.com

Ordering Information:
Quantity sales. Special discounts are available on quantity purchases by corporations, associations, and others. For details, contact the publisher at the address above.

ISBN-13:   978-1-963718-86-7 Paperback Version
               978-1-963718-87-4 Digital Version

PUB. DATE: 05/07/2024

INT. DAY. PLANET ARZON

FADE IN

VOICE OVER

Various military situations were not ideal for Arzon. This once highly developed civilization thought it was immune to most galactic strife. Its fleet had been highly developed and second to none. It ranged the galaxy, much for exploration as the Arzon's had very little appetite for imperialistic spreading like many other civilizations, as their wise men understood the consequences of expanding an Empire too far and wide.

Arzon itself was the by-product of the overambitious spreading of civilization beyond manageable distances. In the great divide that occurred, they were cut off from the Dranzonian Empire and suddenly found themselves isolated and existing in a vast distance that would require travel through the aggressive Revolutionary sectors of space.

It did not take long before the Arzon's discovered they were permanently cut off from all other Loyalist forces. Life continued and, thanks to great distance and seemingly lack of excessive resources, revolutionaries had no incentives to travel to the barren region that had been a drain on the Dranzonian Empire and had not learned to stand on their own two feet, since obtaining all they needed from the Dranzonian Empire was easy to accomplish as they traded intellectual properties with all the resources they needed delivered over vast distances.

When the sudden realization existed, that Arzon was cut off from the Dranzonian Empire, the Arzon's suddenly were thrust into picking up the pieces and began self-sufficiency. No doubt it was rough at first, but thanks to the ample brain power they developed over the years due to the emphasis they placed on education, they slowly engineered their way out of their circumstances and, quite sooner than anyone predicted, built, and designed systems that provided self-sufficiency.

The Arzon's were alone in their solar system. The nearest inhabited solar system existed beyond seven other solar systems, where the Revolutionary Empire had consolidated much of the infrastructure and political systems. Plagued with continuous attrition from war with the Dranzonian Empire, venturing out toward Arzon was neither desirable nor required.

The Arzon's simply were forgotten, and since after learning the mistakes of travel toward Loyalist planets the Arzon's never attempted, it made it much easier for the Dranzonian Empire to forget Arzon existed.

Since the Arzon's were free to develop and would have received the Revolutionary Empire Fleet peacefully, because they had chosen to not arm themselves; they would be treated humanely had that visit occurred, but it did not.

There would never have been any Arzon spacecraft except for the need to get precious materials off nearby mining planets to support life. Hence, the Arzon Space Fleet really began as simply commercial transport for bauxite, iron ore, petroleum distillates that were refined on the mining planets, and vast other natural resources.

The few remaining Dranzonian Empire spacecraft that had made their way to Arzon but could never safely traverse the vast region of Revolutionary Empire space, served a couple useful purposes.

These Dranzonian spacecraft provided the basic essential transportation to the outward lying planets in the Arzon solar system, but they could never be reverse engineered.

Normally such reverse engineering would not be permitted as the Dranzonian Empire was strict about manufacturing all spacecraft at the home planets to prevent proliferation of technology into rebel areas, which ultimately happened without their consent.

Faced with the need to import a vast amounts of resources from nearby planets and since they were conceivably cut off forever from the Dranzonian Empire, the Arzon's selected a couple of the most useful class of transports for disassembly and reverse engineering.

Re-engineering progress took almost three years, but in due time the Arzon's achieved the impossible: they succeeded at copying and building a standard fleet transport that could also be reconfigured with armaments for self-protection.

Because of several intrusions into Arzon space by Revolutionary Empire assets, fear suddenly drove the Arzon's to do what they detested the most: build warships.

Hence the genesis of a powerful fleet began for that one day in the future when they feared they may be forced to defend the planet from Revolutionary forces.

Arzon cities were built at great expense before the Dranzonian Empire fell apart. Arzon was considered a future provincial capital, which would be the stop over for another finger of expansion of the Dranzonian Empire in their direction.

Thanks to the nearby nebula and other astronomical findings, they certainly were on the path to expansion, as people on Earth would think, the great Silk Road to the universe.

The consensus is that if the Revolutionary Empire only sent a modest fleet, the Arzon's might be able to defend their planet. However, if they arrived with a large invasion fleet, the outcome would seem rather bleak. Another good reason to avoid travel through Revolutionary Empire space.

Unfortunately, a diverse society such as the Dranzonian Empire before the breach and breakup left families separated. People made every effort to get home to see their families again. It resulted in travel that ostensibly was restricted, nevertheless.

The five members of the Committee for State Security that formed in the Revolutionary Empire sector called all the shots. They held routine meetings to decide the faith of the New Empire and they subsequently renamed the Revolutionary Empire.

The Revolutionary Empire suddenly discovered interest in Arzon as it lay in the pathway of future expansion. Soon followed high level meetings to discuss the plan forward.

INT. DAY. ZUANSHI-CHENG – REVOLUTIONARY EMPIRE HOME WORLD AND CAPITAL HEADQUARTRS COMMAND CENTER.

REVOLUTIONARY EMPIRE
LEADER NUMBER ONE
We can infiltrate Arzon with our spies.

REVOLUTIONARY EMPIRE
LEADER NUMBER TWO
Not a bad idea since it's almost mandatory that we do and find out what is really going on there.

REVOLUTIONARY EMPIRE
LEADER NUMBER ONE
When is the next blockade runner scheduled to go there?

REVOLUTIONARY EMPIRE
LEADER NUMBER TWO
According to intel sources, a hyperspace runner is clandestinely taking reservations now, due to depart in a couple weeks from Zanziltar and stop at Praxisvlasia to pick up all the Arzon-bound passengers. We could put a spy on that ship before it leaves Zanziltar.

REVOLUTIONARY EMPIRE
LEADER NUMBER ONE
We need to let the ship pass through our zone so that we can get our spy planted on Arzon.

REVOLUTIONARY EMPIRE
LEADER NUMBER TWO
Certainly. We will have exact times and dates within two weeks.

One could equate the Committee for State Security to what occurred on Earth during Napoleon's rise to power. Ultimately the Revolutionary Empire would make the same mistake as the French did, as they were now in the process of anointing Cornelius Xie de Hundan.

The future events the Revolutionaries would experience had amazing parallels to the French in the early 1800s.

A reckless leader led the Revolutionaries down the path of self-destruction when they could simply have consolidated their gains and carved out a new existence in the former crossroads to the Empire.

Immediately upon his coronation, Cornelius Xie de Hundan dispersed the five members of the Committee for State Security to the four corners of the new Empire on fact-finding trips to discover the strength and weaknesses that may pose a threat if the remnants of the Dranzonian Empire they now occupied attempted to recover their vast lost territories. During the Revolution, surprisingly, a lot of military personnel joined in with the Revolutionaries. More spectacular was the number of intelligence operatives who also switched allegiances.

As soon as it became apparent a mutiny occurred in the fleet and over half of all space assets ended up in the hands of the Revolution's Committee for State Security, the foregone conclusion was rather apparent.

One could describe the process similar to rats jumping off a sinking ship back in the wood ship sailing days. Hence Cornelius Xie de Hundan ended up with one of the largest spy networks in the galaxy.

In due time Cornelius Xie de Hundan had meetings with his spy master and got his reports..

GLEN ZHURENSHUO
Your excellency, the transport is leaving Praxisvlasia in
the very near future heading to Arzon.

CORNELIUS XIE DE HUNDAN
Good, make sure we let it sneak through to Arzon.

GLEN ZHURENSHUO
Our forces will be instructed not to interfere with its
progress even though we know it will be traveling
through an area we could easily jump it and commandeer
the ship.

CORNELIUS XIE DE HUNDAN

I'm more concerned about getting a spy to Arzon so we can get an update what they are up to.

GLEN ZHURENSHUO

One of our spies will be on the ship. He'll get the bottom line for us.

CORNELIUS XIE DE HUNDAN

What's his name?

GLEN ZHURENSHUO

Sir, it's best you do not know. We do not disclose our spies' identities to anyone. They are very easy to compromise if people outside our control can identify the individual.

CORNELIUS XIE DE HUNDAN

How will we manage to get a spy into Praxisvlasia and then on to Arzon?

GLEN ZHURENSHUO

We recruited him at Praxisvlasia and trained him at our Zanziltar facility. He's been tested on a few missions. He was part of the Secret Sanctuary City Service establishment prior to the revolution. Once he altered his allegiance to our cause, we asked him to go to Arzon to be able to be useful to us and report the situation there.

CORNELIUS XIE DE HUNDAN

So, he'll be a deep cover operative.

GLEN ZHURENSHUO

Yes, sir.

The black market was alive and well on Arzon. This activity was overlooked because the Arzon's were so desperate for materials, the government looked the other way.

Ships originating at Zanziltar would arrive via Praxisvlasia or some other Dranzonian Empire port loaded with people and trans-shipments to Arzon.

The outlaws that run this operation often described it as the "Pigs and People Run," and the pilots of those ships were called "Hoggers" since there were many cases of livestock shipped in the cargo holds.

Those animals, of course, had to be sedated the entire trip; otherwise, they would injure themselves in the cargo bay of the ship and lose their value to the black marketers who sold such animals to settlers starting up new agriculture activities or simply a restaurant business that wanted to provide some extremely rare meats and poultry, until the world became more civilized.

<u>INT. DAY. SECRET SERVICE BRANCH OF THE MINISTRY FOR STATE SECURITY, DRANZONIAN EMPIRE PRAXISVLASIA HEADQUARTERS</u>

VOICE OVER
The Secret Service branch of the Ministry for State Security in the Dranzonian Empire headquarters in Praxisvlasia had heads up of Evo Kaplan's mission that had already been compromised by Huaiyuansu Ka's recent report to Hari Nuvrean in a Zanziltar safe house.

This mission was deemed so important to the Dranzonian Secret Service that a Department Head summoned a hand-picked person to handle it and deal with Evo Kaplan.

This spy deemed to be one of their premier operatives was none other than the real Blane Jiandie. This would be a dangerous assignment because Reginald Heiqishi had used Blane Jiandie's identity.

Blane Jiandie was dismayed that his long-awaited vacation just got canceled.

Blane Jiandie arrived at room 40 of the Revolutionary Empire Dranzonian code breakers annex. Dranzonian code breakers were hard at work in nearby rooms decrypting and discovering the contents of Revolutionaries communications. This room was selected for this briefing because of its extra security and graphics capabilities.

BLANE JIANDIE
Sir, do you wish to see me?

SECRET SERVICE DEPARTMENT HEAD
Yes, shut the door and come on in and have a seat.

VOICE OVER
The Secret Service Department Head Edgar Boont knew the conversation was not going to be a pleasant one.

The real Blane Jiandie knew people didn't get summoned to see a Secret Service Department Head unless it was an important issue.

Timing was not pleasing because Blane Jiandie anticipated he would soon depart on his vacation he had planned for a while to unwind and drink copious amounts of drug-fortified alcoholic beverages on Fantasy Island, the ultimate tourist destination for single men who were poised to meet a nice woman.

If Blane Jiandie was not able to meet a nice-looking woman, Fantasy Island management would fly into the resort appropriate hostess with impeccable credentials of a pleasure provider as good as anywhere in the galaxy. Fantasy Island operates just like a Japanese Love Hotel.

Blane Jiandie assumed he would meet a very nice lady to spend some quality time and felt secure enough to know he would not be needing the second alternative. But he also knew very few of those single men that arrived would be in fantastic shape like he was, because as part of his requirements for the spy business was twenty hours of hard work out per week to maintain top physical condition.

Once a month Blane Jiandie went on one hundred-mile hikes to measure his ability to self-relocate under arduous conditions, which was often the case in the spy business when one had to bug out when their cover was blown.

Blane Jiandie thoughts of meeting that mysterious woman was brutally interrupted by that unpredictable phone call, several hours prior, just the day after he signed out for leave and would not be back for three weeks, on a Praxisvlasia calendar.

Blane Jiandie knew what type of man the department head was, because people didn't get promoted in this business to a department head level without some extraordinary politics or connections.

No doubt, the department head had been involved in

some of the most wicked experiences bestowed on such mortals during the revolution, when it was not clear who was the enemy and who was a friend. Behind that poker face of the department head wore a mask of steel and a heart of Krypton.

This department head was the type of person who would send his own mother to hell if he thought it would help him get ahead in some way. No dirty task was too much to ask of him.

The department head helped to sift out most of the moles and no doubt killed quite a few innocents just because their loyalty could not be proven beyond a shadow of doubt. In the Secret Service, the post revolution days were a period of cleansing unlike anyone could ever imagine.

The fratricidal event slowly carved the cancer out of the organization and loyalty was a premium. Without loyalty, you would not be allowed to remain in the Secret Service, where nobody got fired— they simply disappeared in ways nobody could ever trace. Since they were part of the secret service, their murders were easily explained to their families: We are very sorry, but your husband was killed in the line of duty fighting the revolutionaries.

DRANZONIAN SECRET SERVICE
DEPARTMENT HEAD EDGAR BOONT

You probably weren't expecting to be called back to work today.

BLANE JIANDIE

I already made arrangements and signed out on leave.

DRANZONIAN SECRET SERVICE
DEPARTMENT HEAD EDGAR BOONT

Yes, I'm aware of that, but something has come up.

BLANE JIANDIE

I just spent two months-worth of my pay for these reservations and transportation.

DRANZONIAN SECRET SERVICE
DEPARTMENT HEAD EDGAR BOONT
I'm aware of that, and you will provide receipts and you will be reimbursed for the loss of the use of those reservations.

BLANE JIANDIE
I realize there is a lot of unsettled business still going on, but we established some relative calm last year and the Revolutionary Empire, or whatever they wish to call themselves, have not spread in this direction and appear to have calmed down quite a bit. I've been working hard for a long time without a break.

DRANZONIAN SECRET SERVICE
DEPARTMENT HEAD EDGAR BOONT
The assignment you will receive will give you plenty of time to unwind, and your disguise will be traveling as a tourist, so to speak, so you will be able to have plenty of down time and enjoy yourself as you carry out your tasks.

BLANE JIANDIE
What exactly will I be doing?

The Department Head Edgar Boont turned on a two-way computer terminal designed so that he could be looking at one screen simultaneously while a guest was looking at another screen on the opposite side so they could share information and discuss matters. Suddenly a picture of a man popped up.

DRANZONIAN SECRET SERVICE
DEPARTMENT HEAD EDGAR BOONT
This is your new assignment.

BLANE JIANDIE
He vaguely looks familiar.

DRANZONIAN SECRET SERVICE
DEPARTMENT HEAD EDGAR BOONT
He should. He is currently hiding out on the planet Zanziltar. You might have seen him out and about. He was a very social person, goes to clubs and entertainment centers routinely.

BLANE JIANDIE
What's his story?

DRANZONIAN SECRET SERVICE
DEPARTMENT HEAD EDGAR BOONT
The man's name is Evo Kaplan. He's a Revolutionary
Empire operative.

BLANE JIANDIE
Is Evo Kaplan working for the Revolution?

DRANZONIAN SECRET SERVICE
DEPARTMENT HEAD EDGAR BOONT
That's what we believe.

BLANE JIANDIE
What is my task with this man?

Blane Jiandie started thinking he would possibly be sent as an assassin.

DRANZONIAN SECRET SERVICE
DEPARTMENT HEAD EDGAR BO ONT
Intel has reported Evo Kaplan has sought and was granted
passage on Toutoumomo de Hundan, a blockade runner
that has a destination to Arzon.

BLANE JIANDIE
Why is he going to Arzon?

DRANZONIAN SECRET SERVICE
DEPARTMENT HEAD EDGAR BOONT
That's where you come in.

BLANE JIANDIE
You want me to find out what Evo Kaplan is doing on
Arzon.
DRANZONIAN SECRET SERVICE
DEPARTMENT HEAD EDGAR BOONT
Precisely.

BLANE JIANDIE
That could take a while. How will I get back?

> DRANZONIAN SECRET SERVICE
> DEPARTMENT HEAD EDGAR BOONT
> We understand the logistics involved will be rough.
> All we can do at this point is promise you we'll find a
> way to get you home.

> BLANE JIANDIE
> The last thing in the world I would want is to be caught
> by the Revolutionaries. We already know what the
> sick bastards do to spies they capture.

The department head handed Blane a small pouch.

> DRANZONIAN SECRET SERVICE
> DEPARTMENT HEAD EDGAR BOONT
> There are some fast-acting pills in there that you can
> take, which will kill you in a few seconds, so you don't
> have to worry about suffering. If you take one of these
> pills you will immediately become unconscious and
> by the time you fall on the floor you would already be
> dead and feel no pain.

Blane took the pouch and put it in his suit coat pocket with sheer reluctance. But he knew some of the sick bastard traitors now working for the Revolutionary Empire's Committee for State Security secret police loved to engage in torture and other cruel and inhumane acts. He knew that if members of the Revolutionary Empire's secret police arrested him in a short period of time, he would have wished he had those fast-acting pills with him.

> BLANE JIANDIE
> When I get to Arzon, how would I communicate with
> the home office? The Revolutionaries have cut off all
> the relay stations, and the last I heard, we have not
> regained communication with the planet?

> DRANZONIAN SECRET SERVICE
> DEPARTMENT HEAD EDGAR BOONT
> When you get off the transport at Arzon, your old
> flame Loraine will observe your arrival. She has been
> briefed on your itinerary and when you check into one
> of the safe houses, she will contact you.

> BLANE JIANDIE
> If communications are cut, how did you contact
> Loraine?

DRANZONIAN SECRET SERVICE
DEPARTMENT HEAD EDGAR BOONT
We have several methods of communicating. Some are slow and some are ultra-fast depending on the urgency. I can't disclose to you how we do it in the event you get captured and tortured to reveal the process.

BLANE JIANDIE
You mentioned I have an itinerary?

DRANZONIAN SECRET SERVICE
DEPARTMENT HEAD EDGAR BOONT
Yes, when you leave my office, you will report down to section Q3, who will outfit you with special gizmos you will take with you and be given your itinerary as well as critical information and egress plans in the event the inevitable happens and we must extract you.

BLANE JIANDIE
When precisely will I be leaving?

DRANZONIAN SECRET SERVICE
DEPARTMENT HEAD EDGAR BOONT
Your departure date and time have not been fixed. The blockade runner is not going to leave until all the seats have been sold or the prices so extreme that he doesn't need to fill all the seats.

BLANE JIANDIE
Will it be a day, a week, or a month?

DRANZONIAN SECRET SERVICE
DEPARTMENT HEAD EDGAR BOONT
Since we can't lock in an exact departure time and date, I suggest you start your vacation that has already been prepaid, which we will reimburse you for, and be ready to deploy within twelve hours' notice.

BLANE JIANDIE
What if I meet a pretty lady and need to stay longer?

DRANZONIAN SECRET SERVICE
DEPARTMENT HEAD EDGAR BOONT

You know you will be on that transport, whether you arrive awake or unconscious.

BLANE JIANDIE
Anything else you wish to tell me about Evo Kaplan?

DRANZONIAN SECRET SERVICE
DEPARTMENT HEAD EDGAR BOONT
Evo Kaplan had been a rather successful Secret Service agent. His character flaw that went unnoticed for a period was his sympathies toward the Revolutionaries. We believe he was recently recruited and has been seen on a couple planets and we believe he conducted missions for the Revolutionary forces.

BLANE JIANDIE
What other information about Evo Kaplan do you have?

DRANZONIAN SECRET SERVICE
DEPARTMENT HEAD EDGAR BOONT
Okay, let's look at this presentation.

The department head started a dossier review presentation that suddenly started streaming on the display in front of Blane. Evo Kaplan's photographs and factoids streamed sideways across the 24-inch 3D screen, which had a narrator discussing the finer points and elucidating the essence of Evo Kaplan.

VOICE OVER
Since Evo Kaplan had worked for the Ministry for State Security in the Dranzonian Empire, there were many data points recorded prior to him changing his personal identity and obtained new credentials allowing him to stay on the planet Zanziltar.

We believe that after Evo Kaplan's recruitment by Revolution forces, he performed various nefarious activities there and may have gone to the resort planet Shen de Huayuan where one of our agents went missing.

The Department Head didn't think it was wise to tell Blane Jiandie that Reginald Heiqishi, who came up missing on Zanziltar, had used his identity, including

cosmetic surgery to acquire his facial features he had
prior to Blane's recent cosmetic surgery.

Otherwise, Evo Kaplan would think he was the same person if they came in contact. Blane had the advantage: he now knew Evo Kaplan's appearance, but Evo had never seen Blane with his new identity he would soon have: Cap Zapatero.

Based on Reginald Heiqishi's debriefing prior to his reckless venture in the heart of the city that ultimately got him killed on a contract to the FIRM by an angry banker. The FIRM, aka Revolutionary Secret Service, required a lot of funds they acquired by performing services such as assassination, racketeering, and the operation of red-light districts. They justified their criminal enterprise as a means of funding all the intel operations they performed against the Dranzonian Empire.

The Revolutionary Empire Zanziltar Operations survived and flourished operating in the Sanctuary City. An element of the Dranzonian Empire Secret Service operating as diplomats out of the Zanziltar Consulate also had an element of success; however, the Dranzonians and the Revolutionaries were never able to go after each other in Zanziltar without being kicked off the planet.

Only those extremely rare moments when they conducted operations such as seizing Reginald Heiqishi while he was drifting around the business district of the city and disappeared in thin air, were there actual casualties in the feud on this planet. More importantly, they were both excellent practitioners of concealment and disinformation and if necessary, the purveyors of lethal actions.

Why Conrad Fanzui disallowed Evo Kaplan from seeing Brenda Broyals again prior to his deployment to Arzon was a mystery. However, Brenda knew why since she was already on her way to another planet on another mission unrelated to the Arzon operation.

Conrad also believed it would be best for the FIRM to keep Brenda Broyals and Evo Kaplan apart as much as possible in the future because they were now fugitives of the Dranzonian Empire with a large price on their heads.

By keeping Brenda Broyals and Evo Kaplan apart, it would force the Dranzonians to expend far more resources to trap and kill them independently than if they were together and a sitting duck target.

Evo Kaplan had his last chance to come home when he was on the cruise ship. From now on his only way home would be in a body bag, and most likely the Dranzonians wouldn't waste the time and effort doing that and would simply put him in a crematorium, disappearing forever if he were captured.

EXT. DAY. FIRM SAFEHOUSE

Immediately after Reginald Heiqishi was eliminated, a VTOL craft came down on the road in front of the abandoned house. The body was carried out and placed aboard and it immediately took off to some undisclosed location where no doubt they had a novel way of disposing of the body. After the body was stripped, it was dropped in the middle of a very large hog farm, where the semi-wild animals had razor sharp teeth and, after smelling the corpse and sampling a few limbs, immediately started fighting over the carcass.

It was about sundown and the farmer was almost a mile away in his farmhouse, listening to the local news on his videoscope and because of his hard hearing was not in a position to hear or see the VTOL craft drop the body. By the time the hogs finished up, there wasn't much left, as the bones were scattered over several acres and the skull was carried off into brush where another type of wild animal finished what the hogs didn't get accomplished.

Due to the large amount of brush surrounding the hog farm, the remains of the skull would most likely not be discovered for hundreds of years. The mystery of Reginald Heiqishi's disappearance would never be solved, though the banker had satisfaction his credits were well spent while his wife simply thought Reginald Heiqishi had simply just enjoyed her briefly and departed.

No matter how hard Glacey Spencer tried to discover Blane Jiandie's (a.k.a. Reginald Heiqishi) whereabouts, there was never any leads including dead ends from the Lantiane Resort, where staff was more than happy to assist finding him for a lot of credits, and they tried unsuccessfully and eventually gave up because he left without a trace. Even transportation records at the space port, which could be purchased by large bribes, rendered no information.

Eventually Glacey Spencer figured out Reginald Heiqishi wasn't the person she thought he was. In fact, she had no idea what he was doing other than the fond memories of what transpired between them while her husband was off with the politician to Orgy Island.

After the VTOL carrying Reginald Heiqishi's body was about out of sight, a vehicle pulled up and one member of the FIRM got out and approached Evo Kaplan.

> FIRM AGENT
> Give us your laser pistol. We can't afford to have
> you captured with a weapon on your way back to the
> FIRM.

Evo handed him the laser pistol quickly, wondering if that was a smart move to do since they could kill him just as easily as he had just done Reginald Heiqishi.

As soon as the Firm Agent took the pistol, he opened the door to the vehicle.

> FIRM AGENT
> Get in the vehicle Evo. These guys will take you back
> to the FIRM.

Evo got in the vehicle, which immediately drove off. There were a couple other vehicles suddenly there. No doubt they were there to sanitize the house to make sure there were no traces left behind.

They too would be gone soon. Traveling down the high-speed corridor placed them back at the FIRM in a short time.

EXT. DAY. FIRM MANSION FRONT ENTRANCE.

The car pulled up front and a security man opened the door for Evo Kaplan, who then got out. He was then escorted to his living quarters on the compound and was soon met by a doctor and a couple of other people.

INT. DAY. EVO KAPLAN'S LIVING QUARTERS.

> DOCTOR
> We are going to give you an injection.

> EVO KAPLAN
> Why?

> DOCTOR
> Because you are most likely suffering from space lag
> and you will be deployed really soon.

> EVO KAPLAN
> What does the injection do for me?

A FIRM agent took over the conversation from the Doctor.

> FIRM AGENT
> This will put you to a deep sleep, almost a coma, and
> we will wake you up in about twenty-four hours.

> EVO KAPLAN
> Then what?

FIRM AGENT
You will be fully rested and given a physical checkup and taken to the space port, where you will be put aboard the Toutoumomo de Hundan, which will be making a stop at Praxisvlasia.

EVO KAPLAN
Is there something I'm going to be doing on Praxisvlasia?

FIRM AGENT
No, this is just a stopover for the transport to pick up more passengers. Do not try to get off the ship at Praxisvlasia. If you do, the Dranzonian Secret Service could possibly capture you and your life will be cut short.

EVO KAPLAN
Why should I be concerned?

FIRM AGENT
Evo Kaplan, you have a price on your head, and you are a Dranzonian Secret Service person of interest in the disappearance of Reginald Heiqishi and Terrshey Wate. You, being a former Dranzonian Empire Secret Service agent, should know how they will treat you if you are captured.

EVO KAPLAN
Shouldn't I eat something before I get this injection?

DOCTOR .
No. It's better that you do not, so that your bowels are not full of material. Since you'll be unconscious, you will not have any hunger pains.

EVO KAPLAN
You want to inject me now?

FIRM AGENT
Correct.

EVO KAPLAN
Okay, what do you want me to do?

DOCTOR
Sit down on the side of the bed, take your shoes off,
and then we'll inject you.

As the doctor prepared the syringe, Evo noticed two large guys suddenly standing on each side of him.

EVO KAPLAN
What's these guys doing?

DOCTOR
When you get your injection, you will collapse within
ten seconds. They are here to make sure you do not fall
and get injured.

Evo watched the female doctor fill up the syringe with a crystal blue liquid from a dispenser bottle. She then directed Evo Kaplan.

DOCTOR
Okay, hold out your right arm and let me see if I can
find a good vein. Make a fist and squeeze.

Evo complied and immediately felt the sting of a needle piercing his arm just like he was getting a blood sample drawn. In about five seconds, the room suddenly started getting darker. At seven seconds the room was all dark except for a small white circle directly in front of him that slowly closed, and it all went black.

The men grabbed Evo as he was collapsing and laid him softly down on the bed. Within a minute, one of the big men walked over to the door and opened it. Several people pushing carts went into the room. These people were advanced cosmetic surgeons. They had advanced techniques where a rich woman could walk into their office and come out the same day looking like someone else.

VOICE OVER
Thanks to advanced drug therapy and new robotic
surgical techniques including three dimensional (3D)
biological printing, a new face could be put on and
when the patient woke up twenty-four hours later,
they would be someone else. They did not tell Evo in
advance they were changing his face because it would
be better for his psychology to simply wake up as a
different person.

Evo Kaplan was gone forever. Just like his enemy

Blane Jiandie, whom he would be facing soon, his identity also changed. All the preparations beforehand were now useless since neither party would know who the other appeared to be. Nobody in the galaxy would see Evo Kaplan's new identity until he arrived at the space port forty-eight hours later. Evo had one of the strangest dreams he ever had.

Evo Kaplan was indeed hallucinating but didn't know it as he was unconscious and almost in a coma from the powerful drugs given him. The beautiful aspect of the knockout drugs was that when they gave him the antidote, he would awake and be awake and alert in fifteen minutes.

The success of this mission hinged on whether they were able to plant a spy on the Toutoumomo de Hundan without detection or attracting any undue attention. Evo Kaplan's new disguise was lifted off a black marketer Krawz Almarip whom the Dranzonian Empire Secret Service knew about, as well as Arzon officials who allowed them to operate since without them, no Loyalist could go between Arzon and the Dranzonian Empire.

VOICE OVER

The black marketer Krawz Almarip, who was given great privileges on Zanziltar, was rather flamboyant and disappeared for days at a time while engaged in various contemptible activities.

The fact Krawz Almarip disappeared then reappeared getting on the spaceship raised no concern since that was his typical behavior. He also had the tendency to not do a lot of talking and usually ignored people outright and only spoke when he wanted something from another party.

The Intergalactic Passenger Transport would have several black marketers onboard who mistrusted each other. The others steered away from Krawz Almarip. They knew he would feel no remorse if he slit their throats if they got in his way.

Krawz Almarip's reputation as a gun slinger was legendary. Part of his finesse with his laser pistol resulted from artificial intelligence that reconciled at a microsecond the target and as he positioned his hand to shoot sliding up and down usually in twenty milliseconds from the don shin position to killing his opponent.

Krawz Almarip's laser blaster was linked to his AI holster that had several sensors and cameras on it to facilitate that deadly fast attack.

Since the real Krawz Almarip worked out as much as any Revolutionary guard, Secret Service, or FIRM personnel, he could carry and manipulate a laser pistol blaster weighing over twice as much as the standard models, which only had enough stored energy for ten shots.

Krawz Almarip's laser blaster could shoot over twenty shots, meaning he wasn't going to run out of options in a dog fight.

Twenty-four hours later as Evo Kaplan—now disguised as Krawz Almarip—was awakened with chemicals to neutralize the sleep-inducing chemicals in his body, he slowly looked around and saw several medical people smiling.

MEDICAL STAFF PERSON
In a few minutes as you wake up you will start to feel some hunger and pain and we will have a meal prepared for you, but before you eat, Conrad Fanzui wants a few words with you. He'll be here momentarily.

True to the notification, a moment later Conrad Fanzui walked in the room carrying a small mirror that one would attribute to a woman putting on makeup. He nodded to the medical staff, who understood they needed to leave the room because they were not authorized to hear what transpired over the next few minutes.

CONRAD FANZUI
Evo, how do you feel?

EVO KAPLAN
They warned me I would develop hunger pains. I'm starting to get them now.

CONRAD FANZUI
Not a problem. They will soon serve you breakfast in bed.

EVO KAPLAN
Any way I can get it.

CONRAD FANZUI
We didn't want to warn you about the preparations we felt we needed to make for your own safety.

EVO KAPLAN
I'm not a coward, just tell me the facts.

CONRAD FANZUI
Your mission will be dangerous enough as it is, and we felt we could not allow you to travel to Arzon with Evo Kaplan's appearance. I know you will probably be upset for a while concerning what we did, but it will provide you with a lot more security.

EVO KAPLAN
What did you do?

CONRAD FANZUI
We gave you the identity of a black marketer named Krawz Almarip who often travels to Arzon. That way you will not stick out.

EVO KAPLAN
Why pick a black marketeer, seems to me that would stand out.

CONRAD FANZUI
We have studied Krawz Almarip and know who he contacts on Arzon and anyone you might encounter; we think we have them identified and how they fit into his smuggling operations.

Conrad Fanzui handed Evo Kaplan the mirror, which he instinctively grabbed and looked at. Evo Kaplan strangely felt the surgery improved his looks. He looked far more urbane and masculine.

CONRAD FANZUI
The doctors informed me the surgery is already seventy-five percent healed and the exponentiators they fed your blood stream with the IV still connected

to your arm will fully heal the cosmetic surgery over the next twenty-four hours.

VOICE OVER

Evo Kaplan was now realizing his life had a new direction. He's always been a spy in his adult life and now he has new masters that will determine his future.

CONRAD FANZUI

As you heal over the next twenty-four hours, you will be given briefings and see images of all his contacts and what they do. Your voice is not too different than his, so we felt no need to alter it.

EVO KAPLAN

I probably can never be Evo Kaplan again, I suppose.

CONRAD FANZUI

Evo Kaplan is now on the Dranzonian Empire Secret Service top ten list of enemy agents to kill on sight. If you want to survive, you must leave Evo Kaplan behind forever.

EVO KAPLAN

Since I don't have much of a family, there probably isn't much of a reason to keep my original identity.

CONRAD FANZUI

If you stay alive and stay in the spy business, you will no doubt have cosmetic surgery a few more times.

EVO KAPLAN

Interestingly, I do not feel any pain.

CONRAD FANZUI

There are painkillers in your IV, but in twenty-four hours you will no longer require any.

EVO KAPLAN

Did you ever go through this procedure?

CONRAD FANZUI

Yes, several times. I was number one of the Dranzonian Empire Secret Service lists to kill on sight. If I leave the planet for a mission, I will get an identity change.

EVO KAPLAN
What happens to the person when you take their identity?

CONRAD FANZUI
We must make sure their identity can never interfere with what we do. They must be exterminated, much along the lines of what you did to Reginald Heiqishi and Terrshey Wate.

Evo Kaplan looked in the mirror again.

EVO KAPLAN
Will Brenda Broyals get cosmetic surgery?

CONRAD FANZUI
You will never see Brenda Broyals again. She has already changed into another person.

EVO KAPLAN
So, is it possible we may pass each other or be involved on a mission and not know the other person is someone we know?

CONRAD FANZUI
I know you care a lot about Brenda. You will not go on missions together, but you will have to trust me. When it's possible to send you both on a vacation together sometime in the future, I will bring you together. You will then discover her new looks.

EVO KAPLAN
How did her surgery work out?

CONRAD FANZUI
She thinks she is far more beautiful than before. We intentionally improved her looks for her pending mission to help her penetrate and exploit her contact on the planet she is now involved in.

EVO KAPLAN
Does that mean exploit with all her resources?

CONRAD FANZUI
A good spy uses all their resources for exploitation if necessary. A good analogy is a lawyer doesn't have to tell the truth; all he has to do is advise his client, so they win the case.

EVO KAPLAN
When exactly do I leave?

CONRAD FANZUI
We have no control over that. The operator will not launch the ship until he has either filled all the seats or extracted enough fees to cover the empty seats.

EVO KAPLAN
How will we know how soon that is?

CONRAD FANZUI
If he doesn't fill the seats in forty-eight hours, we'll buy the remaining seats and tell him to go. We have something important to get from Praxisvlasia, the stop over to Arzon.

EVO KAPLAN
Are you sending important materials?

CONRAD FANZUI
We are shipping contraband for your utilization.

EVO KAPLAN
What is the purpose of the contraband?

CONRAD FANZUI
To bribe officials or to use as barter.

EVO KAPLAN
Wouldn't that make me stand out?

CONRAD FANZUI
Remember, we gave you the identity of a smuggler. They expect you to do it and after you finish eating, trainers will come in and help you start preparing as they school you on a few matters and the personalities

you might run into or those you need to look up, and about Krawz Almarip's prior relationship with them.

EVO KAPLAN
How do you know all this?

CONRAD FANZUI
We get a lot of information from the individual that you have his identity.

EVO KAPLAN
Is this person still alive?

CONRAD FANZUI
Yes, we'll keep him alive until your mission is complete in case, we must get essential information out of him or place his body conveniently in some place to help insure you get out alive.

EVO KAPLAN
He cooperates?

CONRAD FANZUI
After we gave him a couple samples of our advanced interrogation techniques, he would much rather enjoy the good food, wine, and women we supply him than to get back in the swimming pool or the crematorium.

VOICE OVER
Evo Kaplan wondered: did Conrad Fanzui say this as a warning to me a clue what could happen to me if he crossed him?

Conrad Fanzui looked at Evo Kaplan (his identity would stay as Krawz Almarip until the mission was completed).

CONRAD FANZUI
Do you feel you are ready to go on the mission?

EVO KAPLAN
I kind of wish I could have a few good workouts before I leave on the mission.

CONRAD FANZUI
Since we probably have a couple days, you can go out to the workout area tomorrow incrementally between

your training sessions. I'll tell your trainers to give
you three or four workout periods during the day and
I'll have some martial artists there for you to practice
with.

EVO KAPLAN
That's good, I want to work on my timing.

CONRAD FANZUI
Your timing was pretty good on Coy's Ridge.

EVO KAPLAN
Yes, but I've done a lot of travel and had too many
good meals since then.

CONRAD FANZUI
The medical staff will be back momentarily. See you
when you get back.

Conrad Fanzui turned and walked out of the room. A moment later the medical people returned and brought with them a covered cart that brought with it an aroma. Evo Kaplan's hunger suddenly intensified. Shortly after his meal Evo Kaplan succumbed to sleep.

Nobody woke Evo the next day. He awoke on his own and evidently had received a good sleep medication the night before because he did not feel them remove the IV needle in his arm.

All that equipment was gone, and he was alone. Evo got up, did his morning routine S/S/S, then put on gym clothes that were in their usual spot in the closet and running shoes. He dressed and was out the door several minutes later. He started doing his laps, putting his heart into it, knowing he would be on a long space ride soon and better get the maximum workout now.

Evo Kaplan felt he had a lot of energy and no hunger. It was as if he were gliding on air and had never run so easy in his life. The drugs that were still in his body to enhance the healing for the cosmetic surgery had a huge effect on his muscle tissue and prevented the buildup of lactic acid.

After several laps that he usually did, he went over to the workout area and did stretches then some calisthenics and special exercises his trainers taught him. Several women were now running laps as well and by the time he completed his workout they were over to the workout area doing similar calisthenics and special exercises like Evo Kaplan had done.

Evo Kaplan was just about to go back to his quarters, shower, put on his street clothes, and get ready for training, when unexpectedly one of his martial arts instructors appeared.

MARTIAL ARTS INSTRUCTOR
Hello Krawz Almarip.

The martial arts instructor evidently had been briefed on his current name. He knew better than to ask if he remembered him as Evo Kaplan. He could tell by their reaction the women had overheard the name. He had no idea who they were or what they did, but they looked healthy.

MARTIAL ARTS INSTRUCTOR
Okay, let's go through the standard forms!

The forms, which built up the muscle memory and speed, were scientifically designed by ancient elders. Evo broke the man's neck at Coy Ridge with just one chop to the neck in less than one second. It was efficient and it was quiet but may not be the technique he needed the next time, so he had to practice them all.

Going through the martial arts forms burns up energy twice as fast as actual fighting. Most fights last less than three minutes and often use only half the body's energy.

Going through the twenty standard forms, some of which have one hundred and eleven moves, burns up eighty percent of the body's energy in the same amount of time. Evo Kaplan practiced moves from kicking to jumping to punching to twisting and simulated blocks occurred contiguously with no pause until that form was complete. Evo would stop for a moment, announce the next form, and then continue.

Martial arts instructors observe students every day. They see the very best and they also see the not so good as well. They are compelled to help someone because if they do a crummy job on the forms, they might get killed in the line of duty. There was a strong correlation to survival rate with the forms performance. People who had the best forms generally came back alive from missions alive more often.

The instructor knew this and tried his best to convince the practitioners of their fate. Due to scanners and technology, there were many times when you could not carry a laser pistol with you into harm's way. That also goes for the enemy. Hence in 50 percent of all the desperate fights that occur and was in fact a life-or-death manner, it came down to the person knowing martial arts surviving.

In some cases, even though the opponent had a laser pistol, a martial arts expert survived because he was able to disable the enemy before they got a good shot with the laser weapon. Evo knew he was a little rusty because of his recent travel.

The instructor seemed like a pest having him repeat some forms four or five times until he performed them at the level of perfection the instructor required.

At the end of the twenty forms, the instructor knew any further activity would not result in improvement. Evo needed a rest, plus he was advised that about now he needed to shower, clean up, and start receiving his indoctrination for his pending travel.

Evo should have figured by now he was under surveillance all the time and had no privacy. As soon as he was dressed and cleaned up, the doorbell rang. Outside were several people with a cart.

STAFF MEMBER
You will be eating your meal in your room so that you
can receive training while you eat.

EVO KAPLAN
All right.

The staff brought in the cart that doubled as an improvised dinner table. They took one of his chairs and set it next to the improvised table, removed the hood, and exposed an elaborate meal prepared for him.

EVO KAPLAN
The food looks good and smells good.

STAFF MEMBER
It's designed to further help your healing and training.
Please sit down and we will start your training while
you eat.

Another cart rolled in had a screen on it that was covered up until they rolled it about ten feet away from Evo. As soon as the covering material was removed, revealing the display technology under it, one of the technicians pressed a button and it started playing. The narrator to the training started discussing Krawz Almarip.

Within thirty minutes, Evo knew Krawz Almarip's life story, his former girlfriends, and the high points in his life.

The video then started showing all the people he met in Arzon, some of which he would have to seek out to barter and trade for benefits or privileges. Some of the information was only derived a week ago when the real Krawz Almarip got a taste of the crematorium because the Revolutionaries discovered some information he withheld. As one wise person a long ago said, "Trust but verify."

The meal Evo Kaplan ate was highly digestible and the drink he had included energy and alertness formulas. After two hours of training, the staff member made an announcement.

STAFF MEMBER
We are going to take a break now so that you can go work out more, and the doctors will be here momentarily to give you a quick checkup.

EVO KAPLAN
Okay.

The training crew left the room, and the medical people came in immediately after the last trainers departed.

DOCTOR
How are you feeling today, Krawz Almarip?

KRAWZ ALMARIP (a.k.a. EVO KAPLAN)
Pretty good. I felt very strong and fresh when I was running this morning.

DOCTOR
We expected you would, as the drugs wore off that we gave you in the IV to promote healing and sleep.

KRAWZ ALMARIP (a.k.a. EVO KAPLAN)
It was one of my better workouts even though I was probably a little out of shape.

DOCTOR
Would you please take off your shirt so we can look at your neck and shoulders.

Evo complied and the doctors began pawing all over Evo Kaplan's neck and head.

DOCTOR
Looks like you are healing well. All the scar tissue is healed.

KRAWZ ALMARIP (a.k.a. EVO KAPLAN)
Feels good and I think I look better as well.

                    DOCTOR
You have no scars. It would be impossible for anyone
to know you had cosmetic surgery.

          KRAWZ ALMARIP (a.k.a. EVO KAPLAN)
Evo Kaplan grabbed the mirror that Conrad Fanzui
had left him still sitting on his bed. He picked it up and
looked again. I'd say I'm probably ninety-five percent
healed now.

                    DOCTOR #2
Krawz Almarip, you are at least ninety-eight percent
healed. We'll be back later this afternoon to look at
you one more time. So far it looks like the procedure
went well. We'll visit you again to check you before
you go on a mission.

          KRAWZ ALMARIP (a.k.a. EVO KAPLAN)
                  See you then.

EXT. "FIRM" CAMPUS WORKOUT AREA.

Evo Kaplan then put his workout clothes back on and went out to the track and started
running a couple laps. This time it wasn't quite as easy. Those drugs must be wearing
off now. After a couple laps, he went to stretch and do more calisthenics. Just as if
someone was watching him and timing it, the martial arts instructor suddenly appeared
again.

               MARTIAL ARTS INSTRUCTOR
Krawz Almarip, are you ready to do some more forms
now?

          KRAWZ ALMARIP (a.k.a. EVO KAPLAN)
Yes, but I may not be as good as I was this morning.

               MARTIAL ARTS INSTRUCTOR
Okay Krawz Almarip, let's begin.

MONTAGE. MARTIAL ARTS WORKOUT.

Note to the cinematographer:

During the next voice over sequence, a stunt man dressed up like Evo Kaplan
in workout clothes performs some elaborate Karate Kata's. The voiceover

should last approximately one minute. The shoot on the Karate Katas can be a montage of an actual blackbelt performing Katas wearing a mask to look like Evo Kaplan.

VOICE OVER

Evo Kaplan started standard-form number one. It had a strange name given to it by the inventor at some obscure planet such as "Shishido no y ni Tatakai, Taka no y ni Korosu" (Fight Like a Lion, Kill Like an Eagle).

During his martial arts training, Evo Kaplan needed to know how to make each move precisely. He also had to know the definition and pronounce it in the language it originated for promotion through the ranks.

Based on his experience running, Evo Kaplan realized he would probably run out of gas around form number fifteen, which was a very intense movement form that lasted five minutes. It was one of the longest and demanding forms including jumping and landing in a cat stance.

If there was any form that best portrayed a Japanese ninja, it was form number fifteen with one hundred and eleven moves. One hundred and eleven is also known as the magic number. The form number fifteen was referred to as translated from an ancient civilization: Xiong Yu Yi bai Yishiyi Emo Zhandou (Bears Fighting 111 Demons).

Just before Evo started form number fifteen, the martial arts instructor stopped Evo Kaplan.

MARTIAL ARTS INSTRUCTOR

Let's stop for a moment. I want you to do form fifteen well, so before you start, I want you to drink an energy drink.

Everything at the FIRM was scripted beyond belief. No sooner than the martial arts instructor muttered these words, a staff member came walking out with a small bag strapped across his shoulder. He walked up, took the bag off, and handed it to the martial arts instructor, who unzipped the top and grabbed a canned drink that was chilled nicely.

MARTIAL ARTS INSTRUCTOR
Here, drink this.

The martial arts instructor handed the energy drink to Evo, who popped the top and took a nice gulp.

KRAWZ ALMARIP (a.k.a. EVO KAPLAN)
This drink tastes pretty good.

MARTIAL ARTS INSTRUCTOR
It was developed for special forces for moments of extreme stress. We took delivery of a certain amount to help accelerate our training.

MONTAGE. MARTIAL ARTS WORKOUT.

Note to the cinematographer:

During the next voice over sequence, a stunt man dressed up like Evo Kaplan in workout clothes performs some elaborate Karate Kata's. The voiceover should last approximately one minute. The shoot on the Karate Katas can be a montage of an actual blackbelt performing Elaborate Karate Katas. Most Americans have never observed a blackbelt Kata.

You might consider hiring Hanshi Miki who has a Dojo in Carlsbad California as a technical advisor for these Kata's. He probably has some blackbelts to recommend performing them. With a mask or makeup, you can probably make the Karate Ka appear as Evo Kaplan in this sequence.

Shito Ryu Grand Master Minobu Miki in San Diego County — Japan Karate-Do organization (jko.com)

Hanshi Miki Minobu - San Diego Iaido - America Tosa Jikiden Shigetsukai （ アメリカ土佐直傳士月会）

VOICE OVER (MALE)
Evo took his time drinking the energy drink, savoring it. The instructor wasn't annoyed and was glad Evo wasn't drinking it too fast, that way it would have more impact on the outcome of the coming form-fifteen demonstration: Xiong Yu Yi bai Yishiyi Emo Zhandou.

Evo Kaplan finished the contents of the can and sat

it down on one of the picnic tables there that allowed trainees to sit, drink, and rest between sets of exercises. He walked out in the middle of a padded mat where a person could do martial arts training and avoid falling hard and getting injuries. He then started his five-minute Xiong Yu Yi bai Yishiyi Emo Zhandou martial arts form routine.

Evo Kaplan felt amazingly refreshed just as if he had been totally rested. He had more energy, concentration, and emotionally he hung on a plateau that invigorated his ever being. It was as if he knew he could easily pull this off. He suddenly had the psychological advantage, and his spirits were lifted, empowering him to do all one hundred and eleven individual movements in great precision.

The martial arts instructor observed quietly and intently. He had eagle eyes. Just as if Evo Kaplan was operating in a combination of intermittent suspended animation and time lapsed periods, the instructor cogently spotted the quality of each movement and in the back of his head could later recall any criticism he had to give. Since he felt it was a life-or-death matter based on statistics, he would not be cutting Evo Kaplan any slack.

The martial arts instructor would inform Krawz Almarip (a.k.a. Evo Kaplan) in as much precision as he could muster a full critique of his performance. Evo Kaplan continued the form-fifteen without the slightest care in the world for the full five minutes performing the one hundred and eleven moves. Some of the moves are repeated four times for quadrants on the compass. The base one hundred and eleven moves morphed into close to four hundred total moves.

The five different jumps in the routine expended a lot of energy and when the practitioner landed on all fours just like a cat, they had to hold it a brief period solid and not wiggle. Just like in the animal world, a wiggle or movement could betray him.

As Evo Kaplan was near the last ten moves, he felt marvelously refreshed. The energy drink was doing its magic. The instructor predicted the outcome with the drink and based on experience gave it to Evo Kaplan because when you do a poor job in practice, you end up doing a poor job in real combat.

All the exercises and running were video recorded by several video cameras strategically located around the track and workout area. This Xiong Yu Yi bai Yishiyi Emo Zhandou forms routine would be replayed later by the instructor several times at a slower speed to verify his analysis was done correctly and in a future workout, concentrate on the weak areas to improve execution of the forms.

When an operative was killed, part of the investigation went into pulling their workout video and observe how well and competently they were training. They had a team grade their workouts. When they compared to survivors, one thing was crystal clear: the ones who trained more effectively survived at a much higher rate.

Management was thus moved and embraced the notion of installing more quality control into the process. At the end of form number fifteen, the instructor spoke.

MARTIAL ARTS INSTRUCTOR
How do you feel? Can you go full force with number sixteen, all the way?

KRAWZ ALMARIP (a.k.a. EVO KAPLAN)
Yes. I feel great. I think I can do it just fine.

The eighty-nine moves associated with form number sixteen wasn't a challenge. Even though Evo Kaplan was now sweating profusely, his movements and techniques were precise, and his timing was impeccable. At the end of number sixteen the instructor stopped Krawz Almarip (a.k.a. Evo Kaplan).

MARTIAL ARTS INSTRUCTOR
Krawz Almarip, you have done quite a bit in a short period of time. Your body has been severely strained

in performing at the level you are doing. I want you
to drink another energy drink before you start form-
number seventeen.

Evo Kaplan was more than happy to comply because the drink did taste good, and it really seemed to help. The instructor handed Krawz Almarip (a.k.a. Evo Kaplan) another energy drink.

MARTIAL ARTS INSTRUCTOR
Please sit down on the bench. I want you to rest your
legs a bit while you consume that energy drink.

It seemed like a reasonable guidance to Evo Kaplan. The instructor obviously knew what he was doing. The instructor kept Krawz Almarip (a.k.a. Evo Kaplan) at the table for ten minutes.

MARTIAL ARTS INSTRUCTOR
Okay, we better start again, your muscles are building
up lactic acid.

It was pay me now or pay me later and Evo Kaplan knew it. Evo Kaplan continued with the rest of his forms, feeling the best he ever had while doing number twenty, the last one. The crescendo occurred in the last moves. He was finally done and was probably going back to the classroom soon.

On cue walked two men wearing martial arts workout clothes that looked very similar to a Japanese Karate Gi.

MARTIAL ARTS INSTRUCTOR
Okay, now that you have practiced your forms, you
will fight these two men.

KRAWZ ALMARIP (a.k.a. EVO KAPLAN)
Okay.

MARTIAL ARTS INSTRUCTOR
They are professional fighters and are trained in how
to protect themselves. Your job is to defend yourself
against them.

KRAWZ ALMARIP (a.k.a. EVO KAPLAN)
Certainly.

MARTIAL ARTS INSTRUCTOR
We are going to simulate an attack by one where the
other joins in. You must be on the alert for another

enemy showing up and figure out how to deal with the two of them at once.

> KRAWZ ALMARIP (a.k.a. EVO KAPLAN)
> What if I accidently kill them?

> MARTIAL ARTS INSTRUCTOR
> They will know your moves and anticipate them. You will not kill them, but when you hear me blow the whistle that means stop immediately.

MONTAGE. MARTIAL ARTS FIGHT.
Note to the cinematographer:

During the next voice over sequence, three stunt men do the fighting Evo Kaplan is in workout clothes the other two men are wearing clothing that resembles a Karate Gi. There should be shots from various angles including possibly using a drone at about 10 feet in the air circling the fight scene.

The following voice over should take approximately one minute and forty-five seconds.

MUSIC. Background music during the fighting: Johann Strauss Sr. Radetzky March

> VOICE OVER (MALE)
> One of the two men walked over to the side seemingly out of position to offer any threat. The other fighter stepped forward and gave Evo a wakeup-call to his face. Evo did his ninjalike escape, just like he had practiced in form number fifteen to come back for an attack. The smack he received on his face still hurt and it gave him a dose of reality as the two men went at each other.
>
> Evo Kaplan had the added complexity of checking his opponent's moves at blinding speed, as well as keeping an eye on the other person for when he would enter the fray. After five minutes fighting just one person, the instructor gave the nod to the second fighter, who then charged Evo rather quickly.
>
> Evo had to avoid this man because if he had succeeded in tackling him and throwing him to the ground, in real life thetwo of them would kill him very abruptly.
>
> In martial arts the axiom of staying alive is staying off the ground where you will be choked out or kicked by several people with lethal blows.

The jump almost seven feet in the air while maintaining situational awareness of the opponent's location at all times was an extraordinary achievement. The attack was unsuccessful, though the second person proceeded into a profile to assist in coordinated attacks.

So now it was four arms and four legs Evo Kaplan had to block or be worried about. It was now more defense than offense. But he also knew he had to take one of them out to even the odds.

It was time to Kill Like an Eagle. Evo quickly worked out the strategy in his head. He faked toward one fighter and landed on the other a devastating blow. Evo Kaplan knocked the guy out, and now it was down to just Evo and the original fighter.

Evo let his mind scan through the advocacy of the various forms he had practiced with a high level of precision and quickly decided on a strategy and executed it.

The instructor could not ever be so proud as his student showed great finesse in the successful attack and the second fighter was on the ground. Just before Evo would have killed him out of natural response to the series of moves, the instructor blew the whistle a couple times to stop Evo just in time. Otherwise, Krawz Almarip (a.k.a. Evo Kaplan) might have killed the guy.

The two men were immediately attended to by the medical personnel, and the unconscious man was brought back to consciousness. The two men were then carted off to get X-rays and treatment. They knew from past experiences these doctors were extremely good at reducing pain and enhancing the healing. They would be ready for the next guy tomorrow.

MARTIAL ARTS INSTRUCTOR
You did well today. It's time you go back to your quarters and take a shower and change for more classroom training.

KRAWZ ALMARIP (a.k.a. EVO KAPLAN)
All right. On my way.

NOTE TO THE CINEMATOGRAPHER.

The next voice over lasts about two minutes and 30 seconds. Sometimes sound has proven by psychoacoustics has more advantages than visual effects. This Voice over glues the story together.

In the background, with the voice over showing the video depicted in the scene a specific music played would add greatly to the psychoacoustics impact on the audience: [Richard Wagner - Ride of The Valkyries Bing Videos]

VOICE OVER
Evo Kaplan went to his living quarters, took a shower, changed into street clothes, and prepared to receive the trainers. Doctors showed up with the trainers and wanted to check Krawz Almarip (a.k.a. Evo Kaplan) for any injuries sustained in the fighting. The guys Krawz Almarip (a.k.a. Evo Kaplan) beat up were in bad shape.

DOCTOR
Looks like one of the trainers nailed you one good one to your face. You have a good bruise. We'll put some medication on that now, should be okay by morning. Here's a pain killer so that you don't feel any of it.

The doctor handed Evo Kaplan a pill, which he swallowed, and took a drink offered. Soon he felt no pain, but the medication seemed to not blur his thinking ability.

VOICE OVER
The training consisted of more information on the planet, the operation, and now they were getting down to the nitty gritty: exactly what he needed to investigate and precisely how he was going to transmit that information off the planet without being caught.

This mission was all about military intelligence. Evo Kaplan now knew for a fact he was in over his head.

Krawz Almarip (a.k.a. Evo Kaplan) was indeed a major spy involved in military related espionage. If caught he would be executed after they tortured any useful information out of him.

Krawz Almarip (a.k.a. Evo Kaplan) would be very far off where he could expect no help. He was on his own. He had to be careful and patient. Hustling to get a trip home wasn't going to work. He had to be subtle and resounding.

Two hours were jammed full of an incredible amount of data and areas to focus on. The guess work was laid out for him. Krawz Almarip's (a.k.a. Evo Kaplan) job was to confirm what the speculators feared was occurring.

For future planning, they didn't want to step into a trap and lose half the fleet just because they underestimated this outpost that had to be taken down as it was essentially the modern-day pathway to the silk road.

What laid on the other side of the nebula and beyond was distant solar systems that contained valuable planets like Earth?

Evo Kaplan was wondering when the ship was going to leave. He'd like to get at least one more day of workouts before he was stuck on the inter-planetary transport where such physical activity wasn't really feasible.

Suddenly it was time to eat again, and to make use of his valuable time since he could be deploying immediately, the trainers had his dinner brought to his quarters where he dined while receiving more training, more videos, more expose's including information on various types of space craft and what differences there were. Essentially in a few hours Evo Kaplan was shown the video equivalent of the Dranzonian Empire Janes Spaceships.

A half hour after dinner it was decided Evo could go and do some more physical training. This would be limited to running and calisthenics. Interestingly the two women were there again working out. As Evo Kaplan worked on his calisthenics for thirty minutes, a martial arts instructor arrived and had the women both doing martial arts forms.

Better them than me now, Evo thought as he felt for them as they went slowly through all twenty of the forms he had done. They were mostly done when he left the area and went back to his quarters, where he once again showered and felt good.

A doctor came by and looked over his bruised face, put some more ointment on it, then gave him a pill and told him to drink the drink he provided with the pill.

DOCTOR

The pill will make you sleepy. We want you to rest now. We'll wake you up in the morning at the appropriate time.

VOICE OVER

Shortly after the doctor left, Evo Kaplan (a.k.a. Krawz Almarip) felt sleepy and crawled between the sheets. He was soon out like a lamp. He had another one of those strange dreams. But he felt delightful, then he was abruptly awakened to discover several people around his bed.

FIRM STAFF MEMBER

Krawz Almarip, we have some good news for you. Your flight is in a few hours. All your preparations are complete. We have a change of clothes for you to put on now after you use the bathroom. You will then be driven to the space port.

NOTE TO THE CINEMATOGRAPHER.

The next voice over lasts about two minutes and 30 seconds. Sometimes sound has proven by psychoacoustics has more advantages than visual effects. This Voice over glues the story together.

In the background, with the voice over showing the video depicted in the scene a specific music played would add greatly to the psychoacoustics impact on the audience.

[Richard Wagner - Ride of The Valkyries Bing Videos]

VOICE OVER MALE

The moment of reality had finally struck. Evo Kaplan soon to play the role of Krawz Almarip was on his way. Never in the five hundred missions Evo Kaplan performed for the Dranzonian Empire Secret Service did he feel quite as uneasy as this.

DELAY IN VOICE OVER 5 SECONDS FOR EFFECT WHILE THE WAGNER MUSIC CONTINUES PLAYING .

When Evo Kaplan was a patriot spying on the Revolution, being killed in the line of duty didn't bother him. But now possibly dying for the enemy did!

Evo Kaplan playing the role of Krawz Almarip knew this mission was highly scripted and he had to perform the next steps; otherwise, the message that Conrad Fanzui gave him would come to pass: he would wish he were dead.

The staff that had awakened Krawz Almarip (a.k.a. Evo Kaplan) in plenty of time so as not to rush him.

The doctors wanted Evo Kaplan to have good bowel movement, shower, shave, brush his teeth, and feel clean and ready.

Evo Kaplan came out of the bathroom with a towel on and in front of him was a clothing rack with his outfit he would wear to the spaceship. The clothes made him look downright sleazy. He had to look and play the role of the black marketer Krawz Almarip.

As such, the wardrobe they packed for him looked almost identical to what he saw in many of the videos they secretly made of Krawz Almarip so they would have a photographic survey of his natural tendencies and dress. Evo Kaplan said to himself, they did a great job making me appear as Krawz Almarip and not look out of place in the role I will now play.

FIRM STAFFER
Are you ready?

KRAWZ ALMARIP(a.k.a. Evo Kaplan)
I guess I'm as ready as I will ever be.

FIRM STAFFER

We have a cart outside to take you and your luggage to the front entrance.

KRAWZ ALMARIP
Alright.

Krawz Almarip (a.k.a. Evo Kaplan went outside his quarters with the several staff personnel who carried his luggage for him. He got in the passenger side of the electric-powered cart and soon it was underway driving a short distance and around the mansion to the front entrance where a vehicle was waiting for him. The driver opened the door for him, and the staff put his luggage into the rear of the van-like vehicle. They were soon on their way to the space port.

ZANZILTAR TO PRAXISVLASIA, CLAUDETTE RAMSEY ARRIVES

<u>INT. INTERGALACTIC PASSENGER TRANSPORT ZANZILTAR (a.k.a. SANCTUARY CITY) – NIGHT</u>

The driver pulled up to the Zanziltar Space Port, got out and opened the door for Evo Caplan, and handed him his luggage. A porter immediately descended upon Evo, asking him if he could carry his luggage for him.

KRAWZ ALMARIP
Sure.

PORTER
I'm cleared to carry on board with you.

KRAWZ ALMARIP
That's great.

Krawz Almarip walked beside the porter who had his luggage on a small carrying cart. They walked through Customs. The porter was cleared he could walk through with the passengers just for this purpose. They were soon up on the spaceship with the porter helping Krawz Almarip place his luggage in the four-square feet storage he was allowed and cleared to board and assist paying customers on Intergalactic Transport.

PORTER
That will be five credits.

KRAWZ ALMARIP
Charge ten Credits.

Krawz Almarip handed the porter his credit token, which the porter scanned and showed Krawz Almarip the transaction amount. Krawz Almarip approved the transaction with a thumb print on the device.

PORTER
Thank you, sir.

The porter then turned away and walked off the ship and out to the entrance with a big smile from the gracious tip to help the next customer.

THE SONG A SPY IS GONE PLAYS IN THE BACKGROUND.

Note to the director:

A Spy Is Gone is one of Paul D. Escudero's songs that was composed for a future James Bond Song. Since Welcome to Sanctuary City is a Spy Novel, this is the perfect place to debut it. The song requires a concert pianist like Yuja Wang and an orchestra backup and a singer, preferably Jennie Kim.

VOICE OVER
(During takeoff and flying out into space)

Krawz Almarip sat down at his assigned seat and strapped in his safety harness, as he knew the ship would be leaving soon. There were not a lot of people. It was clear the FIRM had purchased all the unsold seats to get the ship underway. Since only half the ship was full, completing preparations were greatly simplified.

EXT. CGI. INTERGALACTIC PASSENGER TRANSPORT LEAVING ZANZILTAR (a.k.a. SANCTUARY CITY) – NIGHT

This transport rolls down the runway and flies out into space like an aircraft. It has huge rocket engines in the back using special fuels for range and velocity.

In no time at all they departed Zanziltar and were soon out in space, heading for Praxisvlasia.

Nobody out of the ordinary was around Krawz Almarip; he got no stares. In the cargo hold were his black-market items, which would provide a lot of credits including some of that energy drink he enjoyed recently during his work outs and Martial Arts Forms.

Krawz Almarip also had a dozen cans of energy drinks packed in his carry-on luggage that would help him improve his alertness, and if he felt he had a reason why he needed to stay awake for long periods of time in route, they would help greatly.

If Krawz Almarip detected surveillance, that would be the case: lack of sleep. He also had a few energy drinks for crewmembers, which Krawz Almarip gave them, according to his interviews. The trip from Zanziltar to Praxisvlasia would not be as boring as it was relatively short.

Expected arrival time at Praxisvlasia Space Port was within seventy-two hours. Since only half of the ship was full of people and cargo (commonly referred to as the Pigs and People run), they had extra fuel to accelerate quicker off the planet and more fuel available to slow down at the other end, which allowed them to travel at a much higher than normal velocity for this leg of the trip.

Most likely they could shave off several hours and arrive as early as just two and a half days. Since a lot of extra seats were purchased to allow an earlier flight, they would not be stuck on the planet waiting for more passengers.

The Intergalactic Passenger Transport would leave Praxisvlasia on its way to Arzon with the posted schedule already advertised.

Being on the planet a few hours would allow a more casual loading, topping off their fuel tanks and those passengers who wanted to get off could stretch their legs in the space port.

Even though this was a blockade runner and a ship that violated a lot of intergalactic laws and regulations, the fact remained it was registered as a Zanziltar Intergalactic Passenger Transport.

Because of intergalactic treaty, the Dranzonian Empire Secret Service would not be allowed to board the ship and detain any passenger. The only way that passengers could fall into their hands would be if they left the ship.

The minute they left the ship to cruise through the terminal, they were fair game. That is one of the reasons why during the FIRM training Krawz Almarip was directed not to leave the ship while it was in Praxisvlasia.

The fact Evo Kaplan was portraying an infamous black marketer Krawz Almarip easily played into the con he had to stay on the ship.

Crew members who had seen Krawz Almarip on trips in the past knew he would not be getting off the ship because they also knew the Dranzonian Empire Secret Service held him as a person of interest. Krawz Almarip had ostensibly engaged in gun running to the Revolutionaries in their formative years.

There was one occasion before when the Dranzonian

Empire Secret Service illegally boarded a Zanziltar Intergalactic Passenger Transport and detained a passenger of reported affiliation with the Revolutionaries.

The Dranzonian Empire Secret Service could not stop the captain of the ship immediately sending off a distress signal. Zanziltar banking officials who then threatened to reveal the bank account information of several Dranzonian Empire officials, including secret rendezvous with organized crime figures and gun runners if the person was not immediately put back on the Zanziltar Intergalactic Passenger Transport.

One of the chief parties involved in the assault on the ship was none other than Reginald Heiqishi and his field operative that had warned him not to do it was none other than Evo Kaplan.

This was one of the events in Reginald Heiqishi's past that grew the animosity toward Evo Kaplan because it almost got Reginald Heiqishi fired. Instead of destroying Evo Kaplan, including a second attempt during Evo's vacation to Shen de Huayuan, the opposite happened when Egor Pataslia's secret police informed the Zanziltar banker Randolph Spencer how Reginald Heiqishi's flagrant affair with his wife Glacey Spencer resulted in a FIRM contract that allowed Evo Kaplan to end Reginald Heiqishi's life.

Evo Kaplan wasn't joyous that he took Reginald Heiqishi's life. In fact, Evo Kaplan had periods of remorse.

However, the scenario played out was necessary for Evo Kaplan to save his own life. Had Evo Kaplan refused to shoot Reginald Heiqishi, it was most likely Conrad Fanzui's men would simply had shot them both and they would have ended up in the same location: the hog farm.

Krawz Almarip (a.k.a. Evo Kaplan) knew it wasn't safe for him to get off the ship. If someone had leaked his new identity to the Dranzonian Empire Secret Service, the facial recognition technology would immediately identify him. Within an hour after DNA confirmation Evo Kaplan would be hauled off to a Dranzonian prison that was no more humane than the Revolutionaries were with their swimming pool and crematorium.

So, what did the real Krawz Almarip do during the delay at space ports en route? It took a while for the FIRM to identify all the flight attendants who flew on this blockade runner, but with insiders working with port authority giving them access to security recordings, and with the use of facial recognition technology, they were all identified. None of them were threatened but they were certainly bribed.

When you live in a den of thieves, being another form of thief was not unexpected. Hence, they were willing participants in discovering everything Krawz Almarip did on those flights so that Evo Kaplan could be trained to copy him to reinforce his cosmetic surgery that took his identity thanks to biological 3D-printing techniques.

Just like the real Krawz Almarip would do, during the flight Krawz Almarip (a.k.a. Evo Kaplan) approached one of the flight attendants Krawz Almarip trusted, Ruth Marradi, and asked her for a favor.

KRAWZ ALMARIP
Ruth, when we land in Praxisvlasia, I want to go to my bunk and sleep while we are on the planet. I sleep much better with real gravity.

RUTH MARRADI
Okay Krawz, understand. Same deal as before?

KRAWZ ALMARIP
Ruth, I'm not sure about the deal. Perhaps I might have something better this flight.

RUTH MARRADI
Those Zanziltar health enhancers are good enough. I can sell them and make get a lot of credits.

Evo Kaplan, during his training, had been informed Krawz Almarip had been giving flight attendant Ruth Marradi a half dozen of these Zanziltar health inducers, which allegedly greatly improved the health of cancer and cardiac patients. Some takers of them claimed they appeared five years younger in a short period of time. Whether true or not, the fact they were willing to pay astonishing amounts for them made it hugely profitable.

KRAWZ ALMARIP
I no longer have those items, but I do have something better. When is your first shift after we leave Praxisvlasia?

RUTH MARRADI
I'll be on duty during Praxisvlasia and twelve hours into the flight.

KRAWZ ALMARIP
So, toward the end of the flight you will be dog-ass tired?

RUTH MARRADI
Probably.

KRAWZ ALMARIP
I'll give you a sample when you wake me up after takeoff. You will not feel tired at all even twelve hours later.

RUTH MARRADI
Okay, I'll give it a try.

KRAWZ ALMARIP
One other thing, make sure nobody snoops around my bunk while I'm sleeping.

RUTH MARRADI
I never have. You can be assured of that. One of my jobs is to always watch the entrance to the ship and I have a direct view of your bunk from there.

KRAWZ ALMARIP
Excellent.

VOICE OVER
Evo Kaplan stayed awake for over a day. He used

the time to reconnoiter the passengers and clear his surroundings for potential Dranzonian Empire Secret Service agents or verify that Conrad Fanzui's men were aboard as watchers.

Just like Brenda during the Coy's Ridge operation, a watcher was probably in the cabin with him to report back any issues that should come to the attention of Conrad Fanzui. Evo Kaplan assumed there was a watcher aboard the ship and might even get off at Praxisvlasia and possibly another watcher come aboard to relieve that person, just to keep him and any possible Dranzonian Empire Secret Service agent from detecting the surveillance.

Krawz Almarip (a.k.a. Evo Kaplan) would probably never know for sure, but he was a good judge of body language and if a watcher was aboard, he would catch that person doing observations. He would then know.

However, there was a distinct possibility a Dranzonian Empire Secret Service agent unrelated to Krawz Almarip's (a.k.a. Evo Kaplan) mission could be put aboard for other reasons, and thus he would be a target of opportunity if Evo could confirm his suspicions in time. The target of opportunity could work both ways. It would be who discovered who first.

After a full twenty-four hours of vigilance, Evo Kaplan went to his bunk, which was in an arrangement with others. To some it might appear as a bunk bed; to others it might seem like stacked coffins. To the pilot and the crew, they preferred people in the bunks as much as possible because they consumed less oxygen, and the environmental controls were easier to maintain if over half of the passengers were sleeping.

For this flight they had the bonus: half the seats were empty, so atmosphere controls operated significantly easier. Evo Kaplan had identified several black marketers who he recognized from his training videos. As expected, they kept to themselves and most likely viewed the other black marketers as a potential threat or even a snitch.

Just like the French officer in the Casa Blanca movie, the crew of the blockade runner saw no contraband, ever!

Krawz Almarip slid his security privacy slide into position and locked it. It had interlocking metal panels that, when locked in place formed what appeared to be a solid wall. A blaster could shoot through it and kill someone, but knives and other weapons would not be strong enough to penetrate.

Inside the bunk with the security privacy slide locked, a person had adequate ventilation with air pumped in and lights they could turn on to read if required. Depending on where the ship was, some communicators worked if a planet was nearby. However, in the open stretch of space they traveled, there would be no planets or any such communications.

VOICE OVER

People like Krawz Almarip and the other black marketers slept in their clothes just in case they had to get out in a hurry. Other travelers would go to the restroom and change into sleeping clothes and be more comfortable.

Evo at least took off his shoes but had them at the foot of his comfortable bed. The mattress sat on a metal tray and was six inches thick and designed for comfort and long hours of sleeping, as some passengers took sleeping pills to pass out for a day or longer to make the trip feel shorter.

Krawz Almarip (a.k.a. Evo Kaplan) was no different and soon saw that white spot at the end of the tunnel getting smaller until he was unconscious. He would wake in about twenty-four hours due to hunger and the need to urinate. His rest period was what the doctor ordered. His dreams were full of color and full of Brenda Broyals, whom he now missed. I must be falling in love with Brenda Broyals.

Just like he expected, twenty-four hours later he awoke due to hunger pains and the incredible need to urinate. As he climbed out of his bunk, he noticed Ruth Marradi who was being bribed to look out for him, seeming somewhat focused on him and the surroundings. She gave him a smile and moved her head up and down once, which apparently was her secret signal, everything was all right. After taking care of his business in the bathroom, Krawz Almarip made his way to the lounge where they served space food.

Due to cramped conditions, atmosphere controls, and other reasons, all food was prepared and in tubes or special containers the flight attendants could roll up into a ball like aluminum foil and place into the recycler press that flattened it, then they slid it through a slit to the recycler storage that would be off-loaded at their destination and traded for credits used to purchase return trip-prepared foods.

The meals and everything aboard Intergalactic Passenger Transports was provided for free, no cash or credits necessary. Krawz Almarip selected the food items he had been schooled to do. Even though he might not like these food items, since the real Krawz Almarip always ate them, Evo Kaplan had to play along consuming those items as to not draw any undue scrutiny by potential passengers who had traveled with him time before, including all the black marketers, who were usually very keen on detecting inconsistencies.

The food items were not bad, just not Evo Kaplan's preference; nevertheless, he consumed them out of sheer hunger and out of professionalism of paying attention to detail like a good spy with an ID transplant would emulate.

The crew did not encourage water consumption because in a full ship, they had to conserve waste storage until they traveled somewhere that wastewater could be dumped, like on the edge of an asteroid field where they would maneuver and then out-chop allowing the debris to hit the asteroids where it would not become a menace to intergalactic travel.

It was also against intergalactic rules and regulations to dump trash and wastewater in shipping lanes because those materials could pose a threat to future transport traveling in the area. On the main asteroid fields found between Zanziltar and Praxisvlasia, there were debris fields of trash, waste, and wrecked space craft. One day as materials prices soared due to scarcity and the profitability of recycling, there would be robotic ships harvesting these rich debris fields as the early years in space travel used much thicker and richer composites.

The scrap value of a first-generation intergalactic transport was worth about five times as much as newer models that used thinner materials with more ingenious engineering. They also had more metal and less carbon nanotubes and graphene content.

VOICE OVER

A female entered the lounge and made her way to the food selectors and grabbed several items and an eight-ounce drink.

The woman sat down with her back to the wall behind her at the next table facing Krawz Almarip and smiled. He returned a smile.

Krawz Almarip had a reputation of latching onto women on his way to far off planets and used them while he was there making his profits. As soon as he had completed all his transactions and collected his credits, he usually hopped on the next space craft leaving and abandoning the woman who thought there was more to the relationship than what existed.

A couple of women out on planets he never intended to visit again would no doubt attempt killing Krawz Almarip if he was ever spotted on their planet. To really play the role of Krawz Almarip, Evo Kaplan had to be flamboyant at times and what would be considered a womanizer.

KRAWZ ALMARIP
Hello. Are you on your way to Praxisvlasia?

FEMALE PASSENGER
No. I'm going to Arzon.

KRAWZ ALMARIP
No kidding! So am I.

FEMALE PASSENGER
What will you be doing on Arzon?

KRAWZ ALMARIP
I have some items I plan on selling.

FEMALE PASSENGER
Seems like a long way to go to sell something.

KRAWZ ALMARIP
Arzon, being a provincial capital and cut off from the Empire, has a lot of need for special equipment and materials. I provide what they need and want and make good money at it.

FEMALE PASSENGER
Have you traveled there often?

KRAWZ ALMARIP
Oh yes, several times. How about yourself?

FEMALE PASSENGER
I grew up in Arzon and was sent to Zanziltar for higher
education and ended up getting hired there for a good
job. The money was right so I stayed.

KRAWZ ALMARIP
Going home to Arzon to visit your family?

FEMALE PASSENGER
Yes, my mother is ill and I want to see her before it's
too late.

KRAWZ ALMARIP
I'm sorry to hear that.

FEMALE PASSENGER
I should arrive in plenty of time to spend some quality
time with her.

KRAWZ ALMARIP
What if the Revolutionaries capture this ship?

FEMALE PASSENGER
I'll plead my case with them and beg them to let me
get to my mother before it's too late.

KRAWZ ALMARIP
There's no transportation between Revolutionary
Planets and Arzon. All that gets to Arzon are these
blockade runners.

FEMALE PASSENGER
I'll stay optimistic and we'll make it.

KRAWZ ALMARIP
What's your name?

FEMALE PASSENGER (a.k.a. Claudette Ramsey)
Claudette Ramsey. How about yourself, sir?

KRAWZ ALMARIP
I'm Krawz Almarip.

CLAUDETTE RAMSEY
Pleased to meet you Krawz Almarip.

KRAWZ ALMARIP
Claudette, same to you. What kind of work do you do
on Zanziltar?

CLAUDETTE RAMSEY
I work as an analyst for one of the large Zanziltar
banks.

KRAWZ ALMARIP
Which one is that?

CLAUDETTE RAMSEY
It's the Zanziltar Central Bank. I work directly for
Randolph Spencer.

KRAWZ ALMARIP
That name sounds vaguely familiar.

CLAUDETTE RAMSEY
Well, since we are alone and I don't have to worry
about the news media recording our conversation, I
can probably tell you why you have heard his name.

KRAWZ ALMARIP
Okay.

CLAUDETTE RAMSEY
There were a lot of media leaks concerning his friend,
a major politician, and him going down to Orgy Island
quite often. And there are rumors now swirling around
that his wife was involved in a scandal at a provincial
planet named Shen de Huayuan. He's been acting
strange ever since there were leaks about all this to
some yellow journalist media sources.

KRAWZ ALMARIP
Sounds kind of shocking.

CLAUDETTE RAMSEY
It was to me when I first heard about it.

Krawz Almarip spent a couple hours chatting with Claudette Ramsey and it was soon apparent to both there was some mutual attraction.

Claudette Ramsey was the type of woman who would like Krawz Almarip even more after she discovered he ran a sordid operation. The psychology of some people created an attraction to negative individuals whether it be pirates, killers, embezzlers, crooked politicians, and lawyers. Perhaps that's what drove her to work for Randolph Spencer?

If it wasn't for the fact, he had Ruth Marradi looking out for him and he missed Brenda, he would have offered Claudette Ramsey to sneak in his bunk with him. It would not be the first nor the last woman to join the twenty-million-mile club with the real Krawz Almarip.

However, part of the caricature he was to develop to emulate Krawz Almarip demanded he follow such a course. Evo Kaplan was briefed and indoctrinated by the FIRM, but also by the Dranzonian Empire Secret Service where he worked as an agent before his purge and eventual defection: all spies use all their weapons as necessary and if a woman had to sleep with a man to fulfill her espionage, she was not sinning, she was merely using some of the tools of her spy craft as the ends justified the means.

That message rings true for all politicians and quite a few lawyers. No doubt there are good people in all professions, but experience shows power corrupts. After a few hours as the testosterone was wearing off and Claudette Ramsey was showing signs of space lag fatigue setting in, she excused herself.

CLAUDETTE RAMSEY
Will you please excuse me, Krawz Almarip. I'm feeling like I want to take a nap. I was awake for many hours and couldn't sleep. I think now I'll be able to.

KRAWZ ALMARIP
Not a problem. I'll be seeing you around.

Claudette Ramsey stood up and walked out of the lounge back toward her seat and bunk. Krawz Almarip went back to his own seat, which reclined forty-five degrees where he could either listen to music or watch entertainment. He saw Claudette Ramsey get into her bunk, which it turns out was the one just forward of his. This might get interesting later.

On the viewer that came down from directly above his seat and provided surround sound and incredible 3D video capability, he selected some entertainment that would prescribe him a journey to a temporal escape. One thing was certain, the blockade runner didn't fly a piece of crap space craft. This was indeed luxury. But he also knew this one cost quite a phenomenal amount. Claudette Ramsey is spending a fortune to get home to see her mother. She might be as corrupt as the banker she works for.

Evo Kaplan started to think about the name Randolph Spencer. He then unexpectedly made the connection. At the captain's dining table on the cruise liner, there was Lady Spencer. That was his wife. And the guy she was flagrantly having a soiree with a Mr. Blane Jiandie, a.k.a. Reginald Heiqishi! It all made perfect sense now. Randolph Spencer is the person who gave the FIRM the contract to kill Reginald Heiqishi.

There are strange twists in life. It was Lady Spencer who delivered Reginald Heiqishi to him so he could exact his sweet revenge. The ironic part of the story it now seems is that Reginald Heiqishi would be alive today had he not purged Evo Kaplan in revenge.

Traveling to Arzon with Claudette Ramsey just spiced up the trip a few notches. He would get closer to her because INTEL on Randolph Spencer just might be of some value in the future. Evo Kaplan started to think he might even find a way to blackmail Randolph Spencer and retire lavishly. Maybe he could use Claudette to help set up Randolph Spencer for blackmail?

Out traveling in space between two worlds is a lonely period. At least they were at the halfway point now. In thirty-six hours, he would be on Praxisvlasia. How would he feel? After watching some parabolic hypnotic series on the view scanner, which is used along with psychoacoustics in synchronization to trigger endorphin releases, Evo Kaplan thought for a few minutes about Brenda and the special time he had with her. Would he ever see her again?

Krawz Almarip was a flamboyant bachelor and fun-seeking guy. Evo Kaplan could not portray him in a melancholy mood so he decided it would be best if he took another one of those special pills and lay down for another twelve hours. Then when he came about, he would only have twenty-four hours to be highly observant of his surroundings. Maybe another meeting in the lounge with Claudette Ramsey?

Evo Kaplan pushed the view scanner up and then stood up to walk around a bit, which is what the real Krawz Almarip would do on these long trips according to the reports. It was also not out of the ordinary for him to go up to the cockpit and talk to the duty pilot and co-pilot. Even though modern-day intergalactic transport ships were fully automated and did not require pilots, the public was never able to accept pilotless Intergalactic Passenger Transports.

There was also union pressure from the pilot's union to not do away with their jobs. It got dicey during the outbreak of the Revolution. The pilot's unions then cemented their positions for good. They had a simple solution: Either agree to the permanent presence of pilots in the cockpit or we'll simply fly all the transports to the enemy! That carried over to even specialized transport such as the blockade runners.

Evo Kaplan had been warned that some of the pilots knew Krawz Almarip, as he had bribed them in the past with women, credits, energy drinks, et cetera. If one of them called him by his name, that was one of them he needed to be very like-minded to and play along as if they were old pals.

Krawz Almarip (a.k.a. Evo Caplan) decided he would now go test the waters of this multi-crew cockpit. These guys ran in twelve-hour shifts and switched out. However, during planet re-entry, they were all in the cockpit sharing the load in communications, navigation, and control. The computer handled the transport space craft, but the pilot had to oversee and apply common sense and judgement in the event some computer glitch occurred, mainly to retain proficiency.

Some transports were all automated; the pilots were too scared to ever control the craft because even the slightest screw-up resulted in termination of their employment. The unions didn't fight it because the junior officers loved the quick promotions when an old geezer was sent packing. The old geezers figured it out: Never come out of autopilot and you have no worries. It took a short period of time to walk past the lounge and up into the forward area. The crew lived up here and they didn't like passengers walking up there, but they knew who Krawz Almarip was.

Krawz Almarip got lucky: it was shift-change, and the outgoing pilots opened the door just as soon as he arrived.

COPILOT
Hello, Krawz Almarip. I heard you were on the flight.

KRAWZ ALMARIP
Yep

COPILOT
Say, come back in about twelve hours with one of your
energy drinks and I'll let you sit in my seat for a while.

KRAWZ ALMARIP
That's great, but when will I get to sit in the left seat?

Evo knew their rankings and that he was talking to the junior right seater.

COPILOT
Well, you know there are two things you never do
on space transports: Sit at the captain's chair in the
wardroom or in his seat in the cockpit.

KRAWZ ALMARIP
But when you make captain, I'm sure we can work out
a deal where I get to just sit there for a moment so I
can see how it feels.

COPILOT
I can't promise you anything I might get in trouble for, but
when I get promoted to captain and you are on my flight, if
you don't tell anyone neither will I.

KRAWZ ALMARIP
All right, I'll make that flight just for you.

COPILOT
Good. Your buddy Captain Buck is at the controls now. He
probably wants to talk to you about some of the schemes
you came up with, or at least one of those fancy energy
drinks that will keep him vigilant for the next twelve hours.

The pilot standing ahead of them at the door held it open knowing Krawz Almarip had
no way to open it, and once it shut those two would be locked in until the next watch
relief. Despite what the public thought, they each did have a piss bottle, but if they had
to poop, they asked a flight attendant to wake up the other captain for a bathroom
relief. And yes, that happened occasionally if the crew got some food-born illness.

In a way it felt kind of spooky. All these guys knew Krawz Almarip well and he had
only limited knowledge of what they had done together, including smuggling and
black marketing. Captain Buck was apparently the worst offender; close to forced
retirement, he wanted that big score so he could stretch his retirement a lot further.

KRAWZ ALMARIP
What the phuc, Buck, Krawz Almarip stated as he had
been briefed that was one of the banters they did and easy
to remember.

PILOT CAPTAIN BUCK
Well, what do you know, here's the Zanziltar Gypsy.

KRAWZ ALMARIP
Are we safe or should I get on my parachute?

VOICE OVER (MALE)
That apparently was another line Krawz Almarip had
used and only became one of the many golden nuggets

he confessed to Conrad Fanzui only after advanced interrogation techniques that compelled him to spill a lot of information. It took him about five tries to realize he couldn't beat their lie detectors.

A couple trips to the swimming pool, feet first in the crematorium where he got some nice burns, then being thrown out of a VTOL at ten thousand feet and held by a small cable got him to be very careful of every word he chose going forward.

Krawz Almarip knew he was dealing with some very sick bastards who gave him the choice of luxury living or a god-awful ending. Based on how well their lie detecting equipment worked, Krawz Almarip had no choice but to cooperate fully.

CAPTAIN BUCK
Did you bring me one of those energy drinks?

KRAWZ ALMARIP
I just now figured out it was shift-change.

CAPTAIN BUCK
You can't look at a chronometer?

KRAWZ ALMARIP
I'll tell you what, if you can have your COPILOT Fursungtarwum hold the door open for me, I'll go back to my bunk and bring us some energy drinks.

CAPTAIN BUCK
Hurry it up, we are behind schedule.

KRAWZ ALMARIP
I'll be right back.

Krawz Almarip walked back to his bunk, opened the four-square footlocker, and pulled out one of the bags he had full of energy drinks he was told would come into great use. This was just one of the uses. He had a small carrying bag he could fold up and put in his rear pocket after delivery. He promptly went forward and almost pissed off a flight attendant who would have stopped him had Fursungtarwum not been standing there holding the cockpit door open.

Moments later Krawz Almarip was sitting in the fourth seat of the six-seat cockpit so he could look and talk to Captain Buck in seat number one. Seat number two was the copilot just ahead of him, seat three was behind the captain. Five and six were behind him and were not occupied unless they were entering the atmosphere in preparation for landing. Having six men in the cockpit helped split up the tasking so the pilot could concentrate on flying, with the copilot assisting. Seats three, four, five, and six maintained situational awareness, weather observation, and affirmative back up to air traffic control and collision avoidance.

All six pilot workstations had similar glass display panels. Complex instrumentation gave these well-trained men extraordinary ability to travel great distance at super high speeds. The rear seaters paid close attention to the Cosmic Spatial Normalizer Data, especially nearing a planet where air traffic could expand exponentially. Praxisvlasia, being the seat of the Dranzonian Empire, had to make extra effort to prevent a sucker punch and therefore had to maintain a credible space force.

Praxisvlasia's enhanced security posture alone created collision hazards. Due to high speeds and Doppler radar, contact correlation was almost impossible without instruments such as the Cosmic Spatial Normalizer, and pilots would not be able to cope.

On board computational equipment processing hundreds of billions of Cosmic Spatial Normalizer Coefficients every second was really doing all the collision avoidance.

The rear seaters were just monitoring the automated process and talking the pilot down to the planet, who sometimes needed adjustments along the way unless he was like one of the old geezers and said the heck with it and allowed the computers to do all the work.

There were actual reported cases of flight crews playing cards during a landing because they had that much faith in the computer, which always gave them a softer landing. With the boys in the cockpit drinking those special energy drinks, a whole new dynamic began.

<u>INT. INTERGALACTIC PASSENGER SPACESHIP COCKPIT.</u>

C.U. DISPLAYS SHOWING COSMIC SPATIAL NORMALIZER DATA

C.U. CAPTAIN BUCK

C.U. KRAWZ ALMARIP

<u>MONTAGE OF C.U. OF COSMIC SPATIAL NORMALIZER DATA, CAPTAIN BUCK, AND KRAWZ ALMARIP DURING FOLLOWOING VOICE OVER AND SUBSEQUENT DISCUSSION.</u>

VOICE OVER
The Zanziltar flagged Intergalactic Passenger Transport was in autopilot and, the Cosmic Spatial Normalizer Data showed no spacecraft ahead at their velocity of 200 million meters per second, which is two-thirds light speed. They couldn't go faster because of the fuel financial constraints to slow down.

A military ship, on the other hand, didn't have to worry about fuel costs and exceeded 300 million meters per second often. It took them several days to make the journey, while a top line military craft would make it in a day.

CAPTAIN BUCK
Are you getting off at Praxisvlasia?

KRAWZ ALMARIP
No, I'm going all the way to Arzon.

CAPTAIN BUCK
Selling some of your wares there?

KRAWZ ALMARIP
If we make it and do not get stopped by the Revolutionaries.

CAPTAIN BUCK
I would think by now that you made enough money to retire.

KRAWZ ALMARIP
Well, yes and no.

CAPTAIN BUCK
Let's start with the no.

KRAWZ ALMARIP
Remember when I told you I was going to take a big
load from Shen de Huayuan to Zanziltar?

CAPTAIN BUCK
Yeah, you were going to get filthy rich.

KRAWZ ALMARIP
I almost made it, but the Revolution caught our ship
and confiscated all the shipment. I could have retired
had I sold the material to my customer on Zanziltar.

**<u>MONTAGE OF C.U. OF COSMIC SPATIAL NORMALIZER DATA, CAPTAIN
BUCK, AND KRAWZ ALMARIP DURING FOLLOWOING VOICE OVER AND
SUBSEQUENT DISCUSSION.</u>**

VOICE OVER
Krawz Almarip knew he would not be caught in a lie
because the Revolution did, in fact, confiscate the real
Shen de Huayuan goods off one shipment recently
when he was abducted by Conrad Fanzui's people.

Pilot Buck and his copilot Fursungtarwum were now
starting to feel the effects of this super enhanced
energy drink.

Aside from giving a person a lot of energy, it also gave
them ultra-sensitivity, which further enhanced their
vigilance and bravery. The energy drink also opened
old memories that were forgotten long ago, that gave
a splendid happiness as they recalled special events in
their lives.

Old jokes were suddenly recalled and soon jocularity
and banter flourished. The pilot Buck and his copilot
Fursungtarwum traded old stale jokes for a while at
the same time the memories flourished, including the
desires to do things they always planned on doing but
never got around to doing.

Sadly, as the drugs wore off that were contained in the
energy drink, so would they lose those desires to do
things they always planned on doing. But for now, and
the remainder of their twelve-hour shift, these pilots
were super animated, and happiness prevailed.

Krawz Almarip was the purveyor of these marvelous moments and memories. Evo Kaplan' portrayal of Krawz Almarip was convincing and Buck and Fursungtarwum were totally consumed and convinced their friend Krawz Almarip was sitting there in seat number three, loosely participating in what was going on.

KRAWZ ALMARIP
I see on the scanners nothing out in front of us.

CAPTAIN BUCK
Towards the end of our shift, we expect to start picking up some Praxisvlasia traffic and so we should start to see some cargo or transport ships.

KRAWZ ALMARIP
Will it be boring until then?

CAPTAIN BUCK
Not really, I got a few more jokes up my sleeve.

CO-PILOT FURSUNGTARWUM
Just what we need, jokes you told fifty times already.

Captain Buck turned to Krawz Almarip.

CAPTAIN BUCK
Krawz, did you meet any pretty ladies on the flight yet?

KRAWZ ALMARIP
I certainly did, and I hope to bag her before we land in Arzon.

CAPTAIN BUCK
You're a slick dog. I wonder how you manage to get all those women?

KRAWZ ALMARIP
Well Captain Buck, it's like this. I studied statistics and probabilities. One way you can control the degrees of freedom is to change the sample rate. I believe increasing sample rate offers you more opportunity.

Buck and Fursungtarwum laughed momentarily, then Fursungtarwum got serious for a minute and asked a great question.

FURSUNGTARWUM
Seriously, Krawz did you ever find a woman you really adored and loved?

This was an easy answer for Krawz Almarip as he allowed himself to think of Brenda Broyals for a moment and knew he didn't have to give any names but would leave no doubt in their minds.

KRAWZ ALMARIP
I think I fell hopelessly in love with a woman. Unfortunately, she and I are heading in opposite directions, and we may never meet again.

CAPTAIN BUCK
That's how we pilots feel.

KRAWZ ALMARIP
Yes, it's a sad life for a traveling guy. We meet suitable partners one week and they are out of our lives forever in just a week.

CAPTAIN BUCK
I always wondered if you purposely meet gals, you know you will not be able to see again.

KRAWZ ALMARIP
Not really, it just ends up that way. I wish a few of them I met were still with me.

CAPTAIN BUCK
But would you give up your traveling gig to be domesticated by a woman?

KRAWZ ALMARIP
For my most recent friend, yes. If she and I could go off somewhere together and live the rest of our lives together, I would be happy to sell my holdings for a reasonable amount and leave all this behind me.

CAPTAIN BUCK
But since that's not possible, do you have designs on one of the passengers?

KRAWZ ALMARIP

Definitely. She lives in Zanziltar, and if we both make it back there alive, I will pursue her with all vigor.

CAPTAIN BUCK

What about the gal you are in love with? What if she comes back suddenly?

KRAWZ ALMARIP

She's rapidly changing. She will not be the same woman when she gets back and may or may not wish to have anything to do with me.

CAPTAIN BUCK

So, you are going to play the odds in your favor and get hooked up with the female passenger?

KRAWZ ALMARIP

At least for a temporary gratification.

CAPTAIN BUCK

Good luck with that one. Let us know how it works out.

KRAWZ ALMARIP

It's already worked out well. We talked for several hours. I like her and she likes me. I think we are meant for each other.

CAPTAIN BUCK

Can a shifty character like you would settle down with her?

KRAWZ ALMARIP

Yes, after I make a big score and move to some tropical planet like Shen de Huayuan.

CAPTAIN BUCK

Have you ever been there?

KRAWZ ALMARIP

Yes, it was nice.

CAPTAIN BUCK

I've never been there but I hear all kinds of good
things. What do you recommend to a person going
there for the first time?

KRAWZ ALMARIP
If you stay at the Lantiane Resort, you will have the
best quality on the planet.

Krawz Almarip then discussed some of the other points of interest such as the Hupu
Waterfalls, club Banma Julebu, the ocean liner tours, Quanqiu Museum, and the
beaches and Barracuda and Cougars that hang out at the swimming pools.

CAPTAIN BUCK
I wouldn't mind a Cougar, but at my age she would
have to be around eighty.

The only interesting aspect of flying out in space between planets going at high speed
was observing the stars and other planets move along the horizon; even though they
were only going two-thirds light speed. It was just enough velocity to see the whole
complexity of the galaxy unfold before their eyes.

KRAWZ ALMARIP
Do you guys ever get tired of being up here in the
cockpit?

CAPTAIN BUCK
Almost every flight we have some excitement.

Captain Buck didn't admit terror as they barely missed several meteorites and space
debris at least once or twice per flight.

VOICE OVER (FEMALE)
The conversations with Captain Buck and the three
other pilots lasted without a break until the next watch
relief. As soon as the oncoming pilot unlocked the
door from outside, Krawz Almarip was able to leave
the cockpit.

Krawz Almarip was a little hungry and decided to get a
snack before he crawled into his bunk for a rest period,
then he would get up and stay up until they landed.
After all the departing passengers were off the ship, he
would crawl into his bunk and rest until takeoff time,
thanks to his prearranged help from flight attendant
Ruth Marradi.

As Krawz Almarip walked away from the cockpit, he made his way into the lounge and unexpectedly ran into Claudette Ramsey.

Claudette wasn't looking quite as cute as when he first met her. She had evidently cleaned up, washed off all her makeup, and now he got to see the natural woman as she really was. Claudette Ramsey new appearance seemed more like a big girl than the woman she appeared as earlier.

INT. INTERGALACTIC PASSENGER SPACECRAFT CAFETERIAS PLIT SCREEN SIDE BY SIDE

C.U. CLAUDETTE RAMSEY AND KRAWZ ALMARIP REPEATEDLY DURING CONVERSATION

> CLAUDETTE RAMSEY
> Hello again.

> KRAWZ ALMARIP
> Enjoy your sleep?

> CLAUDETTE RAMSEY
> Yes, I think I got a total equalizer. I hope I don't suffer much space lag. How about yourself?

> KRAWZ ALMARIP
> I was busy visiting my pilot friends in the cockpit.

> CLAUDETTE RAMSEY
> You know them?

> KRAWZ ALMARIP
> Yes, I've taken many long flights with them before.

> CLAUDETTE RAMSEY
> To Arzon?

> KRAWZ ALMARIP
> No, but to many other locations.

> CLAUDETTE RAMSEY
> From Zanziltar?

KRAWZ ALMARIP
Yes, also from Praxisvlasia.

CLAUDETTE RAMSEY
What were some of your most interesting locations to
visit?

KRAWZ ALMARIP
I'd say the Lantiane Resort on the planet Shen de
Huayuan.

Krawz Almarip noticed the distinct body shift in Claudette Ramsey. He knew he touched a hot button somehow.

CLAUDETTE RAMSEY
What's it like?

KRAWZ ALMARIP
The Lantiane Resort there is the best I've ever stayed
at, and there are a lot of fun things to do.

CLAUDETTE RAMSEY
If I went there, what kinds of things would you
recommend?

KRAWZ ALMARIP
They have good ocean cruise liners worth taking. There
are a lot of good restaurants, one of the Empire's best
museums and the Dewaltracen Art Gallery, exciting
night clubs for dancing, and interesting things to visit
like the Hupu Waterfalls and Guilong Aquarium at
Pangu Bay.

CLAUDETTE RAMSEY
Sounds lovely.

KRAWZ ALMARIP
Shen de Huayuan planet is mildly primitive, but out-
world travelers nicknamed Shen de Huayuan it the
GARDEN OF THE GODS. Are you interested in Shen
de Huayuan?

CLAUDETTE RAMSEY
I wasn't until my boss's wife went there with a couple

of her girlfriends. He got really upset as rumors of a
scandal were circulating.

KRAWZ ALMARIP
How did that turn out?

CLAUDETTE RAMSEY
When his wife first came home from Shen de Huayuan,
Randolph Spencer appeared really upset, then a short
time ago he suddenly acted happy again as if nothing
happened.

KRAWZ ALMARIP
How about the wife?

CLAUDETTE RAMSEY
She's been acting kind of strange apparently.

VOICE OVER
Krawz Almarip knew exactly why Randolph Spencer
appeared happy since he fulfilled the contract to kill
Glacey Spencer's lover and his former despicable boss
Reginald Heiqishi.

Perhaps that might be a way to blackmail Randolph
Spencer? Threaten to tell his wife her husband
arranged to have her lover murdered? The conversation
continued and Claudette Ramsey seemed to get
friendlier.

Claudette Ramsey's smile was genuine, her intelligence was obvious; otherwise,
she wouldn't be an analyst working for Randolph Spencer. Claudette Ramsey was
wholesome and not ugly with her makeup removed. She almost looked like a teenager,
which meant she had many good years ahead of her before she would morph into an
old hag.

Krawz Almarip knew he would not be around to watch Claudette Ramsey grow old.
The sense of affection and attraction intersected Evo Kaplan's (a.k.a. Krawz Almarip)
thoughts, which gave him the ammunition and resolve to lubricate the relationship a
bit and conceivably invite Claudette Ramsey to the twenty-million-mile club in his
bunk.

Evo also started thinking that since Arzon was Claudette Ramsey's home planet, she
could be someone he could exploit and use for his purposes in espionage. Claudette
Ramsey might know people who could further his ability to move around and acquire
information.

VOICE OVER
In a brief amount of time, Captain Buck, and his Co-Pilot Fursungtarwum arrived in the lounge still wearing their uniforms, seeking something to eat before they turned in or did whatever they planned on.

Captain Buck and his Co-Pilot Fursungtarwum gave Krawz Almarip space and realized this woman was his next conquest, another notch in his belt. Observing Krawz Almarip in action with the ladies did more than enough to give Captain Buck and Co-Pilot Fursungtarwum a false sense of reality, as they had no idea they were observing an imposter, a top-level spy from the FIRM.

Captain Buck and his Co-Pilot Fursungtarwum kept their distance and allowed Krawz Almarip the black marketer to continue his conquest. In private later they would make bets on when or if Krawz Almarip managed to get this attractive woman into the twenty-million-mile club.

For the time being, Captain Buck and Co-Pilot Fursungtarwum, now more interested in getting some restful sleep knowing collision avoidance work in the next watch would be a pain in the ass. The two pilots left the entertaining exhibit where Krawz Almarip would achieve his conquest as easily as the lions got to the sheep in Roman coliseums.

They two pilots left the passenger lounge to turn in and knew by the time they came back on watch in twelve hours, the sheep would be eaten alive.

Suddenly Krawz Almarip and Claudette Ramsey were alone.

CLAUDETTE RAMSEY
What are you going to be doing next?

KRAWZ ALMARIP
I'm going to my bunk and rest for a few hours. Want to come along?

CLAUDETTE RAMSEY
What are you talking about?

KRAWZ ALMARIP
Twenty-Million-Mile Club.

CLAUDETTE RAMSEY
What's that?

KRAWZ ALMARIP
Knock on my security privacy slide three times and
I'll unlock it and you can hop in so I can teach you all
about the twenty-million-mile club.

CLAUDETTE RAMSEY
Wouldn't you be ashamed if someone saw me climbing
in your bunk with you?

KRAWZ ALMARIP
Odds are you will never see any of these people again
for the rest of your life.

CLAUDETTE RAMSEY
I would be too nervous to try something like that.

KRAWZ ALMARIP
If you want, I'll have a flight attendant come get you
and escort you to my bunk to make it look all proper.

CLAUDETTE RAMSEY
You have got to be kidding.

KRAWZ ALMARIP
I bribe them well.

CLAUDETTE RAMSEY
Well, first of all, I would never consider doing such a
thing.

In a short while Krawz Almarip and Claudette Ramsey went their separate ways.
Krawz Almarip never assumed that Claudette Ramsey would ever get the wild notion
to join the Twenty-Million-Mile Club; he was merely having fun with her.

INT. INTERGALACTIC PASSENGER TRANSPORT BUNK ROOM.

Krawz Almarip was soon laying in his spacious and comfortable bunk that could
easily hold two people, which sometimes was necessary on the "pigs and people" runs

long distance where there were not enough room for all their luggage so the families gave up a bunk to store all their personal affects and shared a bunk, which had plenty of room as long as one of them didn't hog all the space.

VOICE OVER (FEMALE)
Thanks to the sleeping pill, Krawz Almarip (a.k.a. Evo Kaplan) was soon sound asleep. Evo Kaplan had a restful period and was in a deep dream when suddenly there were three knocks on his security privacy slide. Even though he was well under with the help of the narcotics in the pill he took to enhance sleep, he was also a trained spy, and the three knocks immediately alerted his brain, which swung into action.

INT. INTERGALACTIC PASSENGER TRANSPORT KRAWZ ALMARIP BUNK.

Semi groggy, Krawz Almarip unlocked the security privacy slide and opened it a few inches. The cabin area was somewhat dark, as the flight attendants made artificial nights for the passengers to help them keep a mental semblance of night and day.

Claudette Ramsey had approached Ruth, the right flight attendant, one who had many dealings with Krawz Almarip on past flights and was looking forward to making a lot of money on this flight thanks to his presence and the quid pro quo he was going to provide.

Well, I'll be damned, Krawz Almarip thought for a moment as he saw Claudette Ramsey. Closely behind her was the flight attendant Ruth Marradi blocking the passageway, but also keeping prying eyes away. He then slid the security privacy slide back further, allowing Claudette Ramsey in his bunk, then slid it shut again and locked it. He knew this was going to cost him a little more, but it was worth it as he now would exploit Claudette Ramsey to get a back door to get access to Randolph Spencer.

It was slightly crowded but manageable. The security privacy slide had acoustic baffling as part of its construction. The noise that happened inside the bunk stayed inside the bunk, originally designed so that people could listen to music or play videos without bothering other passengers.

<u>INT INSIDE KRAWZ ALMARIP'S (a.k.a. EVO KAPLAN) PRIVATE BUNK</u>

<u>ANGLE SHOT FROM THE CORNER OF BUNK LOOKING DOWN AT EVO KAPLAN AND CLAUDETTE RAMSEY.</u>

<u>C.U. DURING KISS</u>

<u>AFTER THE KISSING SCENE THEY GET INTO THE SPOON POSITION WHILE LOVE MAKING WITH EVO KAPLAN'S ARMS ACROUND CLAUDETTE CUPPING HER BREASTS WITH HIS HANDS.</u>

> VOICE OVER
> Claudette Ramsey had on a very evocative perfume. Krawz Almarip was big about scents. In the Dranzonian Empire Secret Service he was trained to recognize scents because in some cases scents might come in handy. Just like teaching a sonar technician how to distinguish sound, teaching a spy to recognize scents was just as important. As a spy, Evo Kaplan had to use everything available to him in many instances.

> CLAUDETTE RAMSEY
> Tell me about this Twenty-Million-Mile Club.

Claudette Ramsey statement affected Evo Kaplan in the most provocative manner.

> KRAWZ ALMARIP (A.K.A. EVO KAPLAN)
> Let me demonstrate it first. We can talk about the club's goals later.

> VOICE OVER (FEMALE)
> About then Claudette Ramsey embraced Krawz Almarip and did one thing that was considered offensive to a lot of people: she began kissing him on his lips in the hungriest fashion. Coming from a provincial world like Arzon, this form of behavior was considered normal.

> Vergentia, a Dranzonian Empire World where Evo Kaplan grew up, had similar customs so he wasn't

offended. Men on Praxisvlasia would have kicked Claudette Ramsey out of the bunk. It didn't take the two long to figure out the best way to proceed and soon the twenty-million-mile tango was being performed on a Theme from Paganini.

Claudette Ramsey was long overdue for a physical embrace with a man. As an analyst working for someone like Randolph Spencer, holding other-people's-money image was very important. Claudette Ramsey could not afford any scandals or involvement with any immoral and unethical characters. She had a high visibility job, therefore had an existence as modest and celibate as a Knights Templar.

Krawz Almarip had a scandalous reputation confirmed by Ruth Marradi, which made the lust and desire more intensive and led Claudette Ramsey to act in quite an illogical manner. But Claudette Ramsey realized what Krawz Almarip said earlier as she threw caution to the wind.

You will never see any of these people again for the rest of your life.

A brief period of ecstasy and transcendence into an ulterior lifestyle before Claudette Ramsey had to confront her mother's illness on Arzon made the decision to do this despicable and illogical act even more appealing.

As the splendid euphoria set in from the psychophysical responses manifested by the twenty-million-mile stimulus, Claudette Ramsey achieved a level of gratification that made her feel it was all worthwhile. To her delight she discovered how unusually strong Krawz Almarip was. His muscles were out of this world. Claudette Ramsey had never touched such a strong man in her life before.

Claudette Ramsey had no idea she experienced coitus with one of the most dangerous spies in the galaxy and now near the top of the Dranzonian Empire Secret Service top ten list which equated to kill on sight any way possible and collateral damage should not be taken into consideration in carrying out the execution.

Krawz Almarip sucked all the energy out of Claudette Ramsey before they both collapsed into a euphoric state and drifted into an almost coma-like deep sleep. It was several hours before Claudette Ramsey came to, feeling extremely satisfied and somewhat emotionally attracted to Krawz Almarip. She couldn't believe what she had just done, but she was happy she experienced this physical embrace.

VOICE OVER

Claudette Ramsey realized Krawz Almarip was probably a heartbreaker and here today and gone tomorrow. But she felt invigorated having the courage to try this illogical and, in many ways, considered denigrating toward women, except for those who wanted to live on the wild side and taste the dangerous fruits of a sleazy man such as Krawz Almarip.

Claudette Ramsey would never be able to see anyone like Krawz Almarip on Zanziltar. If Randolph Spencer discovered such a liaison, she feared what that powerful man could do to her.

Claudette Ramsey also thought there was a distinct possibility of strange behavior on the part of Glacey Spencer, his wife, probably thought her husband Randolph Spencer had her lover murdered and disposed. Claudette Ramsey too could experience similar treatment if investors pulled out over a scandal, he attributed to her.

Claudette Ramsey and Krawz Almarip slowly recovered their consciousness and awareness.

CLAUDETTE RAMSEY

I think I should go now. The cabin will be rigged for nighttime for a while, and I would feel better if people didn't see me leaving your bunk.

KRAWZ ALMARIP

No problem, I'll let you get out first and maybe in a while we can meet up in the lounge.

CLAUDETTE RAMSEY
Sounds good.

The security privacy slide was then unlocked and slid open, and Claudette Ramsey slid out. She then went and took care of female matters and took a quick shower and changed. Claudette Ramsey decided that since she was happy to become a member of Krawz Almarip's Twenty-Million-Mile Club, she would put on some makeup for him and be pretty.

Claudette Ramsey morphed into a glamorous banking official and no longer looked like an older teenager when they met soon afterward in the lounge. The lounge allowed passengers to get away from other passengers who preferred quiet and meet family members or friends or new acquaintances to have discussions and avoid upsetting those who didn't want to have to hear noise from others. Krawz Almarip was in the lounge well before Claudette Ramsey, who took her sweet time putting the exclamation point on the inductee to the Twenty-Million-Mile Club.

Captain Buck, had a few hours' sleep, had to get up and use the restroom. He felt thirsty and went to the lounge to get a drink. He found Krawz Almarip there, sitting by himself.

CAPTAIN BUCK
Hello Krawz, how goes it?

KRAWZ ALMARIP
Really good so far. Enjoying the trip, met such a nice
lady.

CAPTAIN BUCK
I saw her with you earlier. She seemed young.

Captain Buck sat down at the table with Krawz Almarip and was enjoying his drink, just taking it easy and getting ready to go back to his own bunk and attempt getting a few more hours of sleep in before he had to go back to the cockpit.

Moments later, while Buck and Krawz Almarip were deep into a discussion about Arzon, Claudette Ramsey appeared, and she was dressed to kill. Claudette Ramsey felt she had to leave a lasting impression on Krawz Almarip to remind him of her stature during the induction into his twenty-million-mile club. She arrived with a flaming smile.

CLAUDETTE RAMSEY
Hello Krawz.

VOICE OVER (FEMALE)
Claudette Ramsey surprised Evo Kaplan (a.k.a. Krawz
Almarip) with her fantastically upgraded elegance.

Claudette Ramsey realized Krawz Almarip was giving her a huge reassessment.

Claudette Ramsey studied body language, her employer felt necessary in the banking industry as an analyst and had to confront corporate execs and quiz them about their earnings statements, she had to know how sincere they were or if they were just blowing hot air up her skirt.

Krawz Almarip did seem to appear thunder struck and striking body reaction to Claudette Ramsey's stunning metamorphism that immediately altered his demeanor and tempered his ego.

Krawz Almarip had no idea he was dealing with a highly educated female analyst working for Randolph Spencer, where her findings could impact trillions of credits in a single day.

Some of Claudette Ramsey's decisions had a net value that exceeded the entire wealth of some planets. She was the cat playing with her mouse Krawz Almarip, just before the kill and the digestion.

One of the galaxy's premier spies just met one of the premier banking analysts for the Switzerland of the galaxy, Sanctuary City, Zanziltar. Claudette Ramsey's clothes were not formal—they were casual— but they were very expensive and exotic and several steps above couture.

The exquisite perfume, attire, makeup, pretty hair, and a beautiful face struck Krawz Almarip so much that he felt weak and wondered if exploiting Claudette Ramsey to get a back door to Randolph Spencer might, in fact, turn out to be a bigger chore than he imagined.

Claudette Ramsey just made her fashion statement.

If Krawz Almarip wanted to swim with the sharks and not be eaten alive, he better be very careful with this woman, who now exposed a side of her that was diabolically quite a departure from his earlier estimate.

KRAWZ ALMARIP
Claudette. this is Captain Buck. He'll be flying us all
the way to Arzon.

CLAUDETTE RAMSEY
Why are you here and not in the cockpit, Captain
Buck?

CAPTAIN BUCK
Claudette, we have three flight crews. We rotate
watches. Normally we only use one pilot and copilot
at a time for a twelve-hour shift, then the second shift
comes in to relieve.

CLAUDETTE RAMSEY
Why so many pilots?

CAPTAIN BUCK
The third set of pilot and copilots is for emergencies,
and they do other functions on the ship in transit and
only work the cockpit with all the other pilots and
copilots when we descend to a planet's surface.

CLAUDETTE RAMSEY
I see. So, you are off watch now?

CAPTAIN BUCK
Yes. I'm off watch and got thirsty so I came to the
lounge to get a drink and I noticed Krawz Almarip
here.

CLAUDETTE RAMSEY
You two know each other?

CAPTAIN BUCK
Krawz Almarip and I have been on numerous flights
together. so I sat down to talk with him for a few
minutes about some of our trips in the past.

CLAUDETTE RAMSEY
I bet those trips were interesting.

**Claudette Ramsey then winked at Krawz Almarip in a way that gave Captain Buck a
notion something had happened between the two.**

CAPTAIN BUCK
Nice meeting you Claudette, but I'm about ready to
go back to bed to get a few more hours sleep before I
must go back into the cockpit as the pilot.

Captain Buck looked Claudette over good and instantly knew this was a quality woman of high taste and stature, and incredibly beautiful. He was even more surprised when she sat down next to Krawz Almarip and gave him a little hug and a smile.

VOICE OVER
I'll be damned, Captain Buck thought. I bet Krawz has
already worked his magic.

Krawz Almarip (a.k.a. Evo Kaplan) understood
instinctively; he only did the Twenty Million Mile
Club action to emulate the real Krawz Almarip, to give
with a high degree of certainty, everyone would be
convinced he was Krawz Almarip who he portrayed in
stealing his identity.

Evo Kaplan also knew he had to draw the line. As a
good spy he would not allow this woman to entangle
him into an emotional bond. But sitting here looking at
her, it would be very difficult not to grow some tendrils
into her in ways he couldn't avoid.

Suddenly becoming the mouse, Evo Kaplan suddenly
had less power than he realized controlling his
emotions.

Claudette Ramsey wasn't a spy; she was just a banking
analyst, but she indeed was a better chess player than
Krawz Almarip, and it would come down to spying
verses analyzing to see who wins the war of the sexes
and love.

Conrad Fanzui would certainly be happy if Claudette
Ramsey could break the spell Brenda Broyals had on
Evo Kaplan. He wanted to break up the two lovers,
as such behavior generally created many problems,
which led to avoiding sending them on the same
mission together and logistics nightmares.

However, the reality was that after this mission, it was

an extremely rare possibility that Evo Kaplan would ever swim with the great white shark like Claudette Ramsey again.

Claudette Ramsey's demeanor was deceptive yet genuine at the same time. Her focus was her mother who was ill, but she also had a life of her own, and living like a modest Knights Templar, like in the past, no longer appealed to her. She wanted to live now. Her bank accounts in Zanziltar were growing exponentially since she was the analyst with insider information, she always knew where to place her bets for sure wins.

VOICE OVER (FEMALE)

As a hobby Claudette Ramsey traded securities at lunchtime and made more income doing so than her seven-digit credit income as a banking analyst. Simply put, Claudette Ramsey was set for life now, with more wealth than she could possibly ever spend. But the downside was she had no mate, and she was lonely. And here Claudette Ramsey was fooling around with such a despicable example of human flesh, a black marketer, a seedy individual who probably had a girl in every port.

But there was something about Krawz Almarip that didn't add up. Claudette Ramsey was a good investigator and would in due time discover who he was and what he really was. They talked for quite a while. It felt so comfortable and refreshing in many ways. Krawz Almarip was a good listener and at times Claudette Ramsey exposed her soul and her life.

Evo Kaplan, on the other hand, could not describe anything about his life. He was in a precarious situation, soon landing on an Empire space port.

Evo Kaplan had to be careful to only reflect upon Krawz Almarip's life, much of it hidden from society as Krawz Almarip himself had changed his own identity several times. The information on Krawz Almarip's life was a hybrid composition. It had so many holes in it that it simply was like Swiss cheese.

CLAUDETTE RAMSEY

Are you going to get off the ship during our stop over at Praxisvlasia?

KRAWZ ALMARIP
I can't leave the ship because the Dranzonian Empire
Secret Service has accused me of gun running to the
Revolutionaries.

CLAUDETTE RAMSEY
Did you really do that?

KRAWZ ALMARIP
I purposely can't remember anything beyond a week
ago. I don't want to remember the past as I strive
forward.

After two hours of chatting, Krawz Almarip wanted to go back to his bunk and sleep.

KRAWZ ALMARIP
I'm getting sleepy. I'm going to go lay down for a bit.
You can join me if you want, but I'll just be sleeping.

CLAUDETTE RAMSEY
They will be turning the lights on in the main cabin. I
think I'll pass. I'm going to go watch some videos. I'll
see you when you wake up later.

Krawz Almarip got his rest period and when he woke up he figured it was time to S/S/S and put on a change of clothes, which would be his clothes for the stopover to Praxisvlasia.

Krawz Almarip took his change of clothes and all the other items he needed and proceeded to one of the empty bathrooms with a shower. After taking care of his business, he stepped into the shower that had three buttons on the wall of the shower labeled wash, rinse, and dry. They couldn't have towels on board for a variety of reasons, so after showering a body blow dryer blowing air down from the ceiling dried a person, including their hair. A person could do multiple wash and rinse cycles, but artificial intelligence cut the time down in half on each subsequent activation to help conserve water.

Eventually when the time got down to a minimum there was a thirty-minute delay so people would be forced to exit the shower. There were no Hollywood showers on this spaceship.

The shower left Krawz Almarip feeling good, and he quickly dressed. One of the items he had was a sleazy male cologne, which was emblematic of what Krawz Almarip usually wore.

Evo Kaplan played the role of Krawz Almarip one hundred percent, including simple items such as a cologne that the flight attendants detested and were getting tired of smelling because it overwhelmed a person if he was near them long, including himself! Evo Kaplan could not stand the smell and cringed every time he put it on, but he knew damn well that spies including himself went through major scent training and this part of his disguise was essential. If he didn't wear the cologne, some people might question his identity.

Evo Kaplan also didn't like the flamboyant hair style that the real Krawz Almarip wore that he now had to wear as part of the disguise.

The hair style included applying a gel-like substance to glue the hair in place. Back on Earth, men of a bygone era would be called "greasers" wearing similar hair enhancers. And finally, the clothing was another item.

In real life most people would not be caught dead wearing Krawz Almarip's types of clothing apparel. On Earth Krawz Almarip would be considered someone who looked like a pimp in the inner cities. One item he did not wear was Krawz Almarip's hat, as he said he normally didn't wear it on the ship, but when he got off the ship, he always wore it to give him those Panama Paul looks.

After Evo Kaplan (a.k.a. Krawz Almarip) completed all his activities in the restroom, he went back to his bunk and restored all his items, then walked forward to the lounge. Not unexpectedly, Krawz Almarip found Claudette Ramsey there reading.

KRAWZ ALMARIP
Hello.

CLAUDETTE RAMSEY
Sleep well?

KRAWZ ALMARIP
Yes, excellent.

Claudette Ramsey sat there looking at her new conquest and immediately knew what she had to do.

As soon as they got to Arzon—and hopefully Krawz Almarip wasn't doing a "hit and run"—she would purchase him some new cologne so he could stop wearing that atrocious smelling stuff he was now wearing.

Other than that, he would be perfect for a female banker's husband. Krawz Almarip (a.k.a. Evo Kaplan) was an intelligent person.

CLAUDETTE RAMSEY
Krawz, are you hungry?

KRAWZ ALMARIP
Maybe a little.

CLAUDETTE RAMSEY
I was waiting for you to eat my meal because I wanted your company.

KRAWZ ALMARIP
It's not much of a meal, but I guess it will have to do.

CLAUDETTE RAMSEY
If you want, when we land on Praxisvlasia, I can get some carry-out meals and bring them on the ship, since you don't intend on getting off.

KRAWZ ALMARIP
That would be marvelous.

The two got their food items and drink and sat back down and proceeded to have their picnic in space. Conversation flowed and Krawz Almarip enjoyed looking at Claudette Ramsey.

Claudette Ramsey was a beautiful woman and while he was sleeping, she redid her makeup and looked and smelled very fresh. If there ever was a time, Evo Kaplan enjoyed being trapped on a ship with a woman like this, including his travels with Brenda Broyals, this was perhaps the most satisfying.

Evo Kaplan (a.k.a. Krawz Almarip) had to keep reminding himself he was a spy and would fail as a spy if he allowed himself to get emotionally intertwined with a person of interest and a future pawn in a blackmail scheme.

Conceivably Evo Kaplan could get enough money out of Randolph Spencer where he could pay for his own cosmetic surgery and live on another sanctuary planet, and if he could find Brenda Broyals and bring her along, that would be just fine too.

But would Brenda Broyals be willing to go? Could she? After several hours the next set of pilots were up and about, eating and preparing to go into the cockpit. All three sets of pilots and copilots would be manning all six seats in their preparation to land on Praxisvlasia.

Captain Buck got his food items and drink and walked over to the table where Krawz

Almarip and Claudette Ramsey were sitting. Observing they had their food trays that had been sitting there for a while, he asked,

CAPTAIN BUCK
May I join you?

CLAUDETTE RAMSEY
Sure. Captain Buck, please have a seat.

VOICE OVER
Captain Buck enjoyed looking at the pretty woman. He could only imagine the intense satisfaction and gratification Krawz Almarip must have had if managed to coax her into joining him on the twenty-million-mile club. He would talk to the flight attendant Ruth Marradi later, whom he knew was taking bribes from Krawz Almarip, and confirm his suspicions.

Claudette Ramsey's disposition clearly articulated a well-satisfied lady. One day he would have to query how Krawz Almarip managed to seduce such intelligent beautiful women. The guy must be a silver-tongue devil!

The meal was considerably more enjoyable while looking, talking, and smelling such a delightful woman. Unfortunately, Krawz Almarip's cologne was a little annoying, but heck, maybe that was the secret!

In all his travels, Captain Buck had met a lot of men talking at bars who bragged about conquest. Krawz Almarip didn't brag, he just did it. The fact these two were heading to the same ultimate destination meant their short tryst could extend into a longer event because it normally took Krawz Almarip a month to dispose of all his black-market items and return on another transport back to Zanziltar.

Captain Buck had the pleasure of transporting Krawz Almarip to planets and back. They had numerous interesting discussions in the past. This trip would obviously be another, and the woman Krawz Almarip had seduced was as glamorous and beautiful as any other he had ever seen him with. She clearly exposed her essence of an Eager Beaver.

Captain Buck hated to leave the couple he was having such a delightful experience talking to. The exceptionally intelligent woman and his old friend Krawz Almarip, but duty called.

CAPTAIN BUCK
I'm sorry to leave you two, but I need to get up into the cockpit now.

KRAWZ ALMARIP
Maybe I can join you guys up there for a brief period.

CAPTAIN BUCK
Go see the chief purser. He can let you in and out later.

KRAWZ ALMARIP
Will do.

Captain Buck stood up and disposed of his meal wrappers and put the tray on a stack that would be later washed by a flight attendant and put back on a dispenser for other passengers.

Claudette Ramsey and Krawz Almarip were alone again in the passenger lounge.

CLAUDETTE RAMSEY
I hope that when you go to visit the cockpit you do not mention you invited me to the twenty-million-mile club.

KRAWZ ALMARIP
No, I would never mention something like that.

Somehow Claudette Ramsey thought that would be the very first thing the pilots, who were called Hoggers for multiple reasons, would ask.

They continued. small talk for another thirty minutes.

CLAUDETTE RAMSEY
Why don't you go visit your pilot buddies? I want to do some more reading.

KRAWZ ALMARIP
Sure.

Krawz Almarip stood up and walked aft, hoping to find the chief purser without a lot of effort. He could be anywhere. Luck was on his side. Not far from his bunk was the Chief Purser conversing with his flight attendant friend Ruth Marradi, discussing items they had to accomplish prior to landing on Praxisvlasia.

While the Chief Purser and Ruth Marradi were talking Krawz Almarip pulled out some energy drinks from his locker and put them in the carrying bag he could later fold up. He then approached the flight attendant and purser.

KRAWZ ALMARIP

Hello Chief Purser. I would like to go up to the cockpit to visit the pilots for a few minutes. Captain Buck said you could let me in.

CHIEF PURSER

Perhaps for about ten minutes because they are going to be getting busy soon tracking inbound and outbound traffic in the space lanes we are approaching.

KRAWZ ALMARIP

All right, that works. I probably only need ten minutes anyway.

CHIEF PURSER

Follow me, Mr. Almarip.

The chief purser knew Krawz Almarip quite well since he had met him on quite a few flights. At one point he was going to tell him he would have to refrain from any more twenty-million-mile club activity since he had received complaints from families whose kids asked their parents questions.

PASSENGER'S CHILDREN

Why is the man and woman going into the bunk together?

Such questions put the parents on the spot to come up with some lie they felt they shouldn't have to tell their children.

Krawz Almarip got away with it on this trip since the craft was only half full and there were no children onboard. The two walked forward through the lounge and crews breathing area and the chief purser put his hand on the palm reader, which scanned it and activated the solenoid activated door lock. He opened the door for Krawz Almarip and admonished him,

CHIEF PURSER
I'll be back in ten minutes. You'll have to leave
the cockpit, as they probably shouldn't have any
distractions as we arrive in the transport lanes.

KRAWZ ALMARIP
No problem.

As soon as Krawz Almarip was in the cockpit standing behind seat number six and
almost against the rear wall, predictably Captain Buck, now sitting in Seat Number
One, turned around to ask a question.

CAPTAIN BUCK
Say, Krawz, did you get that woman up to the Twenty-
Million-Mile Club?

KRAWZ ALMARIP
Well, Captain Buck, you know that gentlemen never
tell.

Krawz Almarip then balled up his fist and stuck his thumb through his index finger and
the next finger, which was a secret symbol between men.

CAPTAIN BUCK
Krawz Almarip, you're a lucky dog.

KRAWZ ALMARIP
Listen, I didn't do anything, I swear, but show her my
stamp collection.

CO-PILOT FURSUNGTARWUM
Krawz Almarip The last time you ever saw a stamp
collection was in grammar school.

KRAWZ ALMARIP
I can't confirm nor deny that!

Krawz Almarip then passed out energy drinks to all six pilots and copilots, who were
eager recipients as the enhanced awareness it created would indeed make the planetary
re-entry far more pleasant.

Krawz Almarip could see over the pilot's shoulders
and onto the Cosmic Spatial Normalizer Display
DATA showing distant contacts they would need to

avoid. It was kind of interesting. The computer display said, "CPA for CTA number 2387 is ten minutes on a course of 155.663.989 and a speed of 0.75 LS." The Closest Point of Approach would be as close as the transport would pass the other ship.

The Contact Target Analysis (CTA) performed on data received via radio beacon information such as its intergalactic hull number 2387 all non-combat ships were required to transmit, or they would lose their immunity from immediate attack.

Transmitting the CTA information also put them in peril in that an enemy ship that wanted to destroy a precious cargo bound to their enemy could be located and destroyed by such exposure.

The CTA derived target course was normalized three vector coefficients that provided a three-dimensional spatialized relative motion, hence three numbers and multiple decimal points. The CTA information traveled the speed of light plus the relative motion combined. Hence the CTA broadcast to hull number 2387 arrived at 1.75 LS.

Like Einstein said, it's all relative, but Einstein didn't appreciate how much combined speeds of approaching ships were above light speed and the images of the approaching ship was delayed by the differential factor the Cosmic Spatial Normalizer resolved.

The pilot's display provided a popup of imagery of hull number 2387 to get an official observation of the structure and hull dimensions of the spaceship.

This cargo spaceship designated CTA 2387 was a 150,000-ton transport that did not do atmosphere penetrations. Its cargo was transshipped via shuttles. Shuttles and space tugs made a lot of money servicing such ships. Captain Buck looked only briefly at the CTA data then closed the window.

The pilot on 2387 was without doubt looking at their own transport hull number 6809. Five minutes later the first glob of CTA data labels on the Cosmic Spatial Normalizer Display (CSND) data started separating and relative motion almost appeared like snow coming toward the windshield on a car traveling in a storm. Just about the time the contact density reached a level the pilots should not be distracted, the chief purser unlocked the cockpit door.

CHIEF PURSER
Krawz, would you please leave the cockpit now?

KRAWZ ALMARIP
Sure, not a problem. See all of you later.

CAPTAIN BUCK
See you later, Krawz.

Krawz Almarip walked aft through crews berthing and into the lounge area where Claudette Ramsey was still reading. I wonder if she's reading some sort of romance novel. Krawz Almarip thought.

He was closer to the truth than he realized and Krawz Almarip's actions on board this space transport was in line with what she was reading! A provocative parallel indeed.

CLAUDETTE RAMSEY
Did you enjoy talking with your pilot buddies?

KRAWZ ALMARIP
Yes. I took them some energy drinks. Helps make the
trip shorter.

CLAUDETTE RAMSEY
You were not with the pilots very long.

KRAWZ ALMARIP
They are now entering the space lanes to Praxisvlasia.
The congestion is beginning, and the pilots must
concentrate and can't be distracted. The chief purser
chased me out of there, but I realized it was time for
me to leave since they were getting busy.

CLAUDETTE RAMSEY
Did they spot any other spacecraft?

KRAWZ ALMARIP
Oh yes, in the space lanes there is a blizzard of ships
they must avoid collision with.

CLAUDETTE RAMSEY
I would think with all the computerization that should
no longer be a problem.

KRAWZ ALMARIP
I'm sure the pilots like to keep up their proficiency just in case they need to do contact management when the computer systems suddenly have a snag.

CLAUDETTE RAMSEY
That seems like a rather remote possibility.

KRAWZ ALMARIP
I don't know what the pilots experience. They obviously want to keep up their proficiency for some reason or another.

CLAUDETTE RAMSEY
Probably.

KRAWZ ALMARIP
How's the book coming?

CLAUDETTE RAMSEY
I'm about halfway done. I want to finish it before we land. I have a few more books to read on the trip from Praxisvlasia to Arzon. Plus, I can get more at the space port terminal.

KRAWZ ALMARIP
I'd get some books too, but something tells me I'm going to have my hands full taking you on additional rides up to the twenty-million-mile club.

CLAUDETTE RAMSEY
You never know, I might just have to take you up to the forty-million-mile club.

Claudette winked at Krawz Almarip as she was relieved his cologne was wearing off a bit and not quite as offensive as he first showed up in. She knew what she had to do. When she was in the tax-free section of the space port shopping, she was going to buy him a cologne she really loved. If she could have sex with that man wearing Chunlang, her utmost favorite, it would all be worthwhile.

They talked for about an hour then Krawz Almarip excused himself to go use the restroom, then came back and wondered if he should invite her to his club or wait for her to invite him to her forty-million-mile club. It didn't take long before Claudette Ramsey put down the book.

CLAUDETTE RAMSEY
You probably didn't take me seriously when I
suggested I could take you to the forty-million-mile
club?

KRAWZ ALMARIP
I would never assume or disbelieve anything about
you.

CLAUDETTE RAMSEY
Okay, come with me. You have your work cut out for
you.

Krawz Almarip followed Claudette Ramsey to her berth, which smelled a lot better than his, and a flight attendant had just rigged the cabin for nighttime operations, which was always done for planetary re-entry so that passengers could enjoy the view of the approaching planet, the moons, and any solar view if they were on that side of the transport.

Evo's favorite flight attendant Ruth Marradi, whom Claudette Ramsey got to know while Krawz Almarip was sleeping and informed Ruth Marradi she had every intention of taking Krawz Almarip up to the forty-million-mile club and teach him a lesson about women.

As Ruth Marradi watched Claudette Ramsey lead Krawz Almarip to Claudette's bunk, she assumed the event was just about to occur for real. Ruth Marradi positioned herself to block off foot traffic in that direction long enough for the couple to assume their pre-launch position to the forty-million-mile destination.

CLAUDETTE RAMSEY
Would you mind taking off your shoes first? Give them
to me and I'll put them in my locker.

KRAWZ ALMARIP
Sure, no problem.

Krawz Almarip shortly handed his pair of shoes to Claudette, who stowed them for him.

CLAUDETTE RAMSEY
You get in first.

The following voice over happens during the love making scene:

Note to the cinematographer. The next two voice overs are concatenated. The first has a male voice and the second has a female voice. This was done for psychological effects.

VOICE OVER (MALE)

Krawz Almarip hopped into Claudette's bunk, and she followed immediately afterward and closed and locked the security privacy slide. Claudette placed her back to Krawz Almarip and initiated immediate spooning.

Between the heavy-laden pheromones in her perfume and a special cream she had just in case she got lucky, Krawz Almarip was soon transfixed into an explosion of gratification unlike he ever recalled.

At first, Evo Kaplan (a.k.a. Krawz Almarip) felt guilty he had expired before Claudette Ramsey could get her gratification, but he was in for a big surprise. There was plenty of room for Claudette Ramsey to turn and reposition herself on the "Pigs and People" mattress.

Claudette climbed up on top of Krawz Almarip and soon demonstrated what lonely women who had to live a private life developed with robotic help: surreal vaginal muscles. Claudette then proceeded to perform unlike anything Krawz Almarip had ever experienced, nor the duration.

Due to the special cream Claudette put on her vulva area, Krawz Almarip was essentially drugged as if he had taken a dozen doses of Viagra. He was not able to stop, and Claudette had the stamina of a Chita that could run seventy miles an hour for prolonged periods.

Chita woman Claudette kept on pounding Krawz into submission. Krawz Almarip just was "trumped" by a woman and he was now a member of her forty-million-mile club.

Moving forward, Evo Kaplan would have a different attitude toward women. After Claudette Ramsey finally ended her Chita burst, the two slowly eased into a post orgasmic evolution of feelings that broke the inner fabric of their emotions.

Krawz Almarip (a.k.a. Evo Kaplan) was in deep trouble now, far more so than he could ever imagine.

Evo Kaplan's thoughts of him breaking a woman's heart was a huge downer on him. It was as if he could mentally think of Brenda Broyals flying off into space, lifeless, as if she was expelled from a crippled ship floating aimlessly to her demise. It was a feeling he never wanted to have again in his life: Breaking the heart of a woman he adored and truly loved.

VOICE OVER (FEMALE)

Claudette Ramsey, the master chess player, was now three moves ahead of Krawz Almarip, playfully having fun with her mouse before she swallowed him whole.

Krawz Almarip was desperately trying to throw himself a life preserver with his vast indoctrination of a spy.

Now Evo Kaplan was failing just as Brenda Broyals herself had when they were doing the Stratospheric Glider test flights for the Coy's Ridge mission. The two were slowly becoming failures as spies because they allowed their emotions to deviate outside the sphere of a spy whose success relied upon compartmentalizing every aspect of their missions and their private lives.

Never shall the two meets, was Axiom number one of the spy businesses. Evo Kaplan's failed to compartmentalize early enough now dangerously slipped over the line. One image he indelibly had printed in his mind now was the girlish look that Claudette Ramsey had when she had her makeup off.

The tender, sweet, and delightful woman had purposely exposed the fabric of Claudette Ramsey's youthful essence unintentionally and just like Brenda Broyals he could not bear to bring himself to break her heart as well.

Caught up in this war of love where there would end up being serious casualties, there was no safe way out.

Evo Kaplan had built his home, and now he had to live in it, for the rest of his life.

It was heartbreaking business, and Evo Kaplan's own heart would also feel the tremors as one or both were stripped away from him forever for reasons out of his control or simply due to failure of the mission he was now just about to execute.

Perhaps there was some satisfaction knowing he would be close to a woman he fell for when he met his demise?

As Claudette Ramsey and Krawz Almarip crossed over that boundary of celestial delights into a realm of unequivocal post-orgasmic paralysis, they jointly succumbed to the psychophysical reaction that induced sleep and were subsequently transcending into another universe or domain that neural processes that were mankind's biggest mystery took them.

The paralysis lasted several hours until they slowly experienced rational and coherent thoughts beyond the dream world.

One stirring aroused the other, which further elevated their awareness of their surroundings. The sleep period had deflated the emotional explosion that a combination of guilt and disturbing consequences flooded Krawz Almarip (aka Evo Kaplan), who had built up remorse from the choking nostalgia that his experiences with Brenda Broyals had just created.

After two hours of sleep and a break from all those thoughts, Evo Kaplan was less incapacitated from the emotions and allowed his training and indoctrination take over his mental processes that fulfilled the need to compartmentalize those emotions as to not interfere with his life-or-death venture that was now unfolding.

Even now though as Evo Kaplan compartmentalized his feelings, he could not help but feel slight sorrow for Claudette Ramsey, who was a special woman and deserved a partner worthy of her.

As soon as Claudette Ramsey was fully alert, she threw Evo Kaplan a lifeline he needed for psychological transcendence to escape the moral dilemma he found himself in.

CLAUDETTE RAMSEY
Now that I have got my spurs into you, why don't we go back to the lounge where I can do some reading and we can hang out?

KRAWZ ALMARIP
Sounds good to me.

The two slithered out of her bunk and got themselves ostensibly together and made their way to the lounge. In passing, Claudette Ramsey smiled at Ruth Marradi, who had raised eyebrows as she Claudette gave the thumbs-up signal while Krawz Almarip was walking forward and out of position to catch the secret semaphore.

VOICE OVER
Claudette Ramsey and Krawz Almarip arrived at the empty lounge, which had been somewhat the case until now.

However, shortly after arrival to the lounge, a couple appeared and obtained their food and drink and sat down at another table.

There wasn't much being discussed between Krawz Almarip and Claudette Ramsey, as Claudette was once again reading.

Krawz Almarip was simply hanging out thinking about what he could or should be doing. Claudette Ramsey was facing the couple and due to the confined space of the lounge, it was impossible to not overhear the other conversation.

This couple were clearly lovers and full of passion and happy they were almost home from their vacation to Zanziltar.

The exposure and carrying on of the two younger lovers were expected to exhibit had an appeal to Claudette Ramsey, which made Claudette's thoughts of just completed forty-million-mile trip feel even more pleasant.

Exposure to love has a strong influence on others. It psychologically creates thoughts and passions that would ordinarily lay dormant and unrecognized.

These influences encapsulated the moment which would be endearing and indelibly etched in Claudette Ramsey's mind. And here her mouse was in front of her as she playfully entertained him, just like a real cat would its prey.

The couple stayed until they were all admonished to take their seats for planetary landing. Krawz Almarip and Claudette Ramsey followed the couple aft to the passenger cabin seating area and took their assigned seats to get strapped in. Krawz Almarip reassessed his plan. He would wait until all the other passengers got off the ship. Krawz Almarip assumed he would be the only one waiting onboard.

KRAWZ ALMARIP
When you finish shopping and come back aboard, I'll
be in my bunk sleeping. If you want to wake me up,
knock three times on my security privacy slide.

CLAUDETTE RAMSEY
Sure thing, sweetie.

Evo Kaplan noticed the tone in Claudette Ramsey's voice. He was now trapped in a whirlpool of love or something else, and he didn't know this woman too well, other than she was a target he planned to exploit to get to Randolph Spencer.

Krawz Almarip (a.k.a. Evo Kaplan) was closest to the window and could raise the window shade and look out. It was certainly dark, but he also observed more and more ships pass by as they approached the planet and the space lanes merged into major space transport paths required for security observations to prevent the Revolution from making a surprise attack.

All ships went down in single file passing space buoys who identified them and verified they matched their CTA data. Otherwise, the Dranzonian Space Force would have an interceptor right on it ready to blast it out of the sky if necessary.

Up in the cockpit Captain Buck and the five other pilots and copilots now witnessed an extraordinary sight they would never have seen five years ago: on the Cosmic Spatial Normalizer Display Data, appearing as a solid stream as the outbound ships were in a perfect line accelerating to precise speeds required until they fanned out a good distance away from the planet and began independent courses to multitudes of different worlds within the Empire and some outside the Empire.

Directly in front of the ship in direct alignment with the planet was a blob that overlaid on top of each other as the arrivals were in perfect alignment as they passed several space buoy identification devices checking registration and originations. This transport would be automatically a ship of interest since it originated in Zanziltar, the Sanctuary Planet, which meant the possibility of money launderers and Revolution spies aboard.

Everyone leaving the ship would be far more scrutinized than arrivals from Empire planets where they were already pre-screened. Captain Buck, up in the cockpit, was merely watching the display graphics as the ship was in full autopilot. Each one of the six pilots would love to grab the controls and fly the ship manually.

Automation was called for because the air controllers in Praxisvlasia demanded absolute abeyance of instructions and any deviation could result in them being shot down over fear of a Revolution ship sneaking in and laying waste to a city or an industrial complex.

Because these spaceships were now in direct sunlight, the outbound ships could be observed and earlier as they were fanning out on new courses pointing their destination planets, the plumes from their rocket exhausts were very bright as the also no longer had speed restrictions.

The ships now passing in single file still under speed restrictions only had small rocket exhausts and plumes were very short and diffused right away. All the CTA information slid by on the departing ships on icons they could expand to read if they wanted. But in reality, it would waste time especially after they passed their CPA and were opening. CTAs would become more important in space traveling through the Revolutionary Empire zone.

The blockade runner would be running dark during the next leg of it's travel. They would not be transmitting any CTA information and under intergalactic convention rules could be considered a warship and attacked without any repercussions. Their only hope was the Revolutionary Guards, or the Dranzonian Empire Space Force would first inquire who they were and where they came from and just detain the ship and the crew for possible criminal prosecution.

In the case of the Dranzonian Empire Space Force detaining the ship, it would be a horror story for Evo Kaplan, so he might as well commit suicide and avoid the torture should that occur. He was prepared to do so. A smart spy always carries a way out with him. Sometimes death is preferred over the treatment a spy receives. He would speculate that since the FIRM was probably Revolutionaries, he would not be subjected to such harsh treatment. At least not until they no longer had any use for him.

Dead ahead was the planet the cockpit crew observed. It was also now being shown on video displays in the cabin, which was done to give the public something to look at and help comfort them at the end of a long multi-day journey.

Part of the departure space lane was in view as well so the passengers could see many ships passing them in the opposite direction. Many miles ahead they were simply growing dots out of the stream of transports departing, but as they got within a couple miles, they buzzed past at very high velocities and only could be observed for a little more than a second before they passed and were no longer in view.

Praxisvlasia slowly grew in size. Meanwhile, Praxisvlasia's moon Yaoyuan de Zhenzhu was then observed off the port side of the transport. Unlike Earth's moon, Yaoyuan de Zhenzhu had many lights on the dark side that were easily observed, showing it was occupied. A large portion of the fleet was on Yaoyuan de Zhenzhu so they would not be all wiped out in a sucker punch and could be quickly launched so that an enemy had to fear being attacked from two simultaneous directions, which complicated any strategy of attacking Praxisvlasia.

Yaoyuan de Zhenzhu also had ample gravity, water, and vast green areas. It could and did sustain life. No people lived on that moon until well over five hundred years ago.

The blockade runner transport Toutoumomo de Hundan slowly closed in on the space port that had a seven-mile-long runway, which allowed large transports to land. It took them some time to slow down, using ground effect on the high-speed wing and forward thrusters.

The transport would arrive into the atmosphere around seventeen thousand miles per hour and continue down at approximately a 45-degree angle, bleeding off speed through dynamic breaking of the auxiliary turbines powering forward facing thrusters.

The amount of dynamic breaking was proportional to speed, so the faster they were going, the more breaking action. When they slowed down below Mach 4.0 the amount of dynamic breaking available was less than 25 percent of initial re-entry speed and had less effect.

The method to bleed off the rest of the speed was simply to fly horizontal for a while; hence the landing patterns were a lot longer than for commercial airliners. Touchdown speed was nearly 300 miles per hour, hence the need for a seven-mile-long runway. Flying four feet above the ground using the ground effect on the wing provided enough friction to effectively slow the transport, usually within three and a half to four miles.

The additional length of the runway was to accommodate ships that had pilots who overshot the runway and had to get down be enough fuel to do a circle and come back and try it again. This only occurred in a manual landing instead of a computer landing, which always touched down exactly on an imaginary point of the runway within a few feet of where any other automated landing occurred.

The transport filled with more light as they were in the atmosphere and slowing down. Soon Evo Kaplan was looking out at the planet and observed sights they passed over. Oddly enough, Evo Kaplan spotted Coy's Ridge and the mansion where the ultra-rich industrialist Abniler Manther lived.

That sight brought back a lot of memories of Brenda, which hit Evo Kaplan in the gut like a ton of bricks. But instead of suffering more remorse, he used his spy techniques and compartmentalized it all and then focused on the mission and a future endeavor with Randolph Spencer.

C.U. KRAWZ ALMARIP (A.K.A. EVO KAPLAN) DURING THE NEXT VOICE OVER.

VOICE OVER

Will I become a "runner" and escape the FIRM? Who would they send to sanction me if they discover I'm hiding out in a distant world paradise?

Brenda perhaps?

As they got closer to the space port, all the landmarks he could see were just like he last remembered them. Too bad corruption landed him in the hands of the FIRM. With the satisfaction of finally dealing with Reginald Heiqishi, he no longer exhibited the bitterness he once had toward the Dranzonian Empire Secret Service.

But Evo Kaplan was a realist; in due time they would attempt to nab him. He wondered why suddenly; he was on the top ten list of Kill on Sight orders? Did the Revolutionaries betray him to coerce him into remaining in their service?

He was having many thoughts and mixed emotions as the transport came down on the runway. It flew just a few feet off the runway without touching down to bleed off the speed using the ground effect, which could either slow you down or allow you to float along forever, depending on the aperture of the wing structure.

Three hundred miles per hour a few feet off the ground is somewhat scary for someone who has never experienced it before. But for a race car driver or a transport pilot, it was a joyous occasion—part of the perks of being in the business. The transport bled off speed pretty quick and at the prescribed speed, the computer automatically deployed the landing gear. Using precise computer control and aerodynamically stabilized landing gear with wings, the contact to the runway was so smooth that even the most sensitive accelerometer could barely pick up the force of the contact.

However, tires on the runway started to slow the Intergalactic Passenger Transport through more dynamic breaking as the electric motors mounted individually on the multiple wheels provided constant reverse pressures. The wheel electric motor generators had more slowing effect than the ground effect earlier, especially when the full weight of the transport was sitting on them.

Just as Pilot Buck hoped, they were down to maneuver speed at the three and a half-mile marker with a perfect landing, allowing them to turn off the main runway onto the service ramp and over to the Intergalactic Customs Terminal.

Looking around, Evo Kaplan could see the passengers were extremely pleased to be getting off the transport and to their ultimate destinations. Claudette Ramsey sat in her seat until all the other passengers had stood up and marched to their bunks to retrieve their personal items out of their lockers. Almost all of them would be leaving and not returning. Only a few would remain for the continuation flight. She didn't need to get into her locker; she was prepared to exit the transport spaceship but wanted a moment of privacy with Krawz Almarip.

Since passengers sitting near Krawz were now gone, Claudette Ramsey sat in one of the seats right next to him.

CLAUDETTE RAMSEY
While I'm off the transport, is there any specific food
items you would like me to get you?

KRAWZ ALMARIP
Surprise me. Pick something you like.

CLAUDETTE RAMSEY
Okay.

KRAWZ ALMARIP
Do you need any credits?

Claudette Ramsey smiled.

CLAUDETTE RAMSEY
Listen, darling, I have all the credits I will ever need.
You are lucky you met me.

Claudette Ramsey then stood up and walked off the intergalactic passenger transport and out into the duty-free zone, looking for souvenirs to give to her mother and friends.

The transport being half empty so many of the passenger lockers would be empty, so there be plenty of room to store her purchases.

Claudette Ramsey realized a little bribe might also help her get one of the flight attendants to help her carry it off the ship since she assumed Krawz Almarip, being a black marketer, would have a lot of his own articles to carry.

The ship was soon empty except for Krawz Almarip's favorite flight attendant Ruth Marradi that always took bribes from him. Krawz Almarip walked to the bunk area and took his shoes off, and hopped in and immediately shut and locked the security privacy slide. He would pop a pill and take advantage of all the down time to sleep so he could do a lot of surveillance on the new passengers and look for potential spies. Especially any that might be sent to find him.

VOICE OVER

Claudette Ramsey walked through the delightful terminal, enjoying having her feet planted back on terra-firma. There were multitudes of shops hawking their junk to gullible passengers. People just passing through always wanted to pick up souvenirs from the Empire's Capital Praxisvlasia to take home.

Everything imaginable was there to purchase. And if you didn't have room on the ship, for a price they would ship it to you on a regular serviced planet carrier. A lot of people traveling to Zanziltar made such purchases. People traveling to Arzon could not take advantage of this service since there no longer was regular service, nor could it be guaranteed since the Intergalactic Passenger Transport to Arzon had to travel through Revolution Empire areas.

It took several hours for Claudette Ramsey to find enough articles. She decided she would re-board, stow her articles in her bunk, then go back out and find some delicacies she could share with Krawz Almarip, her perfect mouse she loved toying with.

Claudette Ramsey bumped into Krawz Almarip's favorite flight attendant Ruth Marradi when boarding the Zanziltar Intergalactic Passenger Transport

CLAUDETTE RAMSEY

Hey, I purchased some souvenirs and need some extra

space for the flight. If you could help me store some of this in an unused bunk for this flight, I'll make it worth your while.

The flight attendant Ruth Marradi, who knew damn well who Claudette Ramsey was and what she was doing with her mouse, smiled.

RUTH MARRADI
The bunk directly above your bunk does not have any reservations for this flight. Go ahead and store it all in there.

CLAUDETTE RAMSEY
Wonderful. Say, I'm going back off the ship to get some food in the courtyard. Is there anything you would like me to get you?

RUTH MARRADI
If you are going to pick up some items, I'm kind of looking forward to Styrolian Sponges served on a bed of Zanziltar Shuidao.

CLAUDETTE RAMSEY
All right I'll get that for you. Say, I have one other question.

RUTH MARRADI
Yes?

CLAUDETTE RAMSEY
Do you know what Krawz Almarip's favorite food is?

RUTH MARRADI
I've stayed at the same hotel with Krawz Almarip a few times and he always seem to order Kao Zhurou.

CLAUDETTE RAMSEY
Okay thanks!

Claudette Ramsey was off the ship and out food shopping. She was lucky she found a restaurant that did takeout that had everything she needed on the menu and didn't have to go to multiple locations.

As soon Claudette Ramsey she was loaded up, she went back to the Zanziltar

Intergalactic Passenger Transport Toutoumomo de Hundan, where she quickly noticed a sign that notified passengers: If you are bringing food items onto the ship, please eat them before we depart the space port so that we can remove all waste products prior to take off.

Claudette Ramsey hoped Krawz Almarip would not be upset if she woke him before takeoff so they could comply with the sign. She went up to Krawz's bunk and knocked three times. She waited about a minute and the security privacy slide slid open and Krawz Almarip appeared to adjust his eyes, focusing in on Claudette Ramsey.

CLAUDETTE RAMSEY
I got your meal, but we must eat it before the ship
takes off so they can dispose of the trash.

KRAWZ ALMARIP
All right.

Krawz Almarip opened up the security privacy slide and hopped out and put on his shoes. Krawz Almarip and Claudette Ramsey headed toward the passenger lounge and met the flight attendant Ruth Marradi on the way.

CLAUDETTE RAMSEY
I brought you what you requested. Would you like to
join us in the lounge?

RUTH MARRADI
Thanks. I have about an hour before we start pre-
boarding new passengers.

The three went to the lounge where they all sat down, and then Claudette Ramsey dished out the contents to everyone.

CLAUDETTE RAMSEY
Good thing I ran into Ruth. She said you like Kao
Zhurou.

Evo Kaplan, mindful this flight attendant knew more about the real Krawz Almarip than he did, simply went along, even though it really wasn't one of his personal favorites, and responded like someone would who liked the selection.

KRAWZ ALMARIP (a.k.a. Evo Kaplan)
Thanks.

Soon they were all eating and Evo Kaplan, eyeballing the flight attendant's meal, sure wished he had the Styrolian Sponges instead. They had only been eating for a few minutes when another flight attendant took Ruth Marradi away for an issue.

RUTH MARRADI
I'm finished. If you guys want to try the Styrolian
Sponges, help yourselves.

KRAWZ ALMARIP
I kind of like those Styrolian Sponges. I'm going to
have some of them.

Krawz Almarip finished half of the serving of Styrolian Sponges and Kao Zhurou.
After Krawz Almarip finished the sponges, he felt full.

KRAWZ ALMARIP
I think I'm done.

CLAUDETTE RAMSEY
Me too. Let me take care of all the trash, dear.

Claudette Ramsey stood up and systematically cleaned off the table, placing each item
in the trash bin that no doubt would get emptied in a short while.

KRAWZ ALMARIP
Thank you for bringing me the meal. It was very
pleasant.

Krawz Almarip gave Claudette Ramsey's a lovely smile.

CLAUDETTE RAMSEY
My pleasure, dear.

VOICE OVER
In many ways, Claudette Ramsey's personalization
of her statements was endearing, but in another way
was also troubling since it spelled out the remarkable
speed with which they had evolved into a relationship
of some sort.

Whether Krawz Almarip (a.k.a. Evo Kaplan) was
ready for a relationship or not, he crossed the line
when he ate the forbidden fruit. Now Evo Kaplan
would have to integrate all those circumstances into
his strategic plan, conducting his mission on Arzon.

Krawz Almarip (a.k.a. Evo Kaplan) also looked at the time, which was shown on
digital displays on the walls in the lounge. He had about thirty minutes before he had

to crawl back in his bunk before customers from Praxisvlasia boarded the transport so they would not see him until they were underway and out into deep space accelerating to Arzon.

By the time the Intergalactic Passenger Transport was accelerating to Arzon, it would be extremely difficult for the Dranzonian Empire to stop and search the craft unless they had a military vessel out in front of them on the path to Arzon.

Claudette Ramsey and Krawz Almarip chatted for about thirty minutes, enjoying each other's company, which included some veiled flirting and cat-and-mouse play time.

KRAWZ ALMARIP

I'm going to my bunk for takeoff. If something goes wrong, I prefer to die in my sleep.

CLAUDETTE RAMSEY

Don't be silly, dear. Nothing is going to happen.

KRAWZ ALMARIP

What are you going to do?

CLAUDETTE RAMSEY

I'm going to stay here and do some more reading until they direct me back to my seat.

KRAWZ ALMARIP

All right, I'll see you in a few hours.

CLAUDETTE RAMSEY

Sleep well, honey.

VOICE OVER

Krawz Almarip stood up and went to his bunk. He looked around. Nobody was within his eyesight. Krawz Almarip took off his shoes put them in the shoe storage locker and climbed into the bunk, which had been remade while he was eating. Probably his bunk was remade by his favorite flight attendant Ruth Marradi, who was not allowed to give her real name to passengers for security reasons. Her name tag only said, "flight attendant."

Krawz Almarip knew the truth: her real name was Ruth Marradi, whom the real Krawz Almarip privately called Ruthless. In the real Krawz Almarip interviews by the FIRM, described all the possible flight crew on CTA number 6809, Evo Kaplan had been advised this was probably the only flight attendant he could trust, though she expected a big payoff.

Krawz Almarip also conveyed Ruthless expected one day to receive sexual favors as well as substantial credits. Sexual favors would become nearly impossible from now on while Claudette Ramsey was aboard the transport.

Perhaps on the return leg if he was able to get back to Zanziltar?

He then took another pill that would put him under for a while.

Pills for this, pills for that. Perhaps the reason why they wanted a six-year contract is they figured that's the duration it would take to burn me out on all these pills?

Evo Kaplan wondered if Brenda Broyals would come to him in his dreams. Will I ever see her again?

CAP ZAPATERO, VOYAGE TO ARZON

VOICE OVER

Cap Zapatero, a.k.a. the real Blane Jiandie, boarded the Intergalactic Space Transport blockade runner Toutoumomo de Hundan. He quickly found his seat and followed all the instructions the flight crew gave, knowing an incident in space would most likely render their ability to return or stay alive somewhat remote.

His first interest was finding Evo Kaplan so he could recognize him or discover if the person was wearing a disguise. If so, then it would take a while to find him.

Evo Kaplan now had one disadvantage. Evo Kaplan didn't know the Dranzonian Empire Secret Service had placed Cap Zapatero, an agent onboard for such purposes. Cap Zapatero was a well-trained spy in the arts and crafts.

Cap Zapatero was a martial arts expert and a clear and present danger to Evo Kaplan. Just like scent training, spies are also trained in audio. Cap Zapatero had spent countless hours listening to Evo Kaplan's voice recorded in several ways.

Cap Zapatero listened hours to a series of Evo Kaplan voice recordings made, both overt and surreptitiously. Evo Kaplan's voice print was indelibly planted in Cap Zapatero's mind just like sonar technician on a nuclear-powered submarine memorizing sounds in the ocean.

Cap Zapatero could distinguish Evo Kaplan's voice with no difficulty. A spy's weakest link is his voice. Through his voice he can be easily tracked.

The FIRM made their biggest mistake in the Arson mission for not altering Evo Kaplan's voice. It would have taken an additional week, which they easily could have extended because the blockade runner was having difficulties finding passengers to Arzon.

Unfortunately, Cornelius Xie de Hundan, the evil Revolutionary Empire dictator, was pushing the Arzon mission too hard out of arrogance but also to support military planning.

One week to alter the voice was easily doable and would not have altered any event except putting Evo Kaplan at risk of detection. Furthermore, they had not yet discovered their double spy, Huaiyuansu Ka, who had already betrayed Evo Kaplan as well as Brenda Broyals, who was also flying into harm's way on another mission.

EXT. CGI. DAY. PRAXISVLASIA INTERGALACTIC PASSENGER TRANSPORT SPACE PORT Toutoumomo de Hundan TAKE OFF. 45 SECONDS

The Intergalactic Passenger Transport Toutoumomo de Hundan was soon heading down the service ramp to the seven-mile-long runway. The spacecraft was heavy because it was full of fuel.

Even though Intergalactic Passenger Transports were designed to take off on their own, space ports like Praxisvlasia had electric catapults to assist getting the ship up to twenty thousand feet where the main propulsion rockets increased power output from fifteen percent to maximum to achieve the required planetary departure speed of seventeen thousand miles per hour. This process, prevented rocket exhaust from damaging homes and businesses.

This launch method also helped reduce the amount of fuel required to reach planetary exit velocity and have a significant amount of reserve fuel for emergencies.

During the launch the rocket engines were throttled up to fifteen percent power as the electric catapult, locked onto electric magnets built into the wheel housing area, provided a shove point that only needed three and a half miles to reach catapult speed.

When the space craft reached catapult speeds after traveling down the runway, computers gave the launch signal simultaneously shifting control surfaces, the electric catapult shut down its electric magnet and the ship quickly rose above it and the runway at supersonic speed leaving behind a mild sonic boom thanks to the wake diffusers.

The passengers all strapped into their seats felt around two "G's" as the ship continued up to twenty thousand feet using fifteen percent rocket throttle settings, before throttling up to maximum power output allowing the spacecraft to reach planetary exit velocity.

Captain Buck and the five other pilots and copilots, who had the long sleep period while the ship was previously waiting at the space port for their launch time, were well rested and fully attentive to detail. The six pilots and copilots, carefully watched their collision avoidance displays that operated off the Cosmic Spatial Normalizer Data that clarified all potential collision threats that would automatically maneuver the ship to avoid any safety concern.

The launch was in autopilot, but at any time Captain Buck could have taken control of the ship, though three seconds would be required for the computer to determine the pilot was making reasonable actions, relinquished control of steering and the auto-throttles. Once the computer released controls, the captain could respond, but most pilots would say it was too late or the pilot would screw up what the computer was doing, as most likely the most prudent act based on algorithms and sensor data.

A navigation system monitor would be a more accurate job description for Captain Buck and the other pilots. Though in an emergency, they could control the ship. As part of their training and licenses, they were required to go to trainers twice a year and go through emergency procedures.

Right around the twenty-thousand-foot mark, Captain Buck watched the auto-throttles slowly increase speed. The idea was not to give passengers a big jerk, so gradual speed increase was necessary. Passengers slowly felt 2.5 Gs as the rocket engines gradually increased to full throttle to efficiently achieve the planetary exit velocity. Once that speed was reached the throttles were throttled down to around fifteen percent, where they fell in line with the outbound formation of transports leaving the planet.

The intergalactic Passenger Transports would remain at fifteen percent power until they went past the outer marker and a good distance to where they could not become a threat to the planet since the Dranzonian Empire Space Force had sufficient reaction time to get a combat vessel up in time to destroy any threat.

In less than thirty minutes they finally reached the outer marker when the throttles were again slowly adjusted to obtain one hundred percent thrust to accelerate to Voyage Management settings.

They were soon accelerating very quickly, but passengers did not feel the gravity consequence as the pilot shifted on the artificial gravity, which was about half of what they felt on the planet. It was more than sufficient to allow walking around on the transport. Looking out to space, a lot of bright rocket exhaust in front of them were spreading as ships maneuvered on new courses toward other planets.

This blockade runner transport Toutoumomo de Hundan had to circumnavigate the planet and turn on a heading nearly opposite of its launch vector. This was good for some of the passengers on the port side of the ship who could watch them pass by their planet Praxisvlasia and its moon Yaoyuan de Zhenzhu.

VOICE OVER

Cap Zapatero watched the planet and the moon and had deep thoughts about his home world and the pending mission. The Arzon mission was full of complications and danger.

Arzon was still part of the Dranzonian Empire and had not yet been invaded by the Revolutionary Guard, but he and everyone else in the Dranzonian Empire Secret Service knew it was only a matter of time. Their luck was going to run out soon.

That eventuality added impetus to figure out exactly what Evo Kaplan was going to be doing on the planet Arzon.

Even though Cap Zapatero (a.k.a. Blane Jiande) could conceivably carry out the top ten-kill on site hit list in route, he had to let Evo Kaplan survive and carry out part of his espionage to discover what he really was doing going to Arzon.

Was Evo Kaplan's mission purely espionage or was there an element of sabotage, and what was the timing of it? Was it to coincide with an invasion? A lot was riding on Cap Zapatero's fact finding.

The flight attendant Ruth Marradi had noticed the attractive Cap Zapatero. She immediately started speculating what this guy was doing heading to Arzon. Since Krawz Almarip is preoccupied with that Trollip Claudette Ramsey, perhaps I can nail this guy?

Ruth Marradi had no shame. In fact, the entire flight crew was somewhat filthy and corrupt, as blockade running wasn't the only illegal thing they were known to do. There had been flights that had no passengers at all on them as they were gun running or human trafficking or transporting children-soldiers.

Child soldiers are typically recruited because they are seen by armed groups as expendable and cheap to maintain. Their ability to handle light automatic laser rifles and pistols, which older children can easily handle, made them ideal to infiltrate.

Dressed up as school children with backpacks made them much harder to detect, and when one child group the Revolutionary Guards used pulled their laser pistols out of their backpacks and killed a group of high-ranking Dranzonian Empire officers during the initial stages of the civil war added to their recognized value.

Hundreds of young women sold to human traffickers were hauled on this ship and it was Ruth Marradi in particular who kept lying to the girls telling them they had been rescued and were on their way home, when in fact they were heading to Orgy Island so a rich banker and his politician friend could experience a group of virgins.

VOICE OVER

Once the safety harness indicator went out in the passenger cabin, Ruth visited all the passengers and explained to them they could now get up out of their seats and go to the restroom, lounge, or their bunks.

Cap Zapatero made a trip to the lounge as an excuse to get up and walk around and observe all the passengers. This flight had a lot fewer passengers than the previous flight.

Cap Zapatero couldn't see how the transport company could possibly be making any money on this flight, then he thought, they must be carrying a lot of precious material in the cargo bay.

It did not take Cap Zapatero long to spot Claudette Ramsey, who was still wearing provocative clothes, had her makeup on, and the perfume didn't hurt either. It seemed rather amusing that such an attractive woman would be flying to Arzon by herself.

Cap Zapatero then made his way up to the lounge and looked around. On a full flight there would already be several people there. But on this thin flight, there was nobody there. One thing was apparent: they would not have any problems running out of food and water on this flight.

Up in the cockpit, the space traffic had thinned out quite a bit, essentially due to very few ships heading in the direction towards Arzon.

In the following day, Captain Buck would be turning off the CTA transmissions for the duration of the flight until they came close to Arzon when he would turn it back on.

Cap Zapatero felt the need to use the restroom. Walking around created a delicate moment in his stomach he needed to resolve.

It was coincidental that Evo Kaplan got out of his bunk about the same time Cap Zapatero was in the restroom.

While EVO KAPLAN was asleep, Claudette Ramsey had requested permission from the flight attendant Ruth Marradi.

CLAUDETTE RAMSEY
Would it be possible if I could change my seat next to Krawz Almarip?

RUTH MARRADI.
Sure, I do not see why not. It's an empty seat and we have an empty flight.

Claudette Ramsey was sitting next to Krawz Almarip's seat when he arrived.

CLAUDETTE RAMSEY
I hope you don't mind. I asked if I could change seats
and sit next to you."

KRAWZ ALMARIP
No problem, I enjoy your company. I'm going to listen
to some music now.

Krawz Almarip lowered the viewer that came down from directly above his seat and provided surround sound and incredible video capability he selected some symphonic music.

The viewer also hid Krawz Almarip's face so that when Cap Zapatero walked by he didn't see who it was. But Cap Zapatero could see a man was sitting next to the gorgeous woman. Probably her boyfriend or husband.

Since it wasn't Brenda Broyals, another Revolutionary Empire Spy on the top ten kill on sight list, it was unlikely to be Evo Kaplan. Especially since their new double spy Huaiyuansu Ka had reported the two were lovers and sent on vacations together paid for out of FIRM funds.

Looking at the man's clothing, he was far too flamboyant. Cap Zapatero knew, the FIRM would never send someone out like Evo Kaplan in such loud outfits that would attract attention.

At this moment Krawz Almarip was listening to music performed by a Gāngqín, which gave a similar sound to an Earth-built Steinway grand piano. Claudette Ramsey was reading a new book she purchased back at Praxisvlasia. If she knew her new lover was a spy, she would be living the life of the person in the new Novel she was reading.

If Claudette Ramsey knew not far from her sat another spy, it would surpass the book she was reading by a wide margin. In Claudette Ramsey's days to come she might come to that realization if certain events occurred, which were terribly likely.

For now, Claudette Ramsey's impetus was, of course, her mother, which she tried to put out of her mind by focusing in on this new love. She had never got carried away with a man like this before and knew that due to his character he would most likely break her heart. But she would live for this day. Strangely, Krawz Almarip didn't seem quite as hideous as his reputation indicated, according to Ruth Marradi.

VOICE OVER
Even Ruth Marradi was taken back a bit. Krawz

For a couple days there was virtually little contact between Cap Zapatero and Krawz Almarip. Cap Zapatero estimated the two were lovers and when he accidently saw her following him into a bunk and quickly shut the security privacy slide and not reappear for another eight hours, he knew it was impossible for this to be Evo Kaplan's Brenda Broyals' lover.

Knowing Brenda Broyals reputation after great study, Cap Zapatero figured Brenda Broyals would kill Evo Kaplan if she ever caught him cheating with another woman. And as deadly as Brenda Broyals was, which Evo Kaplan knew vividly, this man would be the last person on the ship Cap Zapatero would suspect as Evo Kaplan.

For that matter, the crew was quite confident that was the black marketer Krawz Almarip, who took their ship to many destinations. The only thing they would tell you out of the ordinary was Krawz Almarip never fell for a woman. He might have taken a lot of them up to the twenty-million-mile club, but that was always the extent of it.

As more and more people cycled through the lounge, Cap Zapatero made the point to go back there and initiate conversations to attempt possibly recognizing Evo Kaplan's voice.

Cap Zapatero was almost ready to give up his search for Evo Kaplan.

VOICE OVER

Cap Zapatero started thinking: Once again, the Dranzonian Empire Secret Service got fished in by a double spy they thought they controlled.

Another wild goose chase to make them burn up critical assets and displace agents away from where real espionage was occurring. It would not be unexpected that Evo Kaplan arrived on Praxisvlasia and is well positioned while the Empire is chasing him across the galaxy wasting a lot of assets.

Cap Zapatero slowly built up a map he kept to himself and only updated in private as he systematically went through each and all the passengers, and suddenly the only one left he had not heard speak was this man Ruth Marradi said was Krawz Almarip.

Krawz Almarip and Claudette Ramsey had developed a pattern together. They ate their meals based on the clock.

The couple Cap Zapatero identified as Krawz Almarip and Claudette Ramsey did a lot of sleeping together, which was ostensibly headbanging sex in the confines of one of their bunks where they appeared to have visited each together every day.

Cap Zapatero assumed that since there were no passengers in bunks above or below them, Krawz Almarip and Claudette Ramsey probably felt comfortable in engaging in sexual intercourse activity any time they desired.

VOICE OVER

During their next mealtime Cap Zapatero observed Krawz Almarip and Claudette Ramsey heading to the lounge. Cap Zapatero waited a couple moments then proceeded to the lounge where he would appear to get his own dinner.

The couple were not speaking much. It was as if they could communicate in silence just by their presence together.

Claudette Ramsey was liking the way everything was developing and would soon be giving Krawz Almarip her mother's address and contact information so he could get in touch with her and presumably continue the relationship possibly into something more important.

It would be Claudette Ramsey's crowning achievement if she could end up with Krawz Almarip as her spouse in a legal union while her mother was still alive to witness it. Time was running out; Claudette Ramsey couldn't take long. She might even have to be the person to give the proposal if that's what it took.

VOICE OVER

Cap Zapatero was mildly disappointed they were not talking, then something quite extraordinary occurred.

Captain Buck walked out of the crew's berthing and into the lounge. He was getting ready to go relieve one of the crew and take over his twelve-hour shift. The copilot Fursungtarwum followed a short time later.

CLAUDETTE RAMSEY
Hello Captain Buck.

Claudette Ramsey's statement was another interesting data point for Cap Zapatero. This woman knows the crew, how interesting.

Fursungtarwum arrived and after he got his meal and drink and sat down next to Captain Buck, he turned to Krawz Almarip.

> COPILOT FURSUNGTARWUM
> Hey Krawz, you got any new jokes to tell us today, or
> you just going to repeat some of those stale ones?

> KRAWZ ALMARIP
> Fursungtarwum, if I had any new jokes, you would be
> the first to hear them.

Just as if he was suddenly shocked by a lightning strike, Cap Zapatero was suddenly mesmerized. The voice was a perfect match for Evo Kaplan.

Cap Zapatero would eat and drink slowly and get more samples. Cap Zapatero carefully put his hand over his pants pocket and felt the device he had in it: a small black box. It was a high-quality recorder. It could record continuously for forty-eight hours. He only needed a few minutes.

For the next few minutes there was back-and-forth banter between the flight crew and the man referred to as Krawz Almarip, an alleged black marketer.

It would not be out of character for the Revolutionaries to steal a man's identity in an elaborate hoax. They did a fantastic job except for the voice. Also, the woman's voice came nowhere near being anything like Brenda Broyals, so it's not her.

The pilot and co-pilot talked with Evo Kaplan for almost thirty minutes when they suddenly had to make their way to the cockpit. Captain Buck turned around and looked at Krawz Almari.

> CAPTAIN BUCK
> Say Krawz, do you have any more of those energy
> drinks left?

> KRAWZ ALMARIP
> You bet I do.

> CAPTAIN BUCK
> How about grabbing a couple and join us in the cockpit
> for a while.

Krawz Almarip looked at Claudette Ramsey and she instinctively knew and responded.

CLAUDETTE RAMSEY
Krawz, I'm going back to my seat and do some reading.
You should go visit the cockpit.

KRAWZ ALMARIP
All right.

Soon the room emptied out except for Cap Zapatero, who remained as to not give the impression he was bird-dogging them. As soon as Cap Zapatero was alone, he pressed the button on the black box he could feel in his pocket, which stopped the recording.

As expected, Evo Kaplan was gone a while and then came back holding three containers of special energy drinks he had, and continued his way through crews berthing and up to the cockpit where the off going co-pilot was holding the cockpit door open knowing he was bringing a special gift for Captain Buck and Fursungtarwum.

KRAWZ ALMARIP
Thanks, I appreciate you holding the door open for me.

OFF GOING COPILOT
Not a problem. Fursungtarwum promised me that he would
tell me your jokes if they were not old repeats.

Shortly after Evo Kaplan made his way to the cockpit, Cap Zapatero made his way to his bunk where he pulled a small case out of his locker and got up into his bunk after taking off his shoes and placed them in a location he could instantly grab and put on. He then crawled into his bunk and shut the security privacy slide and locked it for his privacy, as he now had a very important task to do.

Cap Zapatero pulled out the black box and took a device out of the case with a small cable and attached it to the recorder. Soon the recorder uploaded the audio files into the device that did voice analysis and voiceprint testing.

A section of conversation was tagged along with comparison files stored on the device. Soon colorized spectrums were being displayed showing the results of the forensic voice analysis.

NOTE TO CINEMATOGRAPHER:

The public is not aware of voice fingerprint analysis to the extent
it has been developed. CIA, NSA, FSB (Formerly KGB), China's
MSS, MI6, Mossad, AIC, DGSE, BND, PSIA, and NIS (South
Korea) utilize such technology. Russia and China have programs
very similar to PRISM. [PRISM - Wikipedia]

The closeup of the spectrographs depicted in this scene should have real time data display and the sound of the voice while Cap Zapatero is verifying Evo Kaplan's voice.

<u>C.U. OF THE SPECTROGRAPHIC ANALYSIS DISPLAY ON THE DEVICE.</u>

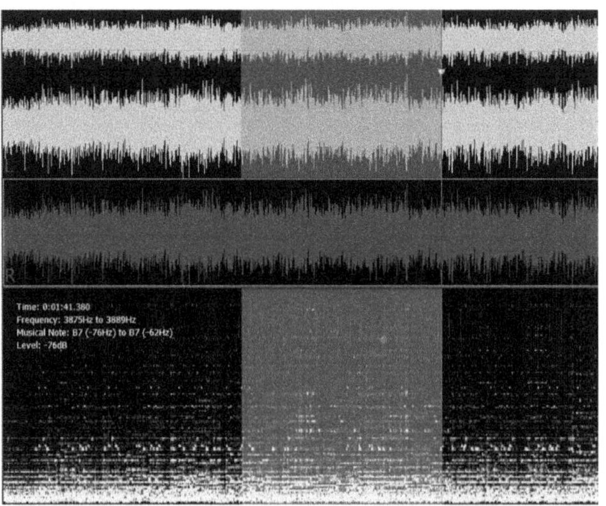

Image produced by this fantastic APP: FFT Sound Analyzer - Audio Analysis Software - Windows & Mac (nch.com.au)

Spectrograph analysis followed by an average tone and pitch analysis, along with statistical analysis that compared results to Evo Kaplan's compiled database, gave off Figure-of-Merit over each word he said. The sequence of Figure-of-Merit percentages on the first ten words were 80, 78, 92, 95, 68, 84, 96, 69, 88, and 86 gave a high average of 83.6 percent probability it was Evo Kaplan's voice.

Cap Zapatero was almost spooked that in just such a short sample he could already determine a match. But he knew better than to get buck fever; he had to analyze the entire contents of the recording to get more degrees of freedom, which would make the predictive elements far more reliable.

On just this one recording, he had 145 words, which he soon tagged and processed. The next results came out rather remarkable. With a much larger sample, the Figure-of-Merit reached 95 percent. Bingo, this is our man Evo Kaplan!

Now Cap Zapatero had to lay low, avoid eye contact, avoid any undue interest in the couple, to give the appearance he was totally disassociated with this Krawz Almarip. Had it not been for the help of Huaiyuansu Ka, the cosmetic surgery was so successful he could have slipped into anywhere in the Dranzonian Empire and done his damage. Had they not got anxious and careless and took care of the voice, he would not have been detected.

If it were not for the fact, the Dranzonian Empire needed to know what Evo Kaplan was going to do on Arzon, he would be dead in a few hours. And as soon as the ship pulled into a Dranzonian Empire Space Port, Blane Jiandie would be transported off the ship by Dranzonian Empire officials and given a hero's welcome for executing one of their most important spies.

Now Cap Zapatero needed to resolve one other misconception reported by Huaiyuansu Ka: Evo Kaplan and Brenda Broyals could not possibly be lovers based on the activity ongoing on this ship. The person of interest, Brenda Broyals, might be someone else who just might be on this ship.

Claudette Ramsey was now a major person of interest because she was having an affair with Evo Kaplan. This had to be the woman Huaiyuansu Ka had reported about just the past few weeks. If so, they have achieved some rather incredibly quick cosmetic surgery, which also is a game changer as they can then more efficiently change identities and get more people inserted behind enemy lines at a much faster rate. This too was a dangerous development that needed to be reported.

VOICE OVER

> Cap Zapatero was now operating with a distinct advantage—the element of surprise. As soon as Cap Zapatero (a.k.a. Blane Jiandie) was able to connect with Loraine, he would be able to set up a surveillance net on Evo Kaplan, who couldn't make any moves without them knowing.
>
> In a short period of time the truth would come out, and they could then make their reports and carry out either an arrest warrant on Evo Kaplan or, if he resisted arrest, perform the "kill on sight" order.

The days quickly passed and by some miracle they managed to avoid the Revolutionary Guard and made their way to Arzon. The ship soon approached the planet, which had nothing like the traffic on Praxisvlasia. Only a few ships left the planet in the entire approach. A ship coming directly from Praxisvlasia was considerably rare these days. Some of the black marketers on Arzon were ready to begin the wheeling and dealing immediately.

Arzon space port had a seven-mile runway, but its electric catapult was not in service. They were lucky they would leave with a mostly empty ship and not need a lot of fuel to get back out in space on the return trip.

As soon as the transport came to a stop at the arrival/departure gate that was quickly opened, the crowd got up and quickly made their way to their bunks to retrieve their belongings and make their way into the terminal and through customs.

Ruth Marradi, true to her word, stood by to help Claudette Ramsey carry all her extra items off the spacecraft and into the lobby.

Krawz Almarip (a.k.a. Evo Kaplan) had his own problem and his hands were full.

Just before they were leaving, Claudette Ramsey gave Krawz Almarip (a.k.a. Evo Kaplan) her local contact information so he could get in touch with her. She had said that because of her mother's health she was staying indefinite and taking a leave of absence.

To avoid any visibility, Cap Zapatero promptly left the ship and went through customs extremely quickly, mainly because he was precleared by government officials. Down in the baggage claim area, his old flame Loraine Rantala was waiting for him.

She approached him because the area had been sanitized and only one possible suspect spy was coming off the ship. She handed him a communicator that would work on the planet in case he needed to call her. All he had to do is state "Call Loraine," as her information was pre-recorded and ready to use.

Evo Kaplan made it through customs rather quickly as well since he was portraying someone customs officials expected bribes from.

Ruth Marradi used her flight attendant credentials to walk Cladette Ramsey through customs, so they made it through quickly as well.

One of the problems of the Dranzonian Empire Secret Service was that with all the purges a significant amount of information was lost, such as five missions Evo Kaplan carried out with his team member Loraine Rantala. Loraine Rantala didn't know Evo Kaplan's new identity because Cap Zapatero had not had a chance to inform her that Evo Kaplan had stolen Krawz Almarip's identity.

Having recently finished one of those special energy drinks, Evo Kaplan was now super aware and focused. Because of his enhanced mental condition, it took Evo Kaplan very little time to spot Loraine Rantala and the man she was talking with who had traveled on the blockade runner Intergalactic Transport Toutoumomo de Hundan.

Evo Kaplan acted like he didn't see Loraine Rantala and slipped out of the airport while Cap Zapatero had his back turned to him losing precious moments while his little head was being enthralled by his old flame Loraine Rantala.

Typically, black marketers would see Krawz Almarip departing the space port where they would contact him and make future rendezvous to transfer materials and credits. Today was no different. A vehicle pulled up to the curb and a man got out. Based on the training it was one of the black marketers he was expected to run into.

BATYLR
Hey Krawz, can I give you a lift?

KRAWZ ALMARIP
Sure Batylr.

Batylr helped Krawz get his articles in his vehicle.

BATYLR
You want to go to the usual location?

KRAWZ ALMARIP
Yep, you know it.

Evo Kaplan had been briefed on the hotels Krawz Almarip frequented. Shortly they were pulling into a hotel that Evo Kaplan knew about from the briefings.

BATYLR
Can we get together later this evening?

KRAWZ ALMARIP
I'm tired. Suffering from space lag, I'm going to just
stay in my hotel today and relax.

The bellhop put Krawz Almarip's items on a cart and took him into the lobby where the receptionist recognized him and knew how he worked it.

RECEPTIONIST
Welcome back, Krawz Almarip. The bellhop will take
you up to your favorite room and we'll take care of the
paperwork when you feel ready probably tomorrow.

KRAWZ ALMARIP
Thanks.

Evo Kaplan was soon in the room with a nagging thought. He had to stay low for a while, since he was followed to Arzon by a spy whom he now could recall, and the

Dranzonian Secret Service female was a spy he knew quite well mainly because she liked practicing her honeypot schemes on her partners like Evo Kaplan who knew his business.

As soon as Evo Kaplan (portraying Krawz Almarip) established communications with Conrad Fanzui, he would report a Dranzonian Empire Secret Service who met another at Arzon whom he identified, meaning he was either bird-dogged to Arzon or that person was sent here for some type of mission.

If there were no other FIRM operations underway on Arzon, which was highly unlikely since Evo Kaplan was being sent here due to lack of information, he had to assume he was the target unless proven otherwise.

The implications of Evo Kaplan being a target at Arzon were huge. It meant the FIRM had been penetrated. There was now a double spy among them, which put them all in jeopardy. If it were not for the fact that they were established at Zanziltar effectively a Sanctuary City and Sanctuary Planet, they would all be quickly wiped out. They still could sustain horrible losses because multiple missions might have already been compromised.

<u>EXT. DAY. BRENDA BROYALS AT ZETA-DALAJIANGYUMI BINGXIAN</u>

VOICE OVER

Conrad Fanzui wasted no time in sending Brenda Broyals and Evo Kaplan in opposite directions. They were both on top ten missions far removed from each other and great distances from Zanziltar as well as Praxisvlasia.

Huaiyuansu Ka's betrayal was now taking on a life of its own. The Dranzonian Empire Secret Service had scrambled agents in the same destinations as Brenda Broyals and Evo Kaplan. The Dranzonian Empire Secret Service thought they had a rare opportunity to take out two Revolution agents currently listed on the order of battle in the Top Ten to Kill any way possible list.

Brenda Broyals had deployed hastily with a team and had been set up by Dranzonian Empire Secret Service thanks to Huaiyuansu Ka's betrayal and logistics support.

The worst possible situation now existed for Brenda. Her contacts on Zeta-Dalajiangyumi Bingxian were also compromised by Huaiyuansu Ka.

Zeta-Dalajiangyumi Bingxian was one of many planets in no man's land between the two Empires that had declared neutrality. If either the Dranzonian Empire or Revolutionary Empire managed to sway many of these neutral planets to pick their side, it no doubt would swing the advantage to that cause, Loyalist or Revolutionaries.

The main reason for the neutrality is these planets, who knew they were on the forefront of taking the full brunt of the punishment if they sided with either Empire, didn't want to see their cities shattered like those that had. The terrible price several planets paid by picking sides was the loss of a lot of their population and the horrible destruction that laid waste to their population centers.

No matter the moral justification in selecting sides, the pragmatic approach and outcome was these planets were not willing to suffer vast destruction simply to switch from one dictator to another.

If the Revolution destroyed a neutral planet, it would wreak severe criticism throughout the galaxy, and they would lose the moral high ground they proclaimed.

The Dranzonian Empire didn't attempt to force their hand simply because they didn't want the bad publicity and really didn't need their help to contain the Revolution, as long as they stayed neutral.

Since Brenda's contacts had been compromised, their safe houses were not safe. The Dranzonian Empire sent in a task force to hopefully catch the spies but in worse case kill them all.

Brenda Broyals' job was to solidify the cooperation with some top-ranking military officials who detested the Dranzonian Empire and were willing to participate in a coup.

The FIRM was to play a pivotal role including assassination if required to ensure the success of the coup these men led.

Because of the compromise, the Dranzonian Empire's Secret Service was able to cherry pick a few members of the coup and convince them to betray the others with the promise that once the existing leaders were wiped out and the bulk of the coup was wiped out, they would then be assisted in seizing power on the grounds they were attempting to restore the government and put down any further attacks.

The Dranzonian Empire really had no intention of assisting these over-ambitious traitors and would subsequently betray them as soon as they no longer had any further use for them, and as soon as they were handed over to patriots their lives would end quickly as well.

Brenda thought she was leading her team into a kill zone. It had all been planned out with impeccable precision and insight. In some ways it looked too good to be true. But like in the case of the recent Chuo Wanpi assassination, personal behavior and traits were the pathway to exploit the path of least resistance.

VOICE OVER
The plan was perfect until it failed.

Zeta-Dalajiangyumi Bingxian was as close to a water world you could find without being a water world. Because of the unique climate caused by a triple solar system and forty-five planets that composed it, rain was frequent and often heavy over almost 90 percent of the planet.

Hovercraft provided the main form of non-air transport on the planet Zeta-Dalajiangyumi Bingxian. There were every derivation of hovercraft types a person could imagine.

The main food staple for the planet was a sorghum type of grain called Zise Gaoliang that was grown in large greenhouses. Even though it rained a lot, the planet was warm and the sunlight strong at times. These extremely large greenhouses built on the side of hills, from the air at twenty thousand feet almost gave the appearance of rice patties.

Planting Zise Gaoliang inside these multi-acre greenhouses into the very muddy soil was done by small hovercraft that had robotic planters precisely delivering seeds to specific levels of the mud.

These small, highly specialized hovercraft did not stir up the mud and created no rough spots so within an hour or so after the plantings, the entire basin of the greenhouse was rendered almost perfectly flat.

Within three days the Zise Gaoliang germinated and green sprouts broke the surface. Within a month the leaves and body of the Zise Gaoliang stood nearly a foot tall.

Flying from above, the transparent greenhouses were green, dark brown, or light brown, depending on what cycle the crop was in.

The muddy basin remained in that consistency with water added every few days to keep the growing conditions accurately controlled by computers and robotic machines until the heads of the Zise Gaoliang reached a point they had fulfilled the head growth and yield expected for harvesting.

The water was then cut off and small trenches were created by a robotic machine around the perimeter of the greenhouse, which facilitated drainage and the collected water was pumped out of the greenhouse.

Because of the heat and direct sunlight, the mud dried up quickly after the drainage and over the next month a wheel-based implement could conceivably harvest the Zise Gaoliang.

However, since the farmers were well equipped with hovercraft, specialized implements were attached to the front of the hovercraft that could systematically, under robot control, enter the greenhouse and harvest the heads of the Zise Gaoliang.

The hovercraft would go back out the same way they came in and haul the load of harvested Zise Gaoliang and dump it into a larger hovercraft waiting outside that would accumulate a load then haul it to a dryer and storage.

The FIRM used souped-up sports model hovercrafts. They could not go as fast as a Terrain Sportster, but they could go practically anywhere. The team had several of them when they set out that morning to execute the plan.

The hovercraft allowed them to cross rivers and lakes, and they proceeded through a menagerie of inland waterways and finally arriving at one of the Zise Gaoliang greenhouses that had just been harvested. All that was left inside this huge greenhouse was stubs of the former plants.

As per the plan, they pulled the hovercraft into the greenhouse where they expected the meeting to occur that would make or break the deal. They didn't know they were driving into an ambush until it was too late.

Dranzonian Empire Secret Service was there with some paramilitary men who were detailed to them from the Dranzonian Empire Special forces commonly referred to as the Space Assault Legion.

These Space Assault Legion special forces, were brought in as tourists but armed by arms smugglers from Zanziltar who had a good track record of avoiding Zeta-Dalajiangyumi Bingxian planetary security forces, performed another one of their "just in time deliveries" at the eleventh hour.

Their concealment was extraordinary, and driving around on hovercraft made it measurably easier to not leave behind a lot of tracks. The density of the greenhouses and all the farm equipment laying around typical of an agriculture community further enhanced the concealment, so the ambush was extremely effective.

The Space Assault Legion were told to avoid shooting the female because the Dranzonian Empire Secret Service wanted to catch her alive, but if she was escaping with no hope of detaining her, then do the head shot or whatever it took to eliminate her.

EXT. DAY. GREENHOUSE.

Brenda driving the Hovercraft pulled into the extremely large greenhouse riding up front on her hovercraft with her sharpshooter riding shotgun behind her, facing the opposite direction in case he had to shoot behind them in the event they had to escape.

Other members of the FIRM's task force were overly cocky and too trustful of what they thought was a well-laid-out plan and contacts. They, of course, had no idea how badly the operation had been compromised. Had they stuck to rules and thumb and proper protocols, they would not have got off their hovercraft and made themselves such excellent targets and would not have concentrated in such a small area within the greenhouse.

The orders were given, and the Space Assault Legion began their assault.

Any other person would have probably tried to go back out the way they came in. Brenda knew they were in a kill zone, and she had to bug out immediately. Those who got off their hovercraft were quickly cut to pieces as the 14.2-millimeter diameter projectiles being shot ripped their bodies apart.

Two other hovercraft whose riders had not got off their machines followed Brenda, thinking she had an escape route. Dead ahead was an opaque greenhouse wall and she had no choice but to blast it to get through it and seek a safe exit as quick as possible.

The Space Assault Legion knew the possibilities existed they could be spotted, and the enemy would try to escape, and had their own souped-up hovercraft at the ready and already manned. They were a little out of position and never thought the FIRM would blast its way out of the building on the other end. Since that was the shortest path to chase them down, they too went through the big hole Brenda created, shooting some miniature armor killers.

Brenda had an evacuation route. She didn't know how badly they were compromised. Without the betrayal, she would have easily evaded the Space Assault Legion.

Unfortunately, the Dranzonians already knew where she would go, so some of the Space Assault Legion were chasing her into the next ambush while others were there waiting in their deadly trap.

The three individuals riding shotgun shooting at the Space Assault Legion landed a few good shots, and of the original ten Space Assault Legion hovercraft that joined into the chase, quickly in short order, half of them were destroyed. Brenda's group were starting to feel better they would manage to get away.

At this point in time the Dranzonian Empire Secret Service had buck fever. They wanted the kill. They arbitrarily decided there was probably no possibility of Brenda Broyals giving herself up. She was exactly the way they analyzed her. She would die fighting and would not surrender. Driving like a bat out of hell, making some dangerous maneuvers and almost throwing her shotgun shooter off the hovercraft, it was apparent that considering she would consider surrendering was a rather foolish idea.

THE LEAD DRANZONIAN EMPIRE
SECRET SERVICE AGENT
If you get a shot at her, take her out. She doesn't plan
on surrendering.

VOICE OVER

A few more good shots and only three Space Assault Legion hovercraft continued in the chase. The odds were now getting closer to even. Freedom was just ahead. If they got past the next five miles, they would be out over a lake where they would be in the clear and could randomly pick their multiple possible exit routes.

The Dranzonian Empire Secret Service and the Space Assault Legion also knew this. They had some serious weapons that might get them caught by the Zeta-Dalajiangyumi Bingxian planetary security forces, but they planned to use them if it came down to preventing Brenda Broyals escape.

Brenda decided at the last minute she would not hit the lake where they originally had planned. It was clear to her now the mission was compromised. While driving and snaking, she controlled the hovercraft with one hand and in an almost impossible fashion communicated on her emergency communicator.

BRENDA BROYALS

We are bugging out. The mission has been compromised. Execute emergency extraction.

VOICE OVER

Brenda Broyals group might all get caught by the Zeta-Dalajiangyumi Bingxian planetary security forces and get bought back by some serious cash bribes, but that was better than being killed by the Dranzonian Empire.

As they got near the water's edge of the lake, they came close to escape.

The two trailing FIRM hovercraft were suddenly blown up by missiles fired from almost a mile away. Brenda felt the heat of the explosion even though she was at least fifty feet ahead and could see the huge flames in her rearview mirror. The three Space Assault Legion hovercraft were still behind her though losing some ground as she was slowly out distancing them.

A specially armed shuttle should appear at any moment to help her get out of the fix. Her rear gunner was suddenly killed by one of the 14.2-millimeter rounds. Brenda Broyals was now the only person left of the original group. She was getting close to the water.

Brenda Broyals knew she had superior water capability and could escape. The shuttle had her in sight, knew that was Brenda, and was coming in as fast as they could, which also alerted the Zeta-Dalajiangyumi Bingxian planetary security forces.

Zeta-Dalajiangyumi Bingxian aircraft were now several miles behind coming in quick to investigate and had seen the two missiles fired blowing up two hovercrafts. Suddenly another missile flew just as Brenda was at the water's edge.

Brenda's world suddenly ended.

The shuttle pilot who observed Brenda getting hit with the missile also detected Zeta-Dalajiangyumi Bingxian planetary security forces in hot pursuit, bugged out, and made a beeline to the mothership.

The Zeta-Dalajiangyumi Bingxian planetary security forces flying an entire squadron came upon the area of the missile launches and spotted the perpetrators on the ground. Knowing they had dangerous missiles and had already blown up three hovercrafts, the Zeta-Dalajiangyumi Bingxian planetary security forces made the determination they had to neutralize the group launching the missiles and quickly armed and launched their own weapons.

The Dranzonian Empire Secret Service agents and the Space Assault Legion personnel who were around the missile launchers rejoicing their success in bagging Brenda Broyals soon discovered the errors in their ways and received similar treatment as the squadron flying up on them out of the sun let go of a lot of ordinances.

Between all the Space Assault Legion and all the high level Dranzonian Empire Secret Service agents killed by the Zeta-Dalajiangyumi Bingxian planetary security forces, even though Brenda Broyals was an important spy, there was a terrible cost incurred in killing her. In addition to losing a lot of their own personnel, they immediately had serious issues by violating the neutrality of Zeta-Dalajiangyumi Bingxian.

If there was ever a time, they could have convinced Evo Kaplan to come back and no longer be a threat against them, that possibility ended with Brenda's death, as his love for her immediately manifested an acute hatred for the Dranzonian Empire Secret Service as soon as he was informed.

Unlike Brenda Broyals, who had no realization her mission had been compromised, Evo Kaplan already knew his was. He had to avoid traps and ambushes. To succeed in falling victim to those situations, he really could not meet anyone. This was turning into the most difficult assignment he ever faced.

Thanks to the Dranzonian Empire Secret Service poor security practices on Arzon, such as a spy meeting another at the space port, Evo Kaplan had what Brenda didn't: advanced warning they were here looking for him.

Evo Kaplan realized their primary mission would be to capture him. Since this was a planet devoted to the Dranzonian Empire, if they did manage to capture him alive, the Dranzonian Empire Secret Service would do their normal methods done after catching a high-ranking spy. The main problem would be getting him past the Revolutionary Zone. And even though the blockade runner was successful on this trip, there was no guarantee they would make it the next time.

Evo Kaplan's only reliable contact to anyone on the planet Arzon was Claudette Ramsey, who was in his long-term plan to get to Randolph Spencer. However, he was starting to have remorse and huge regrets carrying out the affair because he felt in some ways he was stabbing Brenda in the back.

Unfortunately, Evo Kaplan's only chance for survival might be traveling back to Zanziltar with Claudette Ramsey. He was in a tough situation that few spies would ever want to get in. This truly had turned into a difficult mission.

Thanks partly to the fact Cap Zapatero had no quick way of alerting Dranzonian Empire Secret Service he may have identified Evo Kaplan based on voice print analysis before Evo got out of the space port unmolested and far enough down the road for anyone to intervene or discover where he was going.

Evo Kaplan's lodging accommodations were highly confidential, and the hotel received huge special credits payments just like they always did when Krawz Almarip stayed with them. The hotel staff knew Krawz Almarip was a black marketer, and the government was more than likely looking for him, but this one hotel guest paid for what one hundred empty rooms didn't have hotel guests staying there because of the war.

The real Krawz Almarip had set up elaborate methods of transactions. The customer, other than the one that took him to his hotel, never encountered him. That arrangement helped out quite a bit because it meant that Krawz Almarip would not be required to leave the hotel unnecessarily.

Arzon itself had poor security overall. They were living on borrowed time thanks to distance, but that was all changing. All the information they put out on their Worldwide Comnet News compromised their operational security of their planetary defense forces. It was rather incredible for Evo Kaplan that he could systematically figure out the planet's disposition and their defense planning simply by watching Worldwide Comnet News.

The crown jewels the Dranzonian Empire Secret Service missed by Evo Kaplan getting out of the space port unmolested were his three single-use transmitters and three single-use receivers The FIRM provided Evo Kaplan.

Conrad Fanzui didn't plan on sending Evo Kaplan any messages until he heard first from him. It didn't take long for Conrad to get the after-action report and the knowledge that Brenda Broyals was killed in the line of duty for the FIRM. As much as he would like to have sent Evo Kaplan the news of Brenda's passing, her death was nothing more than another statistic; he could not waste a precious resource by initiating one of the critically important communications simply to report her death.

When and if Conrad Fanzui had to reply to Evo Kaplan who sent a message and requested something, at that time he would inform Evo Kaplan of the tragedy. He also knew there was a possibility he had a mole within his organization, which could include anyone, even Evo Kaplan. The only reason why Evo Kaplan wasn't placed on the probable list of moles is that Brenda and Evo were secretly monitored, and he knew how much Evo Kaplan felt for Brenda and would never set her up like that. If it wasn't for Brenda's secret lover's tryst with Evo Kaplan, he would be a prime suspect.

There were others on the list and one that certainly was now under observation was Huaiyuansu Ka. If he was a double spy playing that dangerous game, he too would end up like Reginald Heiqishi and he would give Evo Kaplan the honors of dispatching him. But first he had to know for sure, because two can play the double spy game.

ARZON DEFENSES AND DISPOSITION

Evo Kaplan waited several days to call Claudette Ramsey. Because of his fear of compromise and betrayal, at first, he almost didn't call her. That morning one of the black marketers that had given him a ride to his hotel contacted him. The hotel's guest communicator rang.

EVO KAPLAN
Hello.

ASHTRED
Krawz, this is Ashtred.

EVO KAPLAN
Did you take the delivery?

ASHTRED
Yes, we inspected the cargo, and everything is in order
as you promised. We have made the payment.

EVO KAPLAN
Good. Say, there is something I would like you to do
for me.

ASHTRED
What's that?

EVO KAPLAN
I want a couple of untraceable communicators.

ASHTRED
It might take a day for me to acquire them.

EVO KAPLAN
That's okay. I got a day.

ASHTRED
I'll have them for you by tomorrow morning.

EVO KAPLAN
Thanks.

Evo Kaplan wanted to contact Claudette Ramsey, but decided he would wait until the untraceable personal communicators arrived in the morning. In the meantime, he gathered up all the information Arzon's illogically aired on the Worldwide Comnet News and encapsulated them and get that information into the transmit buffer.

Each day the buffer grew as the voice input was encoded to a compact digital form. Once Evo Kaplan determined he had all the information in the buffer the FIRM wanted, he transmitted the contents of the buffer using the single-use crypto made it unreadable by the enemy or anyone else and transmitted it to an ultra-small drone hiding in space junk almost one hundred thousand miles away.

At an exact time that drone relayed the information, which several days later was received by the Revolutionary Guards intel group on an outlying planet far out of the reach of the Dranzonian Empire.

The intel officer of the frontier group did not have the key to decode the transmission, but what he did have was instructions of who to make sure received the communique. Within a day the encrypted message was received at Zuanshi-cheng Revolutionary Empire home world and capital. That message was then double-encoded and sent immediately to Zanziltar, where only Conrad Fanzui had the key to the code.

Conrad Fanzui, was glad that Evo Kaplan discovered the treachery on his own and was mitigating it. He would then use Evo Kaplan's communications to out Huaiyuansu Ka if he was indeed the mole. Conrad Fanzui was soon talking with Glen Zhurenshuo, the head of Revolution Empire Section, Secret Service, the FIRM.

CONRAD FANZUI

Huaiyuansu Ka might think his treachery is a ticket home to Praxisvlasia, but it's really an invitation to the pig farm.

GLEN ZHURENSHUO

We want that to be confirmed yet. I would like to make sure we know for sure before we kill him.

CONRAD FANZUI

I didn't plan on killing him right away. I'm saving that honor for Evo Kaplan when he gets back, who will probably want to kill him with his bare hands.

GLEN ZHURENSHUO

Based on what we know about the relationship between Evo Kaplan and Brenda Broyals, I'm sure Evo Kaplan will do as well as anyone else in the FIRM to make Huaiyuansu Ka regret his actions.

CONRAD FANZUI

I want to run Huaiyuansu Ka as a double spy for a while. I have some ideas how we can turn this around on the Loyalists.

GLEN ZHURENSHUO

All right. I'm going back to Zuanshi-cheng today. If there is a silver lining, it's that we know we got a mole and can now limit the damage he does.

CONRAD FANZUI

What about our top ten missions? Many or all of them are probably compromised.

GLEN ZHURENSHUO
Assume they have been compromised, except for Evo Kaplan's mission, and bring them all home. Send them to Zuanshi-cheng and we'll run them out of there for a while until you complete your investigation and deal with the mole.

CONRAD FANZUI
I don't want to send them all to Zuanshi-cheng. I want to keep a few of them here to play into my double spy plan.

GLEN ZHURENSHUO
That's a dangerous game to play. You might get a few of them killed.

CONRAD FANZUI
Yes, we might have to sacrifice a few of them in the process, but we can do a lot of damage if they and Huaiyuansu Ka all believe the mission we send them on is the real plan.

GLEN ZHURENSHUO
How will you prevent a lot of casualties?

CONRAD FANZUI
We'll have a second team set up to ambush the ambushers. After we wipe out a few of their teams, they might draw the conclusion their source is flawed.

GLEN ZHURENSHUO
Yea, nothing better than to make them think their source is tainted.

Glen Zhurenshuo left Zanziltar knowing in the face of tragedy was opportunity. Huaiyuansu Ka made the fatal blunder of attempting to outfox Conrad Fanzui, who knew for a fact old age and treachery would overcome youth and skill.

Now it was one of those rare moments where Conrad Fanzui regretted the most and why he strongly opposed agents getting involved with each other the way Brenda and Evo had evolved.

Part of the protocols in communications was the spy in field initiated all communications. The minute he transmitted the single-use buffer, the machine automatically set up a timer on the receiver built into that same black box. A new set of crypto would be used to decode what he soon expected to receive.

After a brief period of time of receiving and displaying the data, the crypto would self-destruct by random numbers, replacing all the crypto and the received text. Once that process occurred there was never again any way to recover the crypto or the text. The process to erase the crypto was a state secret. The process to erase the text was simply a power cycle, which immediately eliminated any information.

It was probably good Evo Kaplan delayed contacting Claudette Ramsey, whom he had grown to like quite a bit. The delay would give him sufficient time to gather his senses after he read Conrad Fanzui's response that stated Brenda had been killed, as her mission was compromised, and they believed Evo Kaplan had also been compromised.

Based on Evo Kaplan's report, which he obtained in the strangely easiest way possible, there was no longer any need for him to stay on the planet and if he could, get on the secret. The process to erase the text was simply a power cycle, which immediately eliminated any information.

Conrad Fanzui then put Evo Kaplan in severe risk. He was willing to risk him because he wasn't sure where his allegiance was, and identifying the mole was paramount. The only near-term option was to use Evo Kaplan.

In a way Conrad Fanzui was betraying Evo Kaplan, but in another sense, he was saving perhaps as many as two hundred agents in the process. Killing one to save two hundred was a price he was willing to pay. He hoped that Evo could save himself. He was a resourceful person. But then on the other hand, Brenda would fear for Evo since she would not be there to save him again.

Evo Kaplan could not contain his emotions. The notice Brenda was dead had a profound effect on him, and he could not help but cry.

Evo Kaplan's remorse and his guilt spilled over. Right at the same time he was having sex with another woman, his lover was being killed. It was a tremendous shockwave through Evo Kaplan's heart. But he knew it was time to attempt returning to Zanziltar.

Evo Kaplan compensated for his depression by a long hot bath, and later a pill that helped him get a restful sleep and escape from the universe for a few hours into an alternate universe where none of these emotions existed.

<u>INT. DAY. ZANZILTAR. FIRM.</u>

VOICE OVER
There was a group of Zanziltar Operations Staff who

worked exclusively for Conrad Fanzui. They were thoroughly vetted and like Brenda Broyals, had been with Conrad Fanzui before the Revolution started. They were compartmentalized from everyone else. Conrad had special means to communicate with them.

Huaiyuansu Ka had no knowledge of the special task force. They were never physically associated with any of the normal Zanziltar Operations Staff. All their logistics were handled exclusively by Glen Zhurenshuo through Mikhail Catamountz. They were briefed by Mikhail Catamountz on their assignment.

Huaiyuansu Ka would have tight surveillance on himself until he either left the planet or was killed, whichever happened first.

Nobody at the Zanziltar Operations Staff knew any of this was going on and Huaiyuansu Ka was growing complacent since he never spotted clever surveillance.

It would not be unexpected to see old men at a library. And if there was an elderly couple looking over pictures of butterflies or birds or a lot of other things, sometimes even a trained spy would not catch the surveillance.

These two old geezers had secret body cameras and microphones built into their clothes. Buttons were cameras and pens and pencils were wireless microphones and sitting across from each other passing books back and forth seemed rather innocuous.

Certainly, spies would not be so loud or obnoxious. Sometimes kids were placed in locations with similar spyware they didn't know they were wearing as their parents thought they were modeling and promoting clothing lines.

The ingenious microphones worked until they went through the wash cycle, but by then they had already provided the information required.

These crazy old men were at the library long before Huaiyuansu Ka and stayed long

after he left so that Dranzonian Empire Secret Service would never suspect they were spying, especially if they were still there several hours after Huaiyuansu Ka.

Just as Conrad Fanzui figured, they would eventually bag more than just Huaiyuansu Ka. They would take out a few safe houses and more Dranzonian Empire Secret Service agents in the process, on Zanziltar and ostensibly elsewhere, through possible interrogations and capture of enemy communications.

By morning Evo Kaplan was in a different mental mood. He had accomplished his mission and as it turned out the fact-finding for the Revolutionaries was far simpler than they estimated, because they were almost in disbelief the amount of critical information released to the press that ended up on the Worldwide Comnet News.

Since the Arzon security apparatus lacked common sense and operational security discipline, all their defense plans, aside from being compromised, they thought they were better prepared to withstand a Revolutionary onslaught when in fact they were pushovers.

INT. DAY. ZANZILTAR. FIRM. CONRAD FANZUI'S OFFICE

Cornelius Xie de Hundan was briefed via long distance neutrino communicator.

CONRAD FANZUI
Evo Kaplan will most likely be on the same space transport returning.

CORNELIUS XIE DE HUNDAN
Send Evo Kaplan my congratulations. Does he have a safe way to get home?

CONRAD FANZUI
If the transport lands again in Praxisvlasia he might get nabbed. Also, we expect a possible Dranzonian Empire Secret Service on that transport who might attempt assassination.

CORNELIUS XIE DE HUNDAN
Perhaps we should stop the transport and board it and take him off, and if he knows who the Dranzonian Empire Secret Service agent is we can nab him?

CONRAD FANZUI
We appreciate your offer, but I must confess Evo Kaplan doesn't know he's working for the Revolution.

CORNELIUS XIE DE HUNDAN
What the hell?

CONRAD FANZUI
As far as he knows, he's working for an intergalactic crime organization, the FIRM.

CORNELIUS XIE DE HUNDAN
When were you going to inform him who he really works for?

CONRAD FANZUI
Based on what he's done for us, doing ultra-risky numerous missions, I planned on divulging that information when he arrived back here and give him the option to tear up his contract or work for the Revolution.

CORNELIUS XIE DE HUNDAN
You would just let him walk out?

CONRAD FANZUI
He knows he can't go back to the Dranzonian Empire Secret Service. He knows there is an order to shoot to kill him on the spot.

CORNELIUS XIE DE HUNDAN
Where would he go?

CONRAD FANZUI
My guess is he would stay on Zanziltar since it's a Sanctuary City and Planet.

CORNELIUS XIE DE HUNDAN
If the Dranzonian Empire Secret Service finds him they will kill him.

CONRAD FANZUI
I think we'll give him an identity change as a way to show our appreciation.

CORNELIUS XIE DE HUNDAN
What do you think he will do if you let him go?

CONRAD FANZUI
It appears to me he's first and foremost a spy. He has it in his blood. He may not be aware of it yet, but I think he'll soon understand it doesn't matter who a spy works for if they want to be the best.

CORNELIUS XIE DE HUNDAN
All right Conrad, I'm going to contact General Guodu Jiaolu and have him prepare to intercept the space transport after it leaves Arzon and get Evo Kaplan off the ship and send him to Zanziltar. He's earned a safe way home.

CONRAD FANZUI
Hopefully he doesn't get assassinated before General Guodu Jiaolu is able to rescue him.

CORNELIUS XIE DE HUNDAN
I'll meet privately with General Guodu Jiaolu and explain the delicate situation to him. He needs to sortie his fleet right away if he wants to be in position to intercept the transport.

CONRAD FANZUI
Thank you, your excellency, for helping.

CORNELIUS XIE DE HUNDAN
Thank you, Conrad. Your services have been exemplary, and I appreciate what you do.

Cornelius Xie de Hundan ended the conversation as Conrad Fanzui was starting to realize Brenda Broyals and Evo Kaplan would be two big pairs of shoes to fill.

INT. DAY. ARZON. EVO KAPLAN'S HOTEL ROOM.

In the morning there was a knock at the door. It was the trusted maid again. She had previously delivered the credits. The black marketers had used her often and she knew better than to cross them because they knew where her family lived, and they lived well because they were taken care of. They, of course, would all quickly disappear if she didn't do as required.

Evo Kaplan saw the trusted maid at the door through the wide-eye spy eye piece, which like some mirrors on vehicles or fancy cameras, allowed a person to see out the hallway and anyone in either direction.

She was by herself as expected and Evo Kaplan opened the door.

                    TRUSTED MAID
                Here's a package for you.

          KRAWZ ALMARIP (A.K.A. EVO KAPLAN)
                      Thanks.

The maid turned and walked away, and Evo Kaplan closed the door. Evo Kaplan felt the package and could feel it contained two communicators.

Evo Kaplan then took the contact information out of his pocket for Claudette Ramsey and called her.

Claudette answered the phone sounding rather subdued.

          KRAWZ ALMARIP (A.K.A. EVO KAPLAN)
                 Hello, Claudette?

Claudette Ramsey was surprised to hear from Krawz Almarip. It had been a few days and she had started to think he had simply enjoyed her body and cast her aside like he probably did most women.

                 CLAUDETTE RAMSEY
             I didn't expect to hear from you.

          KRAWZ ALMARIP (A.K.A. EVO KAPLAN)
          I'm sorry I didn't call earlier. I had to take care of
          business and get over some personal grief.

                 CLAUDETTE RAMSEY
                   Someone close?

          KRAWZ ALMARIP (A.K.A. EVO KAPLAN)
          Yes, I had a lover. She's dead. I've gotten over it now
          and think I can function once again.

                 CLAUDETTE RAMSEY
                 Why did you call me?

          KRAWZ ALMARIP (A.K.A. EVO KAPLAN)
          I probably should not have let myself get so close to
          you. For a man in my business, it's not healthy to get
          emotionally attached to a woman.

CLAUDETTE RAMSEY
You do have a reputation.

KRAWZ ALMARIP (A.K.A. EVO KAPLAN)
There is a lot more there than you know about. Perhaps one day I can reveal more of myself. You would understand then.

CLAUDETTE RAMSEY
Were you expecting to meet up with me and have some more sexual gratification?

KRAWZ ALMARIP (A.K.A. EVO KAPLAN)
No, I wish I could, but I'm leaving on the ship as soon as it departs. I just wanted to call you and tell you that you touched me deeply and have left indelible marks in my memories.

CLAUDETTE RAMSEY
Are you going back to Zanziltar?

KRAWZ ALMARIP (A.K.A. EVO KAPLAN)
Yes, possibly later today or tomorrow if they sell enough seats.

CLAUDETTE RAMSEY
Good.

KRAWZ ALMARIP (A.K.A. EVO KAPLAN)
Are you glad I'm leaving?

CLAUDETTE RAMSEY
No. My mother died before I got here. She was cremated, and I'm leaving, also going back to Zanziltar as soon as I can. I might be on that ship with you.

KRAWZ ALMARIP (A.K.A. EVO KAPLAN)
I will be very happy to see you there if we leave together.

CLAUDETTE RAMSEY
The feeling is mutual, and I'm glad you called me and told me all this. It really helps me a lot.

KRAWZ ALMARIP (A.K.A. EVO KAPLAN)
I'm probably the worst person you could ever meet.

CLAUDETTE RAMSEY
That's okay, as long as you keep coming back to your kitten.

KRAWZ ALMARIP (A.K.A. EVO KAPLAN)
Evo Kaplan was thinking the wrong kind of pussy cat. He didn't realize Claudette Ramsey loved toying with her mouse and planned to toy around a long time with her mouse before she ate it.

KRAWZ ALMARIP (A.K.A. EVO KAPLAN)
I must go now and make those arrangements. I hope to see you on the ship.

CLAUDETTE RAMSEY
Thank you, sweetheart, for calling. This was very important to me.

KRAWZ ALMARIP (A.K.A. EVO KAPLAN)
You are most welcome.

VOICE OVER
Evo Kaplan knew he had to get busy. He had one more meeting he had to do and unfortunately had to be face to face with one of his black marketers to ensure he got a seat on the space transport to leave the planet.

Evo Kaplan understood vividly that he was on his own. He had no logistical support that he was aware of.

Little did Evo Kaplan know Huaiyuansu Ka was betraying him again and that Conrad Fanzui was playing him in a double spy game that put him at severe risk.

As soon as Krawz Almarip (a.k.a. Evo Kaplan) had confirmation he would be on the space transport, ostensibly flying back with the same crew, including Captain Buck, he had to inform Conrad Fanzui with one of the two FIRM single use transmitters that he had. After that use he would be down to one, so he had to make sure everything counted. Those last two transmitters were his perceived lifeline.

Evo Kaplan dressed in Krawz Almarip's flamboyant clothes. His purple shirt and black pants and shiny black boots belonged in some American disco back in the 1970s for those who remembered what it was like.

Evo Kaplan needed to go visit his black marketers' customer, at the Shengmíng Langjie de Fangzi. This business maintained a dubious reputation, where before the revolution men of means often went to experience the best female entertainment the galaxy had to offer.

The hotel always had a private limo waiting to take their upscale clients to various establishments around the city, whether it be for business or pleasure.

With the extraordinary cut back in tourists due to the Revolution, the poor Limo driver received three and possibly four fares a day if he was lucky. He had taken Krawz Almarip to the Shengmíng Langjie de Fangzi several times before, but not within the past three months.

That was expected as the sign of the times. Nevertheless, prior to the Revolution, Krawz was crawling all over the ladies that Shengmíng Langjie de Fangzi who the mob bosses provided for him. Even if he only spent ten percent of his earnings on Arzon, what ended up leftover amounted to a small fortune each trip.

If it were not for the extraordinary need to steal Krawz Almarip's identity so they could place a spy on Arzon, Krawz Almarip most likely would have been here on another black-marketing trip going about doing the many less than Noble acts he was famous for.

The driver instinctively knew where Krawz Almarip wanted to go. There was no mystery to this man Krawz Almarip.

LIMO DRIVER
Krawz, do you want to go to Shengmíng Langjie de Fangzi?

KRAWZ ALMARIP (A.K.A. EVO KAPLAN)
I already think you know the answer to that question.

LIMO DRIVER
Do you have a cold? You sound a little different today?

KRAWZ ALMARIP (A.K.A. EVO KAPLAN)
Yes, I have a slight head cold and I'm taking some good drugs to get over it.

LIMO DRIVER
You might need some good drugs to get over what some of those ladies might give you.

KRAWZ ALMARIP (A.K.A. EVO KAPLAN)
Don't worry about me. I pay big bucks to get virgins each time.

LIMO DRIVER
Are you for real?

KRAWZ ALMARIP (A.K.A. EVO KAPLAN)
You've seen me take some of those women to restaurants in the past, right?

LIMO DRIVER
Yes, sir. You have a delightful taste for women.

KRAWZ ALMARIP (A.K.A. EVO KAPLAN)
I go for quality and yes, they are very expensive. You pay for what you get, right?

LIMO DRIVER
Absolutely. Say, if you are interested, I know my wife isn't all that pretty, but I wouldn't mind renting her out to you.

KRAWZ ALMARIP (A.K.A. EVO KAPLAN)
Rule number one: never mix business with pleasure. You are part of my business. But thanks for the offer anyway.

The limo soon pulled in front of the glamorous Shengmíng Langjie de Fangzi and Krawz gave the poor Limo driver some hefty credits for a tip.

Evo Kaplan had seen pictures in his training of the Shengmíng Langjie de Fangzi. The exterior lighting would remind anyone who ever traveled to Japan the glittery Japanese Pachinko businesses.

Government officials were paid off to allow Shengmíng Langjie de Fangzi conduct its business, and some of the products they sold were carried in by men such as Krawz Almarip who had the business smarts to never cut the "shit" and delivered one hundred percent pure substances.

Products from sexual enhancers to stamina builders came with the reservation. Krawz Almarip didn't need a reservation. Moreover, his money was golden; Shengmíng Langjie de Fangzi owner still owed him plenty for three previous shipments. Times were tough and they were having a tough time paying off their debt.

With the lack of tourists, it would take almost twice as long to sell the products, rent the women, and pay debt owed Krawz Almarip. Arzon businessmen understood men like Krawz Almarip could sell the debt to other organized crime elements on the planet, and they would then be out of business and probably dead soon afterward.

"Bubba," as he preferred to be called, met Krawz Almarip as soon as word passed, he was there. Bubba expected Krawz Almarip because they were receiving his cargo and had planned to plead for more time to service the debt. Krawz Almarip had been a reasonable person and that's why he never ran afoul in Arzon because all the organized crime elements liked the way he operated aloof, no pressure, and reasonable and sometimes suggested great ideas on how they could cope and come back with performance to deal with all their headaches.

Bubba was one of those resourceful men Krawz Almarip used to take care of dirty deeds, sometimes killing someone, or obtaining contraband such as a laser pistol or synthetics used to drug people for nefarious purposes.

Once they were in Bubba's office, fearing this was about collecting money and a significant warning, Bubba started in on making a bunch of apologies and promises.

Krawz Almarip interrupted Bubba.

KRAWZ ALMARIP
This is not about the money you owe me. I want you to
do something for me.

BUBBA
I certainly will if I can.

KRAWZ ALMARIP
It's a simple request and I'm willing to reward you
handsomely for your help.

BUBBA
Okay, what is it?

KRAWZ ALMARIP
I will cancel half your debt and give you an additional
year to come up with the rest of the funds you owe me.

BUBBA
That's quite an extraordinary offer.

KRAWZ ALMARIP
Sometimes timing is important.

BUBBA
Yes, I realize that.

KRAWZ ALMARIP
We have a war going on and I want to get back to
Zanziltar before the Revolutionaries cut off these
blockade runners.

BUBBA
You think they can do that?

KRAWZ ALMARIP
I have my sources, and I give them a fifty percent chance or better.

BUBBA
And what can I do to help you get there?

KRAWZ ALMARIP
The blockade runner intergalactic passenger transport Toutoumomo De Hundan will be leaving here tonight or in the morning, I want to be on it. But because of a few things that came up, I can't be seen making reservations.

BUBBA
I see.

KRAWZ ALMARIP
You remember Captain Buck?

BUBBA
Yeah, the guy you gave all those virgins to.

KRAWZ ALMARIP
Correct.

BUBBA
What do you want me to do with Captain Buck?

KRAWZ ALMARIP
I want you to make my reservation in another name, provide me with fake identity, then inform Captain Buck to be at the entrance of the transport about one minute before they close the door for takeoff.

BUBBA
What for, may I ask?

KRAWZ ALMARIP
I need Captain Buck to make sure I have no problems getting aboard that ship in the event the local law enforcement or government agencies try to take me off the ship.

BUBBA
I'm sure we can do that.

KRAWZ ALMARIP
One other thing.

BUBBA
Yes, Krawz?

KRAWZ ALMARIP
If I make it back to Zanziltar alive, I promise to let you keep half of the half you will still owe me.

BUBBA
You mean I will only owe you one quarter of my current debt?

KRAWZ ALMARIP
You got it. I need to incentivize you.

BUBBA
What about future deliveries?

KRAWZ ALMARIP
My sources say this war will be over in a year and things will be back to normal. We'll pick up then where we left off.

BUBBA
Krawz, you are very generous.

KRAWZ ALMARIP
Bubba, in all these years you have been faithful and honest with me, and now in my time of need I want to reward you for your impeccable honesty and reasonableness. If all my other clients were half as good as you, my life would be far simpler.

BUBBA
Well, we appreciate you too.

Krawz Almarip pulled a communicator out of his pocket and handed it to Bubba.

KRAWZ ALMARIP
This is an untraceable communicator. From now on only contact me with this and don't contact me unless it's an emergency or the exact time to board the Toutoumomo De Hundan.

BUBBA
All right Krawz. I'll make sure of it.

KRAWZ ALMARIP
Bubba, I want you to take me back to my hotel now.

BUBBA
You don't want the girls?

KRAWZ ALMARIP
No, I need to get back and prepare a few things. As soon as you confirm everything, call me with the exact time of boarding.

BUBBA
Will do.

Krawz Almarip followed Bubba out of his office and to the front entrance and informed his manager who ran the Shengmíng Langjie de Fangzi for him:

BUBBA
I'll be back in a few minutes. Me and Krawz are going somewhere.

SHENGMÍNG LANGJIE DE FANGZI MANAGER
Do you want me to send some firepower with you?

The manager was fearful Krawz was taking Bubba out of Shengmíng Langjie de Fangzi somewhere to kill him for not paying his debt.

BUBBA
No, that will not be necessary.

Krawz Almarip, overheard the conversation and responded.

KRAWZ ALMARIP
Bubba, I kind of like his idea of bringing some firepower along if you don't mind. One never knows what he's going to run into.

BUBBA
Sure thing, Krawz.

Bubba turned to the Shengmíng Langjie de Fangzi manager and directed him.

BUBBA
Go get our security detail and have them come with us.

Shengmíng Langjie de Fangzi manager hired former special forces people that had been part of the Dranzonian Empire Space Assault Legion used in pre-revolution days to assist in planet busting when the need arose. Most of them were let go due to government downsizing their military just a few weeks before the Revolution and fratricidal civil war erupted. They were now guns for hire, earning about ten times as much as they earned in the military.

In a few minutes, five men with suits appeared with bulges in their suitcoats, most likely packing a laser shoulder holster. A quick estimation would derive they were all at least six feet and four inches tall, 250 pounds each with forty-inch chests and biceps about the size of most people's legs. In laymen's terms, they looked like tough sons of bitches or professional football players.

Bubba's personal limo pulled up and they all got into it and headed for Krawz Almarip's hotel.

Bubba didn't know what was going on with Krawz Almarip; he certainly wasn't acting normal, but these were not normal times. It was crystal clear that he was in some serious trouble. When criminal enterprises got in trouble with the law, they supported each other. They watched each other's back and when they were mutual benefactors, such as dealing with Krawz Almarip all these years, they would go the extra mile to protect him.

BUBBA
Krawz, I don't know what kind of trouble you are in,
but I know you are in serious trouble by the way you
are acting.

KRAWZ ALMARIP
Trouble is my middle name. I'm always in trouble.

BUBBA
I'm going to have a couple of my men stay with you
and we'll get you to the space port at the designated
time.

KRAWZ ALMARIP
I appreciate that.

The limo soon pulled into the hotel driveway and stopped at the front entrance. Bellhops came over and opened the limo door, happy that some rich person was arriving to spend some money there and help keep the hotel viable.

It's not every day that the hotel staff get to see notorious gangsters. When Evo Kaplan got out of the limo with the two brutes sent along as bodyguards, the bellhops knew the score right away.

The hotel staff all knew Krawz Almarip from many trips to Arzon staying at the same hotel was always involved in shady deals, but they had never seen him associated with big guns of organized crime.

Krawz Almarip also blended in so well with the guns for hire and they followed him just like he was commanding them. The hotel staff also looked at the limo interior while the door was open and could see Bubba, who looked as sleazy as they could get.

The car then shortly pulled out and went back to Shengmíng Langjie de Fangzi where Bubba had to decide what to do about the expensive girls he rounded up for no good reason and all the bribes it took to get them.

Occasionally, a crime boss rewards his dedicated people. In some cases, they buy them a business or help them start a legitimate business such as a restaurant or bar, or in other cases they do some type of magnanimous deed. Bubba turned toward the remaining security staff as they were halfway to his office and addressed them.

BUBBA
I have five keys. There are only three of you here that
will each get a key to a special hostess room to reward
you for your loyalty.

SECURITY STAFF MEMBER
Really appreciate this boss.

BUBBA
I'll save the other hostess room keys for those two
guys protecting Krawz tonight if no harm comes to
him.

SECOND SECURITY STAFF MEMBER
We'll make sure boss.

BUBBA
Consider this your payment in advance to keep Krawz
Almarip safe and alive and get him safely on the
Toutoumomo De Hundan tomorrow.

Bubba handed the three special hostess room keys to these security guys who had a face suddenly that resembled a small boy opening a nice present.

Bubba then went to his office and began all the tasks he knew needed to get done. Just as Bubba figured, after about an hour later, some of his special contacts informed him the Dranzonian Empire Secret Service had flown in a special agent and they were on the hunt for Krawz Almarip, who must have pissed off someone up high.

INTERCEPT!

General Guodu Jiaolu deployed the squadron that would capture the intergalactic transport and offload Evo Kaplan if he was still alive. If he was dead, they would simply destroy the ship to make sure they killed the spy who assassinated Evo Kaplan.

General Guodu Jiaolu was briefed that Evo Kaplan had traveled with a change of identity, both in the credentials he carried as well as the cosmetic surgery to give him the appearance of the infamous black marketer Krawz Almarip.

On the way to the intercept point, members who would board the ship were given briefings that included photographs of Evo Kaplan after he was altered to look like Krawz Almarip. They were also given some distant pictures of not the best quality of a man who Evo Kaplan had managed to photo met by a known Dranzonian Empire Secret Service Agent Loraine Rantala. And just before the fleet departed a special "visitor" came aboard his command ship.

It would never be known why or how Cap Zapatero missed Evo Kaplan leaving the airport that would have allowed them to easily complete the mission. Some speculation was Blane Jiandie got buck fever about possibly ending up in the sack with Loraine Rantala one more time for old sake and was distracted at the critical moment while she laid on her charm.

Whatever the case may be, Blane Jiandie flunked spying-101. In the world of galactic quality spies, you can't turn your back on your opponent for one second and get distracted by a pretty lady, or you just might blow the mission.

Furthermore, the Dranzonian Empire Secret Service blew it by not verifying whether Evo Kaplan knew Laraine Rantala or had ever been on a mission with her. Because of the extraordinary conditions of life-or-death missions where you bond closely with your colleagues, Laraine Rantala would be just about the last person in Evo Kaplan's life he would ever forget since she saved his life a few times and prevented him from receiving some serious injuries as well as participating in lustful transcendental events.

And there she was out in the open meeting up with one of their legends in the Dranzonian Empire Secret Service, sent to take out Evo Kaplan. Brenda Broyals wasn't so lucky, but Evo Kaplan was.

Had Bubba known Krawz Almarip was stolen identity for Evo Kaplan, Krawz Almarip (a.k.a. Evo Kaplan) would be dead by now. Evo Kaplan completed the mission under remarkable risk. Few spies have ever survived a mission they were betrayed where they had to deal with multiple risk factors such as an enemy government and organized crime at the same time.

Evo Kaplan's mission was complete. What he was sent to find out was out in the open, easily obtainable. The Dranzonian Empire Secret Service intel was so poor, they could not fathom how simple Evo Kaplan's mission really was and he could leave so promptly. Krawz didn't need to break into a military headquarters to steal secrets when it was out in the open the way it was on Arzon.

Perhaps it was high expectations that something more nefarious was in the works, like the Coy Ridge break-in that led the Dranzonian Empire Secret Service to think more was to come. The Dranzonian Empire Secret Service had assets positioned all over the planet except the most important spot of all: The Intergalactic Space Port. Nor did the Dranzonian Empire Secret Service think for one minute Evo Kaplan would be returning on the same ship he arrived.

Evo Kaplan almost got away clean and unmolested. It was only due to a fluke and the betrayal made by Huaiyuansu Ka that even gave Dranzonian Empire Secret Service a chance to get any assets on board Toutoumomo de Hundan.

The morning of departure for the Toutoumomo de Hundan intergalactic passenger transport departure, Evo Kaplan received his phone call from Bubba.

BUBBA
Limo is coming your way to give you the ride.

That was it and Bubba hung up. Evo Kaplan needed no more. The two big bruisers took turns sleeping on the second bed in the room. One was outside while the other was snoring.

Evo walked calmly over and grabbed a device out of his luggage laid out like he was packing the night before, and he was ready to go. He walked into the bathroom, which if the bruiser woke up would think he was S/S/S. Instead, he had a buffer loaded with text he could type (or talk was an option too), which would soon be received by

Conrad Fanzui. The message stated he was leaving shortly and would expect the ship to leave soon after he arrived based on prior planning.

As soon as Evo Kaplan hit the transmit button, he knew he only had one lifeline left. That was it; one last communique period. And he hoped he would not need it. He also knew that based on the time it would take to deliver the message and receive back confirmation and further instructions, he would be already out in space in a ship where it would be doubtful he could receive signals on the ship due to solar shielding. In his message he stated he was disrupting the associated receive buffer to make sure it did not fall into enemy hands as he boarded the craft. Hence, don't bother sending a reply.

Just like they drilled this part of the mission repeatedly to perfection, Evo was deposited on the intergalactic space transport. As requested, Captain Buck was there to warmly receive Krawz Almarip and escort him to his seat under another alias. The airport officials didn't have adequate facial recognition to catch Evo Kaplan, because Blane Jiandie let him slip out of the airport before they were able to tag him. Hence getting him back on the ship was a lot simpler than imagined.

<u>INT. DAY. Toutoumomo de Hundan AT SPACE PORT READY FOR DEPARTURE</u>

VOICE OVER

Flight Attendant Ruth Marradi was waiting for a big payoff.

Blane Jiandie, with the help of the Dranzonian Empire Secret Service, tracked Flight Attendant Ruth Marradi down and promised her that if she gave him a tip should Krawz Almarip try to skip town.

As soon as Flight Attendant Ruth Marradi spotted Krawz Almarip sitting in his seat, she went to the access hatch that had an all-weather access that was currently partially open for the nice, beautiful day they were having. She called Cap Zapatero to make the report and collect the reward she didn't realize she would never see.

The ship had completed all its preflight checks, had received permission to takeoff, and Cap Zapatero rushed to the space port in a VTOL and landed nearby and ran to the all-weather access and up the stairs.

Ruth Marradi was ordered to close the door and prepare for taxi and takeoff and was in process of shutting the door as Cap Zapatero slid through, barely missing getting an arm or leg cut off.

The door shutting was automatic, which Captain Buck saw indications in the cockpit. He also knew he had a hot cargo on board and had to get the hell out of "Dodge" right away.

CAP ZAPATERO
You need to tell the captain to stop the transport.

RUTH MARRADI
I'm sorry, it's too late. His cockpit is locked and because of security features will not be able to be opened until thirty minutes after we are airborne, and then only by the chief purser.

CAP ZAPATERO
Damn, I got to get off this transport. I need to contact someone.

RUTH MARRADI
I'm sorry, Cap, but you are stuck on board now, and I seriously doubt the captain will turn around. You will have to get off at Praxisvlasia.

CAP ZAPATERO
That's where you are going?

RUTH MARRADI
Yes, and from there we are continuing onto Zanziltar if we don't get caught by revolutionaries.

CAP ZAPATERO
I need a seat then. Can you do me a favor, which I will arrange for you to be nicely rewarded?

RUTH MARRADI
What do you need?

CAP ZAPATERO
I didn't come with anything including a toothbrush, change of clothes, et cetera. Can you fix me up?

RUTH MARRADI
Believe it or not, people leave some of their luggage
on the transport when they leave. We have some
of their luggage in our lost and found area we plan
on returning to Zanziltar or Praxisvlasia. You can
probably find what you need there.

CAP ZAPATERO
Thanks, I appreciate your help.

RUTH MARRADI
You're welcome.

CAP ZAPATERO
One other thing.

RUTH MARRADI
Yes?

CAP ZAPATERO
Can you find me a seat far away from Krawz Almarip?
I want to avoid seeing him on this flight.

RUTH MARRADI
Sure, he's in the forward passenger compartment.
There are a lot of empty seats in the after-compartment
empty. Go there now since everyone is in their seats;
whichever you pick they will think is your assignment.
If you have any issues, come, and find me.

CAP ZAPATERO
Will do.

EXT. CGI. DAY. SPACE TRANSPORT INTERGALACTIC SPACE TRANSPORT BLOCKADE RUNNER *Toutoumomo de Hundan* TAKING OFF 20 SECONDS.

Evo Kaplan felt a lot better when the transport was heading down the seven-mile-long runway, accelerating as fast as they could until they had to cut power to prevent damage to buildings and homes nearby as they climbed up to twenty thousand feet at fifteen percent throttle settings, which didn't take long. Then they felt the slow increase in pressure in the back of their seats as the throttles were shoved forward slightly as Captain Buck flew the transport in manual mode out in space, enjoying every moment.

Captain Buck didn't have the problem like they did when they were leaving Praxisvlasia on the way to Arzon with heavy traffic where they had to stay at fifteen percent throttle until out past the outer markers.

Arzon, devoid of defenses and common sense, had no such outer markers and from outside the atmosphere the intergalactic transport had no restrictions, plus there wasn't much the Arzon Space Force, which was out of position, could to do stop them at this point. They would never make it within firing range.

Nobody in Arzon knew Cap Zapatero or Evo Kaplan were on the intergalactic transport Toutoumomo De Hundan. However, Huaiyuansu Ka just took the bait that Conrad laid out for him. Nobody in the mansion suspected Huaiyuansu Ka had betrayed their spies except for Conrad, who was now painfully and patiently going through the process to confirm it.

<u>INT. DAY. ZANZILTAR LIBRARY</u>

VOICE OVER

Mikhail Catamountz had his special detail in position and as expected after normal working hours, Huaiyuansu Ka made his way to the library and was amazed the two old geezers were still in the library studying butterflies.

The Dranzonian Empire Secret Service watchers knew the two old geezers had been there for a couple hours and would almost be there at the close of the library and they talked to nobody except themselves. All appearances were, they were safe to proceed.

Hari Nuvrean, of the Dranzonian Empire Secret Service, had been called to the library from the previous message that Huaiyuansu Ka wanted a deal and an extraction, now or never.

Huaiyuansu Ka had handed Brenda Broyals and Evo Kaplan over to the Dranzonian Secret Service, which they got half right but blew the Evo Kaplan part of it.

What it was going to cost the Dranzonian Empire Secret Service now was Huaiyuansu Ka's extraction— today, not tomorrow. Or the deal was off. They would never hear from him again.

Huaiyuansu Ka felt like he was on pins and needles and his wife was just about to walk out the door on him. He was desperate. Time had run out.

Mikhail Catamountz's special detail had some intel a lot of the FIRM's Zanziltar Operations staff didn't have, including the identity of Hari Nuvrean, so he showed up at the library extremely agitated and pissed off because he knew that Huaiyuansu Ka was possibly blowing his cover with his sudden extraordinary demands.

The Dranzonian Empire Secret Service had recently promised Huaiyuansu Ka they would pay his wife a visit and inform his wife that he was being brought back in the Service and was already on a paid mission.

After Huaiyuansu Ka's mission, and as soon as he was extracted would be back at Praxisvlasia with two years of back pay and a promotion.

If that visit didn't cool Huaiyuansu Ka's wife's jets, they would threaten her with the possibility she would simply disappear and nobody would ever know what happened to her, including her kids.

From Huaiyuansu Ka's perspective that visit had not occurred based on his wife's last communique.

The two old geezers saw Hari Nuvrean sit down at the next table with Huaiyuansu Ka.

HARI NUVREAN
What the hell are you doing?

HUAIYUANSU KA
It's now or never. I want extracted now.

HARI NUVREAN
That puts us in a difficult position.

HUAIYUANSU KA
I've been on missions before where it took killing people to get agents extracted. This is Zanziltar. It's a Sanctuary City. It should be simple to fly me out of here.

HARI NUVREAN

This will be very costly for us if we take you out of this building now to one of our safe houses. We are undergoing some type of surveillance right now and may have to shoot our way to a good safe house. And because you ran your mouth in a public place, there is a good possibility someone might have heard you. You put a lot of people in jeopardy. So, what you have better be damn good.

HUAIYUANSU KA

Evo Kaplan is on a spaceship and is off Arzon coming back. That ship, a blockade runner Toutoumomo de Hundan, is scheduled for a stopover at Praxisvlasia. You can board the ship and take him off there.

HARI NUVREAN

When are they scheduled to arrive?

HUAIYUANSU KA

Seven days from now.

What Huaiyuansu Ka didn't know then is he just set off a trip wire. When Hari Nuvrean looked over and heard the noise of the old geezer who was photographing a book with some kind of gadget, chills ran up his spine. Like any good spy, he thought, that might not be a camera. It might be a clever signaling semaphore transmitter. And if it was, the trap had just sprung.

HARI NUVREAN

We need to leave here immediately. Follow me as quickly as you can.

VOICE OVER

Hari Nuvrean didn't know why, but he could feel the tension in the air. When he came barreling out of the library with Huaiyuansu Ka close behind, they knew they were bugging out and probably their cover was blown; soon they all might end up as dead men or worse, in the swimming pool or crematorium.

HARI NUVREAN

Get in, we must leave immediately.

Hari Nuvrean barked the orders to the driver.

HARI NUVREAN
Get us out of here fast.

Within five seconds the limo was moving quickly down the street.

CAR FOLLOWING DURING CAR ESCAPE DURING FOLLOWING VOICEOVER

VOICE OVER

Mikhail Catamountz planned for this scenario. It would be a loose trail.

There were not going to be any major gun battles out in the open in the center of Sanctuary City. They would pick their optimum terrain to accomplish the takedown.

Another complicating factor was Hari Nuvrean had diplomatic protection. But Huaiyuansu Ka didn't.

They had to kill the one without killing the other and could not afford to allow Huaiyuansu Ka off the planet alive for fear their whole Zanziltar operations would be compromised as he could lead them to the facility.

The plan was to allow Hari Nuvrean to drop Huaiyuansu Ka off at a safe house, and after he left, they would take down the safe house, kill Huaiyuansu Ka if necessary, and hopefully catch him alive so he could get some time in the pool and the crematorium.

By the time Hari Nuvrean left Huaiyuansu Ka at the safe house, he was feeling a lot better that no collateral damage occurred. They got away lucky this time. But one thing was certain: They now had to deal with Huaiyuansu Ka.

Hari Nuvrean was in an extreme dilema now because the Revolutionaries would be on the outlook for Huaiyuansu Ka. Any agent seen assisting getting him off the planet would immediately be turned and most likely assassinated.

Soon, Hari Nuvrean posed the question to his superiors.

HARI NUVREAN
Do we want to risk good agents' lives for this traitor?

DRANZONIAN AMBASSADOR
Why such a dismal attitude?

HARI NUVREAN
It possibly may get some agents killed trying to bring Huaiyuansu Ka home, but trying to move him might also create pathways into our organization the revolutionaries might find in the process.

DRANZONIAN AMBASSADOR
Your orders are to get him off the planet and get him back to Praxisvlasia on the next intergalactic transport leaving.

INT. DAY. ZANZILATAR HARRY NUVREAN'S OFFICE INSIDE THE DRANZONIAN CONSULATE.

VOICE OVER
(During the activity filmed below)
While Hari Nuvrean was in his office drafting and encrypting correspondence to the home office requesting further guidance on his next moves, Mikhail Catamountz was already solving the problem for him.

INT. DAY ZANZILTAR AREA AROUND DRANZONIAN SAFE HOUSE WHERE HUAIYUANSU KA WAS SENT.

VOICE OVER
(During the activity filmed discussed below)
Once the Revolutionaries tracked Huaiyuansu Ka to the safe house, they then sent in a field surveillance team to find all the lookouts. A safehouse can have any number of lookouts. They can be a block away, two blocks away, just far enough away to observe an enemy approaching to warn the safehouse to bugout through alternative exit routes, which could be VTOL, limo, Terrain Sportster, or a modified armored car designed to look like a recreational vehicle.

The main difference between a homeowner and a lookout is how often and when they come out of the home and look around. Also, at odd hours of the day, they are exposed. In a pinch assume anyone out and about after 7:00 P.M. in their yards within two blocks of a safe house is a lookout.

Kill them, dispose of the body, and don't look back. As soon as the perimeter is cleaned up quietly and at all points in parallel, you then move into the house using classical storming techniques perfected by a lot of police departments. In fact, it pays to dress like a police officer. Who would know otherwise?

There wasn't much Sanctuary for the Dranzonian Empire Secret Service and because of ongoing issues elsewhere, purposely stirred up by Mikhail Catamountz as a "feint," the Dranzonian Empire Secret Service had to strip personnel away from most of their safe houses to bolster up what was appearing to look like the start of a gangland style turf war in the heart of Zanziltar.

There were only two lookouts at this safehouse, both just a block away in both directions. They both were obvious neophytes, new guys without a lot of practical experience. They would soon discover the hard way the classroom training would make them ill-prepared to deal with the types of attacks they now experienced, silent and deadly.

With the lookouts out of the way, timing was important because without routine status from the lookouts, that constituted a trip wire and a bug-out signal.

Mikhail Catamountz's special squad was the pride of the Revolution. They were partisans first, soldiers second, and philosophers third. Ends justified the means. They would kill every Dranzonian Empire Secret Service agent except for Huaiyuansu Ka, who they wanted to take alive.

They also shot one of the Dranzonians with a dart gun to put him to sleep by orders of Mikhail Catamountz, who planned to use him to work on Huaiyuansu Ka's psyche.

The operation was very efficient and within fifteen minutes from the start, which included taking out the lookouts and breaking into the home and killing all the defenders and taking two of them alive. VOTLS came down and all the bodies were carted off and into the VTOLS, who immediately fled and flew toward the mountains where alternate transportation was waiting.

Later that night, a mothership pulled into a hanger. Two men sedated and mummified were carried by stretcher onto the mothership. The doors were then opened on the hanger and the mothership headed out onto the runway, where it shortly launched and soon was in space on its way to Zuanshi-cheng where Glen Zhurenshuo the master craftsman who knew the exotic methods of the swimming pool would be used to break Huaiyuansu Ka. He would save the crematorium for Mikhail Catamountz to use.

INT. DAY. ARZON. DRANZONIAN SECRET SERVICE FACILITY.

Loraine Rantala began getting worried about Cap Zapatero when he suddenly went to the space port chasing a lead surrounding Evo Kaplan.

Loraine had been "dolling" herself up to possibly rekindle that long lost love who got separated from her when the Revolution got in the way of their romance, and they ended up at the opposite ends of the galaxy with little hope of ever seeing each other again.

Out of the fog of war, a mystery that one could never imagine, here came Blane Jiandie out of nowhere. Had Loraine not been notified the Dranzonian Empire Secret Service used 3D biological printing to cosmetically alter his appearance, she would never know who he was.

One thing is certain, Cap Zapatero (a.k.a. Blane Jiandie) did look amazingly more attractive after the 3D biological printing changed his facial recognition. Cap Zapatero was one goodlooking man. When Blane Jiandie didn't call the office or return, Loraine Rantala wondered, what happened to him?

Loraine Rantala grabbed one of the DranzovideosEmpire Secret Service agents in her office and they proceeded to the space port to find out any information, including ordering the space port to play back all surveillance video so they could see what happened to Cap Zapatero (a.k.a. Blane Jiandie).

INT. DAY. ARZON SPACE PORT.

There were no eyewitnesses who were of much help, but as they started sifting through the video using Loraine Rantala's guidance:

> LORAINE RANTALA
> Take the time of the space craft shove back from the terminal to actual start of boarding and play it back in reverse.

It didn't take long since Cap Zapatero was one of the very last persons boarding Toutoumomo de Hundan intergalactic passenger transport.

> LORAINE RANTALA
> It was amazing he got in with the door shutting without losing an arm and leg by maybe one half second.

> SECOND DRANZONIAN SECRET
> SERVICE AGENT
> Well, we know what happened to him. He's on the Toutoumomo de Hundan intergalactic passenger transport.

> LORAINE RANTALA
> That means Evo Kaplan must be on the Toutoumomo de Hundan intergalactic transport.

Loraine Rantala wondered what her next move should be. With the time that had elapsed, the intergalactic transport was well on its way at hyper-velocities outside of any scanner range or their ability to pursue without getting dangerously close to Revolutionary expanses.

As the investigation unfolded that day, using surveillance video in a number of places that Krawz Almarip visited, they came up with a very short list. The hotel and Shengmíng Langjie de Fangzi. video showed security men from that establishment going up with Evo Kaplan into his hotel room and stayed there overnight.

> SECOND DRANZONIAN SECRET
> SERVICE AGENT
> Why were they protecting him?

> LORAINE RANTALA
> Let's go talk to their boss.

Soon Loraine Rantala was interrogating Bubba, demanding information.

> LORAINE RANTALA
> What kind of items did you exchange with Krawz Almarip?

> BUBBA
> We purchased a lot of his exports. Mostly tourist items.

> LORAINE RANTALA
> Can you prove that?

> BUBBA
> Sure, go see the customs inspector. They take video of all the materials.

That effort came to a dead end. Loraine Rantala informed her partner.

> LORAINE RANTALA
> Evo Kaplan probably used it as a cover as to what his real purpose was being here. The locals may not know it was an imposter Evo Kaplan.

> SECOND DRANZONIAN SECRET
> SERVICE AGENT
> What was his real purpose?

> LORAINE RANTALA
> Good question. Whatever he came for he found out right away.

> SECOND DRANZONIAN SECRET
> SERVICE AGENT
> That means he picked up information. It might be critical to planetary defenses. We somehow must stop him.

> LORAINE RANTALA
> Will the government risk the boarding of a Zanziltar ship in Praxisvlasia?

> SECOND DRANZONIAN SECRET
> SERVICE AGENT
> Maybe they could board them in space and get away with it?

LORAINE RANTALA

The ship could send out distress calls and you would
end up with the same problem, explaining why you
illegally boarded a Zanziltar ship in neutral territory
and removed a passenger.

SECOND DRANZONIAN SECRET
SERVICE AGENT

What could they do about it?

LORAINE RANTALA

Remember, a lot of wealthy Praxisvlasia politicians
keep their wealth in Zanziltar banks. I doubt they
would risk losing their fortunes.

SECOND DRANZONIAN SECRET
SERVICE AGENT

What can we really do about it?

LORAINE RANTALA

Our only hope is that Blane Jiandie can stop him.

SECOND DRANZONIAN SECRET
SERVICE AGENT

Do you think he can kill him on the ship?

LORAINE RANTALA

He wasn't outfitted with specialized equipment; it
would have to be by hand. Evo Kaplan is a martial
artist and can defend himself. He'll have to improvise
a weapon.

SECOND DRANZONIAN SECRET
SERVICE AGENT

Any chance he got his laser pistol onboard?

LORAINE RANTALA

That would simplify it, but then Zanziltar could charge
him with murder if he shot him with a laser pistol.

SECOND DRANZONIAN SECRET
SERVICE AGENT

It's a no-win situation for him.

Two hours after takeoff, Evo Kaplan was feeling a lot better knowing he got off Zanziltar. His next challenge would be making it through Praxisvlasia. He saw Ruth Marradi when he boarded. He'd have to cut another deal with her.

Evo Kaplan suspected she was pissed off because she never got paid when he got off the ship as he promised. But the good news was he had a fortune in credits with him receiving payments from some of the black marketers. He would wait until she came around offering passengers snacks or drinks, then give her one of the credits he had in his pocket he knew was loaded with at least fifty thousand credits.

Evo Kaplan pulled a credit wafer out of his pockets and placed it next to the non-traceable personal communicator he received from one of the black marketers. Personal communicators were designed to do many applications, including read credits and tell the holder how many were left on it.

The first one he checked had fifty thousand credits like he thought. Then as he pulled more of them out, he got the surprise of his life; most of them were 100,000 or 250,000 credits each. He was sitting on a small fortune and could retire with what he held. He shuttered to think what he had stuffed in his personal luggage.

If all the credits he received from the black marketer through his agent were like these, he would have millions of credits. Shaking down Randolph Spencer was probably no longer desired or required.

Evo Kaplan's wait didn't have to be delayed too long. Ruth Marradi walked by, and Evo Kaplan approached her.

KRAWZ ALMARIP (A.K.A. EVO KAPLAN)
Hey, I have something for you I promised.

Ruth Marradi wasn't too happy with Krawz Almarip but looked kind of curious. Evo handed her the credit wafer, which she took and slid it in her flight attendant pocket.

RUTH MARRADI
Do you want anything to drink?

KRAWZ ALMARIP (A.K.A. EVO KAPLAN)
Is there any way you can make Huoshan Xingneng
Drink?

RUTH MARRADI
You mean like they serve on Shen de Huayuan?

KRAWZ ALMARIP (A.K.A. EVO KAPLAN)
Yes.

RUTH MARRADI
Certainly, I can make that drink for you. I'll be back
in a few minutes.

Ruth Marradi went up to the flight attendant's bar where she mixed drinks and first looked at the credit with her communicator. She was exasperated. Fifty thousand credits!

Oh my god! She thought and was suddenly happy like she had not been in a very long time. She started making the drink, smiling, and thinking, Krawz Almarip was true to his word just like he always was.

With a smile on her face and a new uplifting attitude, she realized those fifty thousand credits on top of her salary would allow her to live very comfortably for another twenty years, up until the time she knew she would turn into an old hag and suddenly be living like a pensioner.

As Ruth Marradi gave the drink to the man, she thought was Krawz Almarip, she then started realizing she also had helped someone who might be trying to hurt Krawz Almarip. This new guy on the ship was evidently following Krawz Almarip, most likely for nefarious activity. Perhaps there was an organized crime hit on Krawz Almarip?

Now Ruth Marradi was starting to feel a little guilty for screwing over Krawz Almarip, who had been good to her in the past, over-compensating her for everything. The fact she lived in more expensive apartments and could go to lavish restaurants and buy the latest fashions was due to how this man had treated her over the years for small favors. And now she felt guilty helping a man who she knew, in her heart of hearts, was out to hurt Krawz Almarip in some way.

Ruth Marradi needed to inform Krawz Almarip as soon as she could get alone with him. She would also look over him and warn him if she saw the other man making any provocative moves. Unfortunately, Krawz Almarip was around too many people at the present time to convey to him this critical information. Later in the flight, as soon as she could catch him alone, she would inform him.

About that time, another passenger who had overheard the drink request suddenly requested:

PASSENGER
Excuse me, miss. Can I have one of what he's drinking?

RUTH MARRADI
Sure, no problem, I'll be right back.

In the previous trip, Ruth Marradi had walked down the starboard passageway back to the flight attendant bar. Because she ended up on the right side of Evo Kaplan serving his drink, she ended up walking down the port passageway, where she would be a lot closer to passengers in a wide cabin that gave someone the impression it was the size of a movie studio audience, but the seats were a lot larger with spaces between.

As Ruth Marradi walked thirty paces up the port passageway, she spotted a pretty woman who immediately came to her mind. This is the woman Claudette Ramsey who was fooling around with Krawz Almarip on the flight to Arzon.

She recalled the seat directly next to Krawz Almarip was empty and decided her presence would also help protect him, especially during her sleeping periods.

RUTH MARRADI
Hello miss, I recall you on the flight to Arzon a few days ago.

CLAUDETTE RAMSEY
Yes, and I remember you Ruth.

RUTH MARRADI
Say, I reserved the seat next to your friend Krawz Almarip for you. I'm sure he would like to see you. Why don't you move up there and if you want, I can transfer all your personal effects of your locker up next to his, since that bunk is unused for this flight due to the small number of passengers.

CLAUDETTE RAMSEY
Oh, that would be great. I really appreciate this.

RUTH MARRADI
Follow me please.

CLAUDETTE RAMSEY
All right.

In a moment later, Claudette Ramsey, following Ruth Marradi, was right next to Evo Kaplan. Ruth, smiling hugely.

RUTH MARRADI
Krawz, look who I found.

Ruth Marradi then gestured with her hand and arm toward Claudette.

CLAUDETTE RAMSEY
Hello, Krawz.

KRAWZ ALMARIP (A.K.A. EVO KAPLAN)
Hey, Claudette how you been?

CLAUDETTE RAMSEY
Is it okay if I sit in that empty seat next to you?

KRAWZ ALMARIP (A.K.A. EVO KAPLAN)
Yes, please sit down here. I would love your company.

Evo Kaplan and Claudette Ramsey were both in sour moods for similar reasons. Evo just lost the first true love of his life and Claudette Ramsey just lost her mother who would never be able to see her spouse when that magical day happened.

In their mutual grief, there was a bonding of emotions and appreciation on many levels.

RUTH MARRADI
I'll see you guys later.

Ruth Marradi said, as she knew she should get out of their personal spheres to allow them to have this tender moment together. She could tell there was some immediate body language between the two and it could either explode or lapse into happy time. She didn't want to be around if the explosion occurred and hoped they were on good terms for Krawz's personal protection.

The two knew the other had just suffered severe grief in their lives from losing someone very close to them. For some strange reason the tears forming on Claudette Ramsey wasn't because of her mother, but because she knew Krawz had lost his girlfriend and lover. She must have been someone special to have such tendrils in such a reckless and flamboyant black marketer like Krawz Almarip.

Evo Kaplan, knowing that Claudette had just been through her mother's death, understood her tenderness as well, and the melancholy begat sorrow and more tears. Even though they were in public, not too many people were watching, and Evo Kaplan felt compelled to do something he suddenly desired. He reached out and put his hand on the side of her face, wiping some of the tears away as his own eyes were watering up and pulled her face closer to his and kissed her in the most romantic and provocative way.

Claudette Ramsey knew Evo Kaplan's tears were not fake by any stretch of the imagination; they were genuine, heart-wrenching evocation from a tumultuous event in his life. His tears and his kiss felt genuine and real.

It was the most absolute confirmation of human passion Claudette Ramsey had ever witnessed in her life. As she reflected on this moment years later, she realized it was probably the most important day in her life.

This was absolute confirmation, an unusual galactic traveler who had tasted the seeds of heaven felt genuine love for her.

During the course of events, after the cabin was rigged for night, Evo and Claudette made their way into Claudette's bunk, which proved to be a blessing, as it gave him safety for a few hours.

Evo Kaplan and Claudette Ramsey's time together was an emotional roller coaster, from sorrow to pleasure to sorrow and back to pleasure.

What was different in Evo Kaplan's sorrow for Brenda Broyals was he knew she died in pain.

Spies always die in pain. He knew it was horrific and one of his crying episodes that touched Claudette Ramsey more than almost any time of her life occurred because he allowed himself to dwell on it too much.

Eventually he pulled himself together and encapsulated his past into a compartment in his mind that he would not reopen any time soon. His many periods of meditation, which was an integral part of spy training, paid off, as he soon was able to put the genie back in the bottle for the rest of the trip.

Claudette Ramsey was very amused to watch Evo Kaplan's transcendence into these mental spasms that revealed more about him in five minutes than she had learned the entire time she knew him, though that was in reality short.

Cap Zapatero took to surveillance while the cabins were rigged for nighttime. This was good because in the low lighting it's easier to spy on someone than it is in a well-lit room. Plus, the target of the surveillance very well might be resting peacefully in their chair not yet wanting to get horizontal in their bunk.

After a careful search including a trip to the lounge, he thought the possibility existed Evo Kaplan was not on the intergalactic transport or he might be up in the cockpit again, socializing with the pilots. He went back to his seat and settled down and waited for Ruth Marradi to set him up with some survival equipment, such as a toothbrush, change of clothes from lost and found, and a bunk.

Ruth Marradi provided all she promised but was very careful to place Cap Zapatero in a different bunk room to make sure he didn't accidentally run into Krawz Almarip. Cap Zapatero was in a starboard bunk room and Krawz Almarip was in a port bunk room.

Cap Zapatero stayed vigilant for twenty-four hours walking around looking for Evo Kaplan. Ruth Marradi picked up on the surveillance and having flown billions upon billions of miles, had seen a lot in her day. She knew when someone was up to no good.

Cap Zapatero wanted to remain awake for at least another twelve hours so he could detect Evo Kaplan if he were on board, thinking the man would soon have to visit the lounge and get something to eat. When Ruth Marradi walked into his seating area, he stopped her and asked for a particular type of tea drink that was known to be loaded with caffeine and sleep prohibitors.

Ruth decided she would do otherwise. She had with her some chemicals the crew had to sometimes inject passengers who became unruly. The drugs worked either with injection, which didn't take as much product, or could be drugged in a drink.

The tea that Cap Zapatero requested tasted horrible and would easily cover up the drugs put in it. Ruth Marradi spiked the drink with an amount she knew would put him under for at least twelve hours and possibly up to twenty-four hours.

The only thing that would wake Cap Zapatero at the end of it would be an incredible urge for bowel movements.

In a few minutes, Ruth Marradi gave the drink to Cap Zapatero, then walked away giving him the privacy he most likely wanted. She then made a few trips back over the next fifteen minutes doing odd jobs such as picking up trash someone had accidentally dropped or taking used cups and trash from passengers.

Ruth Marradi observed Cap Zapatero drinking the tea and at one point it appeared he tipped the container as if he was rather thirsty and drinking the final contents, obviously fighting sleep and trying to avoid it, but unfortunately succumbed to Ruth's drugging.

At twenty minutes after serving, Cap Zapatero was lying peacefully back in his seat having the best rest he felt in a very long time.

An hour after Cap Zapatero passed out, Evo Kaplan emerged from Claudette Ramsey's bunk and left her in a deep peaceful sleep. He used the bathroom, felt some hunger, then proceeded to the lounge and obtained a snack and a drink. Timing was everything. Captain Buck was also arriving in the lounge, getting a snack and a drink, and was getting ready to head up to the cockpit for twelve hours.

CAPTAIN BUCK
Hello Krawz, glad you were able to get to Arzon and
off the planet.

KRAWZ ALMARIP (A.K.A. EVO KAPLAN)
I would not have made it without your help. What do
I owe you?

CAPTAIN BUCK
If you have any of those energy drinks on board, I
could definitely use one of them now.

KRAWZ ALMARIP (A.K.A. EVO KAPLAN)
You are very lucky. I only went through about half of
the drinks I brought with me to Arzon. I managed to
get back on the ship with half of them. Let me go get a
couple and I'll bring it up to the cockpit for you.

CAPTAIN BUCK
You might be stuck up there with us for twelve hours.

KRAWZ ALMARIP (A.K.A. EVO KAPLAN)
That's okay. I know you guys have piss bottles up
there."

CAPTAIN BUCK
Yep, and it aggravates the hell out of the chief purser
who is responsible to empty them.

Captain Buck chuckled a bit.

KRAWZ ALMARIP (A.K.A. EVO KAPLAN)
Okay, I'll be back in a couple minutes.

Evo Kaplan left the lounge, went to his locker, and pulled out three energy drinks. He
only had three more left. He would have to conserve them. As he was walking toward
the lounge, Ruth stopped him.

RUTH MARRADI
I need to talk with you about something.

KRAWZ ALMARIP (A.K.A. EVO KAPLAN)
Okay, can it wait? I'm going up to the cockpit to visit
Captain Buck.

RUTH MARRADI
Sure, but when you leave the cockpit come and see
me. I have some important information for you.

KRAWZ ALMARIP (A.K.A. EVO KAPLAN)
Will do.

Ruth was somewhat relieved knowing Krawz Almarip would be safe up there and delay this other person, Cap, from doing nefarious activities.

Evo Kaplan made it to the cockpit and as he got in the co-pilot Fursungtarwum would shut the door and it would be electronically locked and only the purser could unlock it except in an emergency. If the captain hit the chicken switches that would send off distress beacons, any of the crew could then unlock the door and after a sequence of actions, two-man rule stuff, the pilot and copilot could jointly unlock the door.

Just like the real Krawz Almarip, Evo Kaplan sat in seat number three so he could easily talk with Captain Buck and handed drinks to Captain Buck and Copilot Fursungtarwum.

COPILOT FURSUNGTARWUM
This is what I needed.

CAPTAIN BUCK
Hey, that hot chick you met on the way to Arzon came
aboard shortly before you did.

KRAWZ ALMARIP (A.K.A. EVO KAPLAN)
Yes, I've already hooked up with her.

CAPTAIN BUCK
She your new girlfriend?

KRAWZ ALMARIP (A.K.A. EVO KAPLAN)
You might say that.

CAPTAIN BUCK
What ever happened to your girlfriend from Zanziltar?

KRAWZ ALMARIP (A.K.A. EVO KAPLAN)
She was recently killed.

CAPTAIN BUCK
How did that happen?

> KRAWZ ALMARIP (A.K.A. EVO KAPLAN)
> I don't know the details of the incident yet, but I intend to
> find out who was responsible and make that person wish he
> was never alive.

Captain Buck knew better than to continue down that path, as it was going down a rabbit hole real fast.

> CAPTAIN BUCK
> Is this new girlfriend nice?

> KRAWZ ALMARIP (A.K.A. EVO KAPLAN)
> Yes, she is incredible. She has helped me come to terms
> with my old girlfriend a lot quicker than I normally would
> have.

> CAPTAIN BUCK
> I'm really surprised you had a close girlfriend after
> watching you in action all these years.

> KRAWZ ALMARIP (A.K.A. EVO KAPLAN)
> Well, even a crusty ole' black marketer like me sometimes
> stumbles across a magnificent woman who changes our
> destiny and alters our ego.

> CAPTAIN BUCK
> The timing of meeting this new girlfriend seems rather
> auspicious.

> KRAWZ ALMARIP (A.K.A. EVO KAPLAN)
> More than you can imagine.

Evo Kaplan knew the credits he had in his personal luggage were a small fortune and the credits in his pocket were chump change compared to them, and suddenly felt obligated to give something to Captain Buck, who saved his life.

Had Evo Kaplan not made it aboard the intergalactic transport under an alias with Captain Buck's assistance, he would very well be a dead man now or in so much pain he would wish here were dead.

Evo Kaplan reached in his pocket and randomly pulled out a credit cube and handed it to Captain Buck.

KRAWZ ALMARIP (A.K.A. EVO KAPLAN)
Hey Captain Buck, here's a little gift for helping me out
when I really needed it. If you are ever in Shen de Huayuan,
take Fursungtarwum with you and stay at the Lantiane
Resort. I'm sure there are a few Barracuda there wanting
you to go with them to the Hupu Waterfalls.

CAPTAIN BUCK
You sure Fursungtarwum can swim with the barracudas'
without being eaten alive?

Krawz Almarip responded in a mischievous manner, as he vividly understood how
Randolph Spencer hired the FIRM to sting his old boss, Reginald Heiqishi.

KRAWZ ALMARIP (A.K.A. EVO KAPLAN)
After he drinks one of those Huoshan Xingneng drinks,
he'll be ready to take on the Barracudas, but be careful,
their husbands might have a big stinger,

Captain Buck put the credit cube into his pocket and figured it was maybe a thousand
credits or something big like that. He would really get excited if he had known Krawz
Almarip had already given Ruth Marradi fifty thousand credits.

The conversation drifted from travel to broads to harrowing adventures such as getting
out of the way of a cosmic event just in time. The twelve hours went by quickly and
Evo Kaplan had to borrow the piss bottle halfway through. The other men also took
their turn at the rear of the cockpit in semi-privacy.

The Cosmic Spatial Normalizer Coefficients feeding the display panels had not
indicated any significant detections during the entire past ten-hour period. The
conversation and the energy drink went a long way toward overcoming the boredom
and loneliness often felt by the crew up in the cockpit.

Since Captain Buck and Fursungtarwum had flown with each other for quite some time,
they knew each other's stories vividly. Anything they had to say or hear by now was
a repeat many times over. They were glad when new events happened or interesting
characters such as Krawz Almarip flew with them and brought new dimensions and
new stories. They had no idea what was yet to unfold. Nobody, including Evo Kaplan,
expected the Revolutionaries to suddenly show up.

A soft frequency sweeping alarm suddenly brightened on the display as the cosmic
spatial normalizer coefficients doing statistical analysis on cosmic noise suddenly
discovered correlated signals. Uncorrelated signals from space junk and debris posed
no threat. Correlated noise, on the other hand, constituted a valid signal of some type.

Automatic trackers were suddenly engaged and because the ship was traveling at extreme speeds calculations were automatically producing a clarifying picture of the probability of the range, speed, and direction the signals were traveling.

A single signal would not manifest much concern and a different alarm. But this unexpected shrill sounded of a shifting frequency and annotation on the display was no less than a trip wire, which caused Captain Buck to swing into action. The first thing Captain Buck did was give Fursungtarwum orders.

> CAPTAIN BUCK
> Fursungtarwum, initiate a crew recall and have the purser report to the cockpit immediately.

Intergalactic Passenger Transports who come across military ships from time to time do not want to upset their passengers even when they encounter potential harm. The alert and recall are all handled discretely and quietly.

The purser received his notification immediately and saw the nature of it was quite severe.

Any pilot or co-pilot who was thinking of getting a few extra hours of rest was soon mistaken and didn't like to be called back to the cockpit under these circumstances, because it meant a probable disaster was unfolding. Space travel was still dangerous, especially with the Revolution going on.

C.U. COSMIC SPATIAL NORMALIZER DISPLAY, AND PEOPLE IN THE COCKPIT DURING VOICE OVER.

> VOICE OVER
> The Cosmic Spatial Normalizer Coefficients were soon painting a cluster on the surveillance displays, which meant one thing for sure, which Captain Buck understood vividly.

> CAPTAIN BUCK
> It looks like a squadron or larger formation.

Evo Kaplan suddenly felt quite alarmed.

> KRAWZ ALMARIP (A.K.A. EVO KAPLAN)
> Any idea who it is?

> CAPTAIN BUCK
> They have not hailed us yet, but it appears they know we are here and are painting a beeline toward us.

When the Revolutionary Guard Squadron reached about one fourth of a PAU (Praxisvlasia Astronomical Units, the distance from the home planet and its sun is one PAU), they were finally hailed.

Any intergalactic transports who took on passengers from Praxisvlasia were required to have an emergency evacuation access hatch on both the top and bottom of the hull so passengers could be rescued in space. The redundancy served the purpose of allowing rescue if one of the major surfaces remained intact after a collision or accident whereby the hull was not breached to the point of losing its atmosphere.

A lot of warships carried shuttles specifically for this purpose and to take in custody enemy who were defeated after a major battle.

The Cosmic Spatial Normalizer Coefficients were processed by a classifier system, which derived the source of the radiator, usually a radar or neutrino scanner. Sometimes enemies would use infrared and ultraviolet. They needed to know who to outrun and when. Also taken into consideration was the geometry of the intercept.

Captain Buck, knowing their intercept geometry was too perfect and as a result there is virtually no merit in trying to outrun them.

Shortly the purser opened the door and the other pilots and copilots arrived and took chairs three through six. The purser, who knew Krawz Almarip, announced.

SHIP'S PURSER
I'm sorry, Mr. Almarip, but I'm going to have to ask you to
leave the cockpit. Our crew will be busy now and you are
no longer permitted in the cockpit.

KRAWZ ALMARIP (A.K.A. EVO KAPLAN)
Understand.

Evo Kaplan left the cockpit and made his way back to his seat, where he discovered
Claudette Ramsey sitting patiently waiting.

CLAUDETTE RAMSEY
Ruth told me you went to the cockpit to visit with your
pilot friends. Did you have a good time?

KRAWZ ALMARIP (A.K.A. EVO KAPLAN)
It was fun, just like old times.

Evo Kaplan lied to cover up the extreme stress he now had, fearing what would happen
to him based on which Empire boarded the intergalactic transport real soon.

Up in the cockpit, the situation was not looking good. Captain Buck knew that within
fifteen minutes the ships would be close enough to where the passengers could see
them.

Everyone on the ship knew this was a blockade runner. There would be instant panic
in the ship. The more astute travelers knew the intergalactic transport was flying black,
meaning it was not transmitting its CTA signals, which then allowed warring parties to
declare it a warship and attack it without any repercussions.

But Captain Buck felt this was a setup; someone already knew and planned it in
advance. A sophisticated ambush of some sort.

The surveillance displays were lit up like a Christmas tree. There were no more
tripwires. Simply put, Intergalactic Passenger Transport was no match for even a
single space warship. And here closing in on him fast was an entire squadron of space
warships.

Captain Buck's latest instructions from the Revolutionary Guard Commander he was
now communicating with:

REVOLUTIONARY GUARD COMMANDER
Maintain speed and course. We will be sending over a
mating shuttle on your upper escape hatch. We expect
you to receive our boarding party and comply with

> their instructions otherwise you will leave us no choice
> but to blow your ship into trillions of molecules.

The ships didn't need to slow down in the vacuum of space. Actually, they could go faster, but the blockade runner limited their speed for fuel economy since they had to take off without the assistance of an electric catapult.

Captain Buck turned to the purser and directed him.

> CAPTAIN BUCK
> Go get the emergency crew and have them stand by
> the upper escape hatch.

> SHIP'S PURSER
> What about the passengers sitting in that area?

> CAPTAIN BUCK
> Relocate all the passengers to the after-cabin area. We
> have plenty of room for them back there.

Evo Kaplan was near a window that was lead impregnated for radiation hardening but transparent, and looked out in the direction he thought he might see the ships arrive. He sat there silently semi-meditating, realizing there wasn't anything he could do about it.

The display consoles automatically shifted to collision avoidance modes and the ship might have done emergency maneuvers except Captain Buck wisely put the controls into manual override on all collision settings. There were times due to cosmic disturbances they would have had to do that. Lucky, they had the feature because he knew whoever this was would most likely shoot first and ask questions later if they suddenly maneuvered.

In due time it didn't take Evo Kaplan a lot of eye strain to see at a distance light from the approaching squadron. Flying far from any other ships, the squadron put their running lights on so that other Revolutionary Guard ships could see each other and avoid collisions.

Even though the Revolutionary Guard had sophisticated sensors and radars, when they got close, they preferred to shine light on the intergalactic transport so that the entire squadron could easily see their target and observe any sudden threatening movements.

<u>EXT. CGI. SPACE. REVOLUTIONARY SQUADRON ARRIVING. INTERLACED WITH THIS SEQUENCE OF CONVERSATIONS.</u>

Passengers were getting a little irritated as they were all being relocated to the after-seating area. Due to the sudden crowding, another passenger accidentally bumped into Cap Zapatero from his drug-induced sleep.

Coming back to reality, Cap Zapatero felt his stomach turning and he needed to get to the bathroom quickly or there would be embarrassment. He abruptly got up and made his way there. Thank God they were not all occupied!

Cap Zapatero missed out on the big surprise as he was in the toilet doing his business. The Revolutionary Guard were close and turned on all their searchlights onto the intergalactic transport. Suddenly the cabin was so bright it was almost like daytime.

CLAUDETTE RAMSEY
Are we in trouble, Krawz?

KRAWZ ALMARIP (A.K.A. EVO KAPLAN)
Seems so. I'm sorry.

CLAUDETTE RAMSEY
Why should you be sorry?

KRAWZ ALMARIP (A.K.A. EVO KAPLAN)
I think this is about me.

Claudette Ramsey looked at Krawz Almarip in total disbelief. She knew he was an intergalactic smuggler and black marketer but couldn't see how he possibly could have triggered any of these incredible sights with multitudes of lights shining on them from obviously military space warships.

In a while the Revolutionary Guards and Captain Buck coordinated their activities quite efficiently. Everyone on the Revolutionary Guards ships were happy the cool captain was following instructions carefully so this would not have to evolve into a bloody encounter, realizing innocent people were on the ship, simply heading home from visiting families.

They were all formerly of the Dranzonian Empire, and a lot of people felt there had already been too much killing. A stalemate had been somewhat reached and multitudes of people and planets wanted a negotiated settlement, not a hard victory.

<u>EXT. CGI. SPACE. SHUTTLE LEAVES REVOLUTIONARY COMMAND SHIP AND FLIES OVER AND MATES TO THE INTERGALACTIC PASSENGER TRANSPORT.</u>

In a few minutes the shuttle was coming over. On board was an interesting person. Captain Buck had been informed and ordered:

REVOLUTIONARY GUARD COMMANDER.
Present Krawz Almarip to the boarding party when
they arrive.

The purser sent flight attendant Ruth Marradi to get Krawz Almarip and bring him to the cockpit. A moment later she was at Evo Kaplan's seat.

RUTH MARRADI
Krawz, Captain Buck asks that you please come to the
cockpit. He needs to talk to you.

KRAWZ ALMARIP (A.K.A. EVO KAPLAN)
All right.

Claudette Ramsey had a sudden look of fear in her face as Evo Kaplan stood up to follow Ruth Marradi forward to see Captain Buck.

About then Cap Zapatero was coming out of the bathroom, fully relieved and astonished that all the passengers on the ship were crowded back in his after-cabin area and all the glaring bright lights coming from the windows. Just as he focused ahead, he observed the flight attendant Ruth Marradi leading the man he was looking for, Krawz Almarip, walking away with her, and the woman he had seen on the previous flight with him sitting there looking as if she were in panic.

The passengers were starting to get unruly, and some were in hysteria as the rumor mongers were saying:

PASSENGER
These were Revolutionary Guards ships and will kill
all of us!

But for a long while nothing happened, just the strong lights. Eventually the captain came over the intercom:

CAPTAIN BUCK (via INTERCOM)
Ladies and gentlemen, there is no reason to panic or
be upset. We do have visitors as you see outside your
window and a matter that is ongoing will be resolved
shortly and we'll be continuing our transit unmolested.

Our visitors have directed us not to slow down and
to continue to our destination. There will be a shuttle
operation shortly. Stay in the after cabin and do not
interfere with the crew in any way.

As captain of this ship, I have full legal jurisdiction
over anyone on board this ship, so please comply.

**After the captain finished his announcement, hopefully to calm the passengers, he
turned to Evo Kaplan, whom he had always known as Krawz Almarip.**

CAPTAIN BUCK
Krawz, I'm very sorry for what I must do. The
Revolutionary Guards are sending over a shuttle to
take you off this ship. You must go or everyone else on
this flight would be killed.

KRAWZ ALMARIP (A.K.A. EVO KAPLAN)
Okay Captain Buck, I'll gladly go, but can you do me
a favor?

CAPTAIN BUCK
Sure. Krawz.

KRAWZ ALMARIP (A.K.A. EVO KAPLAN)
Do you remember the woman on this flight you met
talking to me named Claudette Ramsey.

CAPTAIN BUCK
How could I possibly forget such a beautiful woman?

KRAWZ ALMARIP (A.K.A. EVO KAPLAN)
I am in love with her. Tell her I will do everything in
my power to get back to her. To please wait for me and
give me some time.

CAPTAIN BUCK
Sure, Krawz. I'll be happy to give her the message.

About that time the Purser entered the cockpit.

SHIP'S PURSER
Captain, we are fully mated with their shuttle. For
some reason they are sending a man down to talk to
Krawz before they leave.

CAPTAIN BUCK
All right, let him come aboard. There's not much we
could do to stop them anyway.

The Purser showed a most critical face.

SHIP'S PURSER
Krawz, please follow me.

In the forward area of the lounge is where the emergency escape hatch existed. The emergency hatch ladder was assembled very quickly as it unfolds and clicks into place. Since both ships were former Dranzonian Empire designs, all the normal escape equipment functioned interchangeably.

Evo Kaplan was standing next to the purser and Ruth Marradi when the hatch opened by remote control from the cockpit and a man suddenly stepped down.

It was a unique situation and thought of at the last minute because the FIRM didn't know for sure Evo Kaplan knew who he worked for and wanted to save his life for all that he had done, including losing the love of his life who gave the supreme sacrifice for the cause.

As soon as the person stepped down onto the deck and turned around, Evo Kaplan had one of the biggest surprises of his life. There standing in front of him was Mikhail Catamountz.

KRAWZ ALMARIP (A.K.A. EVO KAPLAN)
You were the last person I would expect to come here.

MIKHAIL CATAMOUNTZ
I came to get you back to Zanziltar safely.

KRAWZ ALMARIP (A.K.A. EVO KAPLAN)
I appreciate that.

MIKHAIL CATAMOUNTZ
Let's leave now so this ship's captain can calm down
a few nerves.

KRAWZ ALMARIP (A.K.A. EVO KAPLAN)
Are we going directly to Zanziltar?

MIKHAIL CATAMOUNTZ
Pretty much, but you'll be transferred to a non-combat
ship then shuttle down to the planet.

KRAWZ ALMARIP (A.K.A. EVO KAPLAN)
Is there any possibility I can bring someone along with
me?

VOICE OVER

Blane Jiandie arrived and upon return to Praxisvlasia went through a debriefing process and check. The Dranzonian Empire Secret Service performed neuro biopsies and neuroplastigraph lie detector tests as well as blood checks for drugs and poisons. A spy could be hit without knowing.

The Dranzonian Empire Secret Service knew that Blane Jiandie, traveling under the alias of Cap Zapatero, could have been betrayed at any moment.

Post-mission analysis was critical because it might imply several things such as the method of betrayal and now that Huaiyuansu Ka was missing, it was quite feasible the Revolutionaries learned of the operation through information obtained from him.

The fact, Blane Jiandie was almost in a panic to get off the planet Zanziltar during his return further substantiated there was clearly an element of fear and possible compromise he didn't divulge for compelling reasons.

The neuroplastigraph lie detector utilized the plasticity of the brain. Essentially the equipment and the expert operator rewired a person's brain in a way they couldn't control so that real information could be obtained without the suspect preventing it.

To some progressives, neuroplastigraph was felt as a supreme violation of human sanctity, and that nobody would be entitled to privacy in the future. The fear of big brother crept upon the masses as this technology slowly leaked out.

The combination of all the tools and testing soon gave a clearer picture of what happened.

TOXICOLOGIST

Toxicology test results showed Blane Jiandie wasn't poisoned, but he certainly was drugged.

With the help of hypnosis and neuroplastigraph technology, an after-action report with remarkable accuracy was soon composed.

BLAINE JIANDIE'S SUPERVISOR
It appears that a flight attendant named Ruth probably
may have drugged Blane Jiandie. Tell me about it.

TOXICOLOGIST
The fingerprint on the chemicals obtained through the
neuro biopsy registered it as an extremely rare chemical
code-named Gateway that only the Dranzonian Empire
Secret Service who engineered and designed it, know
of it and Gateway rarely use in espionage.

BLAINE JIANDIE'S SUPERVISOR
How such rare and priceless chemicals ended up in
the hands of a flight attendant Ruth Marradi is clearly
a mystery.

BLAINE JIANDIE'S SUPERVISOR'S ASSISTANT
Unfortunately, the intergalactic transport was halfway
to Zanziltar before we knew most of the details.

BLAINE JIANDIE'S SUPERVISOR
It would have been nice to have known when they
stopped at Praxisvlasia.

BLAINE JIANDIE'S SUPERVISOR'S ASSISTANT
If we ever came across flight attendant Ruth Marradi
again, she would be taken to a secret location and
given the same treatment the Revolutionaries would
give someone to get the truth out of them.

BLAINE JIANDIE'S SUPERVISOR
If we discover the source of Ruth Marradi's Gateway
chemicals, we'll have to shut them down.

INT. SPACE. REVOLUTIONARY GUARDS CRUISER STATEROOM

While Evo Kaplan was in the stateroom aboard the Revolutionary Guards Cruiser on
the way to Zanziltar, he had a private discussion with Claudette Ramsey about their
future.

KRAWZ ALMARIP (A.K.A. EVO KAPLAN)
You probably are wondering why the Revolutionary
Guards pulled me off the intergalactic transport. I
know this is probably troubling for you.

CLAUDETTE RAMSEY
Well, Krawz, it's unheard of that nothing like this ever happened before that I'm aware of. It is a little unnerving."

KRAWZ ALMARIP (A.K.A. EVO KAPLAN)
Claudette, I will tell you a lot about it if you want, but I must warn you: the more I tell you, the more I put your life in danger.

CLAUDETTE RAMSEY
Why would you want to tell me such things?

KRAWZ ALMARIP (A.K.A. EVO KAPLAN)
First of all, I think I have fallen in love with you.

CLAUDETTE RAMSEY
Do you really mean that?

KRAWZ ALMARIP (A.K.A. EVO KAPLAN)
I will not lie and say I wasn't recently in love with another woman, but she's now dead. If she were still alive, you and I wouldn't be here together.

CLAUDETTE RAMSEY
If you were in love with this other woman then how did you come onto me so quickly?

KRAWZ ALMARIP (A.K.A. EVO KAPLAN)
At first it was really rough on me, but I had to pull myself together to do things, which I'm willing to discuss with you now so that you know who I am, and you understand the risk you take being in my company.

CLAUDETTE RAMSEY
Krawz, I know you live a strange life and there is a lot about you I do not know. Some people would say you are an unsavory character and have probably broken a lot of hearts in your days, but I'm not fond of ordinary men.

KRAWZ ALMARIP (A.K.A. EVO KAPLAN)
That's good to know.

CLAUDETTE RAMSEY
I can have all the ordinary men I want. But yet, I know
I would never be satisfied with them.

KRAWZ ALMARIP (A.K.A. EVO KAPLAN)
Does that mean you would settle down with an
unsavory character like me?

CLAUDETTE RAMSEY
Sure, you are rough around the edges. You probably do
a lot of illegal things. And no doubt you have enemies.

KRAWZ ALMARIP (A.K.A. EVO KAPLAN)
That I do.

CLAUDETTE RAMSEY
All I will say now is that if you can keep me moderately
safe, I'm willing to be your woman and take on risk.

KRAWZ ALMARIP (A.K.A. EVO KAPLAN)
That's understandable. So, in doing so, I have to tell
you who I really am.

CLAUDETTE RAMSEY
Krawz, who are you?

KRAWZ ALMARIP (A.K.A. EVO KAPLAN)
I'm what you would call a spook.

CLAUDETTE RAMSEY
What does spook mean?

KRAWZ ALMARIP (A.K.A. EVO KAPLAN)
I'm a spy. I'm good at what I do, and the Dranzonian
Empire Secret Service has me on their top ten Kill on
Sight list.

CLAUDETTE RAMSEY
Have they tried to kill you?

KRAWZ ALMARIP (A.K.A. EVO KAPLAN)
Yes, they have tried to kill me multiple times in the
past but failed. There is more. Do you want me to
continue?

CLAUDETTE RAMSEY
Yes, I do.

KRAWZ ALMARIP (A.K.A. EVO KAPLAN)
It will place you at more and more risk the more I tell
you.

CLAUDETTE RAMSEY
I'm willing to take it if you truly love me.

KRAWZ ALMARIP (A.K.A. EVO KAPLAN)
I do love you.

CLAUDETTE RAMSEY
Then you can tell me.

KRAWZ ALMARIP (A.K.A. EVO KAPLAN)
I'm not Krawz Almarip. I'm using his stolen ID.

CLAUDETTE RAMSEY
Does that include the looks?

KRAWZ ALMARIP (A.K.A. EVO KAPLAN)
Yes. The intergalactic organized crime syndicate I
work for has the best cosmetic surgeons we know of
in the galaxy. They can give me someone else's looks.

CLAUDETTE RAMSEY
Okay, they did a good job on you.

KRAWZ ALMARIP (A.K.A. EVO KAPLAN)
They will soon be changing my looks again because
I'm in existential danger. So, to extend my ability to
survive, I must go through a metamorphism.

CLAUDETTE RAMSEY
How will I know who you are in the future?

KRAWZ ALMARIP (A.K.A. EVO KAPLAN)
It's very important we have a few secrets among
ourselves that nobody else knows.

CLAUDETTE RAMSEY
We already have quite a few of them.

KRAWZ ALMARIP (A.K.A. EVO KAPLAN)
When I meet you the next time, I will look different.

CLAUDETTE RAMSEY
That's okay if I know it's you.

KRAWZ ALMARIP (A.K.A. EVO KAPLAN)
My name will change again as well.

CLAUDETTE RAMSEY
Mine will not!

KRAWZ ALMARIP (A.K.A. EVO KAPLAN)
For now, it's probably safe you can keep your name
and identity since you work for Randolph Spencer and
live on Zanziltar.

CLAUDETTE RAMSEY
How soon will I get to see you when we get back to
Zanziltar?

KRAWZ ALMARIP (A.K.A. EVO KAPLAN)
I'm not really sure, but there is something else I must
now confess.

CLAUDETTE RAMSEY
What's that?

KRAWZ ALMARIP (A.K.A. EVO KAPLAN)
I have a six-year contract to fulfill. I almost have the
first year completed. I will not be permitted to leave
the FIRM until I complete my six years.

CLAUDETTE RAMSEY
And after that?

KRAWZ ALMARIP (A.K.A. EVO KAPLAN)
I will leave the FIRM, shake their hands, and promise
them I will never see them again.

CLAUDETTE RAMSEY
Will they let you go?

KRAWZ ALMARIP (A.K.A. EVO KAPLAN)
Hopefully the Revolution will be over by then so there would be no point in keeping me around.

CLAUDETTE RAMSEY
We can surely hope.

KRAWZ ALMARIP (A.K.A. EVO KAPLAN)
One other thing.

CLAUDETTE RAMSEY
Yes?

KRAWZ ALMARIP (A.K.A. EVO KAPLAN)
In one of my bags there is a large number of credit cubes. It's a fortune.

CLAUDETTE RAMSEY
How did you obtain that wealth?

KRAWZ ALMARIP (A.K.A. EVO KAPLAN)
A lot of businesspeople on Arzon owed the real Krawz Almarip a lot of money. I sent the word out that if they made a partial payment, I would cancel the rest of the debt.

CLAUDETTE RAMSEY
Did they agree to that?

KRAWZ ALMARIP (A.K.A. EVO KAPLAN)
Yes, that's how I obtained all those credits.

CLAUDETTE RAMSEY
What happened to Krawz Almarip?

KRAWZ ALMARIP (A.K.A. EVO KAPLAN)
We'll never know. He just will not need his former identity any longer.

Just about the time Claudette Ramsey was thinking about celebrating their bourgeoning relationship, there was a knock at the stateroom door and the steward outside.

STEWARD
Sir, I hate to disturb you, but Mr. Catamountz would like to speak to you.

KRAWZ ALMARIP (A.K.A. EVO KAPLAN)
All right. One minute please.

Evo Kaplan looked fondly at Claudette.

KRAWZ ALMARIP (A.K.A. EVO KAPLAN)
I'll be right back.

Evo Kaplan opened the door the rest of the way.

STEWARD
Follow me please.

Evo was led to the shuttle bay where Mikhail Catamountz stood with a couple other men in plain clothes.

MIKHAIL CATAMOUNTZ
Evo, your presence has been requested at Zuanshi-cheng. You and I and these two gentlemen are going to shuttle over to a fast frigate and go there now.

KRAWZ ALMARIP (A.K.A. EVO KAPLAN)
What about Claudette Ramsey?

MIKHAIL CATAMOUNTZ
We are taking her back to Zanziltar, where she will be able to return to her normal life.

KRAWZ ALMARIP (A.K.A. EVO KAPLAN)
Can I go tell her I'm leaving?

MIKHAIL CATAMOUNTZ
I'm sorry, you must leave now.

KRAWZ ALMARIP (A.K.A. EVO KAPLAN)
Can I send a message to her from the steward here?

MIKHAIL CATAMOUNTZ
What's the message?

KRAWZ ALMARIP (A.K.A. EVO KAPLAN)
Tell her I know how she feels, and I will miss her until I see her again. I will try to see her as soon as I can.

Mikhail Catamountz turned to the Steward and directed him:

> MIKHAIL CATAMOUNTZ
> Go to Claudette Ramsey's stateroom and repeat to her
> what this gentleman just stated.

> STEWARD
> Aye sir, right away.

EXT. CGI. SPACE. SHUTTLE LEAVING THE CRUISER THEN FLYING OVER AND DOCKING IN THE FAST FRIGUIT.

The men climbed into the shuttle and were soon deposited onto the fast frigate. The fast frigate soon maneuvered out of formation and accelerated like few other ships in the squadron could match.

EXT. CGI. SPACE FAST FRIGATE ACCELERATED SO FAST IT APPEARS TO "JUMP" TO ITS DESTINATION.

A half a day later, the fast frigate arrived at Zuanshi-cheng and the four men in civilian clothes were shuttled down to the planet. With wartime conditions, the frigate could not be spared as a taxi service to the planet surface in case it was needed to repel borders.

EXT CGI. SPACE SHUTTLE LEAVES FAST FRIGATE AND TRAVELS DOWN TO TOLKAMERE FOUNDATION

The shuttle landed at the prestigious Tolkamere Foundation and was soon surrounded by heavy security.

Mikhail Catamountz led the men out of the shuttle and were soon escorted into the nearby building that had opulence and ebullience among a few people that were there, apparently waiting on them.

Evo Kaplan had no idea what Cornelius Xie de Hundan appeared like and was the last person he would ever expect to meet.

> CORNELIUS XIE DE HUNDAN
> Welcome to Zuanshi-cheng, Evo Kaplan.

> EVO KAPLAN
> Thank you.

> MIKHAIL CATAMOUNTZ
> Cornelius, Evo Kaplan may not know who you are.

CORNELIUS XIE DE HUNDAN
Be my guest, inform him.

MIKHAIL CATAMOUNTZ
Evo Kaplan, this is Cornelius Xie de Hundan, the
leader of the Revolution.

Evo Kaplan was automatically in suspense, fully integrating all the information in his mind to process the sudden knowledge he was standing just a few feet away from the brutal dictator. He felt tense, but at the same time he had no fear. Brenda's death changed everything. He no longer had any expectations; he would just roll with the punches and fulfill his six-year contract then leave.

Evo Kaplan bowed at the emperor to give him respect whether he liked him or not. The emperor noticed the subtle and respectful nature of Evo Kaplan, who was living up to all the stories now confirmed.

MIKHAIL CATAMOUNTZ
Let me introduce you also to Revolutionary Guard
Force Commander, General Guodu Jiaolu.

Evo Kaplan turned and bowed to the general, who had more than likely just saved his life by pulling him off the intergalactic transport before Blane Jiandie could assassinate him.

Evo Kaplan had been informed on the Fast Frigate a lot of information he wasn't aware of and felt quite ill thinking a powerful spy had been on board the Intergalactic Passenger Transport to kill him and might have, if the Revolutionaries had not showed up right when they did.

EVO KAPLAN
General Guodu Jiaolu, it appears you saved my life
by rescuing me and getting me off that Intergalactic
Passenger Transport before Blaine Jiandie would be
able to assassinate me. I owe you, my life.

GENERAL GUODU JIAOLU
Evo Kaplan you earned the rescue many times over.
Your valent operation at Coy's Ridge has a huge
impact on our future.

Cornelius Xie de Hundan, who was a busy man with a war ongoing, didn't have time to dither and simply announced:

CORNELIUS XIE DE HUNDAN
I asked Mikhail Catamountz, who recruited you for
the FIRM to bring you here to personally thank you
for your harrowing mission to Arzon that had been
compromised by a mole and placed you at severe risk.

EVO KAPLAN
I appreciate your kind words.

CORNELIUS XIE DE HUNDAN
I'm also sorry for what happened to your very special
friend Brenda Broyles. I was informed by Mikhail
Catamountz the two of you were very close. and I'm
very sorry for your loss.

EVO KAPLAN
Thank you for your understanding.

CORNELIUS XIE DE HUNDAN
Brenda Broyals was truly one of our national heroes
who served the Revolution with dignity, inspiration,
and complete dedication.

EVO KAPLAN
Now that Brenda Broyals is no longer with us, I no
longer must hide what that relationship was. She
trained me to be a better spy, but she also was the
love of my life. I've never been that close to a woman
before. I hope to one day get my hands on the people
that killed her.

MIKHAIL CATAMOUNTZ
Evo, if you stay with me, I promise to do my best to
deliver that person to you or arrange for you to visit
him.

EVO KAPLAN
Thank you. I look forward to that opportunity.

Cornelius Xie De Hundan could see Evo Kaplans eyes water up a bit. He knew he
struck an emotional nerve in Evo Kaplan. Perhaps this is why he has done such stellar
operations and never complains?

CORNELIUS XIE DE HUNDAN
Mikhail Catamountz informed me you two have some
unfinished business to attend. Later tonight when you
are free again, I'm having you both brought back here
to the Tolkamere Foundation where I will host a dinner
in your honor.

EVO KAPLAN
Thank you, sir.

CORNELIUS XIE DE HUNDAN
You are all dismissed.

Cornelius Xie de Hundan turned around and walked back to a door leading to a different area where he had the general staff working on war plans and the invasion of Arzon.

Mikhail Catamountz turned toward Evo Caplan.

MIKHAIL CATAMOUNTZ
Follow me, we have somewhere to go.

The two men were soon whisked away in a limo that drove for about ten minutes before turning into a parking garage under an old looking building.

INT. DAY. FIRM INTERROGATION CENTER

They were escorted to a large open room that happened to have a swimming pool.

Oddly there were a dozen people there and it appeared they were taking a man out of the pool who had been tied up in an elaborate outfit including his eyes taped over, so he was effectively blinded.

The person sat down in a chair as the people removed the restraints and helmet and apparatus he had evidently been wearing for a while. Soon, he was sitting there semi-naked with his hands restrained to the chair arms and his legs locked to the chair's forward legs.

Evo Kaplan was brought up and asked to stand immediately in front of the prisoner.

The medica examiner checked the prisoner's medical conditions, such as blood pressure, heart rate, and a few other critical functions.

DOCTOR
The patient appears to be in stable condition. I'm
going back to my office.

Mikhail Catamountz, standing a couple feet away from the man now shivering and obviously distressed person.

Mikhail Catamountz then nodded at the two assistants attending and they immediately pulled the tape off Huaiyuansu Ka's face.

It took Huaiyuansu Ka a few minutes to stabilize his vision, as he was still terribly disorientated. As soon as he could focus on people's faces, he immediately recognized Evo Kaplan and let out an animal-like scream.

The psychological conditioning they did to the mole Huaiyuansu Ka using Evo Kaplan for this final moment at the neurological trigger point did exactly as the doctors had predicted.

Seeing Evo Kaplan's face who he knew the FIRM knew he betrayed as one of the first images after being pulled out of the pool created the effect they wanted as soon they had him babbling and telling them every secret he knew, including all his contacts and people he knew in the Secret Service.

Huaiyuansu Ka, and the Dranzonian Empire Secret Service agent who had been taken from the safe house at the same time with Huaiyuansu Ka were moved to another part of the building that had a crematorium.

This was the final act. Evo Kaplan didn't know if they were doing it to coerce him or just allowing him to see the results of how they dealt with someone who betrayed one of their spies like Brenda Broyals.

The Dranzonian Empire Secret Service agent didn't know what was in store for him; he was soon restrained and positioned on the dolly apparatus that had rollers making it easy to roll partially or all the way into the crematorium.

In due time the man was being moved on the roller's feet-first into the crematorium. He was tied down but could talk, scream, cuss, et cetera.

In about thirty seconds as his feet were beginning to get third degree burns, he was screaming and almost going into shock. They pulled him out and doused his feet with buckets of ice water.

The Dranzonian Empire Secret Service agent was pulled off the dolly and Huaiyuansu Ka placed on it.

> MIKHAIL CATAMOUNTZ
> Now it's time for Huaiyuansu Ka to pay for what he did to Brenda Broyals. We will allow Evo Kaplan to operate the lever and dump him all the way into the fire.

Huaiyuansu Ka was now crying like a baby, begging, and whimpering. Evo Kaplan thought he should just send him in to shut him up.

> EVO KAPLAN
> Listen, Huaiyuansu Ka if you do not shut up, I will shove the lever forward and put you all the way in. So, stop crying and yelling and shut up now or else.

Evo Kaplan then looked at Mikhail Catamountz.

> EVO KAPLAN
> Killing these two men serves no useful purpose. They are already prisoners. I think you have already extracted all the useful information from them. My recommendation is to throw them into prison then release them after the war is over.

> MIKHAIL CATAMOUNTZ
> You had no remorse of killing five people on recent missions.

> EVO KAPLAN
> They were tactical and strategic assets that needed to be eliminated. But these two helpless men are not in any position to do any further damage to your cause.

> MIKHAIL CATAMOUNTZ
> Huaiyuansu Ka betrayed Brenda Broyals and she was

killed. He betrayed you and you would have been killed had we not got you off the blockade runner.

EVO KAPLAN
In the future I will do my fair share of killing, no doubt. It's all part of participating in this fratricidal war. At some point in time the war must end, and the killing stopped. Honor Brenda Broyals by placing these two spies in prison until the war ends. Then we all must learn how to get along together again.

MIKHAIL CATAMOUNTZ
You wouldn't mind going back undercover?

Mikhail Catamountz put Evo Kaplan on the spot. All three lives depended on his answer, and he knew it.

EVO KAPLAN
There is nothing that says I've stopped being a spy just because you took me off that blockade runner and saved my life. It's all part of being a spy.

MIKHAIL CATAMOUNTZ
Does that mean you will conduct missions as well as you have in the past?

EVO KAPLAN
I faithfully signed a six-year contract with you, and I know that Conrad Fanzui will continue sending me on missions that C will design what I do. My contract is with the FIRM, and I consider you three the authority that I answer up to in fulfilling my contract. I know what the fine print of being a spy curtails.

MIKHAIL CATAMOUNTZ
I kind of gathered that would be your attitude.

EVO KAPLAN
It is.

MIKHAIL CATAMOUNTZ
And even though I gave you the opportunity to kill Huaiyuansu Ka, who is responsible for Brenda's death, you declined.

EVO KAPLAN
Killing and assassination for a spy in tactical and strategic operations is a necessity, which I've done. These men are prisoners and provide no value dead.

MIKHAIL CATAMOUNTZ
It seems to me they are of no value alive as well.

EVO KAPLAN
This is what I would recommend. After you are satisfied you know everything they did as a Dranzonian Empire Secret Service Agent, have that information in a relational database and in the future do a comparison with new information that you discover along the way and get more perspective from them.

MIKHAIL CATAMOUNTZ
What if they lie to us or refuse to cooperate willingly.

EVO KAPLAN
If you ask them questions after we have spared their lives and they lie to you, then I would say at that time go ahead and kill them. They have already had one chance by us sparing their lives.

MIKHAIL CATAMOUNTZ
You wouldn't mind if we kill them in a painful manner then?

EVO KAPLAN
How you deal with them in the future is of no concern to me. I need to move on forward to future assignments and complete my missions in a way that you will know I was professional and effective as well as an accomplished spy.

MIKHAIL CATAMOUNTZ
That goes a long way in resolving any concerns I may have had. However, I must admit I was somewhat disappointed you didn't kill the man responsible for Brenda's death.

EVO KAPLAN
Don't worry, I'll take my revenge out on someone you haven't captured such as the real killer and his boss.

MIKHAIL CATAMOUNTZ
I have no doubt you will.

EVO KAPLAN
Since I think we are done here, would it be possible for me to see Claudette Ramsey again before I go on another mission?

MIKHAIL CATAMOUNTZ
Yes, we can make that arrangement for you as a reward for your spectacular mission. But first I'm afraid we will have to change your identity after you have dinner later with Cornelius Xie de Hundan and Glen Zhurenshuo.

EVO KAPLAN
Thanks, I appreciate your help.

MIKHAIL CATAMOUNTZ
I have one question to ask you, though.

EVO KAPLAN
What's that?

MIKHAIL CATAMOUNTZ
How did you respond when you found out Brenda was killed.

EVO KAPLAN
I cried like a baby.

MIKHAIL CATAMOUNTZ
I thought so.

The men left the room and the building with astonishing looks on the two prisoners' faces. Huaiyuansu Ka was instantly a changed man. The Dranzonian Empire would not have been so kind to prisoners if it had been the other way around. They would have most likely killed two prisoners to avoid the lengthy legal system process that might take two decades.

ASSASSINATION

VOICE OVER
The Tolkamere Foundation on planet Zuanshi-cheng that shared the same name with the city (like New

York City, New York) was a sprawling facility and former center for higher learning.

Because many of the Revolutionaries spawned their culture at the Tolkamere Foundation, it slowly evolved from a university to the center of the Revolution government.

Since the Dranzonian Empire maintained its center of government and all the buildings and facilities centrally located at Praxisvlasia, the Revolutionaries had to build their government and infrastructure from the ground up.

Since the Tolkamere Foundation was a center for higher learning, it had significant telecommunications and data-processing networks that streamed live out to vast parts of the galaxy.

So, confiscating a bourgeoise institution like the Tolkamere Foundation and quickly modifying it as a Revolution command post simplified a lot of the communications woe.

The faculty and administrators had lofty towers to live in and their office spaces often exceeded the luxury of intergalactic corporate board rooms. In essence the Revolutions officials became spoiled, lazy, over-paid, and put in their positions by political cronyism and patronage.

The Revolutionaries were quite satisfied they inherited such vastly superior "digs" to live and work out of.

In comparison, Dranzonian government office spaces were pigsties.

Parts of the Tolkamere Foundation complex was reserved and restricted to high-ranking Revolutionary government personnel and Revolutionary Guards senior officers for security reasons.

There were other reasons, such as preventing the masses from discovering they were living quite well, when the majority of the Revolutionary Empire was living modestly and paying hefty taxes to support the insurrection and toppling of the Dranzonian government.

In one of these luxury high rises, Evo Kaplan was taken so he could rest and freshen up. He knew there was a possibility there would be some media coverage, which meant the Dranzonian government would soon see him socializing with Cornelius Xie de Hundan and Glen Zhurenshuo.

Evo Kaplan didn't know it yet, but he would also soon be standing face to face with what was considered the most powerful war lord in the galaxy since Cornelius Xie de Hundan's promotion, that being General Guodu Jiaolu.

He thought it was rather kind of ironic he was being exposed as a Revolutionary Empire national hero, which would immediately filter back to the Dranzonian Empire Secret Service. But he knew this identity would probably end tonight. And he was alright.

In the private settings of the ivory tower, Evo Kaplan was placed in with a couple of bodyguards. Several scanty clad women were brought in to help with Evo Kaplan's rest and relaxation.

One of the ladies suggested Evo Kaplan take a nice hot bath before she gave him a massage. Evo Kaplan felt kind of grimy and readily agreed. He was soon in a large tub with side jets for a massage that could hold six people easily. He was quite surprised as the two women now alone with him disrobed and got in the tub with him now full of bubbles smelling really good and started to massage him right in the tub.

These lovely women started doing massage therapy for him like he never experienced before. The particular bubble massage they were doing surpassed any concept of a NURU massage because his body was reacting to the chemicals in the soap that in addition created the bubbles but gave him somewhat of a narcotic effect.

PLEASURE ASSISTANT
I need to wash your hair and prepare it for the hairdresser later.

EVO KAPLAN
Alright.

Even though Evo Kaplan was semi-stressed and fatigued before entering the tub, he soon felt fully rejuvenated and responded quite happily to the treatment the women gave him. The women did not push sex onto him, but their instructions were to please him if he so desired, which they were more than happy to do since Cornelius Xie de Hundan treated them with spectacular gifts and rewards quite often if they did such acts for his special guests.

Evo Kaplan wasn't interested in these two women; he was more concerned about seeing Claudette Ramsey, whom he had some emotional attachment to, because a spy's life was often nearly finished at any moment in time. He would like to see her again at least one more time.

EVO KAPLAN
Would it be possible for me to get out, dry off, and just
lay down and take a nap?

PLEASURE ASSISTANT
Sure, but we must wake you up in a couple hours so
you can dress and be ready for the festivities.

EVO KAPLAN
Two hours will be good.

One of the women got out of the tub and announced.

PLEASURE ASSISTANT
Evo Kaplan, please remain in the tub a short while we
dry off and put our clothes back on.

Evo waited patiently, noting these women's nude bodies were flawless. Moments later one of the two pleasure technicians announced:

PLEASURE ASSISTANT
Let us help you stand up.

The two women seemed to be unusually strong for such petite looking women. They stood Evo Kaplan with ease, wrapped a towel around him, and the other said, "Let me dry your hair," as she then toweled his hair, drying it in the process while the other took towels to his body drying him off. A pleasure assistant soon provided Evo Kaplan undergarments of the type he preferred wearing that fit perfectly.

They then walked Evo Kaplan over to a king-sized bed and pulled back the sheets and blanket for him to get in. He crawled in the bed and found a comfortable position where he was soon resting very nicely since the bath salts had done their magic and helped sooth him and allow restful sleep. The two women turned out the lights and remained in the event he woke and requested anything such as a drink of water.

If Evo Kalan became in the mood for transcendence into splendid euphoria, they were more than capable and willing to perform functions that Cornelius Xie de Hundan ordered them to perform, should Evo Kaplan want such female affections.

Two hours went by exceedingly too fast. Evo Kaplan rested well but he wanted more. He didn't know it, but his space lag was catching up to him.

Evo Kaplan's grieving for Brenda Broyals on the intergalactic transport blockade runner took a lot out of him. And in his lonely environment, where he could trust nobody and most likely could be killed at any moment, his restless behavior, and memories he fought to avoid kept reoccurring no matter how hard he tried to block them out or meditate them away.

Just like the special assistants had stated, in two hours they had to wake him to prepare him. Cornelius Xie de Hundan wanted his special guest to look especially sharp. The entire Empire would become aware of this man, a new Revolutionary national hero.

VOICE OVER

In a way Mikhail Catamountz was taunting the Dranzonian Empire Secret Service, as he knew simply by giving the Revolutionary media and more importantly the propagandists access to Evo Kaplan, the enemy would immediately know who it was, especially since they had an agent on the intergalactic transport poised to kill him.

Another situation he knew the Dranzonian Empire Secret Service were acutely aware of, the man who betrayed Evo Kaplan and Brenda Broyals was in the hands of the Revolutionaries and was most likely being coerced into revealing all their contacts and associates, plus operational guidance in procedures, methods, and materials.

The Dranzonians scored a big hit on Brenda Broyals, but the price they had to pay was just now being added up. One thing they fully understood as they researched Evo Kaplan deeper and deeper, his former supervisor Reginald Heiqishi had indeed misrepresented him in the purge and as the facts were expunged, it appears they in the process gave the enemy a deadly agent.

As the Dranzonians started tallying up the potential espionage and sabotage Evo Kaplan had already done along with the number of assassinations, including

Reginald Heiqishi, they now speculated Evo Kaplan had performed, the results were overwhelmingly catastrophic.

If they sent out more hit teams, there was a growing concern that a person who took his lover's death personal might be much harder to kill than the price they were willing to pay.

Someone with a little common sense suggested that concern initially got a lot of negative responses, but at a much higher level, it became quite an astonishing decision. Of course, those throughout the agency would never have any way of knowing Randolph Spencer's involvement.

VOICE OVER

The bankers on Zanziltar were starting to sweat Revolutionaries might win the Civil War. Their biggest fears were somewhat based on fact, is that everyone had a price. And they were always looking for information from policy makers what their next move was.

Someone close to Cornelius Xie de Hundan and in the inner circle who had stored his wealth in Randolph Spencer's bank, vacationing and traveling through Zanziltar to get to a premier planet only as a guise to do his banking, was afraid his own fortune would be confiscated as a result and wiped out.

In a private discussion with Randolph Spencer, the revolutionary official informed Randolph Spencer about the details of the Revolutionaries' long-range plans.

The Revolutionaries would confiscate Zanziltar banks as soon as the war was over, and they achieved a unilateral surrender from the Dranzonian Empire.

Astute Revolutionaries such as Conrad Fanzui and Mikhail Catamountz realized that if Cornelius Xie de Hundan seized the Zanziltar banks, there really would be a second Revolution, as too many powerful people would be hurt and want to overthrow it and return all of it to the Dranzonians. Then all would be lost.

What really mattered was how Glen Zhurenshuo

would respond when they discussed the ramifications of confiscating all the Zanziltar banks.

While Evo Kaplan was sleeping restfully those couple of hours, a meeting was held.

Randolph Spencer, acting as a go-between met with the Dranzonian Secret Service Agent Hari Nuvrean in his bank office headquarters, where he knew no bugs could be planted and would be detected immediately if they were.

Randolph Spencer made a proposal to Hari Nuvrean an idea that Conrad Fanzui and Mikhail Catamountz jointly came up with and soon had Glen Zhurenshuo tacit approval.

Evo Kaplan would be given a laser pistol tonight and he would kill Cornelius Xie de Hundan. Krawz Almarip, who was still in the FIRM's custody, kept in really good shape and condition, would be brought to Zuanshi-cheng on a high-speed frigate where the two would be exchanged.

Evo Kaplan would then go back to Zanziltar, where his appearance would be restored as Evo Kaplan and returned to Praxisvlasia and given his job back working for the Dranzonian Empire Secret Service that is if he wanted to be restored to his past life.

Evo Kaplan still had Krawz Almarip's identity; even the palm prints were transferred with 3D biological printing.

After two hours of rest, Evo Kaplan was awakened and being pampered in his dress, hair style, manicured, shaved, teeth cleaned by professionals, and showered with exotic cologne that would make every woman nearby instantly horny.

Evo Kaplan received the royal treatment and when the professionals were complete and he was ready to be escorted to dinner, Mikhail Catamountz arrived.

MIKHAIL CATAMOUNTZ
I need to take you somewhere for a few minutes for a quick discussion about the evening and the plans.

Mikhail Catamountz and Evo Kaplan left the building and were soon on a VTOL Skycar that quickly took them to a safe house. People within the government had to protect themselves from the government, especially a dictator. This was one of those use-once safe houses and never go back. It was that crucial they gladly lost this valuable safe house asset for this meeting and subsequent operation.

Once inside the safehouse alone, Mikhail Catamountz started the discussion.

MIKHAIL CATAMOUNTZ
Evo Kaplan, the FIRM is willing to make a deal with you.

EVO KAPLAN
What kind of deal?

MIKHAIL CATAMOUNTZ
How would you like to have your contract torn up and
returned to the Dranzonian Empire fully restored as Evo
Kaplan?

EVO KAPLAN
That couldn't be possible. I would be immediately arrested
and executed.

MIKHAIL CATAMOUNTZ
We have made a deal with them. We are going to ask you to
do an extraordinary task, that is additionally important for
us, but it is also even more important for the Dranzonian
Empire. That's why they agreed all the way to the top.

Evo, fearing this was going to be an extraordinary event, was suddenly not feeling safe or exuberant any longer. He knew such an incredible deal had to involve some real heavy-duty actions. He also knew this would most likely be the absolute worst mission of his entire career.

Mikhail Catamountz handed Evo Kaplan one of the new styles, miniature laser pistols that had incredible power.

EVO KAPLAN
I've used one of these TOP SECRET MXL-55 laser pistols
before. They were only good for three shots, but they
would burn a big hole through the person they shot and
instant death.

> MIKHAIL CATAMOUNTZ
> Correct. This will fit well in your suit. It's designed with a
> special pocket to evade sensors.

Evo Kaplan knew this laser pistol model well. It was one of the super top secret MXL-55 laser pistols, designed by the Dranzonian Empire Secret Service for their agents going into extremely dangerous situations. Sadly, Evo Kaplan discovered that technology had already been compromised.

> EVO KAPLAN
> When I used one of these MXL-55 laser pistols in the past.
> They are considered state secrets.

> MIKHAIL CATAMOUNTZ
> We get our toys from wherever we can.

> EVO KAPLAN
> Who do you want me to kill?

> MIKHAIL CATAMOUNTZ
> Cornelius Xie de Hundan.

Evo Kaplan was now starting to really wonder whose side he was on. It no longer made any sense.

> EVO KAPLAN
> If I kill Cornelius Xie de Hundan, I'm a dead man. Why
> should I want to do that?

> MIKHAIL CATAMOUNTZ
> We are bringing Krawz Almarip here. He will arrive in
> plenty of time to switch with you. You will kill Cornelius Xie
> de Hundan with this ultra-small laser pistol, immediately
> drop it to the floor, and raise your hands.

> EVO KAPLAN
> That means I'm a dead man.

> MIKHAIL CATAMOUNTZ
> We have a good plan that will keep you alive.

> EVO KAPLAN
> And what exactly is that?

MIKHAIL CATAMOUNTZ
We will give you a special pill to then bite and swallow
that will knock you out and put you in a coma. You
will be placed in a hospital in an intensive care room.

EVO KAPLAN
I will be very vulnerable then and easy to kill to hush
me up.

MIKHAIL CATAMOUNTZ
While you are still unconscious, your body will be
quickly switched with the real Krawz Almarip, who
will have serious memory loss because of the drugs
he'll receive.

EVO KAPLAN,
Well that makes me feel a little better about the plan.

MIKHAIL CATAMOUNTZ
You will be taken back to our Zanziltar facility and
restored to Evo Kaplan.

EVO KAPLAN
Why would you do that?

MIKHAIL CATAMOUNTZ
We'll then take you to the space port and send you
back to Praxisvlasia, where the top leaders have given
you clemency and will tell those below them all the
things you did were part of an elaborate plan to get to
Cornelius Xie de Hundan so that you could kill him in
the role of a double spy.

EVO KAPLAN
Does that mean I'll be able to see Claudette Ramsey
again?

MIKHAIL CATAMOUNTZ
Sure, why not?

EVO KAPLAN
If I do this for you, I'm retiring as a spy. I'm not going
to work for the Dranzonians. I would rather spend my
time with Claudette Ramsey.

MIKHAIL CATAMOUNTZ
In a way that makes me feel good that we would not have to spar in the future because you are a good spy and if you were working for the Dranzonian Empire, you would be a serious problem for us.

EVO KAPLAN
Thanks for the adventure, but after this I like the idea of being retired and enjoying precious hours with Claudette Ramsey.

MIKHAIL CATAMOUNTZ
A well-earned retirement I will say.

EVO KAPLAN
It's too bad Brenda Broyals isn't here to enjoy it with me.

MIKHAIL CATAMOUNTZ
Evo, I'm sorry to inform you she would not have given up the spy business to be with you. It was in her blood.

Pause for effect. Music Soundtrack with superior psychoacoustics exploitation ensonifies the moment.

Note to the director and cinematographer:

This moment during the pause for effect requires superior music soundtrack and psychoacoustic exploitation that must be done with great effect.

The 2019 academy award winner for best movie by the Korean film director Bong Joon-ho in PARASITE, utilized superior psychoacoustics exploitations and that's how he won. Other than exemplary psychoacoustics exploitations, PARASITE was really not significantly better than the other block buster movies, but superior psychoacoustics exploitations and appropriate sound effects gave it an edge.

The key to success in this movie will be a combination of great psychoacoustics exploitations and CGI implementation to give the actors the backdrop to make them shine.

C.U. MIKHAIL CATAMOUNTZ

MIKHAIL CATAMOUNTZ

Sure, she fell in love with you, and she told me herself, but she also conveyed to me she had something she had to do, and romance could not get in the way of the Revolution.

Another pause for effect.

C.U. EVO KAPLAN

Evo Kaplan remained speechless taking it all in.

MIKHAIL CATAMOUNTZ
She gave you up for her career. She was still in love with you when she died, but she had a mission to perform and her love for you was not going to get in the way.

EVO KAPLAN
I see. Thanks for clarifying that. It makes it a lot easier for me to live with her death.

MIKHAIL CATAMOUNTZ
It's not your fault. You too were an innocent victim of treachery.

EVO KAPLAN
All part of the business it seems.

MIKHAIL CATAMOUNTZ
That's why we wanted to give you the opportunity to deal with Huaiyuansu Ka who betrayed you.

EVO KAPLAN
What will eventually come of Krawz Almarip?

MIKHAIL CATAMOUNTZ
Since we must guard Huaiyuansu Ka and the other gentleman you requested we not kill, adding a third person to their jail cell will not make much of a difference.

EVO KAPLAN
Will he be let go after the war is over?

MIKHAIL CATAMOUNTZ
Yes, because he's not guilty of any crimes other than some black marketing, but that's not a good enough reason to kill him.

EVO KAPLAN
Thank you, I'm glad you are letting him live.

MIKHAIL CATAMOUNTZ
Evo, there are not many spies like you who are so benevolent. A lot of your peers would soon kill all three. But I appreciate your humanity, because that's where we need to take this Revolution, where our government is fair, and we eliminate corruption.

EVO KAPLAN
Ok, let's get the show on the road. Can you do me a favor? I would like you to give me a hint when to shoot Cornelius Xie de Hundan.

MIKHAIL CATAMOUNTZ
All right, in memory of Brenda Broyals whom we both felt very highly of, when I say to you, I'm very sorry what happened to Brenda Broyals, that's the cue to commence shooting.

EVO KAPLAN
Let's go.

VOICE OVER
The two left the safe house and the FIRM special assistants to Mikhail Catamountz, who were compartmentalized, also left, abandoning it forever. In days to come a real estate person would be selling it to an unsuspected buyer.

The VTOL Skycar took Mikhail Catamountz and Evo Kaplan back to the Tolkamere Foundation that had a VTOL landing pad near the building where they were scheduled to have dinner. It was almost like a dream for Evo Kaplan.

Evo Kaplan didn't know if he was being set up to do someone's dirty work, then be killed immediately. He didn't know if the pill that Mikhail Catamountz gave him wasn't being used to poison and kill him immediately to permanently silence him. He was now operating on pure faith. But strangely when he almost died in the Stratospheric Glider, he was operating off pure faith.

One thing Evo Kaplan knew looking into mirrors before departure was that he looked his very best. This whole makeover made him look and feel exquisite. And as he walked into the heavily secure event with several well-dressed ladies, he couldn't help but notice they were giving him the evil eye.

The special pocket deceived the weapons scanners. Evo Kaplan was very amazed to see the design had paid off handsomely, as he now knew there was no prevention against this new generation of laser pistols.

Before long, Evo Kaplan was seated at the table with the devil himself, Cornelius Xie de Hundan. There were the upper class of society all around him—bankers, industrialists, politicians, and people that would be seen on information and entertainment viewers every day.

The food was soon served, and Evo hoped that Mikhail Catamountz would not mention Brenda Broyals until he at least had the dessert.

It became slightly nauseating during the meal as Cornelius Xie de Hundan showered Evo Kaplan with accolades and bragging about how they had recruited one of the Dranzonian Empire Secret Service agents as one of their most successful spies.

Mikhail Catamountz must have sensed he wanted dessert before the shooting. After finishing the creampuffs filled with an elaborate mixture, including some narcotics for a good buzz, Evo Kaplan turned toward Mikhail Catamountz with a very slight nod.

MIKHAIL CATAMOUNTZ
I'm terribly sorry for what happened to Brenda Broyals.

EVO KAPLAN
Me too.

Evo reached in the special pocket, gripped the laser pistol, and before anyone could even see his martial arts speed move, the laser was burning a hole into Cornelius Xie de Hundan's chest. As promised it was truly one hell of a powerful laser with only three shots. Evo Kaplan did all three laser shots, burning a hole clear through Cornelius Xie de Hundan's chest and heart.

Cornelius Xie de Hundan then fell over, blood shooting on several women's dresses near him; they immediately started screaming at the top of their lungs. Evo Kaplan dropped the laser pistol and swallowed the pill. He took a sip of water. About the time security officials tackled him, he was already unconscious before he hit the floor.

Medical personnel were immediately brought in to perform a triage, but as soon as they saw the hole in Cornelius Xie de Hundan's chest, they knew he was dead. Laser pistol shots in the middle of the chest like this that instantly cooked the heart were usually lethal.

The security officials who tackled Evo Kaplan quickly discovered his body was limp; he gave no resistance.

MIKHAIL CATAMOUNTZ'S SECURITY DIRECTOR
He must have swallowed a poison pill. I think he's dead!

Security Officials quickly emptied out the room, taking everyone to a nearby ballroom where they were identified and questioned. Soon they slowly were let go and escorted out of the building and sent home expressing utter horror in what they observed during the assasination.

Emergency responders put Evo Kaplan on a stretcher and took him to a VTOL Sky ambulance. He was flown to a nearby Revolutionary Guards Military Hospital where doctors immediately attempted to revive him, and eventually discovered a small pulse.

CHIEF SURGEON
He's barely clinging to life.

Glen Zhurenshuo, Conrad Fanzui, and Mikhail Catamountz jointly arrived and sought the chief surgeon to get a prognosis.

CHIEF SURGEON
Not sure he will make it. His pulse is extremely
weak. We have him on life support, and we are doing
toxicology to discover what poison, if any, he took so
we can apply an antidote if we discover it in time.

Revolutionary Guard Force Commander General Guodu Jiaolu arrived shortly with his attaché and approached the three spymasters and nodded. He was in on it too and had a lot of wealth in Zanziltar and would be poised to move the body in a few hours after they tightened up security.

The two old men who had been looking at butterfly pictures in the library at Zanziltar and sitting on park benches at Praxisvlasia when Evo Kaplan was being recruited walked in wearing doctor uniforms.

The chief surgeon was informed these Revolutionary Guard doctors would be taking over the case for security reasons. Other staff members also showed up shortly as the entire floor was sealed off and all patients moved to other parts of the hospital.

Special equipment was being moved in for a poison specialist, who would oversee the treatment to ensure they got the assassin back alive to enable them to do a thorough investigation and interrogation.

As soon as all conditions were met and security boundaries were in place, one of the two old doctors pulled a case out of the cart just now brought in. He opened it, pulled out a syringe, and walked over and gave Evo Kaplan an injection.

Within five minutes Evo Kaplan was coming out of his coma and starting to respond and become aware. Mikhail Catamountz bent over and whispered.

MIKHAIL CATAMOUNTZ
Good job, we are getting ready to move you now.

The handlers let Evo Kaplan slowly come out of the toxicity, then wheeled a strange-looking cart over. It had a door to it.

MEDICAL HANDLER
Get up and get inside the cart. You will be taken down
to a van and taken to a shuttle.

VOICE OVER
Evo Kaplan complied with his instructions and got
into the cart. They closed the cart door, and he was
immediately wheeled out and taken down and out to a
shuttle, and then out into space.

Another cart more like a coffin came in and they opened it and moved a body onto the bed. This person was dressed in hospital gown and laid down and quickly restrained, even though he was unconscious from being drugged.

Another FIRM doctor put an IV in the real Krawz Almarip that would sedate him and help make his memory fuzzy for weeks if not months.

When Evo Kaplan got into the shuttle, it took off heading into space at the same time Mikhail Catamountz handed him a change of clothes. He had a makeup artist put on a wig and a hat and some dark glasses. The quick makeover went far in changing his identity.

General Guodu Jiaolu went with them, and they all boarded the fast frigate after the shuttle docked in the shuttle bay. They soon proceeded with a high-speed transit to Zanziltar that would reach a lot quicker than most people knew possible.

In the span of twelve hours, Evo Kaplan had arrived at the FIRM and was unconscious, going through 3D biological printing surgery. His body had a tough time because he had gone through a lot stress from all the drugs and antidotes.

The doctors knew the stresses Evo Kaplan experienced and went as easy as possible, extending the time of the operation to avoid heavy doses of various drugs needed as part of the remarkable 3D Biological Printing to change his facial features back to Evo Kaplan. It took Evo Kaplan two days to regain consciousness. He was very weak, as all the surgery and drugs took a lot out of him.

The Revolution Empire was reeling in post assassination incriminations and dirty politics. The five members of the Committee for State Security were recalled and took a couple weeks to arrive back on Zuanshi-cheng to help put an end to the chaos that had erupted.

A strange calmness occurred on the front lines between the Loyalists and the Revolutionaries; it was as if something put the fire out of the Revolution.

Claudette Ramsey was wondering what the disposition of Krawz Almarip was. But she had nobody to call. All she knew is they had been wrapped up in some rather significant event, especially to get a ride home on a Revolutionary Empire military space craft. Then afterward nothing but silence.

Nobody attempted to contact Claudette Ramsey. She took Krawz Almarip's luggage to her office where it would be safe because she had special cabinets, she locked up with encrypted locks to prevent sensitive customer information from being accessed by unauthorized individuals.

INT. DAY. ZANZILTAR. RANDOLPH SPENCER'S OFFICE.

Several days passed and unexpectedly Randolph Spencer called Claudette Ramsey and asked her to come to his office. When she went inside, she almost felt like she saw a ghost. There was no other than Mr. Catamountz standing there with Randolph Spencer in a somber mood. She almost felt like panicking, but decided to play cool and discover what was transpiring.

> RANDOLPH SPENCER
> Claudette, please have a seat.

Randolph Spencer then nodded to Mikhail Catamountz, who also took the hint to sit down as well. Randolph Spencer then walked back over to his desk. And as soon as the secretary shut the door offering them privacy, it all unfolded.

> RANDOLPH SPENCER
> Mr. Catamountz has something to tell you about Krawz Almarip.

Claudette turned to Mikhail Catamountz, intently observing his every word with great interest.

> MIKHAIL CATAMOUNTZ
> We assume that since you had your experience on intergalactic transport you knew that Krawz Almarip was probably involved in a lot of serious matters.

CLAUDETTE RAMSEY
That became quite apparent when you took us off the intergalactic Passenger Transport.

MIKHAIL CATAMOUNTZ
Indeed, he was. For your own safety we can't reveal what that was all about, other than to say it was a rather extraordinary event for an extraordinary man.

CLAUDETTE RAMSEY
I quickly came to that conclusion.

MIKHAIL CATAMOUNTZ
In the business that Krawz Almarip is in, he has had to undergo significant cosmetic surgery. In essence, he's a spy. Or shall I say, he was.

CLAUDETTE RAMSEY
What does that mean?

MIKHAIL CATAMOUNTZ
As part of a remarkable mission Krawz Almarip just successfully concluded, which was of grave importance to the Empire, as a reward for this extraordinary achievement, he's officially retired and will no longer face risk like he has in the past.

CLAUDETTE RAMSEY
Mr. Catamountz, may I ask you why you are telling me all this?

MIKHAIL CATAMOUNTZ
The reason why I'm coming to you is to inform you that first and foremost, who you knew as Krawz Almarip is truly in love with you. You are all that matters to him in his life. He puts you above everything else.

As Claudette Ramsey listened, she suddenly got slightly emotional; hearing these powerful words from a third party added a significant impact to the statements. Krawz Almarip must have felt strongly about me by divulging it to Mr. Catamountz.

MIKHAIL CATAMOUNTZ
The reason why I've come here today is to inform you he has received cosmetic surgery. He has been given back his original identity. His real name is Evo Kaplan.

CLAUDETTE RAMSEY
Will I get to see him again?

MIKHAIL CATAMOUNTZ
He doesn't know you are here, but Mr. Spencer and I felt you knowing the whole story that you would trust meeting a person who looked different than a person you saw just a few days ago. We asked him to come here so that you will see him and know it's really Evo Kaplan who you knew as Krawz Almarip. He's not a fake; it's the real Evo Kaplan who loves you dearly.

CLAUDETTE RAMSEY
What about our future?

MIKHAIL CATAMOUNTZ
We will not interfere with your relationship with Evo Kaplan and what you two decide to do with the rest of your lives, but I felt it would only be fair for you to know that's the real person you got to know and had a significant relationship in your life, even though he does not look like the person you met.

CLAUDETTE RAMSEY
I could imagine he looks different if he had significant cosmetic surgery.

MIKHAIL CATAMOUNTZ
Are you okay with this?

CLAUDETTE RAMSEY
Sure, I want to see him and look into his eyes

A moment later the secretary knocked on the door and opened it.

ANNE (RANDOLPH SPENCRE'S SECRETARY)
Mr. Spencer, there is a gentleman, Evo Kaplan, you requested visit you. He's in the lobby. Would you like me to invite him in?

RANDOLPH SPENCER
Yes Anne, bring him in.

A moment later, Evo Kaplan, appearing exactly how Mikhail Catamountz first saw him during recruiting back at Praxisvlasia walked into the office. There was a charged atmosphere between Randolph Spencer and Evo Kaplan because they both knew Randolph had contracted Reginald Heiqishi's assassination and Randolph knew Evo Kaplan did Reginald Heiqishi's killing.

Evo Kaplan looked away from Randolph Spencer, realizing he was responsible for his return to society and the termination of his six-year contract early. But he paid dearly. He then focused his interest on Claudette Ramsey, who stared at him and burned holes through his eyes to the back of his head because her stare was so intense.

The atmosphere got stranger by the minute as the two intimate lovers looked at each other. It was anyone's guess how it would turn out.

CLAUDETTE RAMSEY
Is that really you?

EVO KAPLAN
Yes. This is the real me. I've been unmasked. You now
know the real me.

CLAUDETTE RAMSEY
No, I will never know the real you, but that's okay. I
know enough about you. It might take a while to get
used to your new looks.

EVO KAPLAN
These are my old looks.

CLAUDETTE RAMSEY
That too.

Claudette Ramsey turned to Mikhail Catamountz.

CLAUDETTE RAMSEY
I need to thank you for saving Evo Kaplan's life and
also being here today to make sure I knew he wasn't
an imposter.

MIKHAIL CATAMOUNTZ
Evo Kaplan has done a lot for me. I owe him a lot
more than this.

CLAUDETTE RAMSEY
If you wouldn't mind, Mr. Spencer, I would like to request permission to take the rest of the day off.

RANDOLPH SPENCER
Claudette, please take the rest of the day off. You have been through a lot lately.

CLAUDETTE RAMSEY
Thank you, Mr. Spencer.

CLAUDETTE RAMSEY
Evo, your luggage is in my office. Let's go down there so I can give it to you.

EVO KAPLAN
Sure.

Evo turned to Mikhail Catamountz.

EVO KAPLAN
Mr. Catamountz, you did a lot for me, and you helped me when I was in great deal of need. I hope that I paid back to you for all the good things you did for me and improved my life.

MIKHAIL CATAMOUNTZ
Evo Kaplan, I've been paid back ten-fold with your efforts. You are an extraordinary individual, and you will be sorely missed.

Evo Kaplan held out his hand to Mikhail Catamountz.

EVO KAPLAN
I will always admire you, Mr. Catamountz. You and I know what you pulled off. I don't know what to say other than I was fortunate working with the very best probably that ever lived. I learned a lot from you.

MIKHAIL CATAMOUNTZ
A teacher's proudest moment is to see his student achieve. You make me proud.

Mikhail Catamountz shook hands with Evo Kaplan, then Claudette Ramsey and Evo Kaplan departed Randolph Spencer's office.

The two first stopped in Claudette Ramsey's office where she unlocked her secure cabinets and removed the three pieces of luggage.

EVO KAPLAN
I have a lot of credits in one of those suitcases. Do you
think we have enough time where I can deposit them?

CLAUDETTE RAMSEY
Sure, we'll go down to the lobby and get an executive
banker to open you an account and make the deposit.

Randolph Spencer's bank was not surprised anytime someone came in with a large number of credits because they were known as one of the easier banks to launder money. The executive banker took the couple into his office where they were able to set up the account.

INT. DAY. ZANZILTAR RANDOLPH SPENCER'S BANK EXECUTIVE BANKER'S OFFICE.

EXECUTIVE BANKER
How much money do you wish to deposit, sir?

EVO KAPLAN
I've never counted it. I just know it's a lot of money.

The executive banker wasn't quite ready for what unfolded but having Claudette Ramsey there helped smooth the way considerably.

They pulled out the credits and the banker rolled the cash value of the credit into an account. The first token contained 250,000 intergalactic credits.

As Evo handed the executive banker the next ten credit tokens, they all contained 250,000 credits each. And they still had a good-sized bag left to empty. Claudette Ramsey was slowly becoming seriously astonished halfway into the bag. Five hundred thousand credits were really getting this executive banker quite animated. Before the bag was half empty, Claudette Ramsey realized Evo Kaplan was a very wealthy man. He didn't need her; he had his own money! He just wanted her! And now she had a whole new outlook. After all the credits were accounted for, Evo asked the question.

EVO KAPLAN
Can I put a designated person to receive all these funds
if I'm suddenly deceased?

EXECUTIVE BANKER
Certainly, but that person will have to come into the
bank and sign a form for us.

EVO KAPLAN
She's here already. Claudette Ramsey.

Claudette was so shaken by Evo Kaplan's generosity and devotion during such a short whirlwind love affair, she suddenly broke down and started crying. It was an emotional moment, but she soon regained her composure and signed the documents. The executive banker had never witnessed such an astonishing event in his life.

The couple left the bank afterward and Claudette took Evo Kaplan to her home where they could spend some private time. Claudette, who was already somewhat wealthy from bonuses and incentive pay from customers, had a maid, Elsie, whom she sent home for the rest of the day.

INT. DAY. ZANZILTAR. CLAUDETTE RAMSEY'S HOME.

Claudette's luxury home was void of one thing: a full-time male component. Perhaps, finally, one had arrived. The lovemaking was incredible, and it did not take long for Claudette to become accustomed to Evo Kaplan's looks.

Evo Kaplan was relieved concerning one item: He had made a fortune, although ill gotten, and he also had a female to give it all to in the case something happened to him. He was ready for the inevitable.

After a few days, Mikhail Catamountz sent the two old guys to visit Evo Kaplan to remind him that his ticket was paid for a trip back to Praxisvlasia. His safe passage was guaranteed by both parties (Revolutionaries and Dranzonians). But as Evo Kaplan thought about it more and more, Evo Kaplan realized, he was best suited to stay in Sanctuary City, Zanziltar.

Evo Kaplan conveyed to the two old gentlemen.

EVO KAPLAN
I do not feel I could trust the Dranzonian Empire.

OLD GENGLEMEN
Why makes you think that?

EVO KAPLAN
It just did not add up to me. The Dranzonians will simply allow me to be restored in view of the fact they probably knew by now I probably killed Reginald Heiqishi and was involved in Terrshey Wate's disappearance.

OLD GENGLEMEN
They have sent through top diplomatic channels a certified legal binding copy of your restoration and pardon.

EVO KAPLAN
If they discovered I stole the Dranzonian Empire's new proton gravity disrupter weapon plans, they might not fulfill their end of the bargain.

OLD GENGLEMEN
But we have their guarantee.

EVO KAPLAN
I've had singlehandedly done too much damage. It means I might have to sleep with one eye open the rest of my life.

OLD GENGLEMEN
How do you feel about the Revolution?

EVO KAPLAN
I have no reason to fear the Revolutionaries. I've done a lot for them.

The old man suddenly started smiling.

OLD GENGLEMEN
I think I have an idea.

EVO KAPLAN
May I ask what's your idea?

OLD GENGLEMEN
You could permanently move to some far away world like Shen de Huayuan where we can protect you. But first you will have to go through an identification change.

EVO KAPLAN
May I ask what's your name?

OLD GENGLEMEN
I'm Earls.

EVO KAPLAN
Mr. Earls, could you please inform Mr. Catamountz I
would like to have a meeting with him.

MR. EARLS
I shall inform Mr. Catamountz right away.

EVO KAPLAN
Thank you, Mr. Earls.

The two gentlemen left, and soon Claudette Ramsey was looking at Evo Kaplan.

CLAUDETTE RAMSEY
Why do you wish to talk with Mr. Catamountz?

Claudette Ramsey appeared slightly animated, if not showing slight irritation.

EVO KAPLAN
I think I want to change my identity again.

CLAUDETTE RAMSEY
Why?

EVO KAPLAN
I think Evo Kaplan is too well recognized by too many
people, and if I'm going to disappear, I need to become
someone else.

CLAUDETTE RAMSEY
You'll arrange that through Catamountz?

EVO KAPLAN
Yes, I can pay for it myself. I don't need to do a quid
pro quo to obtain it.

CLAUDETTE RAMSEY
But you are out of the spy business, correct?

EVO KAPLAN
Definitely.

In a while Evo Kaplan also decided to divulge his intentions to Claudette.

EVO KAPLAN
I've decided I'm going to permanently move to Shen de Huayuan. With my wealth, I can live well there and be away from most of the turmoil that exists in this ongoing civil war.

CLAUDETTE RAMSEY
I can't move to Shen de Huayuan. My life is here in Zanziltar.

EVO KAPLAN
You can come and visit me as often as you wish.

CLAUDETTE RAMSEY
Maybe in a few more years I can retire and think about moving there.

EVO KAPLAN
I'll be waiting for you. I have nowhere else to go.

The rest of their day was anticlimactic, as the two pondered each other and the fractures and stresses imposed on long distance relationships.

It really wasn't what Claudette Ramsey wanted. But she instinctively knew Evo Kaplan's calculations and perceptions had derived the need to leave his Sanctuary City Zanziltar. Perhaps he felt he needed to leave to stay alive?

Later in the afternoon, Earls returned and met with Evo Kaplan.

MR. EARLS
Here's a communicator token for a special connection. Mr. Catamountz asked me to give this to you and you may contact him using that token. Do you have an untraceable communicator?

EVO KAPLAN
Yes, I do.

MR. EARLS
Very well. Give him a call when you are ready. He's waiting to hear from you.

EVO KAPLAN
Thank you.

Earls left and Evo Kaplan would never see him again.

Evo Kaplan put the token in his pocket then went over to one of his three pieces of luggage, opened one of them, and removed the untraceable phone he obtained on Arzon. He then turned to Claudette Ramsey.

> EVO KAPLAN
> I need to go for a walk by myself. I'm going to that park a few blocks away. I'll be back in a while.

> VOICE OVER
> If one could categorically state Claudette was not having a good day, it might be said that was an understatement, as her emotions were getting all twisted as she pondered everything that suddenly transformed around her.
>
> This was not just a whirlwind love affair, it was drenched in intrigue, heavy emotions, and so much unexpected that it was seemingly impossible for her to cope. In a way she was a victim, an innocent bystander in the galactic hemorrhage of fratricidal warfare.

It was extremely rare for an individual to encounter a real spy. It was even rarer to encounter a spy, assassin, and saboteur of the stature of Evo Kaplan.

It all started out that Claudette Ramsey lusted for a sleazy man that women sometimes like to experience.

But as Krawz Almarip morphed into Evo Kaplan, she got more than she bargained for. Claudette Ramsey suddenly realized that if Evo Kaplan moved to Shen de Huayuan, it might be the ultimate solution, as it would give her some distance for her anxiety she now developed. Perhaps she would visit him from time to time. That is, unless he found another woman.

EXT. DAY. ZANZILTAR PARK

Evo Kaplan walked to the park and on the way remained ever vigilant in his spy mode. He quickly concluded spies never retire. They can never escape. There are always going to be tendrils to the spy business.

When Evo Kaplan reached the park, it was semi-empty, and he selected a small bench far away from anyone and pulled the token out of his pocket. The token was nothing more than a business card with an RFI chip in it. He held the token next to his communicator and placed a call.

This was a self-destruct token and as soon as the communicator recognized the number and programmed it into the numbers database, the token self-destructed. There were no smoke or other indications of self-destruction. The fuse links in the data storage on the RFI were destroyed making all data zeros and ill retrievable.

MIKHAIL CATAMOUNTZ
Hello, Evo. Mikhail Catamountz knew who was calling by the encrypted caller ID.

EVO KAPLAN
Thanks for taking my call.

MIKHAIL CATAMOUNTZ
What's up?

EVO KAPLAN
I've decided I want an identity change and I want to move to Shen de Huayuan.

MIKHAIL CATAMOUNTZ
You don't want to return to Praxisvlasia and reclaim your former life?

EVO KAPLAN
No. The real Evo Kaplan has too much history with the Dranzonian Empire Secret Service, and I do not trust them.

MIKHAIL CATAMOUNTZ
That's probably a good thing.

EVO KAPLAN
I think if they ever discovered some of my espionage, they would come down hard on me.

MIKHAIL CATAMOUNTZ
The fact you stole some important military equipment design documents would obviously seriously irritate them.

EVO KAPLAN
Yes, and when I worked there, they usually eliminated irritations."

MIKHAIL CATAMOUNTZ
So, what do you want me to do in regard to this move
and change of identity?

EVO KAPLAN
I can pay for the surgery myself, but I would prefer
your doctors for the job because I know I can trust
them to protect my new identity.

MIKHAIL CATAMOUNTZ
For our doctors to work on your identity change and to
achieve all the logistics associated with it would cost
far more than you can afford. And I know how much
money you put in Randolph Spencer's bank.

EVO KAPLAN
How do you know that?

MIKHAIL CATAMOUNTZ
Let's just say we have a working relationship with
Randolph Spencer. He provides us with information
and we provide him information. The quid pro quo
works well for both of us, especially since we have the
Zanziltar Operations Center.

Evo Kaplan suddenly realized he was being recruited for another mission. And now he understood the game he was in. He was forced to pick sides and neither of them would ever let him go. He was doomed as a spy for the rest of his life.

Mikhail Catamountz understood the human condition quite well. Having controlled some of the best spies in the galaxy including those dearly departed like Brenda Broyals, he didn't believe for one minute Evo Kaplan was ready to retire from spying. He was after all first and foremost a spy. He lived for the thrill and excitement involved.

Mikhail Catamountz understood Evo Kaplan quite well. Claudette Ramsey was a temporal love affair that would not last. Claudette Ramsey would not be able to handle the stresses of being around Evo Kaplan as she discovered more about what went on in Evo Kaplan's past.

Evo Kaplan and Cladette Ramsey breakup was inevitable. Mikhail Catamountz rightfully estimated Evo Kaplan knew the best way to lament the past was to go do another mission of extraordinary complexity requiring extreme valor like he demonstrated in the past. Mikhail Catamountz had more missions for Evo Kaplan to perform.

EVO KAPLAN
Okay, if I agree to do one more job for you, then how soon and how long?

MIKHAIL CATAMOUNTZ
You would be deployed in a few days as Evo Kaplan, and since you want to go to Shen de Huayuan, you can go there as you are, look for a place to settle down, do the job, then get your identity change and return there and live there the rest of your life if that's what you want.

EVO KAPLAN
All right, I'll be ready to go in a few days. But I want to take Claudette Ramsey with me to show her Shen de Huayuan to convince her to move there with me.

MIKHAIL CATAMOUNTZ
That's fine, but you cannot divulge to her we are deploying you again.

EVO KAPLAN
Understood.

MIKHAIL CATAMOUNTZ
Fine, someone will pick you up exactly three days from now. You will know it's us because the vehicle will pull up in front of Claudette Ramsey's home exactly at nine o'clock. Wear a suit with a red tie and the driver will say, "Mr. Kaplan, that's a beautiful red tie."

EVO KAPLAN
Got it.

MIKHAIL CATAMOUNTZ
Goodbye.

Mikhail Catamountz ended the call.

Evo Kaplan walked back into Claudette Ramsey's home, and she instantly had that curious look on her face when he arrived.

<u>INT. DAY. ZANZILTAR. CLAUDETTE RAMSEY'S HOME.</u>

> **EVO KAPLAN**
> I want you to take a few days off and go with me to Shen de Huayuan.

> **CLAUDETTE RAMSEY**
> I'm not sure Mr. Spencer can spare me for a few days.

> **EVO KAPLAN**
> Call him tomorrow and I'm sure he'll be accommodative.

Arrangements were made and interestingly, Randolph Spencer was very agreeable with Claudette Ramsey taking some time off when she called.

> **RANDOLPH SPENCER**
> You need some time off; I know you have been through a lot.

> **CLAUDETTE RAMSEY**
> What about my analysis on those trade deals I've been working on?

> **RANDOLPH SPENCER**
> Hand that over to Perry Black. He will finish the reports as you have already done most of the hard work.

> **CLAUDETTE RAMSEY**
> Okay, thanks.

> **RANDOLPH SPENCER**
> Enjoy your time off.

> **CLAUDETTE RAMSEY**
> I will.

In a few days after they were packed and ready to travel to Shen de Huayuan.

> **CLAUDETTE RAMSEY**
> Why are you wearing that ridiculous red tie? Don't you think it will make you stand out?

> **EVO KAPLAN**
> When we get on the intergalactic Passenger Transport, I'm going to change into some casual clothes.

Moments later the doorbell rang. The LIMO DRIVER looked a lot like Earls partner that looked at butterfly books within the library when they busted Huaiyuansu Ka.

> LIMO DRIVER
> Mr. Kaplan, that's a beautiful red tie.

> EVO KAPLAN
> Thank you. I'm going to take it off now because Claudette doesn't like it.

C.U. CLAUDETTE RAMSEY DURING VOICE OVER

> VOICE OVER
> Claudette Ramsey had an evil smile now because she realized she had influence over Evo Kaplan, and it was simple things like this that mattered as it indicated to her Evo Kaplan would listen to her comments and take them seriously. Of course, Claudette Ramsey was unaware it was a semaphore Mikhail Catamountz arranged so that Evo Kaplan who has a price his head would know its safe to get into the Limo.

Because of Evo Kaplan's new wealth and not knowing Claudette Ramsey was extremely wealthy, he had no problems obtaining a reservation for a bungalow at the Lantiane Resort for their stay as partners. Claudette Ramsey had a social profile because of her close work with Randolph Spencer which qualified the couple to be given such exquisitely expensive amenities. Based on one phone call from Mikhail Catamountz to Conrad Fanzui, Egor Pataslia was alerted to this visit and would play a role in all of it during Evo Kaplan's stay at Shen de Huayuan.

INT. DAY. LANTIANE RESORT

In a way, staying at the Lantiane Resort produced some negative psychological effects because it brought back memories of Brenda Broyals. But at the same time Evo Kaplan was very familiar with all the amenities and how it served his purposes. Some of the tourist things he did with Brenda Broyals be repeated, mainly because they were fun, and he felt Claudette would enjoy it.

INT. DAY. LANTIANE RESORT BEACH BAR AND RESTAURANT

Eventually they wandered into the resort's restaurant bar by the pool. The same band was performing and some of the Barracuda were still active. The three Barracuda were surprised to see that man again, but they also took note he was with a different woman.

As the barracuda talked among themselves, they focused their attention on Evo Kaplan.

SPARKLES
There was something about the man that had changed.

GLACEY SPENCER
His whole demeaner is not the same.

MONICA
He seems more laid back, less high strung.

SPARKLES
Monica, do you honestly think you can sneak him away from that hot flame he is with?

GLACEY SPENCER
I wonder, what happened to that blonde he was with the last time we saw him?

SPARKLES
He must have a lot to offer. That's the second pretty woman we've seen him with.

MONICA
One thing for sure, he's always with a woman who looks spectacular.

GLACEY SPENCER
That man's definitely a good dancer. When he was with his prior lady friend at the Banma Julebu they put on quite a show.

MONICA
His name is Evo Kaplan.

GLACEY SPENCER
You know him?

MONICA
Yes, now that he's back I'll get another chance if I can get him away from that woman for a while.

Evo Kaplan was now on the Barracuda radar. Their inquisitiveness drove great interest and intrigue.

At breaktime the singer Sheri approached the table acting very friendly.

SHERI
Are you having a good time?

EVO KAPLAN
Yes, may I buy you a drink?

SHERI
Yes, thank you.

Sheri sat down, looking good as ever, but her perfume seemed to turn off Claudette Ramsey, who thought, she smells like a cheap whore.

There was some acute jealousy that erupted. Women have a way of sensing other women's intentions or appetite for men, especially if it's that man they are with.

The small talk was highly predictable.

SHERI
Enjoying your vacation?

EVO KAPLAN
Certainly.

SHERI
How long are you going to be here?

EVO KAPLAN
For a while.

Actually, a long while, Evo Kaplan thought and smiled.

Claudette Ramsey started thinking, wouldn't it be so convenient for Evo to be here without me? This woman sure seems to want to get her digs into him.

Another minor irritant was the fact the bar singer floosy was at least ten years younger than Claudette. Claudette realized that as she grew older and turned into an old hag, this spring chick would be there wanting action.

The mere thought of Evo Kaplan canoodling with this bar singer floosy added to the irritation Evo started to detect in Claudette.

Shortly after the band started performing, Claudette requested they leave.

CLADETTE RAMSEY
Can we go somewhere else?

EVO KAPLAN
Sure.

This late in the afternoon, there were not that many options, so Evo stopped the waiter going past and asked.

EVO KAPLAN
Excuse me, sir, can you tell me if the Dewaltracen Gallery is still open and what time do you think it closes?"

WAITER
Yeah, it's still open and usually doesn't close until around 9:30 in the evening.

EVO KAPLAN
Thank you.

WAITER
You are welcome.

After the waiter stepped away, Evo Kaplan informed Claudette of an idea.

EVO KAPLAN
I want to take you to a nice place I think you will like.

CLADETTE RAMSEY
Sure, I want to get out of this place, and I do not like the music."

EVO KAPLAN
All right.

Evo led Claudette out to the curb in front of the Lantiane Resort and a Limo was right there to give them a ride.

The Limo driver recognized Evo Caplan and knew that if a man came back this often with good-looking women each time, he obviously had some wealth. As he dropped them off at the Dewaltracen Gallery he notified Evo Kaplan about the plan to pick them up when finished.

> LIMO DRIVER
> Here's a pager. Press the red button when you want me
> to pick you up.

> EVO KAPLAN
> Thanks.

INT. DAY. DEWALTRACEN GALLERY

Evo Kaplan escorted Claudette Ramsey inside the Dewaltracen Gallery and started walking around all the exhibits.

Evo gave Claudette an exclusive tour. Eventually they walked in front of Mathematician Agstavar's famous artwork.

> EVO KAPLAN
> This is the most precious artwork in the gallery and
> perhaps in the galaxy.

> CLADETTE RAMSEY
> Yes, it's a brilliant illustration of creativity and full of
> imagination.

Evo recalled the time he met Egor Pataslia here and what he had elucidated about the long-deceased Mathematician Agstavar's work and repeated it.

> EVO KAPLAN
> It is said there are exactly one thousand, one hundred,
> and eleven objects in the artwork depicting all the
> demons in the afterlife."

> CLADETTE RAMSEY
> Do you believe in the afterlife?

> EVO KAPLAN
> I may smell like an atheist, but I wear the cologne of
> a galacticist.

> CLADETTE RAMSEY
> What's your galacticist mean?

> EVO KAPLAN
> A galacticist is a departure from an agnostic.

CLADETTE RAMSEY
In what way?

EVO KAPLAN
An agnostic view that certain claims—particularly metaphysical and religious nature such as whether God, the divine, or the supernatural exist—are unknown and perhaps unknowable.

CLADETTE RAMSEY
A galacticist knows something special?

EVO KAPLAN
A galacticist simply thinks the universe is simply too big for us to understand with our limited knowledge. Even though it's right before our eyes, our limited intellect gives us the ability to understand it almost as coherently as a seagull begs for food when you feed them. They squawk and make noise and you instinctively know they want you to feed more of the food you have to offer, but they have no idea where the food comes from or anything about you.

CLADETTE RAMSEY
Will we ever know?

EVO KAPLAN
I think there is a time and place for everything. If there is a God, God will make us aware of things when he thinks we are ready.

CLADETTE RAMSEY
Give me an example.

EVO KAPLAN
We know all about planet Earth that lies far beyond Arzon and the Nebula near it, but Earth knows nothing of Shen de Huayuan. One day they might when the Empire decides to reach out to them.

They walked around carefree, and Claudette enjoyed every minute of it, smiling, unwinding, and becoming slowly less agitated from the singer who was flaunting herself onto Evo. Suddenly she started feeling hungry.

CLAUDETTE RAMSEY
Is there someplace nearby where we can have dinner?

EVO KAPLAN
I know of a nice restaurant and bar that has great food
and we can dance afterwards.

CLADETTE RAMSEY
That sounds fun. Are we dressed for it?

EVO KAPLAN
Not really. Let's go back to the resort. They can dress
you up quick and nice. They can also dress me.

CLADETTE RAMSEY
They can provide garments to wear.

EVO KAPLAN
Yes, their guest services are fabulous. They will put
you in a couture dress within a half an hour and redo
your makeup and hair.

CLADETTE RAMSEY
I suppose I can wait a little for dinner. I'm not quite
that hungry yet. Sure, let's go back and get dressed up.
But I do have my own clothes.

EVO KAPLAN
They have good fashion designers. Let her school you
on your wardrobe tonight, you will like it. And if you
want, you can buy it and take it back to Zanziltar.

INT. EVENING LATIANI RESORT BUNGALOW.

In due time they were back at their bungalow calling guest services. Within five minutes after the call, Inchalchary and several technicians arrived at the door. They had several carts for both Evo and Claudette.

FASHION DESIGNER
Let me take a couple measurements on the lady.

Amazingly Claudette Ramsey's measurements came very close to matching Brenda Broyals. Inchalchary wondered what happened to the other woman, though this one was slightly prettier.

Just as Evo promised, in thirty minutes they were both dressed superbly, and Claudette was utterly shocked a resort had a fashion "pit crew" that worked as efficiently as this group. Little did Claudette know they dressed Barracudas and Cougars all the time.

EVO KAPLAN
Okay, let's go.

CLAUDETTE RAMSEY
What about all these people and all this stuff they have
laying around?

EVO KAPLAN
They will take care of everything.

CLAUDETTE RAMSEY
All right honey.

Evo and Claudette were soon back out front of the Lantiane Resort heading to the Banma Julebu with reservations.

EXT. EVENING. BANMA JULEBU RESTAURANT AND NIGHTCLUB.

By the time they reached the restaurant, the line had formed, and many had been waiting a long time and apparently were pissed off. Evo was dressed impeccably in a phthalocyanine blue suit like what he wore once before. It made him look quite distinguished and handsome.

Claudette's couture miniskirt carried a Madam Zraklevin design label on it, which meant it in addition to being couture and exotic, it had never been seen in public or copied. Claudette had nice legs and the only thing most men wanted when they saw her in the outfit was the dress be a tad bit shorter.

Evo Kaplan walked up to a gentleman who appeared to be the head security man.

EVO KAPLAN
Sir, I have reservations for fifteen minutes from now,
and the line is too long.

At first the man started giving Evo Kaplan a run around, then out of nowhere a man stepped forward. Evo Kaplan remembered the man. He was one of Egor Pataslia's men who helped throw Terrshey Wate's body over the side of the cruise liner during that tumultuous cruise when he and Brenda Broyals took that cruise.

EGOR PATASLIA'S AGENT
I will escort him to the elevator.

The security manager, almost looking in disbelief and a sense of shock, responded.

SECURITY MANAGER
By all means.

Egor Pataslia's operative escorted Evo and Claudette directly to the elevator, and he had another man with him as a backup. No punks were going to mess with these well-dressed but dangerous-looking men. Several regulars in line knew the couple being escorted had to be involved with some nefarious activities to be given the red-carpet treatment.

To add insult to injury, Egor Pataslia's operative would not allow anyone else in the elevator with the couple and sent them up alone.

When the elevator door opened that faced the Maître d' and only the couple was in the elevator, he knew these people were special if security sent them up alone. Respect was pouring out of his persona immediately.

MAÎTRE D'
What name is your reservation made under?

EVO KAPLAN
Evo Kaplan.

MAÎTRE D'
This way Mr. Kaplan,

The maître led Cladette Ramsey and Evo Kaplan to one of the best tables in the restaurant with a nice window view and facing the dance floor and stage directly.

Soon waiters appeared with water, menus, and complimentary champagne. Evo also had an excellent view of the bar and the twenty barstools and the crowd forming there, drinking, and preparing for dancing, storytelling, and general all-around seduction of women in the rarified challenge of romance. Unfortunately for the guys, some of them were seduced and didn't know it.

After placing their orders, Evo observed the older gray-haired man and his two bodyguards walk to the end of the bar, where a few individuals next to those bar stools were agitated they had been reserved for someone.

As Evo Kaplan reflected, his first thought was the Mathematician Agstavar's artwork and the explanation that Egor Pataslia had given about the one thousand, one hundred, and eleven objects in the artwork depicting all the demons in the afterlife. And here he was only a few feet away, the head of the Revolutionaries Shen de Huayuan intel and spy operations.

It didn't faze Evo Kaplan because he thought this was simply his location for some recreation, eyeball liberty, drinking, and conversation. The evening moved along, with pleasant conversation with Claudette Ramsey, good music from a live band not playing excessively loud so they could hold a conversation, and the food was rather remarkable.

After dessert and cleaning off the table, the bands changed, and the dance entertainment period began. Most of the diners were slowly filing out and dancing couples and groups filtered in. The booze started flowing and in due course it was a happy time as the performers put on their best act of the night.

Between the drinks, the wonderful music, and the atmosphere that Evo created with his gentle smile and warmth and affection, Claudette was moved and transformed into a genial plateau as she ascended the boundaries of her persona into new territory begat by Evo Kaplan.

When a certain tune that would allow slow dancing and closeness as observed by the other dancers, Claudette requested:

CLAUDETTE RAMSEY
Could we dance to this tune?

EVO KAPLAN
Sure.

Soon they were out on the dance floor, responding to the evocative oscillations and resonance between the music and their souls. Romance flourished and history escaped this temporal and effervescent transcendence allowing them a period tranquility and dreamlike moment.

As Claudette reflected on this moment, she realized she never ate the mouse that got away. The cat lost this battle. She may never catch the mouse, but from time to time she would play with it just as if she had an appetite. She knew one thing that most women didn't: She knew Evo Kaplan loved her and in spite of the god-awful scenarios he lived, she had to live for today and enjoy every moment of it.

Egor Pataslia looked on watching the two lovers. He knew that Evo Kaplan had matured into a galactic class spy. He was lethal and quite interesting, as he had followed him around extensively on Shen de Huayuan with Brenda Broyals.

They had been videoed and recorded often. Their rooms bugged and filmed. He knew of all their actions and from his perspective genuinely believed Evo Kaplan had been in love with Brenda Broyals, whom he knew was now deceased in the line of duty.

To see the remarkable recovery and activity Evo Kaplan now demonstrated further convinced Egor Pataslia how good a spy Evo Kaplan could become because his behavior indicated he in no way was affected by Brenda's death.

Many people would be dysfunctional for a while, which is understandable. But in the case with Evo Kaplan, his remarkable activity included assassinating one of the top leaders in the galaxy so soon after Brenda's death and showed a remarkable skill of compartmentalizing emotions, which a good spy had to do. Spying had to come first, everything else second.

Egor Pataslia was eyeing retirement himself, but he needed to turn over his FIRM to someone with extraordinary cunning, courage, intelligence, and drive. Egor Pataslia realized he was looking at such a man. Egor Pataslia had also been informed by Mikhail Catamountz that Evo Kaplan intended to permanently locate to Shen de Huayuan. It would take him about five or six years to groom Evo Kaplan for the job. His time was running out he needed to get this turnover done and retire.

But first, Evo Kaplan had another assignment. Egor Pataslia had no idea what it was other than to be ready. His logistical support of Evo Kaplan's future mission had already begun. A special envoy would be arriving soon to secretly give Egor Pataslia his marching orders.

For tonight, Egor Pataslia enjoyed watching the lovely couple fully integrate their emotions into each other. Egor Pataslia knew that Evo Kaplan learned of Brenda's death in the middle of a mission and had he not been emergency extracted directed by the man whom Evo Kaplan himself soon afterwards had killed, he would also be dead.

The irony of killing the man who saved your life was apropos of the spy business. At first it seemed a good deal to Evo Kaplan, as it did indeed result in the termination of his six-year contract.

However, as Evo Kaplan worked through the logic of the citizenship restoration as part of the deal, he concluded what Egor Pataslia had also figured out. The Dranzonians would never really forgive Evo Kaplan and as they discovered more of what he had done; their promise of allowing Evo Kaplan's citizenship restoration was nothing more than a promise that might not be honored.

Evo Kaplan took the smart way out and remained at Sanctuary City. Unfortunately, in a place where the density of intrigue was extensive, sleeping with one eye open the rest of your life didn't seem worth it. Evo Kaplan figured out he needed to relocate somewhere safer.

Egor Pataslia did have one task to perform tonight. When Evo Kaplan visited the men's room, he would meet up with him there and pass on a message and a communications token. Evo Kaplan was just about to receive his orders and the final transformation of his life— that is, unless Egor Pataslia had something to do about it. He couldn't see wasting one of the best spies languishing on a holiday resort planet when he could be enjoying what he did the most: applying his spy craft.

Predictably Evo Kaplan had to excuse himself to go to the men's room. As soon as he walked out of sight, Egor Pataslia and one of his bodyguards followed. The bodyguard waited outside to stop anyone going in for a few minutes so the men would have privacy and not be interrupted.

Evo Kaplan had completed his business and turned to wash his hands, and there stood no other than Egor Pataslia.

EVO KAPLAN
I didn't think I would see you ever again.

EGOR PATASLIA
Nor did I.

EVO KAPLAN
Is this a social call?

EGOR PATASLIA
Here's my communicator token. Call me in a few days
when you get time.

EVO KAPLAN
All right.

EGOR PATASLIA
One other thing, you will have a visitor in a few days.
I suggest you call me before he gets here so I can make
arrangements that fits into your busy schedule."

EVO KAPLAN
Certainly.

Egor Pataslia turned and walked out of the restroom. Evo Kaplan knew it was probably about that time he would have to earn his change of ID. He also knew it would be hazardous; his ultimate freedom would not come cheaply.

Evo Kaplan went back to his table where Claudette Ramsey was there, all smiles and getting a lot of happy stares from men who had seen her short dress on the dance floor.

Tonight, Claudette was certainly eye candy. The couture designer Inchalchary had worked her magic and Claudette felt more alive than ever before in her life.

Claudette recalled talking with her girlfriends when they were out and about nothing certain floozy's showing off their assess and acting like tramps. Now, she was dressed like one and loving every minute of it, as she knew when she looked in the mirror back at their bungalow the transformation was utterly remarkable and extremely sexy.

Claudette hoped it effected Evo Kaplan in a major way because she now had some pent-up emotions, she wanted to let loose in an orgasmic eruption to put an exclamation point on how she felt and what they had gone through to get here.

After more dancing and a few more drinks, Claudette was in the mood for some big "A." She moved over to Evo in his seat and whispered.

CLUDETTE RAMSEY
Take me back to our room and make passionate love
to me.

Evo got the message loud and clear and signaled to the waiter to come over so he could get his bill and pay and leave.

WAITER
Yes sir, what may I get you?

EVO KAPLAN
I would like my check please.

WAITER
Sir, everything has been taken care of. You can leave
when you wish.

Evo was slightly amused, but then it dawned on him that Egor Pataslia was sitting at the bar and may have made those arrangements. After Evo stood up and he and Claudette were halfway across the restaurant heading for the elevator, he looked over toward Egor Pataslia, who gave him a subtle nod.

<u>INT. NIGHT. LATIANI RESORT BUNGALOW</u>

Back at the resort a while later, Evo Kaplan performed exactly how Claudette had envisioned and as they both soon transpired into a cloud of splendid euphoria, time appeared to hang in a spell like a temporal anomaly. There was no conversation; they just heard each other's heartbeats.

The next day Evo took Claudette on a cruise, figuring he was safer this time. As he observed the clientele, he quickly noted four of Egor Pataslia's men on board the ship and they were apparent everywhere he went. This cruise was far more enjoyable, and Claudette got into the grove real fast.

As expected they stopped at the various places the previous cruise did except, they did one additional stop at the Hupu Waterfalls. Evo timed the rainbow he knew they would see and as soon as that incredible view appeared, he grabbed Claudette Ramsey and kissed her like there was no tomorrow.

Evo Kaplan's behavior struck Claudette Ramsey and the correspondence to the simultaneous stimulus had a mystical effect on her as she immediately felt the moistness and the desire that went with it. Claudette could think out of the box like anyone and chose to be brave and whispered something in Evo's ear that reported the impact on her and the desires it had created. She could not wait to get back to the ship.

After the passengers were shuttled from the visitor landing pad back to the cruise liner via VTOL Skybus, the ship got underway and continued along the coastline. One of the stops at Shenhuaban de Baozang would be at an area where Evo Kaplan would like to move.

After they finished their romantic tumult and took a refreshing shower and clothed themselves, the captain made the announcement over the intercom.

SHIP'S CAPTAIN VIA INTERCOM
Ladies and gentlemen, we are now moored at
Shenhuaban de Baozang. We'll be here for two and a
half hours so that you can go sightseeing, find a nice
restaurant, or look for souvenirs.

As the passengers left the ship, each person was informed by the purser and his assistant:

PURSER
At fifteen minutes before we pull the brow and get
ready to leave, the ship will toot five blasts on the
ship's whistle.

The ship's whistle had already been used a few times, and the passengers all knew what it sounded like, as it had similar properties like a foghorn that was very loud to get the attention of other ships to hopefully prevent a collision.

EXT. DAY. SHENHUABAN DE BAOZANG VILLAGE CRUISE LINE PIER.

Evo Kaplan and Claudette Ramsey stepped off the ship onto the pier and walked toward the shoreline.

> CLAUDETTE RAMSEY
> Are we going to get on one of those tourist buses?

> EVO KAPLAN
> No, we are going to walk around the waterfront area.
> I saw some real estate offices the last time I was here.

> CLAUDETTE RAMSEY
> Why look at real estate here?

> EVO KAPLAN
> This is where I want to live.

> CLAUDETTE RAMSEY
> It looks kind of interesting.

> EVO KAPLAN
> It truly is an artist's paradise as you will see shortly.

As they walked around, predictably they spotted no less than a half dozen real estate offices that had beautiful pictures on the walls depicting properties. Looking up on the hillside, one could gather some real money living here off the beaten path.

They only had two and a half hours, but they were close to the ship, so they would hear the ship's whistle and be back in plenty of time.

> CLAUDETTE RAMSEY
> Are we going to find a restaurant?

> EVO KAPLAN
> Let's look at some houses. We can eat on the ship later.

> CLAUDETTE RAMSEY
> All right.

As they walked through the real estate offices and looked at prices, none were more than 500,000 credits. Evo Kaplan could afford to buy any of the homes. Safety was in numbers in case his future identity was ever blown, so he mentally made a note to choose one near the downtown seaport village complex. There were several homes for sale, and as Evo Kaplan looked around, he could tell no matter which one he purchased, it would take some effort in restoration.

But Evo Kaplan ostensibly would have a lot of time on his hands. He could fix a few of them up to help spruce up the area a bit to make it look less depressing to those who were used to living in luxury but didn't want to live up on the hill sides where it was obvious some wealthy individuals had homes.

Evo Kaplan asked one of the realtor ladies.

EVO KAPLAN
Could we look at a couple of these homes?

REALTOR
Sure, which one would you like to look at first?

Evo looked at a couple and picked one based on the view of the bay and the pier and was slightly elevated for protection against high tides and storms. They went there. A family was home but wanted to sell and were more than happy to allow them in on short notice. Evo looked around and knew what he had to do.

This home was large enough he didn't need to do much construction. It would be 90 percent repairs and a lot of paint. They soon cooled their heels and went to another home, then took a good look. It was a smaller house, single story.

Evo immediately knew what he could do: turn the entire house into a garage for all the different types of vehicles he would come to own and build new on top of it after bracing the walls with stronger beams to weather storms and foul weather. They looked at a couple more homes and then it was time to go back to the ship.

EVO KAPLAN
We'll be back in a couple of weeks. Do you think these
homes will still be for sale?

REALTOR
They do not move very quickly. I'd say four of the five
will be available in a couple of months.

EVO KAPLAN
Good, we'll pick one out, but I'll have to recondition
the house I move into. What I will probably do is buy
two, so I have a place to live in while I work on the
other, and when I get it done, I'll redo the original
home I plan to move into.

                    REALTOR
                Sounds like a plan.

                  EVO KAPLAN
        How do you get supplies for construction projects?

                    REALTOR
        Three ways actually: by ship, vehicles on the
        transcontinental Hiway, or by VTOL Sky trucks.

                  EVO KAPLAN
        No problem getting construction materials here?

                    REALTOR
        Not really. Shipping via the ocean is far cheaper
        though but takes slightly longer.

                  EVO KAPLAN
        I see. Thanks for showing us around. I'll be back in
        probably a month to purchase one of these homes.

                    REALTOR
                We'll see you then.

The realtor had no way of knowing if she should believe the person who might have just been fooling around and not a serious buyer.

Claudette Ramsey and Evo Kaplan made it back on the ship with plenty of time to spare.

INT. DAY. CRUISE LINER PENTHOUSE.

Just as Claudette Ramsey and Evo Kaplan were about to decide on an early dinner, a porter rang the doorbell to their sea cabin suite.

                    PORTER
        Sir, this is your invitation from the captain to dine with
        him tonight.

                  EVO KAPLAN
                Thank you.

The cruise liner captain previously advised by a couple of Egor Pataslia's men that Evo Kaplan was under their protection and that four agents would be on board for the cruise. Also, Evo Kaplan's partner traveling with him, Claudette Ramsey, worked directly for and was a special analyst for Randolph Spencer.

The captain then added Claudette Ramsey and Evo Kaplan's names to the captain's table for dinner that evening.

Evo Kaplan and Claudette Ramsey did not come prepared and dressed for a formal dinner at the captain's table.

When Claudette was starting to melt down with apprehension that she would not be able to attend for that very reason, Evo suggested.

EVO KAPLAN
Let's call guest services and see if they can help.

Just like at Lantiane Resort, guest services had a fashion designer at their sea cabin suite within five minutes with a couple assistants.

We are here to help dress you for the captain's table tonight. We will put you in the sort of clothes the captain advises us that he prefers to see his guests wearing.

Claudette joked:

CLAUDETTE RAMSEY
I hope that does not imply low cleavage and short dresses.

FASHION DESIGNER
No miss. The captain prefers to see women fully clothed or completely naked, nothing in between.

Evo Kaplan piled on with a smirk on his face:

EVO KAPLAN
Just like me.

The fashion designer opened the rolling cabinet doors to show the evening gowns. Their colors and designs were definitely eye-catchers. Even if the woman was ugly, the dresses on the rack were so pretty that it would create a feeling of appreciation to the average observer.

These were exquisite couture designs. Very few people had ever seen these evening gowns before. The designer had restrictions to never bring the same couture designs on a cruise within the year. That was easy since the person wearing the garment, or another passenger often requested to buy it. Most likely it would not be available again.

Madam, first thing is first. We must give you a bath, wash your hair, and work on your nails and makeup. We will show you each garment and then you can try on which ones you might choose from.

                    CLAUDETTE RAMSEY
                    Sounds good to me.

                    FASHION DESIGNER
          Sir, we would like you to go into the other room where
          your needs will be met.

                    EVO KAPLAN
          We only have one bathtub.

                    FASHION DESIGNER
          That's okay. Ladies first, then you can bathe, and we'll
          wash your hair as well.

The bath they put Claudette in was loaded with minerals and narcotics. If she had any aches and pains, they were gone.

Claudette Ramsey had elevated endorphin activity in her brain. Her cheerfulness expanded along with her frame of mind. The couture designer did this little trick because a happy customer was much easier to deal with than someone feeling anxiety over the social event they were preparing for.

As such, drugging the customer in the bath, it made the process at least 50 percent more efficient and prevented a lot of lost time over paranoia, narcissism, and bipolar sequences that erupt during a high-pressure event scheduled to be in public with a lot of exposure to notable individuals.

If Evo Kaplan thought he was going to have to wait a long time to get in the tub, he was sadly mistaken. Claudette's bath was not designed to soak in for enjoyment; it was a physical preparation with timing, and within ten minutes her hair was washed, she was clean and sparkling, and out getting toweled off by two exotic young women from a distant planet.

These young fashion workers' faces were incredibly beautiful and their bodies so small and sleek, weighing at the most ninety pounds. Their small size in no way conveyed their brilliance and hard work.

These fashion experts were master hair and makeup artists and would soon transform Claudette to the same extent as they had other women who soon found their mates far more attracted to them with an incredible makeover.

Within a minute after Claudette's exit of the tub, Evo Kaplan was right in there and the two ninety-pounders were almost completed washing his hair and applying special cream to his hair they messaged in and then rinsed out. He would soon find his hair softer than he had ever experienced in his lifetime, as those alien compounds had amazing effects.

While they let Evo Kaplan rest in the tub for five minutes enjoying the absorption of the chemicals and narcotics applied improving his disposition measurably, they shaved him and cut his hair, giving it a slight stylish trim to get it more in line with galactic hair trends.

Evo Kaplan was then helped from the tub, dried off, and quickly helped put on his undergarments.

The fashion designer opened the clothes rack cart, exposing suits most appropriate for the top men in the galaxy. Looking at the rack, Evo Kaplan noticed one suit that looked rather appealing and pointed to it.

EVO KAPLAN
What color is that?"

FASHION DESIGNER
That's Charleston green.

EVO KAPLAN
Where did that name come from?

FASHION DESIGNER
We could never discover, but there are rumors that the Wollenites did a visit to the planet Earth and picked up materials the Earth people stated was Charleston Green.

EVO KAPLAN
One day I would like to visit planet Earth.

FASHION DESIGNER
It's rare planet Earth in the Scullian Sector get visitors because they are very far away.

EVO KAPLAN
They're lucky they can avoid all this fratricidal civil war going on. I'll try that one on.

In a few minutes, Evo Kaplan was looking like a Viceroy or better, with matching shoes provided.

They started on Evo Kaplan after Claudette, but it took her longer. The fashion designer knew they needed to be at the captain's table at exactly 7:00, so she made sure there was a cushion in the time to make the deadline. And as predicted, it all came together, and the couple was then ready.

You may now leave and go to the first-class dining hall. Your reservations are confirmed at the ship's officer's podium next to the entrance to the captain's private dining area.

Evo Kaplan and Claudette Ramsey departed their suite and the professionals cleaned up all items before they left, including dry cleaning and hanging the previous clothes they had worn in the closet.

<u>INT. EVENING. CRUISE LINER FIRST CLASS DINING HALL.</u>

When they left the suite several minutes later, the suite was put back to ready to rent status, with fresh towels and sheets and bed made ready for sleep later that evening.

The ship was familiar to Evo Kaplan since it was the same exact ship he had taken on the previous cruise, and thanks to the artificial intelligence, the ship's officers at the podium already knew who the guests were when they approached.

SHIP'S OFFICER
May I escort you to the captain's table, Miss Ramsey?

CLAUDETTE RAMSEY
Yes, you may.

Claudette loved the pomp and circumstance like treatment of the two distinguished-looking cruise line officers.

Evo Kaplan followed a couple steps behind and was led up onto a stage-like area behind the tall bullet-proof glass wall where the captain could look out on first class dining hall and view any passengers.

Claudette Ramsey and Evo Kaplan's names were on a little card adjacent to their place settings. Evo and Claudette would be sitting across from each other so they could have conversations as well as those across the table from them.

Claudette Ramsey and Evo Kaplan were seated at the third set of placemats away from the captain. The closer you set to the captain, the higher in the food chain you belonged.

Evidently couple number one and two were extraordinary individuals who turned out to be competing bankers and knew Randolph Spencer quite well.

They also knew who Claudette Ramsey was, since she was the analyst and one that kept them on their toes as her competition was fierce and omni-potent.

THE CAPTAIN'S ASSUMPTION

By 7:00 the dining hall was full. The background music, which was light and fresh, was suddenly interrupted. Just like Evo Kaplan remembered, a military march almost identical to Franz von Suppe "Light Calvary Overture" was played by the small orchestra that sat in the area in front of the tall glass wall.

The captain and two military escorts in dress uniforms marched down the long corridor and stopped just before the orchestra and large glass window, did an "about face," and turned around facing the diners.

The music tailed off to a quiet room that had been previously loud and engaged in numerous parallel conversations.

The captain began his speech, which Evo Kaplan remembered from the previous cruise.

> SHIP'S CAPTAIN
> On behalf of my crew and I, we would like to thank you all for choosing this adventure and I hope you have a good experience while we are cruising. The weather report is good, and we expect to have calm seas tonight to make it a very enjoyable evening. We shall be arriving at noon tomorrow at your demarcation point. I hope you all have a safe and glorious evening.

Just like on cue from the side, a steward walked up to the captain and his two escorts with a glass of champagne on a velvet-covered tray and presented the glass to the captain.

> SHIP'S CAPTAIN
> I would like to toast to all of you and hope your evening is filled with joy and happiness.

He has this speech memorized, Evo Kaplan thought.

The captain tipped his glass and consumed the contents.

SHIP'S CAPTAIN
Don't rush, in three hours this room turns into a dance hall,
and you are all invited to stay and partake. For those of you
with the desire to try your luck at gambling, our casino is
next door, just aft of the dining hall with access from the
main deck on the port and starboard sides.

Evo Kaplan knew this was almost a carbon copy routine the ship did on each cruise.

Then on cue the orchestra began playing another portion of the march sounding clearly identical to the portion of the Franz von Suppe LIGHT CALVARY OVERTURE that radiated a sense of militarism, and continued as he walked past the two ships officers by the podium and entrance to the captain's table behind the bullet-proof glass wall. As he arrived at the end of the table, he bowed and sat down. The march music played by the orchestra faded and soon they were playing light music again with violin, cello, and other solos.

The captain had a rap sheet on every guest. He was amused he had a former intergalactic trader at his table, the FIRM provided him as part of his cover until he got his next identity change. Oddly enough the captain seemed to think he had seen this man before and halfway through the third course it came to him. This man was under observation from Egor Pataslia's men when a passenger came up missing that turned into a cold case. And here the person of interest and Egor Pataslia's men present again. Well, well, well....

And to make it even dicier, Evo Kaplan was here with Ms. Claudette Ramsey, a high-profile analyst for the major banker, Randolph Spencer, and sitting next to two of his competitors. Hopefully there would be no skullduggery on this voyage.

Dinner conversation was in four or five groups. At this end of the table, the two bankers were too interested in each other and didn't feel the other guests were worthy of their precious time and ignored them, chatting with the captain now and then, who spent the majority of his time flirting with the first four women, who had all received major fashion designer makeovers making them temporally far more attractive than they would appear in the days to come.

Nobody seemed to pay attention to Evo Kaplan, which he didn't mind since he didn't have much, he wanted to share with them.

The ship's captain did, however, take great interest in Evo Kaplan and out in first-class dining he also observed four men he knew were well armed and protecting this person. All the circumstances added up to this person being of immense importance.

What happened on the ship a while back was now being overshadowed by the news coverage of the assassination of Cornelius Xie de Hundan. The killer was currently in a hospital recovering from an attempt of self-poisoning to prevent capture and revealing who he worked for. Reports published in the media stated the man was a well-known mobster and heavily engaged in black marketing.

The ship's captain, remembering Evo Kaplan, wrote his name down in his diary later that night, and went back to pages recorded in the past at the time of Terrshey Wate's disappearance and wrote Evo Kaplan in the border area of the page.

One day when the Dranzonian Empire took credit for the assassination of Cornelius Xie de Hundan, and declaring their spy Evo Kaplan as the killer, he would go back to those pages and re-read them and naturally drew the conclusion that Evo Kaplan was involved in the disappearance of a man named Terrshey Wate.

The time flew by, and dinner and dessert courses completed as the music played on. The captain politely excused himself and exited a side door. As if on cue, the officers at the podium controlling access to the captain's private dining area left as well. Evo knew that was more than reason to exit, but when he suggested they leave.

CLAUDETTE RAMSEY
Could we stay and dance? I feel so good tonight.

EVO KAPLAN
Sure.

Evo smiled at Claudette, who he realized looked exceedingly attractive tonight.

It wasn't long before the orchestra started playing local compositions designed for dance with a tropical flare to it. There were ladies in first class dining dressed for such music, and in due time were swinging their hips enticing their partners and, in the process, showing off. These were not the type of songs to dance to with the apparel they wore.

Nevertheless, in due time a very nice sounding song was played, with a female singer appearing resonating the dance floor with her diva quality, which gave Claudette Ramsey all the motivation she needed to entice Evo Kaplan to the dance floor.

Because of the beauty and compelling suggestiveness that resonated, friends in groups that were on the ship took the time to catch photographs of their friends dancing who happened to be near Evo Kaplan and Claudette Ramsey.

In months to come when the investigation revealed Evo Kaplan was Cornelius Xie de Hundan's assassin, passengers who took the photograph of the couple in the background who recognized the face in their pictures were soon socializing that information with friends and relatives. They would yarn stories and embellish the evening aboard the cruise liner for another generation.

For this night, the love and joy overflowed. It was a night to remember for Claudette Ramsey as they progressed into more dancing fortified by mysterious cocktails that had a unique buzz to it. Evo thought they would have an early evening but was diabolically proven wrong by the energetic partner he had who was out for a lot of fun.

Another factor motivating Claudette Ramsey's actions was the true and genuine intentions Evo Kaplan gave and delivered. One thing she knew more than anything: this man was a man of action, had been around the galaxy, and had done far more than any man alive, and what he said he was going to do he delivered with great fidelity.

Claudette Ramsey knew Evo Kaplan would never waver in his commitment, but at the same time Claudette Ramsey couldn't possibly come to grips with the complexity of Evo Kaplan's life and how difficult it was to simply disengage from the spy business. This was Evo Kaplan's swan song and soon his new life where he would morph in the artist fishing village was all he wanted, nothing more and nothing less. A future place and time where he could have the love of his life with him and cherish each day.

Even though she was glamorously dressed in such a way one would expect a person to be more reserved, conservative, and less spontaneous outbursts of energy, Claudette got into the grove of the music and with the total delight of dancing with her prince, she savored every moment of it.

Claudette Ramsey completely fulfilled her desires in this social setting in a pleasurable celebration of their partnership and moved her body in a physical tapestry appreciated by other men watching, resulting in one or two gentlemen getting an elbow in the ribs by their spouses.

Eventually the night had to end, and they left first class dining and returned to their sea cabin suite.

<u>INT. NIGHT. CRUISE LINER PENTHOUSE.</u>

Inside the suite was clean and impeccable. The cruise line staff had completely cleaned it and prepared it for their sleep period that was to unfold.

In due time Claudette Ramsey and Evo Kaplan were in bed and sound to sleep as the late hour and fortified elixirs caused their sleep patterns to be enhanced before any thoughts of horizontal tango or transcending into splendid euphoria could manifest.

They probably would have slept for twelve hours had the captain not ordered deployment of the hydrofoils and made an announcement:

CAPTAIN (SHIP'S INTERCOM)
The ship will proceed to high speed and all outside
doors are being locked to prevent people from being
blown overboard.

Soon the thousand-foot-long ship was racing along at 140 knots per hour heading back to an area just off Lantiane Resort. The vibrations woke Evo Kaplan and in due time they also interfered with Claudette Ramsey obtaining any further sleep.

Knowing her time was limited and she would soon be heading back to Zanziltar, leaving Evo Kaplan behind to perform some mysterious function, Claudette Ramsey decided she needed to get as much out of Evo Kaplan while she could.

Claudette Ramsey actions soon left no doubt in what she wanted to do, as Evo soon felt the stimulus, she applied that created the dynamic and subsequent activity. Their lovemaking had elements of love, lust, desire, and attraction that pulled them closer together. They lived for now. They had been through a lot together in such a short time.

Claudette might never had allowed Evo Kaplan to get this close to her had she known he was a cold-blooded killer, assassin, spy, saboteur, and all the rest. In the future she would have to learn how to deal with it and compartmentalize her emotions, but for now the misperceptions allowed this transcendence into a love bonding in the mysterious ways of nature to enjoy this moment like there is no tomorrow.

What if you knew you only had a short, limited time to live? Would you act any differently? Claudette was acting and living in such a way.

<u>INT. DAY. CRUISE LINER FIRST CLASS DINING HALL.</u>

When they completed all their activity, they did their morning routine and cleaned up. Feeling a slight hunger, they decided to proceed to the first-class dining hall, where brunch was being served.

The Maître d' escorted them to a table by the window. When they were seated and ordered morning drinks, Evo had a view looking aft and Claudette looking forward. Evo observed the rooster tail the ship was putting out with its hydrofoil. The cloud of water spray was impressive. People observing from a distance could see it took a while for that cloud of water to disperse several minutes later. The wake from above viewed by an aircraft was impressive. This hydrofoil cruise liner was clearly a mechanical marvel.

Evo Kaplan looking closely at Claudette Ramsey's face and noticed how in just a few weeks she had gone from a fatigued banker analyst in melancholy on her way to seeing her dying mother, to a woman seemingly full of vitality and someone that had undergone a spiritual uplifting.

From Claudette's perspective, she had just eaten the mouse. The chase was over.

They consumed their meal in a reflective silence, both knowing they would be separated again shortly as Evo Kaplan had to go earn his way home. His identity change would come just in time, though neither of them, including the FIRM could predict the propaganda the Dranzonians would soon sponsor.

Their goal was twofold. Agitate the Revolutionaries and possibly demoralize rank and file, and at the same time spoil their asset from now on, making him a galactic terrorist and impossible to ever be used again. Even though they were unsuccessful in killing him, they at least would prevent him from operating easily as he had been in the past. It was felt that by exposing him they would at least neutralize him. Unfortunately, they underestimated 3D biological printing techniques and advanced skin grafting processes created out of it.

After a couple more days of enjoying the tropical paradise, they checked out of the resort and were taken to the Shen de Huayuan Space Port.

<u>EXT. DAY. SHEN DE HUAYUAN SPACE PORT.</u>

Here they sadly split apart. Claudette went back to her job, and Evo Kaplan went to an outlying planet where Egor Pataslia's men briefed him on his mission. A visitor arrived with the toys for the mission. It was none other than "C."

This mission was probably as dangerous as the assassination of Cornelius Xie de Hundan. He would become a saboteur.

> AGENT "C"
> You will be brought in by a shuttle to a relay station. Your job is to get high explosives carried in this backpack to the station that is guarded by several hundred Dranzonian military.

> EVO KAPLAN
> That sounds like a force too large for one guy to handle.

> AGENT "C"
> They work in shifts.

> EVO KAPLAN
> Where will I put the explosives?

> AGENT "C"
> It is believed that you will have to enter silently and put the explosives next to key component of the power

plant, which would disable the relay station, that would delay operation by at least several months it is believed.

EVO KAPLAN
Why are we doing this?

AGENT "C"
This is part of a broader plan.

EVO KAPLAN
Will the shuttle pick me up afterwards?

AGENT "C"
With the relay station blown, your only way out will be with a Stratospheric Glider we will send down to an extraction point.

EVO KAPLAN
Why use the Stratospheric Glider?

AGENT "C"
Planners felt after the explosion it would be unsafe to send a shuttle to the planet to retrieve you. The Stratospheric Glider designed for such missions would have a lot of extra life support since it would be a one-way trip with one human aboard it was designed to accomodate.

Evo Kaplan trained for the mission for a week on this strange planet on mockups of the relay station. Finally, it was time to go. They flew up to the mothership in a shuttle carrying the Stratospheric Glider. They were soon on their way.

EXT. NIGHT. ARRIVAL AT RELAY STATION FOR SABOTOGE.

Evo was brought down to the planet on the shuttle and let out shortly after sundown. The shuttle then departed. He was now on a Dranzonian outpost that provided one of the major high-speed repeaters in the Dranzonian Empire's galactic communications network.

Evo Kaplan had to carefully work his way to the relay station. The minute this station went down, there would be intense curiosity by the Dranzonians. And of course, if he was caught performing sabotage, his life would be cut short. He knew he would run into rovers on the way. He was counting on the garrison troop mentality:

They will never attack here because we are safely well inside the Empire, and they would have to travel a long distance to get here.

Another problem with garrison troops: What does a division commander of shock and assault troops do with slackers and undesirables? For political correctness, they dump them on the garrisons. The officer corps doesn't help the matter either because they are of the same mindset:

> They will never attack here. It's too far out of their way.

The commander of the garrison troops here was an especially poor performer and a career climber. He removed all risks to his promotion. One of his brilliant moves was to lock up all the night vision goggle equipment so he wouldn't have to explain any loss or worry about the maintenance. If he suddenly had a surprise inspection, he could show:

> All his equipment was accounted for and none of the devices ever got lost.

Another huge folly was:

> He didn't issue laser rifles because he didn't want them broken, lost, or stolen either. That was also a huge explanation to his boss should one of their high-power laser rifles come up missing.

Finally, since he didn't believe he would ever be attacked, he gave the security sweepers and rovers projectile shooters.

> But since he had to account for every bullet and write a letter explaining the loss of any ammunition, the rovers had to come back to the control tower to get ammunition only after they signed out for it and had a compelling need for it. The rovers and security sweepers were defenseless.

Evo Kaplan didn't know why he had the advantage, but in the after-action report it would go a long way to explain why he wasn't shot and killed.

The rovers had poor search patterns and reporting requirements. There was no responsible party really checking up on them. Some watch officers sincerely believed they all found good spots and slept out there and only came back for watch relief. Therefore, if a rover didn't report back within the one-hour requirement, it wasn't considered a big deal since none of them did!

Unlike his adversaries, Evo Kaplan did have night vision goggles on. That allowed him to travel quicker and more upright. Traveling at around two miles per hour didn't take Evo Kaplan long to come across the first rover. Because of poor watch standing practices, the watch totally ignoring his surroundings came up by a tree to take a leak (that's what they do when they have to really pee) and began urinating on the tree trunk.

The first security rover Evo Kaplan encountered was feeling real good releasing his load on a tree trunk, then suddenly, the security rover's lights went out. His neck was broken, and he was unconscious. Evo pulled the security rover off the trail and into some brush that hid his body well.

Evo Kaplan continued another fifty yards closer to the communications relay station where two sentries were sitting down on what appeared to be a concrete slab used to hold back part of the hillside. Due to their position and orientation, this would be a hard one to deal with. But "C" had given Evo Kaplan some toys that would help. Evo Kaplan carried a dart gun with a laser pointer and a night vision scope. He could load two poisonous darts at a time and shoot them individually.

Evo got into a position to minimize exposure in case the enemy turned on a searchlight.

Using the dart gun scope, he pointed the laser at the first man's neck, then pulled the trigger. The poisonous dart found its mark and the man slowly started gasping and bent over. Just as the second man looked at the first the poisonous dart went right into his Adam's apple. This man crumpled over right away. Ten seconds later the two security rovers lay dead.

Evo Caplan moved on searching all around with his night vision and saw only people on the far side of the facility, now too far out of range to stop him even if they saw him. Evo Kaplan was fully dressed in black heat signature reducer clothes to help reduce his thermal image.

Evo Kaplan walked quietly to the back fence expecting to have to work twenty minutes cutting a hole in the chain link fence. However, to his chagrin, due to incompetence and negligence the back gate was unlocked, though shut. The rusty lock hanging there appeared to not have been engaged in months.

Evo Kaplan simply had to open the gate and walk over to the large cylinder-shaped machine that was the heart of the communication repeater's power plant. He simply slid down an access flap on the side of the backpack, pressed two buttons simultaneously, and held them for three seconds, which enabled the timer and the tamper proof device. If someone touched the bag twenty seconds from now it would automatically detonate and do what it was intended damaging the power plant taking down the Dranzonian communications relay station.

Evo Kaplan also pressed another button on a device in his pants pocket. The shuttle and mothership were notified, bomb placed and would go off with a timer or if someone tampered with it. Either way the relay station was going down.

Evo Kaplan had five minutes to get away and head for the designated Stratospheric Glider landing zone, where he could climb into it and escape as quickly as possible.

Evo Kaplan sprinted carefully, looking ahead with the night vision goggles that were about one-inch thick and strapped on like an electrician's head lamp. Because of starlight and parasitic lighting from behind him on the compound, the night vision goggles turned night into daylight.

Evo Kaplan knew the route well because he had trained for a week on a simulated installation laid out almost identically. He reached a point in the road and knew now to climb up the hill from here about two hundred feet where a rocky outgrowth existed and a flat area ideal for landing the Stratospheric Glider happened to be. The Stratospheric Glider was on the way.

In his headset Evo Kaplan could hear a strange intermittent beeping sound that started out with a long pulse width that got shorter and changed pitch as the Stratospheric Glider got closer. This was an audio-cue to help him prepare and deal with surface threats at the landing zone so as to not interfere with is take off.

The beeps in the alert audio started getting shorter and shorter between pulses with the pitch shifting upwards. And just like in training, he knew from the sound sequence of the sound beeps the Stratospheric Glider was now less than a minute away.

The explosion would be a good diversion. Just as the beeps slowly shifted into an almost steady tone, a low frequency vibration began.

<u>EXT. CGI. NIGHT. NEARBY COMMUNICATIONS REPEATER SITE STRATOSPHERIC GLIDER TOUCHING DOWN LANDING VERTICAL ON 3 LEGS. 15 SECONDS.</u>

The explosion combined with the power plant failure added to a very loud and bright conflagration exactly at the time the Stratospheric Glider rocket engines slowed and stopped on the surface of the flat area.

Evo Kaplan walked over and put his hand on an area near the nose of the vertically orientated stratospheric glider that was a palm reader. The machine opened. Evo Kaplan stepped into the stratospheric glider, then pressed the button to shut the hatch and automatically began preflight checks and automatically launched moments later.

EXT. CGI. NIGHT. COMMUNICATIONS REPEATER SITE

Three…two…one…zero. Evo Kaplan felt the Stratospheric Glider start climbing into the air, accelerating as it went.

The explosions at the communications repeater site continued for several minutes and the flames became quite bright as fuel and heat from the catalytic transducers could not shut off causing the vast amounts of fuel pumping into the power plant to continue ignition.

The Stratospheric Glider velocity was supersonic within two minutes and in twenty minutes it was in space traveling near the mating zone of the shuttle.

EXT. CGI. SPACE. STRATOSPHERIC GLIDER LANDING IN SHUTTLE GLIDER BAY. 15 SECONDS.

The shuttle flew to the mothership and landed in the shuttle bay allowing it to depart the area as quick as possible, knowing military ships were being vectored in to investigate.

EXT. CGI. SPACE. SHUTTLE MATES WITH MOTHER SHIP AND MOTHERSHIP ACCELERATES TO LEAVE AREA. 20 SECONDS.

Timing was everything. Military ships were approaching from far away, and FIRM would bug out with about a minute to spare as the Dranzonian frigates were no match for the FIRM's mothership designed for speed in espionage support missions.

As soon as the shuttle was aboard, the captain moved the throttles fully open, and the mothership then accelerated at a perpendicular angle to the onrushing Dranzonian frigates.

EXT. CGI. SPACE. DRANZONIAN FRIGATES CHASINvG FIRM'S MOTHERSHIP.

The Firm's mothership quickly opened the range, though leaving behind quite a wreck at the communications repeater site. It didn't take long for the Dranzonian frigates to curve toward them, but by then the mothership carrying Evo Kaplan to safety had exceeded the range to which there could not be any opportunity for them to catch it. Had the Dranzonian Frigates arrived just a minute earlier, Evo Kaplan would be dead.

INT. SPACE FIRM'S MOTHERSHIP COCKPIT

After one-hour high-speed run on the present course, the Mothership Captain directed the CO-Pilot to make course changes.

MOTHERSHIP CAPTAIN
Change course towards the Cat's Eye Nebula.

The CO-Pilot operating flight controls in manual mode changed course as they knew there would be ambushes ahead if they didn't.

COPILOT
Course change is complete. Anything showing in the
Cosmic Spatial Normalizer?

MOTHERSHIP CAPTAIN
I can still detect the Dranzonian Frigates chasing
us and had we not changed course we would soon
be flying into a hornet's nest of Dranzonian space
warships this new Coxeter Convolver Clarifier system
recently installed easily detected.

The Mothership Captain could have flown in autopilot that would take his audio commands, but he knew the copilot enjoyed every moment he could manually fly the mothership.

The CO-Pilot concentrated on flying the mothership allowing the Mothership Pilot to concentrate on observing Cosmic Spatial Normalizer Coefficients and the new Coxeter Convolver Clarifier carry on equipment recently installed.

CO-PILOT
Random course selections will no doubt force the
Dranzonians to commit a large force to box us in.

MOTHERSHIP CAPTAIN
The Dranzonians will leave themselves open to attack
which General Guodu Jiaolu's Revolutionary Guards
are no doubt observing for such an opportunity.

Soon the random course selection placed them far away from any Dranzonian fleet ships. But the Mothership Captain decided he would have the CO-Pilot perform a sophisticated maneuver: a Copmoc-Drylunsky Maneuver just in case they were being shadowed.

MOTHERSHIP CAPTAIN
Go ahead and perform a Copmoc-Drylunsky Manuever.
The Copmoc-Drylunsky Manuever produced a Three-
Dimensional Schläfli Matrix that would enhance the
probability of the Coxeter Convolver Clarifier and
Cosmic Spatial Normalizer systems to locate and
identify any possible clandestine trailers that could set
them up for an ambush.

Copmoc-Drylunsky Manuever which was very complicated at high speed. It might also create some excess Gs, so the pilot passed out on the intercom.

CO-PILOT
Everyone make sure your safety harnesses are latched
in, the ship will be taking excessive angels.

Evo Kaplan not knowing anything about what the ship was undergoing could only vision the worst possible scenario, the enemy was upon them and this was a survival maneuver. As the moments passed on feeling the Gs from the radical course changes brought about by the Copmoc-Drylunsky Maneuvers, Evo Kaplan had significant emotions and said to himself, if I get back alive, I'll be very happy to be retired.

At the conclusion of the Copmoc-Drylunsky Maneuvers the Mothership Captain informed the CO-Pilot.

MOTHERSHIP CAPTAIN
Coxeter Convolver Clarifier and Cosmic Spatial
Normalizer systems hold no contacts. It appears the
enemy has returned to their bases.

The captain realizing his special passenger and the crew could probably use some reassurances now after what he put them through announced over the intercom:

MOTHERSHIP CAPTAIN
This is the captain speaking. I'm pleased to inform
you we are now alone in space. We have left the
Dranzonian Frigates chasing us far behind and it
appears the Dranzonians have given up the chase and
are returning to their bases. I expect the remainder of
this voyage to be far more pleasant. Carry on.

The Dranzonians were now had to cope with a much bigger issue: One of their major relay stations was just knocked out and they had effectively lost communications to over half the galaxy.

Evo Kaplan was soon relaxing after the captain's announcement vie the mothership intercom. Evo Kaplan was thinking he had not really done such a big job, but to the FIRM, it was a huge job and one of the top ten they didn't have such a talented spys available to do.

<u>EXT. DAY. ZANZIL SPACE PORT. FIRM'S MOTHERSHIP LANDS AND PULLS INTO A HANGER. 15 SECONDS. 2 SCENES LANDING AND PULLING INTO THE HANGER.</u>

The mothership made the rest of the way to Zanziltar unmolested and Evo Kaplan was met inside a hanger by the FIRM and taken by a van to the facility where he would get his just reward. His final change of identity. Paid in full.

EXT. DAY. ZANZILTAR FIRM OPERATIONS CENTER

Conrad Fanzui was waiting for the van when it pulled up.

> CONRAD FANZUI
> Job well done, Evo.

> EVO KAPLAN
> Thank you, but I didn't feel it was all that difficult.

> CONRAD FANZUI
> You think that but that's only because everything all
> worked out. It doesn't always. You have some doctors
> waiting for you. Let me walk you there.

Evo went into the medical facility and was soon stripped down, scrubbed head to toe, and put in a hospital gown and wheeled to a 3D biological printer operating room. He was soon put under and was unconscious as the machine started working on him. His fulfillment had finally come true. He would never be Evo Kaplan again. Working through Randolph Spencer with Claudette Ramsey, all of Evo Kaplan's bank accounts were changed to his new identity with Conrad Fanzui looking out for one of his best spies ever.

INT. DAY. RANDOLPH SPENCER'S OFFICE IN ZANZILTAR

The surgery and the recovery were completed in a couple days. On the third day, Mikhail Catamountz and Evo Kaplan, with his new identity of Jerimiah Clifton, met in Randolph Spencer's office. Claudette Ramsey was brought in to see his new identity. In the future she would know it was him.

> CLAUDETTE RAMSEY
> Wow, they keep on making you look better.

> EVO KAPLAN
> Hopefully this is the last time."

> CLAUDETTE RAMSEY
> I hope so, as well.

> EVO KAPLAN
> I'm leaving today. Going back to Shenhuaban de
> Baozang on Shen de Huayuan to buy a house or two.

> CLAUDETTE RAMSEY
> I wish we could spend some time together before you
> go, but I know you need to leave here immediately.

EVO KAPLAN
I'll be waiting for you there to come visit me any time
and if you decide to move there, you know you will
make me very happy.

CLAUDETTE RAMSEY
Thanks, I appreciate that.

Jerimiah Clifton, a former friend of Randolph Spencer who was recently diagnosed with a serious brain tumor, had called Randolph to inform him he was going to go to a special needs center in a few days to accelerate the end of his life so that he would not suffer the growing conditions the inoperable brain tumor posed.

When Mikhail Catamountz contacted Randolph Spencer for help in creating Evo Kaplan's new identity about the same time, Randolph had the solution for both.

The real Jerimiah Clifton secretly went away with the FIRM's help and without suffering. Since Jerimiah Clifton had no living relatives or a family, the identity switch was seamless and easy. Since the doctors had a living person to acquire all the three-dimensional reader and printer coefficients, they could do a complete identity transfer.

There were no recorded retinal scans of Jerimiah Clifton; only his voice required tweaking and was easily obtained. His dental records might become an issue in the future, so a break-in was accomplished, and all his dental records were stolen and destroyed.

Randolph Spencer, who knew Evo Kaplan had taken care of one of his problems and might consider contracting him again should another arise, asked Jerimiah Clifton (a.k.a. Evo Kaplan):

RANDOLPH SPENCER
Can I give you a ride to the space port?

JERIMIAH CLIFTON (a.k.a. EVO KAPLAN)
Yes, I appreciate that.

Evo Kaplan then turned toward Mikhail Catamountz.

JERIMIAH CLIFTON (a.k.a. EVO KAPLAN)
When I first saw you at that park bench when I was
hungry, I had no idea you would turn my world upside
down and give me another phase in my life. I've had
quite a few unique experiences since then.

MIKHAIL CATAMOUNTZ
I knew what I was getting when I recruited you. I had
high expectations, and you did not let me down. I hope
you have a happy life in Shen de Huayuan.

The men shook hands.

RANDOLPH SPENCER
I'll escort all of you all out of the building.

The group took the elevator down to the first floor. Claudette Ramsey used Evo
Kaplan's new name to get used to it.

CLAUDETTE RAMSEY
Goodbye Jerimiah.

Claudette Ramsey wasn't going to accompany them to the space port. She had to be
careful seeing him in public or she too would end up with an identity change.

Mikhail Catamountz, without saying a word, departed the group at the elevator exit
and walked directly out front to a waiting limo and its driver shut the door immediately
after he got in the car and quickly drove off.

Bank security had Randolph Spencer's limo just outside the entrance by the time they
approached the door.

The two men got in and the car drove off.

RANDOLPH SPENCER
It's good that we had this time alone. I wanted to say a
few things to you.

Evo Kaplan nodded.

RANDOLPH SPENCER
You probably do not know who you work for. Most of
them don't.

JERIMIAH CLIFTON (a.k.a. EVO KAPLAN)
I do not follow what you are saying.

RANDOLPH SPENCER
To help set your mind at ease, you are not working for
the Revolution.

JERIMIAH CLIFTON (a.k.a. EVO KAPLAN)
No?

Evo Kaplan was now dumbfounded, but this was getting more interesting.

RANDOLPH SPENCER
The interface is, of course, through Catamountz and Fanzui, but their puppet master Glen Zhurenshuo works for the Banking Cartel.

JERIMIAH CLIFTON (a.k.a. EVO KAPLAN)
The FIRM works for the banking cartel?

RANDOLPH SPENCER
That's correct.

JERIMIAH CLIFTON (a.k.a. EVO KAPLAN)
I see it now. You keep the civil war going to maximize profits and to restrain power and make sure no dictator takes over.

RANDOLPH SPENCER
That's correct. That's why we had to eliminate Cornelius Xie de Hundan; he was getting too powerful.

JERIMIAH CLIFTON (a.k.a. EVO KAPLAN)
It now makes perfect sense. I guess it's a good thing I'm retiring now.

Randolph Spencer started chuckling.

RANDOLPH SPENCER
You expect me to believe that?

JERIMIAH CLIFTON (a.k.a. EVO KAPLAN)
It's true. I'm hanging up my spurs and calling it quits.

RANDOLPH SPENCER
I'll make a prediction Evo Kaplan. You will go to that sleepy village of Shenhuaban de Baozang and live there for a while and get bored. Your enemy is time off.

JERIMIAH CLIFTON (a.k.a. EVO KAPLAN)
I've had too many close calls. This is it for me.

RANDOLPH SPENCER
Something tells me we'll be having another meeting again one of these days and you will humbly submit that I was right.

JERIMIAH CLIFTON (a.k.a. EVO KAPLAN)
I think that once I get Claudette moved to Shenhuaban de Baozang and we get our first house rebuilt and live nicely, there will be no desire to get back in the fly by the seat of your pants routine.

RANDOLPH SPENCER
Evo Kaplan, do you honestly want me to believe that Claudette will move to Shenhuaban de Baozang and be happy there? She's a city girl. She needs all this, or she will go insane. Even if I do let her go to you, I do so with no reservations. You know why?

JERIMIAH CLIFTON (a.k.a. EVO KAPLAN)
Why?

RANDOLPH SPENCER
Because it will not take long for her to figure it out and she will be right back working for me.

JERIMIAH CLIFTON (a.k.a. EVO KAPLAN)
What makes you think that?

RANDOLPH SPENCER
She's not in lust with a carpenter wannabe. She lusts for the grizzly spy that you are. It's the seedy part of you that she's in love with, not a future domesticated male.

JERIMIAH CLIFTON (a.k.a. EVO KAPLAN)
You really think so?

RANDOLPH SPENCER
Your retiring has just killed the man she was in love with. Furthermore, now you even look different!

JERIMIAH CLIFTON (a.k.a. EVO KAPLAN)
Well, if you ever take a trip to Shen de Huayuan, I hope

you can take time to stop at Shenhuaban de Baozang
to visit me. I'd like to see you again.

RANDOLPH SPENCER
The feeling is mutual.

Jerimiah Clifton departed the limo with serious number of credits for his immediate needs and would set up local accounts and do wire transfers from Randolph Spencer's bank for future needs.

Many Zanziltar people had vacation homes in Shen de Huayuan and required long-distance banking. Randolph Spencer was one of the leading bankers supporting the banking industry of planet Shen de Huayuan.

The intergalactic transport flight to Shen de Huayuan was uneventful, as Evo Kaplan felt more secure with a change of identity. He would not be recognized. Also, Jerimiah Clifton, his new identity, didn't have many friends and no relatives, so the odds of meeting one of them were extremely remote. Evo Kaplan was now about as spooky as he could be.

As part of his change of identity, a significant event for Evo Kaplan was just unfolding.

The FIRM had to kill an Evo Kaplan look alike to give the appearance Evo Kaplan was finally wiped out. It didn't take long.

Another spy the FIRM felt discovered another Huaiyuansu Ka type double spy and traitor, someone the Dranzonian Empire Secret Service had likewise purged, and the FIRM recruited, was given Evo Kaplan's identity, and set up on a mission and assassination.

The Dranzonian Empire Secret Service, despite their outright lie they would receive Evo Kaplan in open arms and restore his status, was given tips that Evo Kaplan was alive and well in Zanziltar. The FIRM went to Claudette Ramsey and asked for her assistance in being seen with an Evo Kaplan in public so they could help hide Evo Kaplan forever and at the same time they would eliminate an insider threat Claudette was not informed about for her own safety and mental health.

The chance to get involved in intrigue enthralled Claudette, who eagerly agreed.

The betrayed double spy now with Evo Kaplan's identity, was assigned to meet with Claudette Ramsey at a particular restaurant they knew Evo Kaplan would easily be detected by Dranzonian Secret Service agents who frequented the establishment, including Zanziltar Consulate Hari Nuvrean, an actual Dranzonian Empire Secret Service agent still operating under diplomatic immunity.

Once detected, the Dranzonian Secret Service swung into action just like the FIRM expected. The real Blane Jiandie and not an imposter volunteered for the assignment, as he eagerly wanted to redeem himself for his failures associated with the Arzon mission.

The Dranzonian Empire Secret Service made a fatal blunder in that they had left Blane Jiandie with his altered identity of Cap Zapatero. Therefore, Cap Zapatero was easily detected with facial recognition and followed when he arrived in Zanziltar, the Sanctuary City.

Once they tagged Cap Zapatero, they were able to quickly and systematically identify his entire team put in place to support the mission that soon unfolded.

<u>EXT. EVENING. ZANZILTAR (SANCTUARY CITY) DOWN TOWN BUSINESS AREA.</u>

Cap Zapatero yelled half a block away.

CAP ZAPATERO
Hey, Evo Kaplan!

There were only a few vehicles streaming by, as all the business clientele had departed past normal working hours.

The double spy, now converted to Evo Kaplan's identity, instinctively turned around to see who was calling his manufactured name as he walked down the downtown area late in the evening as he was being sent to a stake out assignment nearby.

Cap Zapatero and another man were together and closing on their target. The Evo Kaplan look alike spy had walked into the kill zone. Just as it was scripted, a couple men suddenly appeared in front of the Evo Kaplan look alike, blocking his exit route in that direction, and suddenly there were a couple men across the street. The Evo Kaplan look-alike spy knew that if someone called his alias name Evo Kaplan, it was bad news, and his training now effected his next moves. Based on rule of thumb, his only route to safety would be toward the two men who called out his name. He had to time it carefully or he would die.

The double spy turned around and walked towards Cap Zapatero and the other man.

DOUBLE SPY WITH EVO KAPLAN'S IDENTITY
What do you want?

Just as the double spy asked the question, he pulled out his laser pistol and shot Cap Zapatero in the chest, instantly killing him.

About that time, he and the other man traded shots and killed each other at the same time.

The other four men converged on the dead men lying on the sidewalk. Another moment a van pulled up to a screeching halt. Dranzonian support personnel hopped out and grabbed their two dead colleges and threw them into the van leaving Evo Kaplan's corpse behind because they could ill afford being caught with it after signing the agreements with the Revolution.

Before they bugged out, one of the Dranzonians verified the Evo Kaplan look-alike double spy was not wearing a mask and his body camera showed his face and the nice hole in the man's chest. Just to make sure he couldn't be revived, he put his laser pistol up to his head and prevented any chance of revival.

The FIRM purposely let the Dranzonians get away with their two dead agents' bodies. They killed two birds with one stone. They eliminated a mole and killed two Dranzonian Secret Service Agents in the process. Evo Kaplan's demise was now complete. The Dranzonians would never again go looking for him.

Blane Jiandie was buried with full honors. To give the appearance they had nothing to do with Evo Kaplan's murder, they announced his role in the assassination of Cornelius Xie de Hundan and he was working for the Dranzonians which Mickail Catamountz knew otherwise.

EXT. DAY. SHEN DE HUAYUAN.

Jerimiah Clifton arrived in Shen de Huayuan without much personal effects. He would help the local economy at Shenhuaban de Baozang purchasing everything he needed there, of course at elevated prices of a tourist town.

EXT. DAY. SHENHUABAN DE BAOZANG VILLAGE

There weren't many choices of hotels in Shenhuaban de Baozang, but they at least temporarily put a roof over Jerimiah Clifton's (a.k.a. Evo Kaplan) head and his room was comfortable and clean, though it had no amenities like he was used to.

After a nice meal around noon, Jerimiah Clifton went to the real estate office he had been at and saw the homes he wanted were still available.

JERIMIAH CLIFTON
I want to buy both these homes.

REALTOR
How will you pay for them?

JERIMIAH CLIFTON
With credits.

The real estate agent was utterly stunned, and her paycheck just got a lot thicker.

REALTOR
How soon do you want to make the purchase?

JERIMIAH CLIFTON
Right now.

The realtor almost fainted but pulled herself together.

REALTOR
Would you like to go look at the properties now?

JERIMIAH CLIFTON
No. I saw them recently.

REALTOR
When was that?

JERIMIAH CLIFTON
I was on a cruise ship that came in.

REALTOR
I see.

REALTOR
Where are you from?

JERIMIAH CLIFTON
Zanziltar.

REALTOR
What did you do there?

JERIMIAH CLIFTON
I was part of the banking cartel.

It now made perfect sense for the realtor, who now added it all up.

REALTOR
Why are you buying two houses?

JERIMIAH CLIFTON
I'm going to live in one while I rebuild the other.

REALTOR
There are some luxury homes for sale up on the hillside.
Why not look at one of them? For the price you are paying
for these two homes, I can get you into one of them.

JERIMIAH CLIFTON
No, I want to be centrally located near downtown where I
can walk everywhere I need to go.

REALTOR
All right let's start filling out the paperwork, then we'll go
meet the owners and let them know you have made an offer
of the listing price.

JERIMIAH CLIFTON
Thank you.

That evening there was a lot of celebration in Shenhuaban de Baozang as two families
desperate to get un-trapped and move the hell out of there had their dreams come true
by some city slicker, who just paid almost double what the homes were worth.

Because this was a cash transaction, the processing took a week and Jerimiah Clifton
was the new owner. As stipulated in the contract, the previous owners needed about
fifteen days to pack and remove all their personal effects.

Jerimiah Clifton noticed a couple of Egor Pataslia's men he recognized loitering
around the community. One day during lunch at a local restaurant, he approached
them as the place was almost empty.

JERIMIAH CLIFTON
Do you guys have any home construction skills?

EGOR PATASLIA'S AGENT
No why?

JERIMIAH CLIFTON
I want to hire you. Be in work clothes tomorrow by 9:00
A.M. and we'll be ready to begin.

Egor Pataslia's men laughed, but the next day they were in work clothes, looking not quite so happy. It appeared that when they reported to Egor Pataslia about the conversation, he quickly responded in a joyful manner:

Egor Pataslia's men arrived at Jerimiah Clifton's hotel the next day with a sour look on their faces and truly pissed off at Jerimiah Clifton.

Jerimiah Clifton knew he and these men didn't have the skills necessary to do the construction he wanted and went ahead and hired a contractor on the basis he had to use him and his associates as laborers.

The contractor was not happy with the proposal but when he was informed privately, they would work for free, he really changed his attitude quickly because to have three free mature grown men as gophers and hammer operators made his day.

The contractor had his own architect and any friction he received from zoning and building inspectors was magically quelled in unscrupulous ways this contractor couldn't quite fathom.

The new dwelling was built with extreme safety and security in mind. Even the concrete bunker designed to withstand tsunamis, hurricanes, or possible wars was an extravagance not expected.

Evo noticed Egor Pataslia's men were not happy living in the crappy hotels, so he got another bright idea and bought two more houses, allowing two more families to escape, and quickly had them remodeled and gave the two Egor Pataslia's men sets of keys where they could be more comfortable. One of them immediately moved his girlfriend in, who ended up working at one of the tourist venues.

In due time that new house took shape, and the impressive architecture changed the skyline of Shenhuaban de Baozang Village and added measurably to the village's image.

Eventually the construction was completed, and the cleanup and landscaping began. Suddenly the downtown Shenhuaban de Baozang area looked measurably better. More Tourists now seemed inclined to go ashore and business activity improved.

Eventually Jerimiah Clifton was able to move into his new home as the furnishings slowly trickled in via the cruise liner cargo delivery. When it was finally done and one hundred percent ready, then and only then did he invite Claudette Ramsey to visit. He wanted to make sure everything looked perfect for her.

At the same time, they started on the second home. It would be built with similar features and just as majestic. Because of the dramatic facelift the town was starting to show, real estate prices started picking up and the realtors loved Jerimiah Clifton.

Jerimiah Clifton then did his next big project: he purchased another four run-down homes nearby and immediately started renovating them. When approached by townspeople about what he was going to do with the four homes, he said that was a big surprise to wait until the renovations were complete.

Shenhuaban de Baozang Village now looked quite different as the metamorphism manifested an altogether different image.

With eight handsome looking homes in the downtown area Shenhuaban de Baozang Village area it felt like a new town.

Right about the time the second home next door to his primary residence was completed, the four homes he purchased recently were finally renovated and he took no time fully furnishing them. A family could move in with almost nothing.

He then went to visit the local school principal, who was having issues recruiting good teachers, and informed him:

> JERIMIAH CLIFTON (a.k.a. Evo Kaplan)
> The next four teachers you recruit can stay in my four fully renovated homes for just one credit a year stipulated in the contract as long as they maintain their position as a teacher in your school. If they decide to stop teaching in your school, the contract is terminated.

> SCHOOL PRINCIPAL
> Are you serious?

> JERIMIAH CLIFTON
> Absolutely. I hope this helps to improve your recruitment of good teachers.

> SCHOOL PRINCIPAL
> You better believe it will when they find they only must pay a single credit to rent one of those homes that had such a lovely renovation.

> JERIMIAH CLIFTON
> Those homes are fully furnished. They can arrive with nothing and keep their existing homes wherever they may be.

Near the end of the school year, Jerimiah Clifton gave the principal checks for one thousand credits each to give out to each teacher in the school. After that none of them entertained leaving. The village now slowly evolved to a healthy tourist destination that had everything except excellent hotels.

Jerimiah Clifton took care of that and privately met with one of the hotel owners and said he would privately fund their reconstruction and modernization. To make up for their loss of revenue during reconstruction, he assured them a guaranteed stream of income. Just like the rest of the downtown areas, a new face on hotels started having a dramatic impact on the image of Shenhuaban de Baozang Village.

It took a while for Claudette Ramsey to come and visit Evo Kaplan at Shenhuaban de Baozang Village. Evo Kaplan suspected Claudette Ramsey might have found another lover.

But the truth of it was, the propaganda that Dranzonian Empire put out on Evo Kaplan's assassination of Cornelius Xie de Hundan had a dramatic impact on Claudette Ramsey's psyche.

Claudette Ramsey now started to understand who Evo Kaplan, now known as the alias Jerimiah Clifton, really was. She loved Evo Kaplan (a.k.a. Jerimiah Clifton) dearly, but she also felt Evo Kaplan's world was too dangerous for her, even though Evo Kaplan ostensibly retired from the spy business.

Claudette Ramsey made that faithful journey to Shenhuaban de Baozang, almost regretting going, but when you are in love with someone, it's hard to get over it.

EXT. CGI. DAY. SHENHUABAN DE BAOZANG VTOL LANDING PAD.

Claudette Ramsey arrived by a VTOL Skycar and Jerimiah Clifton met her at the landing pad. She, of course, was nervous; it had been a while since they had seen each other.

EVO KAPLAN(a.k.a. JERIMIAH CLIFTON)
Welcome to Shenhuaban de Baozang.

Claudette Ramsey looked deeply into Evo Kaplan's eyes and knew he was a much different man than she had imagined. Here was a galactic famous killer everyone thought was dead, as the news media had well publicized his untimely death, shot, and killed in a shootout in Zanziltar.

CLAUDETTE RAMSEY
Thank you for inviting me.

EVO KAPLAN
Let me put your luggage on the electric cart.

Soon they were heading to Jerimiah Clifton's (a.k.a. Evo Kaplan's) home and the townspeople who caught glimpses of Claudette Ramsey were in awe.

One of the shop owners commented to her friend as they were socializing when Jerimiah Clifton and Claudette Ramsey drove past.

LADY SHOP OWNER
So that's the mysterious princess?

As they pulled up to the home, Claudette commented.

CLAUDETTE RAMSEY
This place really looks different now.

EVO KAPLAN(a.k.a. JERIMIAH CLIFTON)
Yea, we've put some work into it all right.

CLAUDETTE RAMSEY
Your home's architecture is exquisite. I've never seen anything so beautiful.

Across the street was another home so immaculately crafted that gave a glistening aura to it. Claudette Ramsey liked this home being situated in such a nice area if she were to live here.

INT. DAY. EVO KAPLAN'S SHENHUABAN DE BAOZANG VILLAGE HOME

They entered the home. Jerimiah Clifton introduced his butler, Andy.

EVO KAPLAN (a.k.a. JERIMIAH CLIFTON)
Andy is one of Egor Pataslia's men providing around-the-clock protection.

CLAUDETTE RAMSEY
WHO's Egor Pataslia?

EVO KAPLAN (a.k.a. JERIMIAH CLIFTON)
Egor Pataslia is one of the top security officials for Shen de Huayuan.

Claudette Ramsey suddenly started feeling alarmed with Evo Kaplan's revelation about his butler being someone important in Shen de Huayuan's security apparatus.

Jerimiah Clifton (a.k.a. Evo Kaplan) didn't know it yet, but Egor Pataslia had plans for him. His current setting was perfect for the cover. The town was slowly evolving into another FIRM.

ANDY
Good morning, madam. I will put your luggage in the
guest room.

Jerimiah Clifton (a.k.a. Evo Kaplan) didn't want to spook Claudette by showing any sexual demands as they had not been together in a while.

CLAUDETTE RAMSEY
Thank you.

EVO KAPLAN (a.k.a. JERIMIAH CLIFTON)
Would you like to rest before we go out and do
anything?

CLAUDETTE RAMSEY
I didn't sleep well coming here.

EVO KAPLAN (a.k.a. JERIMIAH CLIFTON)
Are you hungry?

CLAUDETTE RAMSEY
No, just sleepy.

EVO KAPLAN (a.k.a. JERIMIAH CLIFTON)
Let me show you to your bedroom where you can rest.
There is a little box with a red button on it. Just press
it if you need anything.

CLAUDETTE RAMSEY
Thanks.

A well-dressed man in a suit was standing by the guest bedroom door. He had been wearing construction worker clothes just a few weeks prior and was one of Egor Pataslia's men.

EVO KAPLAN(a.k.a. JERIMIAH CLIFTON)
This is Rocu. He'll remain outside your bedroom door
for your personal safety.

Claudette's luggage had been moved into the guest room, and she was starting to haveregrets coming as she kept analyzing her situation.

Just like in her business practices she learned from some of the best traders and wealth managers in her firm, If the trade or transaction doesn't feel right, don't do it. There are plenty of other opportunities.

Hearing the security arrangement only made Claudette Ramsey feel less secure as shewent into the guest bedroom and shut the door.

Claudette got between the sheets that smelled really good, just like the nice, clean room. She didn't know it, but she was the first person to ever sleep in that bed, as it was reserved exclusively for her.

Claudette Ramsey's mental hang-up was that when Evo Kaplan was posing as Krawz Almarip, a sleazy intergalactic black marketer, she had some lust for that kind of guy. But Claudette Ramsey now knew Evo Kaplan was a cold-blooded murderer, an assassin, and recently the most wanted man in the galaxy until the FIRM did a great job of faking his death, there was just too wide of a chasm to cross to feel comfortable being around him. She was dog-tired but could not sleep.

Claudette Ramsey pressed the red button on the little box on the furniture next to her bed, which Evo Kaplan immediately knew occurred because of the low-level chimes in his personal office and den. He made no assumptions of why she was paging him, but he went to her immediately.

Evo Kaplan opened the door and entered.

> EVO KAPLAN(a.k.a. JERIMIAH CLIFTON)
> Yes Claudette, what can I do for you?
> CLAUDETTE RAMSEY
> I'm very tired but I can't sleep. Do you have any medications that would help?
> EVO KAPLAN(a.k.a. JERIMIAH CLIFTON)
> Yes, I'll be right back.

Evo Kaplan had some pills he was given several times he kept that would provide really good sleep and a clear head when he woke up. He grabbed a bottle so that Claudette could read the instructions. It said take just one per eight-hour period.

He went back to the guest room with an unopened chilled glass bottle of water and handed her the pill container and the bottled water.

Claudette looked at the instructions as well, took a pill, and drank half the bottle of water. She then laid back, hoping sleep would come fast. Evo walked over and kissed her on the forehead.

Claudette smiled only out of politeness; inside her she almost felt like she was being kissed by the devil himself.

Love is a funny thing. It appears like magic, and it can also disappear like magic. Her little mouse had grown to an oversized rat that she could no longer play with. The situation was intolerable as she fell into a restful sleep a lot quicker than she imagined.

One of the problems of the psychotropic drugs in the sleeping pill she swallowed, though designed to induce sleep and calm nerves and act like a tranquilizer, it also allowed an intelligent person with a high IQ to have vivid dreams. Since Claudette was borderline genius, her dreams were intense and portions brightly lit. Her mind manufactured visions of Evo Kaplan killing people.

Entertainment had always as far back as people could remember shown factionary programs that fed into her dreams. Due to Claudette's mental state, she could not separate fact from fiction. In her dream state it was all fiction as if she had transported to a parallel universe.

The evilness poured out of Evo Kaplan, a gangster, a murderer, a despot criminal. And in her dreams this murderer was having sex with her. At first it felt good, then it felt horrible having intercourse by such an evil person. She mumbled in her sleep please stop, please stop. And by the grace of the Supreme Being, it all stopped. She was suddenly floating, feeling better than ever. Her feelings were warm and friendly, happiness prevailed. It was a calm moment as her demons had temporaneous departed.

She would have kept on sleeping, but in eight hours two things occurred: she suddenly needed a bowel movement, and she was getting hungry, both of which brought her out of her slumber. She did feel amazingly better and clearer headed.

Even though her dream started out as a nightmare, it ended peacefully, but she knew what it meant. She needed more time before she could possibly make any decision on continuing her relationship with Jerimiah Clifton (a.k.a. Evo Kaplan). After Claudette used the bathroom, she dressed and went downstairs looking for Evo Kaplan.

Rocu was still there guarding her door if that was any consolation.

CLAUDETTE RAMSEY
Is Jerimiah downstairs?

At least she was smart enough to use his new name but could see where in a pinch she might screw up in public and call him Evo.

ROCU
Yes, Claudette, he's down in his study.

CLAUDETTE RAMSEY
Thank you.

ROCU
You are welcome.

Claudette Ramsey found Jerimiah Clifton (a.k.a. Evo Kaplan) dutifully working on projects in his study. His dress had changed quite a bit. He no longer looked like a city slicker. He was now like the population here, artists and backdoors men.

Claudette Ramsey didn't notice it before, but Evo Kaplan's hair was longer and shaggier. He had changed. He was no longer that cute youthful-looking spy. Working outdoors for almost a year rebuilding these properties had weathered his face and created wrinkles. In a way he looked more distinguished, but in another way he looked more sadistic, almost evil.

CLAUDETTE RAMSEY
So, this is where you hang out now?

EVO KAPLAN(a.k.a. JERIMIAH CLIFTON)
Sure is. Keeps me busy."

Claudette noticed he had a private library with books on shelves all over the room.

CLAUDETTE RAMSEY
Did you read all these books?

EVO KAPLAN(a.k.a. JERIMIAH CLIFTON)
Not yet, but I will eventually. Would you like to eat
at home, or would you like to go to a café along the
waterfront?"

                    CLAUDETTE RAMSEY
I would love to go to the waterfront. That sounds fun.

              EVO KAPLAN(a.k.a. JERIMIAH CLIFTON)
Okay, I'm ready, just let me say something to Rocu.
I'll be right back.

Jerimiah Clifton informed Rocu they would be going out so that he didn't have to waste his time hanging around upstairs.

The two left the home and walked down to the waterfront a short distance away. Evo took Claudette to a nice restaurant that had plenty of seating, but was a mad house just hours earlier while the cruise liner was in.

<u>INT. DAY. SHENHUABAN de BAOZANG VILLAGE WATERFRONT RESTAURANT.</u>

Claudette Ramsey and Evo Kaplan were seated at a table next to the window so they could see the harbor that was mostly empty but had a couple small fishing boats.

              EVO KAPLAN(a.k.a. JERIMIAH CLIFTON)
How is everything back at Zanziltar?

                    CLAUDETTE RAMSEY
About the same. Not much has changed. How about
you? What have you been up to?

              EVO KAPLAN(a.k.a. JERIMIAH CLIFTON)
Well, I helped build two houses and restore six others.

                    CLAUDETTE RAMSEY
You turned into a construction worker?

              EVO KAPLAN(a.k.a. JERIMIAH CLIFTON)
It kept me busy.

                    CLAUDETTE RAMSEY
This Village looks totally different now.

              EVO KAPLAN(a.k.a. JERIMIAH CLIFTON)
Yes, it had some improvements and some of the people
that moved out are trying to move back.

CLAUDETTE RAMSEY
I bet they were sad they left.

EVO KAPLAN(a.k.a. JERIMIAH CLIFTON)
You can say that again. Their friends and relatives still live here. They come back now and then for visits and unfortunately can no longer afford to buy back the houses they sold me. The prices have more than doubled since they left.

CLAUDETTE RAMSEY
It seemed a lot cleaner and polished when I arrived.

EVO KAPLAN(a.k.a. JERIMIAH CLIFTON)
I've helped a dozen families paint their homes and replace windows with more modern types and repaired the sidewalks and helped the city repave all the streets in the downtown area.

They ordered and had their meal. Claudette seemed a little strange and not herself. It was as if she was resisting Jerimiah Clifton; perhaps that was part of the issue since he no longer appeared like Evo Kaplan. He knew something was wrong, but figured he'd eventually figure it out.

After dinner they went for a walk around the community, down the boardwalk and then down out on the pier that went almost two thousand feet to accommodate the big ships that pulled in. They watched the sunset together then walked back to Jerimiah Clifton's home.

Looking up the hillside, there were spotted numbers of homes where the last moments of sun struck reflecting brightly off the large windows. From this vantage point one could see there were far more homes up on the hillside than you would notice during the day thanks to the sun's reflection.

INT. DAY. EVO KAPLAN'S SHENHUABAN de BAOZANG VILLAGE HOME.

Back at Evo Kaplan's (a.k.a. Jerimiah Clifton) home they went to the main living room and sat down. Nice furnishings abound, thanks to Krawz Almarip's fortune he collected on his mission to Arzon.

Claudette Ramsey knew what Evo Kaplan wanted at that moment and figured she might as well get it over with, and sometime in the morning she would tell him she was going back to Zanziltar.

Claudette Ramsey needed to reflect and think about their relationship and decide if she could cope living with a cold-blooded murderer and assassin. Claudette unexpectedly announced:

CLAUDETTE RAMSEY
Let's go up to the guest room and make love.

Evo was more than ready and would tell anyone:

EVO KAPLAN
I was born ready.

They went up to her bedroom and shut the door. Rocu repositioned himself outside the door, doing his everlasting vigilance.

For the moment Claudette was able to compartmentalize and block all those horrible thoughts out of her mind as she was soon engulfed in passionate lovemaking. Evo Kaplan, who indeed loved her, performed in a couple manners, one out of pure lust and the other as an emotional bond to the only woman in his life.

Evo Kaplan appreciated Claudette Ramsey more than she could imagine. Due to his stature in life, his personal history, and the risk of uncovering his identity, finding another woman to be part of his life would be virtually almost impossible.

After several hours of releasing pent-up emotions in the physical embrace, they collapsed in each other's arms. Evo Kaplan passed out into a primordial slumber while Claudette, suffering from space lag, easily achieved a resting sleep feeling close and secure to this wonderful man she knew down deep in her heart she loved.

In the morning, they both stirred at the same time. Evo got up dressed and went downstairs to meet with the chef he brought in for Claudette's stay to make sure he was well prepared for their breakfast.

After seeing the chef had some delightful baking and wonderful breakfast items produced, he then went to his own bathroom and completed his S/S/S, then dressed in a more moderate but attractive attire.

Claudette dressed and looked rather pretty, but knew she had to do what she needed to right away at breakfast.

They were seated and halfway through breakfast when Claudette dropped the bomb on Evo Kaplan.

CLAUDETTE RAMSEY
I want to go back to Zanziltar today.

EVO KAPLAN
Is there something wrong?

CLAUDETTE RAMSEY
A lot of things have happened. When I met you, I really didn't know who you were. You turned out to be someone other than I met.

EVO KAPLAN
I'm sorry about that.

CLAUDETTE RAMSEY
I will admit that when we first met and I thought you were Krawz Almarip, a sleazy intergalactic black marketer, one side of me lusted for you. I suppose a lot of women like bad men.

EVO KAPLAN
What caused you to change your mind?

CLAUDETTE RAMSEY
When I got to know you better, I discovered you were a lot more than that. I never thought I would ever meet a man such as you, and in normal life I would avoid people like you. But I didn't know a lot about the things you had done then.

EVO KAPLAN
You were with me when some of that happened. I thought you were okay with me especially after my identity change and retirement.

CLAUDETTE RAMSEY
The news media has reported that you have committed some serious crimes. I know some of it is true because of my relationship with you. It's not every day a Revolutionary Guards in major combat ships remove a passenger off an intergalactic transport.

EVO KAPLAN
We were getting along fine after that incident.

CLAUDETTE RAMSEY
I was also startled to learn my boss Randolph Spencer is involved in the FIRM, which is an intergalactic organized crime syndicate, and you are their hired killer.

EVO KAPLAN
I do not work for anyone; I'm really retired now.

CLAUDETTE RAMSEY
That's what you claim but I'm not sure they will ever stop calling you.

EVO KAPLAN
I'm retired from all that so we can be together here.

CLAUDETTE RAMSEY
I know you care a lot about me. I can tell you have feelings for me, but I need some time to think about whether I want to be part of all this. I already fear I'm in too deep as it is and already fear for my life.

EVO KAPLAN
I'm retired from all that so we can be together here.

CLAUDETTE RAMSEY
If you are ever identified, no doubt someone will be sent to kill you and I could be collateral damage if I'm with you when that happens.

EVO KAPLAN
I have a lot of protection here. You would be safe.

CLAUDETTE RAMSEY
I now have nightmares thinking about what you have done. I'm not sure I can cope with all that. I'm going to go back to Zanziltar and continue with my life as I had before I met you. I need some time to think about it and adjust. I can't promise that I will ever come back.

Evo just looked into her eyes, not knowing what to say.

CLAUDETTE RAMSEY
I will tell you I know for a fact you are the first man

I've loved in my lifetime. It's been a bittersweet experience.

Evo knew this would not end well.

CLAUDETTE RAMSEY
Please let me go and give me some time and space. If I think I can handle it I will be back. If not, then you will never hear from me again."

EVO KAPLAN
I understand what you desire. I will make all the appropriate arrangements. I'll be back in a few minutes.

Evo went to his study and shut the door. He made a few phone calls and then came out a few minutes later.

EVO KAPLAN
A VTOL Skycar will arrive at the landing pad in about twenty minutes. I'll ask Rocu to get your luggage and bring it down and we can take you to the landing pad and see you off."

CLAUDETTE RAMSEY
You're not mad at me?

EVO KAPLAN
No, I love you and you are right. I need to give you some time. If it feels right to you, then you will come back.

CLAUDETTE RAMSEY
You are a sweet person, Evo. That's why I like you so much. You are a perfect gentleman.

EVO KAPLAN
Thank you, you are also a very sweet person as well.

In a few minutes Rocu came down with the luggage and the three of them went out to the electric cart and loaded the luggage and went to the Heliport landing pad.

EXT. CGI. DAY. SHENHUABAN DE BAOZANG HELIPORT LANDING PAD

Just as promised the VTOL Skycar arrived in twenty minutes and landed. They loaded

Claudette's luggage onto the airframe and then Evo Kaplan gave her one last hug and a tender kiss. He then helped her into the VTOL Skycar, then stepped back as it soon revved up its engines and took off. In twenty minutes, she was at the space port.

<u>INT. DAY. INTERGALACTIC PASSENGER TRANSPORT SPACE PORT</u>

A kind gray-haired gentleman met Claudette Ramsey as she stepped out of the VTOL Skycar.

EGOR PATASLIA
Claudette, I'm a friend of Jerimiah Clifton. He asked me to come here and help you get on the next intergalactic transport. There is one due to depart in thirty minutes. You have an electronic boarding pass, seat assignment, and are precleared through customs. Let us help you with your luggage.

CLAUDETTE RAMSEY
Thank you.

Claudette was surprised Evo Kaplan's friend, and his helpers were allowed to escort her to the Intergalactic Passenger Transport and carry all her belongings for her making her departure much easier.

After Claudette was situated on the intergalactic transport the flight attendant was with them.

FLIGHT ATTENDANT
Gentlemen you must now leave as we will be leaving soon.

EGOR PATASLIA
Not a problem Madam, Claudette's belongings are all stored in her bunk area, we are ready to leave.

CLAUDETTE RAMSEY
I'm sorry sir I forgot to ask you your name.

EGOR PATASLIA
Claudette, I'm Egor Pataslia.

CLAUDETTE RAMSEY
Egor Pataslia, thanks for your assistance and promptly getting me on a flight to Zanziltar.

In a way it was a sad day for Egor Pataslia, that such a fine person and extraordinary spy like Evo Kaplan had failed in love with this beautiful woman who was deserting him, but on the other hand it was a blessing in disguise as he had plans for Evo Kaplan.

Egor Pataslia knew his days were numbered and he needed to turn over his legacy to someone worthy of carrying it on like Evo Kaplan.

Unlike other spy agencies who grew so they could demand more funding and promotions, Egor Pataslia realized early on that when a spy agency gets too big, that opens windows of opportunity for the enemy to penetrate. Even though a smaller agency could only do a lot less, the chances of compromise were much slimmer.

Egor Pataslia's employees were handpicked and cultivated over a lengthy period. There might be some resentment from some of the locals being passed up for an outsider.

Unfortunately, Egor Pataslia's employees only thought in terms of provincial thinking. A future man in charge of Shen de Huayuan's FIRM needed galactic insights and knowledge of the bigger inter-galactic picture; otherwise, they would not be able to cope with future external threats.

The group, though, would accept Evo Kaplan mainly because they knew he was the best spy that Mikhail Catamountz had ever ran. Conrad Fanzui also knew none of his subordinates had ever carried out a high-level assassination of someone like Cornelius Xie de Hundan and survived, though the two waring Empires believed Evo Kaplan was killed on Zanziltar.

TIME FOR A VACATION

Randolph Spencer was eventually forced to go on vacation with his wife to Shen de Huayuan. He figured one month with her, and he would be free to go for the rest of the year doing his own business with his politician buddy routinely flying down at Orgy Island.

INT. DAY. LANTIANE RESORT

Randolph Spencer soon found himself at Lantiane Resort and to add to his irritation, his wife's two best friends happened to be there at the same time. The three Barracudas were back together, and he was stuck with all three.

It only took a few days to knock out visits to any of the attractions Randolph Spencer wouldn't mind visiting, then his wife and her two friends were insistent upon taking the overnight cruise. Grudgingly Randolph Spencer went along.

INT. DAY CRUISE LINER HYDROFOIL SHIP.

Randolph and Glacey Spencer along with Sparkles and Monica were soon aboard the tourist hydrofoil ship cruising at 140 knots per hour heading up the coast. If nothing else, the novelty of a fast liner gave Randolph Spencer slight satisfaction. He bit his lip and went along, and because the two other women were without an escort, he was stuck with all three of them and no male to converse with.

Eventually the thousand-foot-long ship slowed, retracted the hydrofoils, and pulled into Shenhuaban de Baozang. All three women had been here before, but not recently. When they got off the ship, Sparkles commented to Glacey Spencer.

EXT DAY SHENHUABAN DE BAOZANG VILLAGE

> SPARKLES
> Wow, this place has really changed.

Walking off the pier and heading toward one of the cafés on the pier, Monica noted with sheer exasperation, remembering the run-down area just a year or so ago.

> MONICA
> I wonder who lives in those two mansions?

> RANDOLPH SPENCER
> I know the owner quite well.

> GLACEY SPENCER
> Oh really? Who is it?

> RANDOLPH SPENCER
> It's a short walk. Let's go over there and ring his
> doorbell. I kind of would like to see him anyway.

Randolph was brainstorming how he might be able to convince Evo Kaplan to continue the voyage with them the rest of the day so that he would have someone to talk with.

They walked up to the mansion Randolph knew Evo Kaplan lived at and rang the doorbell. Randolph and the three women were well dressed.

INT. DAY. JERIMIAH CLIFTON'S HOME IN SHENHUABAN DE BAOZANG

Rocu was on duty and answered the door.

> ROCU
> How can I help you?

RANDOLPH SPENCER
I'm Randolph Spencer from Zanziltar and a friend of
Jerimiah Clifton. We just got off the cruise liner for a
few hours and was walking by and wanted to say hello
to him.

ROCU
Sure, come on in.

Rocu led them Randolph Spencer and the three women into the front living room,
which boiled over with opulence.

ROCU
I'll be right back. Jerimiah is in his study.

Rocu went to the study, knocked on the door then opened it.

ROCU
Mr. Clifton, you have visitors, a Mr. Randolph Spencer
with three ladies.

Jerimiah Clifton walked out of his office with Rocu down the hallway and into the
open area and was almost shocked to see of all people Randolph Spencer.

JERIMIAH CLIFTON (a.k.a. EVO KAPLAN)
Hello Randolph, good to see you.

RANDOLPH SPENCER
Jerimiah, this is my wife Glacey and her two friends,
Sparkles and Monica.

Jerimiah shook each of the lady's hands, recalling their names and welcoming them
one by one, and when he said Monica, she responded.

MONICA
Monica is my nickname, I'm really Theolonabatress
von Surret, but I like to be called Monica.

JERIMIAH CLIFTON (a.k.a. EVO KAPLAN)
Randolph, what brings you to Shenhuaban de
Baozang?

RANDOLPH SPENCER
We just got off the cruise liner for a few hours.

JERIMIAH CLIFTON (a.k.a. EVO KAPLAN)
I see. Going to find a restaurant or go on a tour?

RANDOLPH SPENCER
The ladies want to go to a café on the waterfront.

JERIMIAH CLIFTON (a.k.a. EVO KAPLAN)
Sounds fun.

RANDOLPH SPENCER
Say, Jerimiah, why don't you go with us? We can have
a good visit.

Randolph was almost pleading, as being stuck with the three Barracuda wasn't his cup of tea. If he could share the misery with someone else, it would help improve his day.

JERIMIAH CLIFTON (a.k.a. EVO KAPLAN)
Sure, why not?

The group then walked the short distance down the waterfront where Randolph asked:

RANDOLPH SPENCER
Which one of these places would you recommend?

Jerimiah responded, looking at the sign, The Crow's Nest.

JERIMIAH CLIFTON (a.k.a. EVO KAPLAN)
This one right here is good.

INT. DAY. SHENHUABAN de BAOZANG VILLAGE THE CROWS NEST RESTAURANT.

They went inside The Crow's Nest Restaurant and had lunch and the ladies asked Jerimiah a bazilian questions, which he answered by his memorization of the life and times of the real Jerimiah Clifton, a noted recluse and consummate bachelor.

The three Barracuda knew Jerimiah Clifton was a perfect fit and were shocked to learn he only lived a short distance away from their resort. Their little calculators in their heads started analyzing the prospects and they each wondered who would win the cat fight to get their digs into Jerimiah Clifton first.

RANDOLPH SPENCER
Say, Jerimiah, I have a really good idea. Why don't
you go with us on the ship for the rest of the cruise.

The three Barracudas quickly seconded.

Randolph Spencer thought it wouldn't be such a bad cruise, after all, if he could spend some time with the real Evo Kaplan, the mysterious spy and greatest assassin of all times. The amusement would be well worth it. Plus, Randolph Spencer thought Evo Kaplan might get lucky with one of the Barracuda – Monica.

Jerimiah Clifton owed Randolph Spencer his life. Without him, he could not have made the elaborate identification switches and disappeared like a true spook. Only for that he tacitly agreed.

> JERIMIAH CLIFTON (a.k.a. EVO KAPLAN)
> Sure, I wouldn't mind going, but I want to go home
> and change my clothes first and clean up a bit.

> RANDOLPH SPENCER
> All right, we'll go back to the ship from here and find
> the purser and get you a suite, so you have a place to
> sleep tonight."

> JERIMIAH CLIFTON (a.k.a. EVO KAPLAN)
> What if the ship is all booked up?

> RANDOLPH SPENCER
> Don't worry, everyone has their price. I'm sure there
> are some people on the ship that wouldn't mind getting
> paid a lot of money to spend the night in a hotel here
> if necessary and continue their voyage in the morning.

> JERIMIAH CLIFTON (a.k.a. EVO KAPLAN)
> I'm sure you are right.

Monica didn't let this opportunity to ace the two other barracudas pass and jumped in.

> MONICA
> (a.k.a. THEOLONABATRESS von SURRET)
> Jerimiah, I have two bedrooms, in my penthouse on
> the ship, I'll tell the Purser you are my guest.

> JERIMIAH CLIFTON (a.k.a. EVO KAPLAN)
> Monica, I'm sure I can find a cabin on the ship, but
> thanks for the invitation in case I need one.

The group broke up and Evo Kaplan went home and cleaned up and changed and informed Rocu what he was doing. Rocu immediately reported it to Egor Pataslia.

                    ROCU
Mr. Pataslia. The cruise liner pulled in and Evo Kaplan
met with Randolph Spencer who invited him to travel
with him on the rest of the cruise so they could
socialize.

                EGOR PATASLIA
I'm delighted Evo Kaplan will be going on a cruise
with Randolph Spencer. The situation between Evo
Kaplan and Claudette Ramsey makes him miserable.

                    ROCU
How are we going to handle this voyage?

                EGOR PATASLIA
Put a task force together immediately and you four
men there now go aboard the ship on a security detail.
Go to the Captain and advise him like we have before.

EXT. DAY. CRUISE LINER BOARDING ENTRANCE.

When Jerimiah Clifton arrived on the ship, the purser was there to personally meet him
and take him to his suite.

                SHIP'S PURSER
Welcome aboard Mr. Clifton. Randolph Spencer made
your reservations. Please follow me so I can take you
to your suite.

        JERIMIAH CLIFTON (a.k.a. EVO KAPLAN)
                Thank you.

The sea cabin suite was next door to the three Barracuda and Randolph. The cruise
ship was happy to sell four suites on this cruise because half of them were empty due
to the continuation of a slight recession caused by the ongoing Revolution.

                SHIP'S PURSER
I was asked to give you a couple of messages.

        JERIMIAH CLIFTON (a.k.a. EVO KAPLAN)
                Sure, what are they?

                SHIP'S PURSER
First, Randolph Spencer asks that you meet him down

at the first-class lounge, and secondly, you have been
invited to the captain's table for dinner tonight.

JERIMIAH CLIFTON (a.k.a. EVO KAPLAN)
Thank you. Which way to the lounge?

SHIP'S PURSER
Let me escort you.

JERIMIAH CLIFTON (a.k.a. EVO KAPLAN)
Thanks."

INT. DAY. CRUISE LINER FIRST CLASS LOUNGE.

Sure enough, there was Randolph Spencer sitting at a sofa by himself. On the sofa
next to him was a ship's RESERVED sign on it so that some grumpy customer would
not sit there because Jerimiah Clifton was expected any minute. A waiter was also
standing by.

As soon as Jerimiah Clifton approached, Randolph Spencer stood up and greeted him.

RANDOLPH SPENCER
Good to see you made it, Jerimiah.

JERIMIAH CLIFTON (a.k.a. EVO KAPLAN)
It was kind of good your ship pulled in and I had a
chance to visit.

RANDOLPH SPENCER
Definitely. Say, I'm sorry that Claudette Ramsey
didn't work out.

JERIMIAH CLIFTON (a.k.a. EVO KAPLAN)
She needs time to adjust. She's a quality woman, well
worth waiting for.

RANDOLPH SPENCER
I like your attitude. I agree with you, she's a fine
woman. Smart too.

JERIMIAH CLIFTON (a.k.a. EVO KAPLAN)
Are you enjoying your cruise with the three lovely
ladies?

RANDOLPH SPENCER
Good thing I ran into you. They were about to drive
me nuts.

JERIMIAH CLIFTON (a.k.a. EVO KAPLAN)
Well, it's the least I could do for you for all you have
helped me with.

RANDOLPH SPENCER
The pleasure is all mine. You earned my respect
because you delivered. There are not too many men
in the world who have gone through what you have.

JERIMIAH CLIFTON (a.k.a. EVO KAPLAN)
I'm a failure where it counts with my lovers. Seems I
can't hold on to them.

RANDOLPH SPENCER
You might want to consider that a blessing in disguise.

JERIMIAH CLIFTON (a.k.a. EVO KAPLAN)
Why do you say that?

RANDOLPH SPENCER
You have never had the chance of any of them going
stale on you.

JERIMIAH CLIFTON (a.k.a. EVO KAPLAN)
Is that what happens?

RANDOLPH SPENCER
Sure is.

The conversation continued until suddenly a ship's officer approached Randolph
Spencer.

SHIP'S OFFICER
Excuse me Mr. Spencer, your wife requests you return
to your suite to get ready for dinner.

RANDOLPH SPENCER
See what I mean?

Randolph stood and looked at the ship's officer.

RANDOLPH SPENCER
Thank you, sir, for the message.

Jerimiah Clifton stood and instinctively followed Randolph back to their suites that were next door to each other. They separated and went into their own suites.

<u>INT. DAY. CRUISE LINER PENTHOUSE.</u>

When Jerimiah Clifton was alone in his suite, he looked in the mirror and wondered if he looked appropriate for the captain's table. He wasn't sure, so he called guest services and within five minutes a fashion designer and her assistants arrived.

FASHION DESIGNER
Mr. Clifton, I understand you wanted a fashion consultation.

JERIMIAH CLIFTON (a.k.a. EVO KAPLAN)
Yes, please come in.

Once inside, the fashion designer lady evaluated Jerimiah Cliftons current clothing for a few minutes.

FASHION DESIGNER
I do not believe your outfit is becoming of you for the captain's table. I know I can make a remarkable improvement.

JERIMIAH CLIFTON (a.k.a. EVO KAPLAN)
All right. Let's see what you can do.

Just like they had done before, Jerimiah Clifton (a.k.a. Evo Kaplan) was in the tub getting scrubbed and feeling suddenly a lot better. He was dried, pampered, and worked over in the most professional manner. The designer opened the cart door, exposing the suits she anticipated would be perfect for him. He looked them all over and asked:

JERIMIAH CLIFTON (a.k.a. EVO KAPLAN)
What color is this one?

FASHION DESIGNER
This is a 'Drakes Neck' color.

JERIMIAH CLIFTON (a.k.a. EVO KAPLAN)
It looks rather exotic.

FASHION DESIGNER
This color pattern came from some frontiersman who visited distant solar systems and came back with samples.

JERIMIAH CLIFTON (a.k.a. EVO KAPLAN)
Do you know what planetary system it came from?

FASHION DESIGNER
We have no way of confirming it, but the legend indicates it came from planet Earth.

JERIMIAH CLIFTON (a.k.a. EVO KAPLAN)
I'll wear that one.

Soon Evo Kaplan was dressed and looking very handsome. He looked in the wall-length mirror and was happy with what he was seeing. He would feel good tonight.

FASHION DESIGNER
Okay, it looks like you are ready to go.

JERIMIAH CLIFTON (a.k.a. EVO KAPLAN)
Thank you. This was a very good job you did.

FASHION DESIGNER
You are most welcome, Mr. Clifton.

No sooner than the fashion designer and assistants left, than the doorbell rang. It was Monica.

JERIMIAH CLIFTON (a.k.a. EVO KAPLAN)
Good evening.

MONICA
Randolph informed me that you offered to escort me to the captain's table.

JERIMIAH CLIFTON (a.k.a. EVO KAPLAN)
Sure, why not?

Evo allowed the Barracuda to conduct her invented story that she made up to make sure she elbowed Sparkles out of the way and took custody of the fresh meat.

Moments later Sparkles, who lost the race, and Randolph and Glacey Spencer appeared, and the group trudged forward to the first-class dining room.

<u>INT. EVENING CRUISE LINER FIRST CLASS DINING HALL.</u>

Evo Kaplan did a strategic move as they arrived at the door: He opened it even though a doorman was there, he acted as if he were holding it open so that Randolph would take the lead with Glacey, and he would then settle back behind with the other two ladies on each side to put the best face forward.

Sparkles was extremely appreciative of his gentlemanliness, as she knew Monica had a knock-out body and Jerimiah Clifton would no doubt want to knock her socks off long before he would entertain an old hag like her.

The officers at the podium were alert and ready, and knowing a distinguished guest such as Randolph Spencer was approaching, they were very professional in their greetings. The group received multiple escorts to the captain's table, where there were more staff on hand waiting. Half of the staff were extras brought in to pamper the Spencer party.

Shortly the music stopped and suddenly the military march almost identical to the Franz von Suppe "Light Calvary Overture" was played by the orchestra and the captain marched very dignity like down the middle of the dining hall. Just like Evo Kaplan observed on previous cruises, the captain toasted the diners then walked over to the podium where he was escorted by two officers to his table.

After all the toasts and proclamations, the captain sat down and asked everyone at the table to introduce themselves and where they were from.

In approving the captain's table list and briefings from Egor Pataslia's security detail, the captain was once again surprised that this unusual man was sitting next to Randolph Spencer in seat two across from three of the wealthiest women probably in the galaxy. Even though the man had changed his appearance, the captain knew this had to be the same person.

Because of his top-secret briefings from the company as well as the planetary security apparatus, the captain was aware of advances in 3D biological printing. Even though it was not public knowledge, some of the top-secret details implied spy agencies had already gone to 3D biological printing, which would eventually make security tricky as it would defeat facial recognition technology.

The captain knew his life would be in jeopardy if he ever uttered to anyone his speculation that Jerimiah Clifton was Evo Kaplan, perhaps the most famous spy and assassin of all times.

If Evo Kaplan had escaped the Clutches of the Dranzonians and successfully changed his identity, the captain thought that was okay too. Like most people within the Revolutionary Empire, Cornelius Xie de Hundan was considered a despot and as he increasingly strengthened his dictatorship, he was making more lives miserable.

Therefore, if this was truly Evo Kaplan, he would be the last person to inform authorities as his mission was beneficial to society greatly. Also, his disappearance act was the greatest hoax ever perpetuated, which also added to Evo Kaplan's mystique.

This suddenly was turning into one of the more memorable moments in the captain's life, dining with and sitting side by side with Randolph Spencer and Evo Kaplan who were apparently taking this cruise together.

After dinner the ladies insisted on staying to dance. Randolph appreciated Jerimiah Clifton even more doing a lot of the dancing so he didn't have to and could concentrate on enjoying refreshments.

Jerimiah Clifton didn't mind the dancing; he needed to get back into shape and was now living too much of a sedentary life. Recently as he looked at himself in the mirror, he was disgusted in what he saw. He knew he was long overdue to get back into physical fitness and this cruise was a perfect way to kick it off.

While he was sitting down resting and having a drink, listening to the captain talk to Randolph after the captain returned to socialize with guests, which was rare, Jerimiah Clifton felt the buzzer of his personal communicator. He had a message, which he could read on a text screen and avoid the miniature holograph others might see and hear.

C.U. JERIMIAH CLIFTON'S (a.k.a. EVO KAPLAN) COMMUNICATOR

The text was from Claudette Ramsey:

> VOICE OVER Claudette Ramsey's voice)
> I'm very sorry, but after giving it great thought. I've decided I can no longer see you. I want you to know I was truly in love with you, but due to the nature of our lives and who we are and where we have been. I do not wish to be in your sphere any longer. I take this stance with huge regret and sorrow.
>
> If you truly love me, then give me this. Do not attempt to contact me. Give me my space and let me live free in my world and my place and time. You will always be in my memory. Thank you for the love you gave me. Claudette.

Evo Kaplan was stunned, full of sorrow and regret. In such a short time he lost two women he loved. These were incredible women, rare and unique, irreplaceable. His heart was broken, but he would reflect and meditate and get on with his life. In some ways he should be happy to just be alive, as she said in her farewell, where they had been and what they had seen.

Just like a good spy, Evo Kaplan immediately went to the backup plan. Thanks to his many hours of meditation and soul-searching transcendence into plausible realities, he recoiled and glazed the evening with rarified friendliness and compassion to others.

Even the poor hag Sparkles, who could afford to ease up on a donut or two a day, was having a super time as Jerimiah Clifton danced with her in the quality he had obtained by Brenda's finesse.

Around 2:00 in the morning, Randolph Spencer had more than he could take. The captain was long gone, cramming a few hours of sleep in before he had to give the orders to deploy the hydrofoil and speed up to 140 knots per hour.

RANDOLPH SPENCER
Okay, everyone, I'm sorry but I must get some sleep.

Randolph growled the words and the women thought he had just taken away their Christmas as they were just warming up.

Jerimiah Clifton likewise added his escape routine:

JERIMIAH CLIFTON
I'm developing a headache. I need to lay down too.

Sadly, the group exited the exciting dance going on, the band playing greatly because the crowd had been so enthused all night long.

The group went to their separate suites and called it a night.

INT. NIGHT. CRUISE LINER PENTHOSE.

Evo Kaplan was thinking about jumping into bed and getting some sleep when the doorbell rang. He looked through the security eye piece and saw Monica standing outside.

Evo Kaplan opened the door.

JERIMIAH CLIFTON (a.k.a. EVO KAPLAN)
Hello.

MONICA
May I come in?

JERIMIAH CLIFTON (a.k.a. EVO KAPLAN)
Sure.

He shut the door after Monica entered the suite and was amazed that Monica immediately started undressing and asked.

MONICA
Can you unhook my dress?

Jerimiah Clifton reluctantly unhooked the dress and it fell to the floor, revealing nothing underneath. She was completely naked and smartly walked into his bedroom and crawled into his bed.

This was not a good night for Evo Kaplan, who was miserable over the loss of the love of his life. He had no lust or desire for sex.

He undressed, crawled in bed with Monica, put his arms around her with her back to him, and she instantly thought he would spoon her when he simply hugged her and fell asleep.

At first Monica was unhappy, but then she remembered it was very late and felt sleepy herself. She was soon resting well and being hugged all night long felt good.

Monica awoke before Evo Kaplan and started thinking it would be a scandal if someone found out she spent the night with him, so she got up, dressed, and went back to her own suite.

Evo Kaplan was awakened while she dressed and eased herself out of his suite. He was glad she was gone and glad he had not touched her. He went back to sleep and rested peacefully until suddenly he heard the announcement of the high-speed run and the vibrations starting from the hydrofoil operation.

When he woke up and finished his morning routine, he walked over to his closet and saw that the butler Charles had hung up all his clothes and the designer's suit was gone, probably already returned.

<u>INT. DAY. CRUISE LINER 1ST CLASS DINING HALL.</u>

Evo Kaplan dressed and made his way to the first-class dining hall and ordered a hot caffeinated drink while he observed the rooster tail the ship was putting out. A thousand-foot-long ship on hydrofoils left an impressive wake, mostly ocean spray in the air several hundred feet.

Over at the other side of the first-class dining hall was Rocu, sitting there watching him and giving him a nod, which was comforting knowing everything was all right.

In a while Randolph found Jerimiah Clifton (a.k.a. Evo Kaplan).

RANDOLPH SPENCER

Hey, that was a wonderful performance you did last night. The women all love you. They are very pleased to associate with you.

JERIMIAH CLIFTON (a.k.a. EVO KAPLAN)

That's good. I like them too.

RANDOLPH SPENCER

A man can't go wrong being friends with those three women, if you know what I mean.

JERIMIAH CLIFTON (a.k.a. EVO KAPLAN)

Yes, they are quality women. They are smart and seen a lot in their lives. You can have a good conversation with them.

RANDOLPH SPENCER

That is true. But its hell on a man when you got all three of them to take care of.

JERIMIAH CLIFTON (a.k.a. EVO KAPLAN)

I can imagine.

About that time the captain walked into the dining hall. He was doing his morning routine, socializing for a few minutes with the passengers to give them a friendly face of the company.

SHIP'S CAPTAIN

Hello gentlemen, enjoying your trip?

RANDOLPH SPENCER

Yes, captain, we appreciate your companionship last night.

SHIP'S CAPTAIN

It was my pleasure. Have you guys seen the bridge before?

RANDOLPH SPENCER
No. we haven't.

SHIP'S CAPTAIN
Why don't you come with me? I'll give you a quick
tour.

RANDOLPH SPENCER
That would be fantastic.

The captain led the men up a stairway and to a door that had a cypher code he typed in, then suddenly a solenoid shifted unlocking the door and he opened it and went in.

INT. DAY. CRUISE LINER BRIDGE

Suddenly one of the watch standers announced:

WATCH STANDER
Captain is on the bridge.

SHIP'S CAPTAIN
As she goes, carry on.

The captain walked through an open area that had a lot of room so the captain and discrete guests could monitor operations. Sometimes company inspectors would stand back here monitoring bridge activity and write reports.

The bridge had half a sphere of view. Going at their speeds there was no need to be concerned about shipping behind 090 degrees or 270 degrees relative because the high probability there could be no collisions.

The vast-large circular window allowed them almost a full 180 degrees view and there were several cameras showing video on monitors above the windows, which magnified any surface contacts.

When a contact became a contact of interest such a potential collision, a red lit banner around that display started flashing and an audio alarm giving a half second audio sound, which automatically shifted the rudder for collision avoidance in three seconds if the helmsman did not alter course.

If multiple collision threats suddenly appeared, auto throttles would also change speed and if the shipping density got severe, the ship would de-hydro and slow to a surface speed until all collision threats were managed.

Looking at the oncoming ocean flying at 140 knots was quite a sight. With the wave action it was almost hypnotic. The twelve officers on the bridge getting ready to slow down and return to port were very professional and attentive to their jobs, totally ignoring the visitors.

SHIP'S CAPTAIN
You guys are lucky. You will get to see us slow down.

The captain made the announcement over the intercom.

SHIP'S CAPTAIN
The ship will be slowing.

He then ordered the officer of the deck, Slow to ahead one-third and retract the hydrofoils when the proper speed has been obtained.

The officer did a repeat back on the orders then took all appropriate actions and soon the ship slowed and lowered into the water and became a surface ship again. The hydrofoils were retracted, and the captain announced:

SHIP'S CAPTAIN
Ladies and gentlemen, the ship has slowed. All doors
are unlocked, and permission is given for passengers
to access the outdoor deck areas.

The captain then turned to Randolph.

SHIP'S CAPTAIN
Mr. Spencer, your special VTOL Skycar you requested
will be arriving in ten minutes. I suggest you get
your party together and report to the VTOL deck for
departure.

RANDOLPH SPENCER
Thank you, captain, I appreciate your hospitality.

SHIP'S CAPTAIN
The pleasure is all mine.

The captain shook his hand, then he shook Evo Kaplan's hand and gave him an extra double squeeze on the hand as if to signal Evo Kaplan.

I wonder if he knows who I am? Evo asked himself.

The Ship's Captain escorted the men back down to the first-class area then returned by himself back to the bridge to make sure flight operations were going to move smoothly. A number of VTOL Sky-buses would soon be streaming aboard the VTOL deck to onload passengers returning them to various resorts and hotels.

Evo walked with Randolph Spencer to the VTOL deck, which was restricted and fenced off. The waiting room doors were guarded by employees who only allowed those to exit who had clearance for specific VTOL craft.

RANDOLPH SPENCER
Can I give you a lift to the resort or your home?

JERIMIAH CLIFTON (a.k.a. EVO KAPLAN)
There is a security detail with me. We all need to get
on the VTOL Skybus together. I have transportation
arranged.

RANDOLPH SPENCER
All right. We'll be seeing you again, and thanks a
million for entertaining the ladies. I really needed your
help.

JERIMIAH CLIFTON (a.k.a. EVO KAPLAN)
The pleasure was all mine.

Randolph Spencer and the three Barracudas got onto what looked like a souped-up VTOL Skycar. It flew as fast as it looked.

<u>EXT. CGI. DAY. EVO KAPLAN AND 4 SECURITY MEN GET INTO VTOL AND FLY OFF THE HELO DECK OF THE SHIP. 15 SECONDS.</u>

Evo Kaplan was back home in Shenhuaban de Baozang thirty minutes after a memorable night. He was already missing Claudette Ramsey, but he remembered vividly what she said. "If you truly love me, please do not contact me."

Evo Kaplan would go on with his life without Claudette Ramsey.

Later that night Evo Kaplan received a visitor at his home. It was none other than Egor Pataslia himself.

Evo Kaplan didn't know it, but the Shen de Huayuan security apparatus including Egor Pataslia opened all mail and monitored all communications. Egor Pataslia knew that Claudette Ramsey had said good-bye to Evo Kaplan forever. He had to strike while the iron was hot. Evo Kaplan was in a vulnerable mood. It was time to visit and pitch him.

JERIMIAH CLIFTON (a.k.a. EVO KAPLAN)
You are about the last person in the world I would ex-
pect to see.
EGOR PATASLIA
Not after you sell me that house next door.
JERIMIAH CLIFTON (a.k.a. EVO KAPLAN)
That's my guest house for visitors.
EGOR PATASLIA
When was the last time you had visitors?
JERIMIAH CLIFTON (a.k.a. EVO KAPLAN)
You have a point there. I doubt you are here just to buy
that house.
EGOR PATASLIA
Smart guy. We have some other business.
JERIMIAH CLIFTON (a.k.a. EVO KAPLAN)
What could that be?
EGOR PATASLIA
I'm getting too old for this job. I need to turn over within
five years, as I will have to retire about then. Right now,
the only person around I think can run this operation is
you. But I will need about five years to groom you.
JERIMIAH CLIFTON (a.k.a. EVO KAPLAN)
I'll have Rocu get you a set of keys for the house next
door. Consider it paid in full.
EGOR PATASLIA
I like the way you think. It simplifies everything.
JERIMIAH CLIFTON (a.k.a. EVO KAPLAN)
I'll be an eager student. I know I have a lot to learn.
EGOR PATASLIA
It takes time. I think we can get it done in five years
SHERI AND EVO KAPLAN FINALLY EVOLVE
The next day Randolph Spencer called Evo Kaplan

EXT. CGI. DAY. SHENHUABAN DE BAOZANG VTOL LANDING PAD. EVO CAPLAN GETS IN VTOL AND IT TAKES OFF 15 TO 20 SECONDS.

In about thirty minutes, the VTOL Skycar landed at the Shenhuaban de Baozang VTOL landing pad and Jerimiah Clifton got on and it promptly left. In a short period, the VTOL arrived at the Lantiane Resort landing pad.

EXT. CGI. DAY. LANTIANE RESORT VTOL RESORT LANDING PAD. EVO KAPLAN DEPARTS THE VTOL AND WALKS INTO THE RESORT. 20 SECONDS.

Jerimiah Clifton (a.k.a. Evo Kaplan) walked into the resort and went to the front desk, who had his reservation and facial recognition technology acknowledged:

EXT. CGI DAY. LANTIANE RESORT SWIMMING POOL.

Jerimiah Clifton (a.k.a. Evo Kaplan) went down to the pool area where he figured he would run into the Barracuda. And sure enough, there they were.

He figured that Monica felt she had some unfinished business to attend to. Since Evo Kaplan's lover Claudette Ramsey dumped him and he was now free to roam, if the conditions were right, he might just fulfill Monica's fantasy.

Jerimiah Clifton did his formalities.

They all responded.

THREE BARRACUDAS
(In a chorus)
Hello Jerimiah.

Evo Kaplan could tell the three barracudas were tickled pink of his presence, and he would humor them for a while since he still felt some sense of obligation to Randolph Spencer for helping him put his life in order; otherwise, he would surely be a dead man.

Feeling he lacked exercise Evo Kaplan decided to go for a swim. So, Jerimiah Clifton (a.k.a. Evo Kaplan) jumped in and started swimming.

VOICE OVER
One thing Monica picked up on quickly was Jerimiah Clifton's swimming style. It was a carbon copy of someone else she had seen, a man named Evo Kaplan. Strangely Jerimiah Clifton's body seemed like Evo Kaplan who she had seen swimming before as well.

Suddenly, Monica had a flashback of a man with two different women. Could this be Evo Kaplan with reconstructive facial surgery? That thought sent shivers down Monica's spine.

Evo Kaplan spent a couple hours with the ladies, not having much to say but being polite and performing suntan lotion application often as the three barracudas kept asking for more loving Jerimiah (a.k.a. Evo) touch, especially when he ran his hand up inside their thighs almost touching their private parts..

Eventually the music started playing in the pool bar and restaurant. A familiar voice was singing.

Evo Kaplan excused himself from the ladies and went into the bar restaurant. There she was, Sheri, looking as good as ever. At the break Sheri went to Evo Kaplan's table, as he looked familiar.

JERIMIAH CLIFTON (a.k.a. EVO KAPLAN)
Hello.

SHERI
I think we have met before.

JERIMIAH CLIFTON (a.k.a. EVO KAPLAN)
We certainly have.

SHERI
I thought so.

JERIMIAH CLIFTON (a.k.a. EVO KAPLAN)
Have a seat. Let me buy you a drink.

SHERI
All right.
They talked for a few minutes then Sheri went back
to work.

During her next break, Evo Kaplan asked Sheri:

JERIMIAH CLIFTON (a.k.a. EVO KAPLAN)
Do you like going to the symphony?

SHERI
Sure.

JERIMIAH CLIFTON (a.k.a. EVO KAPLAN)
Do you ever get any time off?

SHERI
Yeah, a couple days a week.

JERIMIAH CLIFTON (a.k.a. EVO KAPLAN)
When is your next day off?

SHERI
Tomorrow.

JERIMIAH CLIFTON (a.k.a. EVO KAPLAN)
I have a really good idea.

SHERI
What's that?

JERIMIAH CLIFTON (a.k.a. EVO KAPLAN)
Come up to my penthouse tomorrow around 5:00 P.M.

You don't have to be dressed up. I'll have a fashion designer there to fit you out for the symphony. After the symphony I'll take you to dinner.

SHERI
Is this for real?

JERIMIAH CLIFTON (a.k.a. EVO KAPLAN)
Yes, don't tell anyone and come to my penthouse, room 222. Should be easy to remember.

SHERI
All right, I wouldn't mind going to the symphony. But can you tell me your name?

JERIMIAH CLIFTON (a.k.a. EVO KAPLAN)
Sure, Jerimiah Clifton.

SHERI
Okay Jerimiah. If you promise to be respectful and treat me decently, I'll go.

JERIMIAH CLIFTON (a.k.a. EVO KAPLAN)
I don't want to spoil my reputation by mistreating you, I'll be a good friend.

SHERI
I like your attitude, I'll go.

Jerimiah Clifton went back to the pool and hung out with the three Barracuda for another couple hours, then went back up to his penthouse and took a hot bath. In the middle of it, Charles knocked on the door and entered.

CHARLES
Mr. Clifton, Randolph Spencer has an invitation for you.

JERIMIAH CLIFTON (a.k.a. EVO KAPLAN)
All right, after I finish the bath, I'll read it.

After his bath he read the invitation. They were to go to a dinner and dance club in a couple hours. Fifteen minutes later there was a knock at the door, and no other than designer Inchalchary with her cart and two assistants.

Since Evo Kaplan was already bathed, all he needed was some hair styling, a shave, and the proper men's cologne and a nice outfit. The designer showed him what she selected for him, and he picked a Dark Byzantium suit with matching shoes. As soon as he was dressed, the fashion designer and staff departed, and Evo Kaplan asked Charles to inform Randolph Spencer he would be waiting for the group down at the pool bar and restaurant.

<u>EXT. EVENING. LANTIANE RESORT POOL BAR AND RESTAURANT</u>

Evo Kaplan figured he would have a drink and listen to Sheri singing. His usual seat was empty, giving him an excellent view of the performer. When she saw how distinguished Jerimiah Clifton appeared, she was more than ready for tomorrow night. She had great attraction for him. If Jerimiah Clifton lived up to his promises—the symphony, restaurant, etcetera— she would just about be about ready for anything.

Timing was everything. Sheri had another break and was able to get close and visit Evo Kaplan. His cologne almost hypnotized her. She was truly letting herself go.

Randolph escorted the three ladies to the front entrance and suddenly said:

RANDOLPH SPENCER
Oops, I forgot something, I'll be right back.

Just as soon as Sheri started singing again, Randolph Spencer entered the bar and grabbed Evo Kaplan and led him out front of the resort where a limo was waiting for them.

The group went to a bar and restaurant dance club Evo wasn't aware of. It was nicer than Banma Julebu, but there were also fewer patrons. It too had live bands and a great view. The seating at the large circular table was a male between each woman.

The food was fabulous and soon the dancing started.

Evo, being the good spy he was, planned to drug Monica that night because he wanted her to get sleepy and go to bed and not chase him. He wanted to save it for Sheri, as he felt something was developing.

Evo Kaplan always liked Sheri. She could sing well, and she was very pretty. Unfortunately, due to opportunities in a tourist Mecca, Sheri had to be a performer to survive and didn't have opportunities to really get involved with a man.

The three Barracudas enjoyed dancing with Evo Kaplan all night long until Randolph was getting tired and had enough. While the three ladies went to the restroom, Evo Kaplan drugged Monica's drink. In the lady's room they had to work out an agreement that Sparkles would not get in Monica's way. There was some anxiety going on in the bathroom as the ladies conspired with Glacey being the referee.

By the time the women returned, the drug in Monica's drink had diffused nicely so she would not pick up a taste from it. She was getting thirsty from the dancing and finished the drink rather quickly and asked for a refill.

Randolph watched Evo Kaplan do the drugging and smiled because he figured it out. He didn't want to have to deal with her tonight.

In fifteen minutes, Monica started yawning. Randolph smiled. He made a mental note to talk with Evo Kaplan. He had some ideas for his own wife!

The group made it back to the resort a short while later and Monica was so sleepy she went into her penthouse and laid down on her bed without taking off her dress and slept until late in the morning.

Evo Kaplan went down to the beach in shorts and running shoes and made some laps getting some exercise. He would avoid the Barracuda today and contacted Randolph privately to advise him he had a hot date and would not be available that night.

Randolph, knowing Evo Kaplan was terribly upset with the loss of his lover, Claudette Ramsey, was glad he might have found someone else.

At 5:00 P.M. the penthouse doorbell rang. Charles had been notified by Jerimiah Clifton that Sheri would be arriving about that time and to have the fashion designers up immediately after she arrived.

Sheri thought she was cute enough as she was, but to make Jerimiah Clifton more comfortable by wearing fancy dress was okay to her as well.

Couture designer Inchalchary with her cart and two assistants arrived and took Sheri into the bathroom and gave her a bath, which almost confused her since she was already cleaned up and dressed for success.

INCHALCHARY
You need these special bath salts so that you will wear the
clothes better and aid us in getting you ready.

SHERI
Okay, whatever it takes.

Sheri soon started feeling better.

When they scrubbed the makeup off her face it upset Sheri, knowing she spent over two hours putting it on. Soon, however, she was done feeling better and she was sitting in a chair getting her nails and toenails done.

In the other bedroom of the suite, Jerimiah Clifton was also getting similar treatment, being well prepared. He picked out a bistre-color suit with matching shoes.

Finally, they were both ready to go. The designers and staff departed, having cleaned up smartly, and Jerimiah Clifton looked at the time.

JERIMIAH CLIFTON (a.k.a. EVO KAPLAN)
Perfect timing for us to get to the symphony on time.

SHERI
I'm so excited I know the symphony will be such a
wonderful time.

As they left Sheri and Evo Kaplan left the penthouse, the three Barracudas came down the hallway in the opposite direction, just back from the pool bar restaurant. They spotted Jerimiah Clifton (a.k.a. Evo Kaplan) and the gorgeous creature he was with. They almost wanted to go cry; there was no way they could compete with that exquisite beauty.

Some of the resort employees that knew Sheri saw her with the gentleman all dressed up. She looked glamorous with the full-length gown on a B'dazzled Blue with Golden Stars and streamers running lengthwise.

Sheri's hair made up looked so pretty and princess like. The real gems she was wearing were on loan and insured. She was worth a million credits because she was wearing a million credits worth of gems.

Sheri and Evo Kaplan had no worries about Sheri being robbed for the gems because Egor Pataslia's men were always within eyesight of Evo Caplan and if someone approached them, they would make their presence felt immediately and they had much better AI controlled laser pistols that would quickly wipe out any assailants.

As they approached the Limo, the driver opened the door for them, and they headed off to the symphony. They were soon seated, and Sheri was having the time of her life, looking so good, feeling so good, and with a gentleman who could have easily seduced her with hello and had sex with her simply by inviting her to his penthouse.

But instead, he was treating her like a princess and his idea to scrub her up kind of pissed her off in the beginning, but after the makeup artist explained why during the work it all became sense because of the scientific processes used to apply the exotic markups they used had to be on fresh skin to achieve their purpose. The dress she was wearing cost more than her yearly salary!

One thing Evo Kaplan remembered was his humble beginnings and his near starvation. He simply came out of the gutter and was living well now.

The two-hundred-piece orchestra with two hundred choir members created sound and vibration that cut through the human psyche and transported Sheri to a transcendence she gladly enjoyed. As a musician and a singer, she appreciated these artists on a different level as she could pick out infinitesimally small deviations and exotic sounds that created a psychoacoustic effect the composition derived.

The two-hour performance left Sheri in a frame of mind that was positive and expecting. However, her stomach was in dire need of some food, and she was extremely pleased they were leaving immediately for a restaurant.

Evo Kaplan took Sheri to the Banma Julebu.

<u>INT. EVENING. BANMA JULEBU RESTAURANT/NIGHTCLUB.</u>

Just like any other night, there was an angry line and a security detail. Something strange occurred though. Evo didn't need to approach the security supervisor because one of Egor Pataslia's men, who was advised of his plans for that evening, was ready to escort him to the elevator.

Just as one previous night, no other customers were allowed in the elevator with them. And just like before, the Maître d' knew his name and immediately escorted him to a table with a fantastic and unobstructed view of the band and the dance floor.

The meal was truly amazing for Sheri, as it was the best chef creations she had experienced in a while.

Eventually dinnertime was over, and the band changed out. Dancers were arriving and the mood swung into a lot of happy folks enjoying the ambience of a fantastic club. Evo Kaplan asked Sheri to dance a couple slow dances with him. He was electrified by her touch and her perfume was loaded with pheromones. The designer had whispered in her ear the pheromones in the perfume would make her boyfriend super horny. It worked as she promised.

At the completion of the dance, they sat down for a minute. Evo Kaplan excused himself, got up and walked over to the Maître d'.

JERIMIAH CLIFTON (a.k.a. EVO KAPLAN)
Excuse me, sir, my date is a professional singer. She
has a lovely voice. Could you ask the band if they
would let her sing a song for me?

Evo Kaplan then informed the Maître d' the name of the song a recent popular hit that was now being performed in clubs in the resort community.

MAÎTRE D'
I will ask them for you, Mr. Clifton.

                    JERIMIAH CLIFTON (a.k.a. EVO KAPLAN)
                              Thank you.

In a few minutes the band took a break, the Maître d' talked to the lead singer of the band and soon was pointing at the couple.

                              BAND LEADER
               As good looking as she is, I'll take the chance. Sure,
               when we come back from break, we'll let her sing the
               second song.

                              MAÎTRE D'
                              Thank you.

A few minutes later the Maître d' approached Evo Kaplan.

                              MAÎTRE D'
               Mr. Clifton, the band said she can sing the second song
               when they come back to play after the break.

                    JERIMIAH CLIFTON (a.k.a. EVO KAPLAN)
               Thank you very much. This means a lot to me.

                              MAÎTRE D'
                 You are welcome, Mr. Clifton.

Since it was quiet without the band playing, Evo Kaplan informed Sheri:

                    JERIMIAH CLIFTON (a.k.a. EVO KAPLAN)
               I wanted to do something tonight we would both
               remember the rest of our lives together. I asked the
               band to let you sing a song for me. After they come
               back, they are going to allow you to sing the second
               song for me.

                              SHERI
                 Which one do you want me to sing?

                    JERIMIAH CLIFTON (a.k.a. EVO KAPLAN)
               The one you sing at the club, 'I know you are bad, but
               I will always want you.'

                              SHERI
                             Are you sure?

JERIMIAH CLIFTON (a.k.a. EVO KAPLAN)
Definitely.

SHERI
Okay, I'll try my best.

Egor Pataslia and his two bodyguards came in and sat down at the bar. He looked over at Evo Kaplan and gave a slight nod and immediately looked at the eye candy that was sitting with him.

The band started playing they knew their moment was just about to occur. The song was kind of lackluster, the customers were not overly enthralled with the performance, but at least it was a live band that played a few good songs. After the song, the lead singer announced.

BAND LEADER
Ladies and gentlemen, we have a surprise for you
tonight. A lady from the audience is going to come up
to the stage now and sing you a lovely song.

The singer and band leader held out his hand for Sheri, who got up and walked over to the steps on the side of the stage and climbed up and walked over and the singer handed her the microphone. They had a small huddle and Sheri told him the song which the band knew but didn't have a great singer to perform it.

The audience was mystified with the beautiful woman. And soon the band started playing and Sheri started singing. The words resonated with Evo Kaplan, who grew slightly emotional.

The resort pool bar restaurant had such crappy acoustics that did no justice for Sheri's voice. In this club where they had million credit acoustics, and Sheri's voice was incredible.

The lead singer was stunned. The dancers were suddenly crowding the dance floor and the place was rejuvenated to its former glory. The song was slightly longer than normal—four and a half minutes—and every second counted. Sheri melted Evo Kaplan's heart on the spot. His breaking heart from Brenda and then Claudette was healed tonight.

At the completion of her song there was a standing ovation; the crowd was enthralled and captivated!

That night Egor Pataslia saw a different dimension in Evo Kaplan he hadn't seen before. Sheri's singing seemed to motivate the band, and they were suddenly on fire. Management was delighted and this night would be one memorable one.

Evo and Sheri danced to a few more songs and then Sheri surprised Evo Kaplan.

SHERI
I want to sing one more song for you if that's okay.

JERIMIAH CLIFTON (a.k.a. EVO KAPLAN)
Sure, let me go ask again.

The Maître d' was all smiles admiring the beautiful lady who sang so pretty. It was like a magical moment she brought to everyone. When Evo Kaplan approached him again, it was as if he was hoping he would ask if she could sing again. And when the question came out, the Maître d' responded in the most positive manner.

MAÎTRE D'
Yes, Mr. Clifton, I would be utterly delighted to make
that request.

The band was in the process of just about to take a break when the Maître d' broke their game plan and approached the lead singer and asked:

MAÎTRE D'
Before you guys take a break, could the young lady
sing another song?

BAND LEADER
Damn right she can. Send her right up.

The maître d' walked over to Evo Kaplan's table and announced.

MAÎTRE D'
Madam, the band has requested you sing another song
now.

SHERI
Oh, thank you.

Sheri got up and went back on stage, and as soon as she informed the band leader the name of her song choice which the band knew and she grabbed the microphone, there was already an audience ovation for her reappearance.

When Sheri informed the band leader of the song's name, at first, he was slightly afraid because that song required a dynamite voice to hit all the high notes and hold some of them really long. The song writer and recording star were phenomenal artists, so few bands ever attempted performing it.

Within thirty seconds of starting the piece, Sheri had knocked it out of the ballpark. The crowd was on fire, and so was the band. By the time she finished singing the song, "I Always Wanted To Meet A Guy Like You," Evo Kaplan almost broke down into tears. If the song conveyed her real thoughts, then he knew he was enamored for life if it came true.

The standing ovation was tremendous. Egor Pataslia observed Sheri walk over and give Evo Kaplan a sweet hug that conveyed romance and love. He felt so good for Evo knowing what the poor bastard had been through. Hopefully this lady will work out this time.

EXT. NIGHT. LANTIANE RESORT EVO KAPLAN'S PENTHOUSE

Evo Kaplan took Sheri back to the penthouse and soon they were engulfed in lovemaking that transcended the obvious and eclipsed the unordinary. In the morning, they woke up in each other's arms fully in love.

SHERI
I'm sad because I know you will soon leave and go
back to Zanziltar, and I may never see you again.

EVO KAPLAN
I live in Shen de Huayuan now.

SHERI
You do?

EVO KAPLAN
Yes.

SHERI
Where abouts do you live?

EVO KAPLAN
I have a home in Shenhuaban de Baozang. Would you
like to go see it?

EVO KAPLAN
When?

EVO KAPLAN
Now.

Sheri grabbed Evo Kaplan and kissed him in the most romantic fashion.

They soon got up and dressed and departed the resort.

As they were leaving and walking down the hallway, one of the Barracuda saw them leaving and went back into her penthouse and would soon be communicating with the others about the scandalous affair of Jerimiah Clifton (a.k.a. Evo Kaplan) spending the night with the resort band singer!

EXT. DAY. LANTIANE RESORT FRONT ENTRANCE.

Evo Kaplan walked up to the attendant in front of the resort at the podium where he coordinated all the transportation and asked:

EVO KAPLAN
Can you send a VTOL Skycar to pick us up.

ATTENDANT
Where are you heading?

EVO KAPLAN
We are going to Shenhuaban de Baozang.

ATTENDANT
There will be one in five minutes at the landing pad area.

EVO KAPLAN
Thanks.

True to his word, the VTOL Skycar arrived, and they got in and it flew directly to Shenhuaban de Baozang.

EXT. DAY. SHENHUABAN DE BAOZANG. EVO KAPLAN'S HOME

After they got out of the VTOL Skycar, Evo Kaplan explained.

EVO KAPLAN
We can walk to my home. It's only a little over a block
away.

As they were walking toward the hill there were the haves and the have-nots' homes, clearly stratified. Sheri wondered which one was his and when he walked up to the mansion, she was very surprised.

SHERI
Is this is your home?

EVO KAPLAN
It can be your home too if you want.

SHERI
Do you really mean that?

EVO KAPLAN
You might want to call your boss and tell them they need to
find another singer for the band today.

Sheri held onto Evo Kaplan's hand even more strongly as she was suddenly feeling dizzy from all these sudden revelations. He led her into the mansion and explained.

EVO KAPLAN
I know you might feel uncomfortable for a few days, and
if you like you can sleep in the guest room as long as you
want.

SHERI
No, I better sleep with you, or I might get scared.

FIVE YEARS LATER

EXT. DAY. SHENHUABAN DE BAOZANG. EVO KAPLAN'S HOME

Evo was out working. He had volunteered more and more time along with Rocu and other Egor Pataslia men, painting and landscaping the have-not's homes in the village. He privately donated money to roofing contractors to replace every roof needed in the community. Houses in dire need of repair due to elderly or incapacitated people received facelifts. Grumpiness within the community slowly subsided.

The doorbell rang. Sheri was busy dealing with a couple of her toddlers. The two-year-old was pulling the four-year old's hair. The kids ran her ragged at times but she adored them anyhow.

Sheri opened the door. There was a pretty woman standing there.

SHERI
Yes, can I help you?

CLAUDETTE RAMSEY
Does Jerimiah Clifton live here?

SHERI
Yes, he's not home now, but should be back in about
fifteen minutes.

One of the home watchers contacted Rocu to inform him:

WATCHER
An attractive woman has just rung Jerimiah's doorbell
and his wife invited her in. She looks familiar for some
strange reason.

Rocu informed Evo Kaplan, who decided he better go home and see what that was all about.

Evo Kaplan had on blue denim trousers and a thin shirt and had a lot of paint spilled on his clothes as would be expected.

As soon as Evo Kaplan opened the door and looked inside, there she was. Claudette Ramsey. If hell had frozen over, this would be the day.

Claudette Ramsey didn't know Evo Kaplan had a family. When she broached the subject to Randolph Spencer, she wanted to take a trip to Shen de Huayuan to see Jerimiah Clifton, as she was now having remorse for arbitrarily ending the relationship, he advised her not to go and to forget it.

But Claudette Ramsey was one of those women who couldn't take no for an answer and did it anyway.

Claudette Ramsey observed the family pictures on the fireplace just past where Sheri was standing and now knew Jerimiah Clifton was a daddy and had a family, a couple small kids and a young wife. As soon as she saw his face she knew she had made a terrible mistake.

It was worse than remorse. She had loved this man dearly and because she was a gutless wonder, she threw him to the curb, knowingly breaking his heart.

Claudette Ramsey also knew she had been cruel because the poor man had already had his heartbroken over Brenda Broyals, though the timing would be one thing that would upset her if she knew the whole truth.

As Claudette Ramsey looked around at the kids, she realized, They could have been my kids, and felt utterly miserable.

> EVO KAPLAN
> I didn't expect to see you again.

> CLAUDETTE RAMSEY
> Well, you didn't call.

> EVO KAPLAN
> I complied with your instructions.

> CLAUDETTE RAMSEY
> I'm glad you are alive, and things are going well for you.

> EVO KAPLAN
> Everything okay with Randolph?

> CLAUDETTE RAMSEY
> He's okay, but I think his wife is going nuts. He's been giving me hints. I think he wants to start a romance with me.

> EVO KAPLAN
> Never mix business with pleasure.

It was very awkward. Evo Kaplan and Claudette Ramsey, both knew her remaining in his home was not appropriate, now that she knew what happened to him. The most decent thing she could do now, five years later, would be to leave in peace and forget the past.

> CLAUDETTE RAMSEY
> Well, I wanted to know what happened to you and I'm glad you're well. So, I'm going to be going now.

> EVO KAPLAN
> Good-bye, Claudette.

> CLAUDETTE RAMSEY
> Good-bye, Jerimiah.

Claudette wanted to say Evo Kaplan, but she realized if she did it might cost her life. Because no doubt Evo Kaplan was probably still an assassin.

Claudette would go back to Sanctuary City and forget all about this man. She knew the possibility existed she might have to leave right away and asked the VTOL Skycar to wait at the landing pad for a few minutes and she would be back to tell them to leave or would be leaving with them.

Just before Claudette Ramsey stepped aboard the VTOL Skycar, she turned and looked back. Standing on the mansion's front steps was Evo Kaplan.

One last look and Evo Kaplan was gone forever.

Paul D. Escudero
April 2, 2024

DRAMATIS PERSONAE

Evo Kaplan – Spy working for the FIRM. The central figure in this story.

John Youling – temporary name for Evo Kaplan during training and indoctrination.

Proctor Pugong – Evo Kaplan's temporary ID for the Stonue mission.

Krawz Almarip (a.k.a. Evo Kaplan) – Evo Kaplan's new name for the Arzon mission (stolen identity of a known black marketer)

Jerimiah Clifton – Evo Kaplan's final identity.

Sparkles (Herbert von Karalon's wife -barracuda)

Glacey Spencer (Randolph Spencer's Wife)

Monica (a.k.a. Theolonabatress von Surret, Edgar von Surret's Wife-barracuda)

Shenhuaban de Baozang – future home of Evo Kaplan and tourist town.

Tolkamere Foundation – Former college campus and now headquarters for the Revolutionaries (Revolutionary Empire)

Shengmíng Langjie de Fangzi (house of ill repute on Arzon) Chinese derivation for the business: 声名狼借的房子— Shēngmíng láng jiè de fángzi

Zeta-Dalajiangyumi Bingxian – planetary security forces for that planet.

Dalajiangyumi Bingxian – Chinese deravation: Big enchilada 大辣酱玉米饼馅 Dà là-jiàng yùmǐ bǐng xiān

Sheri – Cabaret Singer at the Lantiane Resort. Becomes spouse to Evo Kaplan.

Loraine Rantala – Loyalist Spy Blane Jiandie's old flame (former girlfriend now on Arzon).

Gangqin – Piano 钢琴 Gāngqín

Cap Zapatero (a.k.a. Blane Jiandie) – the real Blane Jiandie's fake name for the Arzon mission (Zapatero: Spanish: shoemaker; cobbler) Ruth Marradi – flight attendant

Claudette Ramsey – analyst for Randolph Spencer, one of Evo Kaplan's lovers.

Kao Zhurou – Roast Pork 烤猪肉 Kǎo zhūròu

Yaoyuan de Zhenzhu – Distant Pearl 遥远的珍珠 yáo yuǎn de zhēn zhū (Praxisvlasia's moon) Chunlang – Pure Wolf 纯狼 chún láng

Captain Buck – Intergalactic Transport pilot Buck (blockade runner) Fursungtarwum – Intergalactic Transport copilot.

Charles Xianfeng – Charles Pioneer 先锋 xiān fēng (Butler for the Penthouse 4C)

Shenhuaban de Baozang – Fabulous Treasure Island 神话般的宝藏 shén huà bān de bǎo zàng. This is where Evo Kaplan retires and lives with Sheri at the end.

Banma Julebu – zebra club -斑马俱乐部 bān mǎ jù lè bù Fashionable nightclub.

Inchalchary – Lantiane Resort Couture Fashion Designer

Bristol - Lantiane Resort Masseuse

Quanqiu Museum – Global Museum 全球 Quánqiú Huoshan Xingneng Drink – Volcano Performance Drink 火山性能 huǒ shān xìng néng

Lantiane Resort – Blue Swan Resort 蓝天鹅 Lán tiān'é. Shen de

Huayuan's most expensive and exclusive resort where Evo Kaplan and Brenda Broyals stayed during their two -week vacation

Egor Pataslia - the chief of Revolutionary Security for Shen de Huayuan.

Fufen Ray – Manta Ray 蝠鲼 fú fèn

Guilong Aquarium – Turtle dragon Aquarium at Pangu Bay 龟龙 Guī lóng

Hupu Waterfalls – Tiger Waterfall 虎瀑 Hǔ pùbù

Xingning Shizhe – Star gazer -星凝视者 Xīng níng shì zhě name of restaurant.

Dewaltracen Gallery, Shen de Huayuan. Brenda Broyals meets Egor Pataslia here.

Brenda Broyals recent description: "She's built about the same, 125 pounds approximately, currently has blonde hair, and has a strong resemblance to the entertainer Carly Lambardi. Revolutions top Spy trained Evo Kaplan and became his lover.

Hari Nuvrean – Dranzonian Empire Secret Service agent working at the Zanziltar Consulate with full diplomatic immunity.

Huaiyuansu Ka – former Dranzonian Empire Secret Service working logistics for the Revolutionaries at the Revolutionary Empire Zanziltar Operations, became double spy for the Dranzonian Empire Secret Service until he was turned. Huaiyuansu Ka betrayed Evo Kaplan and Brenda Broyals leading to her death.

Doctor Buster – in charge of Stratospheric Glider project.

Chuo Wanpi -顽皮 (wánpí) – Stonue's recalcitrant leader (Chinese: naughty).

Conrad Fanzui – the head of Revolutionary Empire Zanziltar operations the FIRM.

Zanziltar – the Switzerland of the galaxy SANCTUARY CITY.

Xing Ganmao – Revolutionary Empire recruiter/project coordinator

Mikhail Catamountz – Evo Kaplans the Revolutionary Empire recruiter and part of the FIRM'S inner circle.

Vergentia – a Dranzonian Empire World where Evo Kaplan grew up.

General Guodu Jiaolu – Revolutionary Guard Force Fleet Commander.

Arzon – the alien planet near the Orion Nebula.

Revolutionary Empire – the disenfranchised portion of the former Dranzonian Empire

Praxisvlasia – Dranzonian Empire home planet and center of the government.

Zuanshi-cheng – Revolutionary Empire home world and capital (diamond city).

Cornelius Xie de Hundan – Revolutionary Empire Dictator.

Blane Jiandie – Dranzonian Empire Secret Service agent sent to kill Evo Kaplan.

The Dranzonian Empire Secret Service was a branch of the Ministry for State Security in the that had its headquarters in Praxisvlasia.

Glen Zhurenshuo – Head of Revolution Empire Section, Secret Service.

The five members of the Committee for State Security minor role in the book. Molded after the French Revolution.

Reginald Heiqishi – Evo Kaplan's supervisor while working at the Secret Service, and Evo Kaplan's nemesis.

Terrshey Wate – Reginald Heiqishi's partner for the Evo Kaplan operation.

Note: some names and locations are derived from Chinese. To facilitate Chinese readers who might want the translation, that information is provided. I did this out of my respect and admiration of the Chinese language, which I'm constantly learning. Please forgive me if I made a mistake in translation.

Chinese is a tonal language and where I placed the Chinese Mandarin Characters above, the tonal markers are included on the Pinyin, which is the phonetic spelling of the word. Since most of the written text now is in simplified Chinese, I used those Mandarin characters. If you look at "Traditional Chinese Characters," you will discover they do not all match the Simplified Mandarin, which is the standard way newspapers, books, and other print are produced.

You will notice I removed and modified the Pinyin in the story; I did so to minimize transfer issues in the editing process that may occur. I also did it to create hybrid words. However, if you use a translation program and play the actual Mandarin character used you will be able to hear how its pronounced.

Your other option is to become good friends with a Chinese person, who I'm sure would be happy to help pronounce those words for you. You will discover in some cases the words are pronounced very beautifully and elegantly. I hope it enriched non-Chinese readers in some way and possibly motivated someone to learn Chinese. Be patient and it will be worth your while, especially if one day you can converse in Chinese.

Because of MARTIAL ARTS in the Novel/Screenplay, there are a few examples in the Glossary below.

Glossary

Chaofei Jiansuji: super fat reducer 超肥减速机 chāo féi jiǎn sù jī

Martial Arts Form Number One: Shishido no y ni Tatakai, Taka no y ni Korosu. "Fight like a lion, kill like an eagle," 獅子のように戦う、鷲のように殺す.

Martial Arts Form Number Fifteen: Xióng Yǔ Yībǎi Yīshíyī

Èmó Zhàndòu, Bears Fighting 111 Demons" 熊与一百一十一恶魔战斗. [Xióng yǔ yībǎi yīshíyī èmó zhàndòu.]

Shen de Huayuan: planet was mildly primitive, but out-world travelers nicknamed it the Garden of the Gods. A lot of the action takes place on this planet.

Gaoyang: an animal that closely resembles lamb and is prevalent on the planet Zanziltar that lives in the wild in various mountain ranges. Professional hunters are sent out to capture them alive. They are usually fed a high calorie diet to clean out their system of wild foliage prior to butcher and are often used in barbecues or special events.

Zise Gaoliang: Purple Sorghum food type 紫色高粱 Zǐsè gāoliang

Zanziltar Operations Planning Center for special Revolution Spy briefings

Styrolian Sponges: a delicacy far more extravagant than black caviar. Styrolian Sponges was served on a bed of Zanziltar Shuidao, which was very much like rice on planet Earth or Vergentia Xiaomai, which looked and tasted about the same. The Styrolian Sponges were fried and slightly crunchy, but amazingly tasted like black caviar.

Dranzonian Empire's new *proton gravity disrupter weapon when weaponized*

the disrupter caused gravity wave distortion that could lead to significant navigation failures on enemy ships, forcing them out of control where they become sitting ducks for attack.

Coy's Ridge where the Ultra Rich Industrialist Abniler Manther lives

Stratospheric Glider: a one-man space craft used for clandestine insertion and extraction.

Haiwangxing perfume that released unique Pheromones to effect sexual arousal.

Terrain Sportster: high speed galactic mountain bike device did not use wheels.

Wuxing: Capital City of Stonue

VTOL: vertical takeoff and landing

Dumbwaiter: a vertical lift device invented by Jefferson Davis in 1790 for his Charlottesville, Virginia home. It was just a simple device to lift articles to an upper floor. The mechanical dumbwaiter was invented by George W. Cannon, from New York City. Cannon first filed for the patent of a brake system (US Patent no. 260776) that could be used for a dumbwaiter on January 6, 1883. Cannon later filed for the patent on the mechanical dumbwaiter (US Patent No. 361268) on February 17, 1887. Cannon reportedly generated a vast amount of royalties from the dumbwaiter patents until his death in 1897.

[a.k.a.....] also known as

[nll.....] now looking like

CPR: Cardiopulmonary resuscitation is an emergency procedure that combines chest compressions often with artificial ventilation in an effort to manually preserve intact brain function until further measures are taken to restore spontaneous blood circulation and breathing in a person who is in cardiac arrest.

111 is a magic number. A six-by-six magic square using the numbers 1 to 36 also has a magic constant of 111. (The square has this magic constant because $1 + 2 + 3 + ... + 34 + 35 + 36 = 666$, and $666 / 6 = 111$).

The number 111 has a significant amount of study to it. 111 is a perfect totient number. A perfect totient number is an integer that is equal to the sum of its iterated totients. In cricket, the number 111 is sometimes called "a Nelson" after Admiral Nelson, who allegedly only had "One Eye, One Arm, One Leg" near the end of his life.

Occasionally 111 is referred to as "eleventy-one", as read in The Fellowship of the Ring by J.R.R. Tolkien.

The first Pacific (4-6-2) locomotive in Great Britain was the Great Western Railway's No. 111 The Great Bear of 1908, designed by the great engineer George Jackson Churchward.

3D Biological Printing: A process where advanced alien races depicted in this book are able to quickly change the physical appearance of a spy for a mission in the span of a couple days usually.

FORWARD THE SANCTUARY CITY

Many of my fans took Brenda Broyals getting killed in Sanctuary City kind of hard. I have a surprise for them. I'm going to soon publish the sequel to Sanctuary City second screenplay.

The second Novel is titled:

"Revenge at Sanctuary City The return of Breda Broyals"

By the time you read this screenplay, The return of Brenda Broyals screenplay will be at the publisher.

Everyone thinks Brenda was killed based on the first Novel.

The original Sanctuary City text:

Brenda's world suddenly ended. The shuttle pilot who observed Brenda getting hit with the missile also detected Zeta-Dalajiangyumi Bingxian planetary security forces in hot pursuit, bugged out, and made a beeline to the mothership. The Zeta- Dalajiangyumi Bingxian planetary security forces flying an entire squadron came upon the area of the missile launches and spotted the perpetrators on the ground. Knowing they had dangerous missiles and had already blown up three hovercrafts, the Zeta-Dalajiangyumi Bingxian planetary security forces made the determination they had to neutralize the group launching the missiles and quickly armed and launched their own weapons.

What really happened is Brenda Broyals got lucky. People who read Sanctury City do not know this.

The missile strike hit behind Brenda Broyals Hovercraft which lifted up Brenda and flew her into the water unconscious.

The pressure of being underwater and sinking to about 50 feet woke Brenda Broyals up.

Brenda Broyals had an underwater breathing apparatus in her backpack in case they had to jump in the water and swim to safety. They are operating on a mostly water world where everyone travels via Hovercraft.

With the enemy bugging out because the Dranzonians could not risk being captured by the local government nor could the Revolution FIRM people, Brenda swam up the coastline a while, she was able to swim up to a desolated island where she could hide out eat the abundant flora, frogs, and turtles and survive and reflect on what went wrong.

Brenda Broyals knew she had been betrayed. There was a mole back in the FIRM.

Brenda Broyals eventually cycling through various planets works her way back to society and because she's a well-trained spy she was able to steal clothes, CREDITS and find a means to get off the water world planet. Her ordeal could be a separate Novel (3RD in series).

Eventually five years later Brenda Broyals makes her way back to Sanctuary City.

Brenda Broyals spent a lot of time thinking about the betrayal and she was on a war path to kill everyone involved.

Meanwhile, the Dranzonians tracked Evo Kaplan down. They didn't know his next-door neighbor was the former head of the local FIRM spy apparatus.

Dranzonians come in at night and placed explosive charges around Evo Kaplan's home.

Evo was lucky, he had to get up in the middle of the night to defecate and drain his kidneys when the explosion went off killing his wife and 2 kids and damaging him badly including disfiguring him with 3rd degree burns all over most of his face. He looked like the actor in the movie, "The English Patient."

Evo Kaplan slowly clung to life and eventually came back to consciousness. The doctors regrettably informed Evo Kaplan his wife and 2 children passed away from the explosion.

Evo Kaplan was devastated.

Evo Kaplan had retired from the spy business, and his next door neighbor who had communications with the leaders of the FIRM spies had them contact the FIRM in Sanctuary City because he knew they could do all the 3D biological printing and change EVO Kaplan's identity and take care of all the scar tissue that covered most of his face.

Evo Kaplan was sedated and woke up in his former room at Sanctuary City FIRM facility that had grown in stature since he finished his 6-year contract and retired.

Brenda Broyals had been briefed on what happened to Evo Kaplan and how Evo Kaplan was informed she was dead, so that's why he ended up marrying the dead Cabaret Singer.

Only Conrad Fanzui knew this was Evo Kaplan and he informed Brenda Broyals it was him even though he had changed his identity with the 3D biological printing.

Brenda's identity had been changed as well including her voice. She's now known as Sofia Maris.

Conrad Fanzui (Spy master) had a long talk with Evo Kaplan, and it became music to Conrad Fanzui's ears. he knew Evo Kaplan was really pissed off and wanted to get his hands on the spies that killed his family.

What better a spy who has a cause?

Conrad informs Sofia Maris (a.k.a. Brenda Broyals) she will get to work with Evo Kaplan again. But he admonished her: Don't fall in love with him and have sex again, because I don't want to have to separate you like we did before.

So the Dynamic Dual now go deep into the Dranzonian Empire wreaking a terrible toll on them as Evo is working to one day get the opportunity to put a laser pistol shot between the eyes of everyone involved in killing his family.

The Drama begins. 2024 -2025.

Paul D Escudero

March 26, 2024